AT ALL COST

NATHAN T. WHITE

Copyright © 2024

At All Cost
Nathan T. White

All rights reserved. No part of this book may be used or reproduced by any means, graphic, electronic, or mechanical, including photocopying, recording, taping or by any information storage retrieval system without the written permission of the publisher except in the case of brief quotations embodied in critical articles and reviews. Because of the dynamic nature of the Internet, any web addresses or links contained in this book may have changed since publication and may no longer be valid. The views expressed in this work are solely those of the author and do not necessarily reflect the views of the publisher, and the publisher hereby disclaims any responsibility for them.

ISBN-13: 9798340954503

All Scripture quotations are used by permission. Scripture marked (NKJV) are taken from the New King James Version®. Copyright © 1982 by Thomas Nelson, Inc. Used by permission. Scripture quotations marked (NIV) are taken from the Holy Bible, New International Version®, NIV®. Copyright © 1973, 1978, 1984, 2011 by Biblica, Inc.™ Used by permission of Zondervan. All rights reserved worldwide. www.zondervan.com. The "NIV" and "New International Version" are trademarks registered in the United States Patent and Trademark Office by Biblica, Inc.™

Editing / Interior Book Design & Layout / Book Cover Design
CBM Christian Book Editing
www.christian-book-editing.com

Printed in the United States of America

DEDICATION

To God-

Which may be superfluous.

He is the One who calls, gifts, guides, provides, protects, and enables, all in love to complete a life a plan, all for His glory and His beloved to know Him, to love Him, to understand and comprehend Him.

At All Cost

AT ALL COST-

A Timeless Story. Love. Love that Acted. Protected. Guided. Provided. Love that Sacrificed. Love that saw Value where none existed. In a people and place, now forgotten and misunderstood. Love that rescued. Love unshakeable, unfathomable, unrelenting! Love "At All Cost!"

CONTENTS

CHAPTER 1

BEGINNING OF THE END

Darkness cool and inviting, a stab of pain, a flash of light, a ragged gasp!

He had passed out. Shock racked His tortured frame. Fire exploded out to His extremities and the smell of hot desert sand slammed into Him along with the coppery scent of blood! The thrum of blood was in His ears. He was dying. And there was nothing and no one to stop it!

But this was what He had chosen, He and His Father.

Underneath the slow steady thrum of blood in His ears, He heard the drums. No there were no real drums, at which the Romans played, or the Hebrews. But a sure deep bass note as if the very foundations of the world resonated in time with the advent of oncoming death. Or could it be a rage? Rage, the ever-growing onslaught of darkness, and the insatiable hunger to destroy mankind.

The shouts and cries of the Roman guards were mixed with the taunts and jeers of what? His peers, His equals, His people . . . His . . . Creation?

There faintly He noticed the beat again. A steady pronounced beat. He knew it vaguely as a drum of war. A war not many could see, hear, or even interact with. He could because He was the Son of God. His Father and He had a schedule to keep. And He heard Satan's laughter echo amidst the sun, heat, and slow death.

Sounds assailed His ears; the crowd's screams and the ever-increasing thrum of His blood did not cease. *Funny,* He thought, *near death your senses heighten. Too bad it wasn't the opposite of the pain.*

He pushed Himself up on the aching foot. He could not turn His hands to even attempt to grip the roughhewn wood. Each muscle was screaming for relief and help! His thoughts were almost as cloudy as His eyesight. But He did manage to hold His chest higher to breathe a bit easier. Not that breathing easier was possible.

All of Jerusalem stood in front of the Cross it seemed. The smell of fear and sweat. He never knew fear had a smell until now. He had never known any of the things He was feeling, again, not until now. Oh, He knew of life and death and even joy and sorrow. But now, in this place, His suffering was for another reason.

Then came a flash of light, a knife edge of pain, and a figure nearby. He looked through the wash of blood covering His eye. It stung as the sweat and blood mingled near His swollen and bruised cheekbone.

It was Abdias, and Jesus' heart broke. Now this demon looked on in joy. He was the demon assigned among many to gather pleasure from pain and to gain influence over men through torture and harm. All for the goal of thwarting His Father's plan and mankind's rescue.

His mind raced back to before Creation and the life before Him.

Abdias, a *Servant of God,* was moving toward the Throne in the Heavenly realm. He was moving toward the LORD with purpose. He was troubled, his heart ached knowing he had to relay the painful situation. The LORD let him come . . . for the LORD Almighty already knew.

Abdias stopped before the Throne bowed deeply and stood eyes averted.

"Your Majesty, Lord of Hosts," he paused and said, "I have disturbing news." Abdias waited silently.

"Yes, Abdias, what is it?" He knew, that troubles and sorrow must be spoken to begin healing.

"Light Bringer again?"

"Yes, Light Bringer said he did not understand why you have made the stones of fire, uh, the stars so plentiful. The area is so vast and shouts daily praise to Your greatness and awesome power, but is so separate from all the other parts of Creation you have made." He paused, "Even I don't see how these Redeemed will live in the stars. We fly there and move among them freely because you made us so, but I still do not understand. And Light Bringer asks why you want to have these Redeemed in Our realm. It seems He is angry since you already have one that can choose, why more?"

"Abdias, do you understand the plan for creating and how the Redeemed are a crucial part of it?" the LORD answered.

"Not fully, though I know you said I am to help these Redeemed when you say, and protect and help them to become like us. . ." he finished.

The LORD smiled and then spoke again.

"Abdias, The Father of Lights, and I know of all the Sons of God's loyalty and praise, even your adoration, and we thank you. The Redeemed are our concern, and Light Bringer as well. Rest and be faithful because we will need of you soon, once Earth and the rest of the planets are formed, they will require your help, watch and care."

He turned then from the Throne, His raiment reflecting the surrounding light, casting rainbows upon the ground.

A scream of pure hatred and the sight of sand broke the memory.

"If you are the Son of God, then come down and save us all!" the disheveled-looking man spit out. Next to him a child's hand grabbed up sand next to His feet and tossed it in His direction, a mixture of sorrow and learned hatred was in her eyes.

If you only knew, precious one, Family, Nation . . . if you only knew, He thought. *You don't understand and Satan has blinded your hearts and minds . . . just as always.* The drum of war resonated again; His ears carried the cry of rage closer to His heart.

His eyes beheld the crowd, panning with great effort. It seemed the smudges of black had increased, yet, light remained. And of course, Abdias was nowhere to be seen.

Amidst the sting of sweat and blood in His eyes, He made out the forms and faces of John and Peter, along with His mother Mary. She was huddled with Martha and the devout ladies, even Mary of Magdala.

His heart stirred with joy as He beheld them; knowing that she had found her home and acceptance. Along with that, joy in being free from bondage and nightmares, only one other had endured longer. Again His vision blurred and a larger, darker smear appeared next to the group. The smear coalesced into Lucifer himself and anger began to rise in the Son of God's heart as Lucifer leaned in and whispered in His ear. . .

Suddenly, a knife-edged memory flashed into His mind!

He heard the rumblings. Rumblings of growing dissatisfaction and resentment . . . even now hatred. His Omniscience needed no reminder, nor His holiness prompting, for He knew what He must do. Yet, He must be true, right, and just. He knew even Lucifer, as Creation, must be shown grace, even in knowing the outcome. It was hurtful to think part of His Creation was not fulfilling its function or duty. He walked toward the ever-enlarging gathering of the Host, the Sons of God, near the Temple.

He heard the smooth confidence in Lucifer's voice, "So it begins."

He stopped and listened; knowing that the outcome would damage His creation, and yet in the end allow restoration at a higher price that still did not deter His decision. Life was precious, all life. This group before Him was His handiwork; a small part of Himself lived in even them. Just like the Universe He had built, soon others would bear His light too. They would be called - Man, Human, The Redeemed, and Sons of God among other things. And they would choose just like now, but out of love and gratefulness, and even out of hope.

"Gabriel, I am not saying the Father of Lights and the Sons' Creation has fault because you and I both know He makes no mistakes."

Lucifer's words dripped out, "But, is all of this necessary? He made Light, of which I am a part, and these stars and galaxies He named are so numerous and we His host do His bidding always. He is adored and worshipped by all He surveys, is this not enough?" Lucifer paused.

"He is always worthy of all praise," Gabriel said. He turned slightly and was greeted by calls of "True" from the Host behind him.

Lucifer continued as if speaking to a simple creature, "Yes. True, true. Father, asks many things of us. We watch over His Stars and the Heavens. And now He asks us to prepare for these others that will join us somehow, in this realm. And they too shall have choice. Will they have the same garments? Will they have access to the very Throne of God? Are they to stand here beside us as brothers? Are we to teach them? I do not truly understand The Light Father's plan, and I am above His Throne!" He paused again.

The dark seeds of discontent did not show at first, but the pinprick of black flashed briefly and was hidden.

Gabriel spoke again. "Does this truly matter Lucifer? Are we not all part of Creation? Are we not all called to worship the One and the Son? Does it hurt to have stuff of beauty to look upon and whether we teach them or not, are they not as we ...?"

"They," Lucifer hissed interrupting, stopped the swelling rage in his heart, and finished, "are definitely not going to be as us. I was not told that they would fly or as yet have access to our realm. Nor do they even look like we do brothers, nor can they do deeds like ourselves, we mighty ones. Yet, the Father of Lights says we are to help them. Protect them and help them prosper when they appear. Father says they have a glory all their own and it is not the same as ours." He hesitated, if he disclosed too much, he would not get the desired result. "When did The Light Father become displeased with us and our service? He says we are His messengers and His Messengers with Fire, His Authority!" He smiled, as murmurs met his ears. He knew he would hear from Gabriel and maybe a few others soon with voices of dissension, but Lucifer pressed on. "But who are these others? The ones named Man, Redeemed . . . from what? Has the Light Father ever let one of His creation slip? Why then would 'Man' need redeeming? I have always felt the Light Father has loved me sufficiently." Lucifer let the insolence hang, "Do not you feel the same? Oh yes, I know you do. He has provided for our every need, has He not? We have no need for sustenance or sleep. Unlike these others coming, they will need food to live and sleep. Or they may become angry and weep . . . tsk, tsk, tsk," clicking his tongue as he finished.

"That is the Father's business, not ours Light Bringer!" Gabriel charged.

"Yes Gabriel, you are right, but some of us have a different relationship than you with the Light Father. Some even have place above the Throne, yet seem to know so little. . . why? Gabriel, does that trouble you, old soul? Does it disquiet that stout heart you carry within your bosom?" Smiling slyly he continued, "Why would Light Father have the Host in rank? Or even some of them in better raiment, is that not unloving?" He spun in place casting rainbow spears into the sky.

Disquiet was growing and there was a rustling of wings as Gabriel turned to Michael in a harsh whisper, "This is not right! The Light Father must know!"

"I believe, Gabriel, He does look." The Archangel's head tilted in the direction behind and to the left of them, "I do not know what He will now do. Creation has never disputed His Character, Promise, or Word before." Michael finished.

"Light Bringer, may I speak with you?" The Son of God spoke sincerely, waiting for his answer. He scanned the Host before him, sadness spreading over his heart; He tried not to show any emotions on his face yet, to influence in any way the angel's thoughts or actions at this point. He had given them choice, just as He had given Lucifer and soon Mankind.

Some had averted their eyes out of respect, more it seemed from guilt or fear.

How painful this is for them, this choice. And they do not have to ever make that fateful decision. The one faced by the Redeemed. But it pains them to be sure. The Son thought, *How to choose? Who to trust? Where should my allegiance be and my efforts? Is this relationship with my Father and I better than what he would offer? These of the Host; are straightforward and honest. They know nothing of what Lucifer tells but all must be fulfilled. Line upon line and precept to precept.*

He will gather them one more time and then this realm if it were possible would be sundered like my heart.

Lucifer moved through the gathered host with feline grace, belying his size and stature. He fell into step with the Son as they both turned away from the crowd and moved toward the Throne. They walked steadily and surely beside the River of God and the water sang out as it flowed passed. Its song mixed with the sounds of Heaven and other of the Host casting a backdrop of hope, obscuring the seriousness of the moment. The river sang of its own "Life, Healing, Hope" mixed with "Holy, Holy, Holy is the Lord God Almighty! Who was and is and is to come!"

The Angel of Light waited in silence, muscles tense and emotions taught.

The Realm glistened and sparked with shafts of light as they moved beside the River of Life. Light Bringer was surrounded by light; it breathed and moved, and as always, sang! His very garments were softer echoes and swells of the Realm's Music as He continued.

Silently, the Son of God moved. He kept his face a mirror not relaying the inner pain each step brought. Deep in His being the struggle was beginning, *No, not a real struggle yet.* But conflict just the same, holiness, justice, and grace vied for dominance.

He heard accolades as He passed the throngs, Elders, and the Four Creatures, ascending the steps to the Throne Room. He did not alter His path nor acknowledge the praise, not that He missed it or didn't hear it, but for the moment He prepared His heart for what was to come. This would only end in war. Something that had never happened in the Realm; now or ever, nor would it again after.

The Son of God moved to the Throne on His Father's right and sat down.

There was a stillness that permeated the Throne room, as Lucifer stood before the Father of Lights and the Son, unashamedly trying not to look bored with it all.

"Light Bringer, the Son and I sense you are unsettled by the advent of Creation and the future plans for Our Realm." The Father of Lights paused, "Is this true?"

"Well, your Majesties," Lucifer crooned, "I am concerned that some things may affect Our Realm more than you plan, but yes I am."

The Father of Lights turned to the Son, and the Son acknowledged the look and spoke.

"I see, can you enlighten us as to the situation? It seems there is an unease with the Host and we want to alleviate everyone's fears and questions, especially yours." The Son waited.

He knew Lucifer's thoughts already and his internal struggle. He would lovingly speak to him and offer some hope for all of it and then let him choose. He saw the first signs of darkness brewing . . . shifts in light against his garment pulling toward more magenta and crimson.

Lucifer spoke with reserve. "If I may ask then, why was I not told."

The Son of God looked into his eyes, "What were you not told of Light Bringer?"

"Am I or am I not the 'Angel of Light' ?" he questioned.

"Yes and. . ." the Son began, "you have made me the Music Director of Heaven and the one Angel to shine forth, reflecting your Glory, yes?" again questioning.

"All you have made surrounds you and cries out to Your Greatness, Power, Glory, Goodness, and Wisdom, continually, even the Host sees to that also, what more is there need for? I arrange the Host in the Stars of Heaven to shout and make music along with Creations cries. Have we need to increase our efforts or frequency?"

"No, Light Bringer no, the Light Father and I are more than pleased with all you do." The Son said.

"Light Father, Majesties, I was concerned that You all were displeased with my work that You have called me to. And honestly, being over the Throne is a daunting task, one of which I truly enjoy. As well as directing the Host and arranging them to bring the highest of praise continually, and yet, I feel a distance here with you. I was rather surprised that I was not told of Creation completely, and the need for others. As one in authority, I had hoped when possible, to aid you in your endeavors and thus know how best to serve You and the Realm. But, it seems I wasn't needed at this juncture and had to find out about the event from Michael and Gabriel." Light Bringer said.

The Son spoke evenly, "I am glad you enjoy your place above the Throne, it is a place of Honor and authority as you said. But, it seems you feel less than you are to us. Creation was a part of our plan always and even the Light and stars, and more, truly no slight was intended, or even concern on your part is necessary. You are faithful and all that you are attests to your place in our Realm; you alone reflect The Father's light, no one else." God's son could see the flicker of elation, and pride and then watched as Lucifer's face echoed the dying hope in his heart. The Son saw the perceived hurt and the growing mistrust. Then He saw the spiral of that hope end in quiet anger, frustration, and ever-growing resentment.

"I see," Lucifer said, "And what of these . . . what did Gabriel say 'Redeemed'? Are they to join our Host? Or are we to be teachers to them and show them how to conduct themselves in our realm? Because I am concerned that they might not understand their place. They may disrupt the workings in the Realm and I for one feel we are doing fine! I know. . ." He continued quickly, "I will double the Host among the Stars and the Worship will improve you will see, I have been working on a few melodies and harmonies and songs that befit your Greatness! And then, I will find a way to enhance my garment to show more of your light!"

"Light bringer, **Light Bringer**!" The Son interrupted smiling. "You are fine just as you are! And the worship as well; don't you understand. . ."

Lucifer stiffened. He turned slightly from the Throne took a halting step, and turned back with a voice ringing with tension, oblivious to his surroundings.

"I have always done my best. I have worked hard and labored long on the music that fills these spheres and heavens. I have longed for . . . I have sought only to build your Greatness and Glory . . . and of course be appreciated. I have led the Host in song and tasks of your bidding, surely there is more that I can do. And a creature of my talents of course could be utilized often in decisions and . . ." His voice faded.

"Is this. . ." he waved his arms, "not enough?? Surely, our praise is sufficient and am I not guiding the worship and Host? What need have we for these Redeemed? They do not know, they were not there when we saw Light Father speak and Creation begin! Were they there when I was chosen?" His voice rose, "I, Light bringer, to stay above the Throne. To Cover the Almighty, Light Father!" Turning from the Throne, Lucifer appeared as if to shrink and the reflection of light faded for a brief moment. Straightening, he turned back to The Father of Lights and the Son, speaking calmly. "Forgive me your Majesties, I am not myself I need to go and rethink my questions and concerns, I was wrong to disturb you with my questions and the Host. Please forbear with me for a few moments and I will return to You better able to voice my concerns and fears. . . And the questions I have on the matter of Creation and the Redeemed. Excuse me please." He spun on his heel and left the Throne Room not waiting for dismissal.

The Son of God turned to the Father and spoke in a pained voice, "Father, you saw his heart; I know the answer as You, but it must be voiced." He sighed again, "Why Redemption must cost so? If Light Bringer had believed the truth, the steps of Redemption would have changed little, but not the reason for it. And less of Creation would be affected. Yet, now war has come and the sundering."

The Father of Lights looked intently at the Son and said, "We knew of this long ago and we searched far and wide to find the best solution *to Sin*," He spit it out as if the poison of the word spoken would make its effect worse, "This Dear Son is our only choice." He laughed ruefully, "Millennia from now hosts of Angels and even the Redeemed will question 'Our Choice' and the power of sin and its ultimate destruction. More so, many will ask, why? That you Son, wanted to die for them. Their perceived value to Creation and our world will have them question all of it just as Light Bringer, even how much We value them." He continued, "And Redemption is necessary. Their Creation and lives, joys, sorrows, pains, and exultation adds more to the world and their choice to love Us than they will ever know. And for now, it must be. Remember, all that We have in store for them, even in their homecoming. To have them again walk with Us, out of Love and from their own choice, to have once again true companionship. Heaven and all will bring them and Us to the desired end. This must be done. . . **AT ALL COST.**"

Lucifer's body was taut and his muscles straining, as he tried to outdistance himself from the Realm and . . . *What? I have never felt this before. Never have I wanted to . . . escape!* He thought. Yet the urgency was real and the call to fly farther and farther did not diminish with the distance he had traveled. Yet it seemed to grow all on its own, this call to flee or hide away from eyes and hearts and knowing! He glanced behind him and caught the fading rainbow aurora his wake left. Still he flew on. The edges of the Realm passed by him unnoticed and star after star became a flickering marker of distance. Continually his heart and mind screamed *Run, Flee, away! Hide yourself!* He looked ahead and saw the red hyper giant. He pushed further on to land on its surface. Amidst the shifting carbon-helium shell and the flames he stood. He watched as the surface cracked and bled crimson magma and helium, repeating the process it was designed to do, from now, till The Father of Lights said no more! The raging heart of the giant did little to calm his emotions or mind. Nor did it end the urgent call to flee. He waited, struggling, thoughts racing. He fought the urge to crack open the sun shell and hide beneath its surface.

I have never felt this! Why do I flee? I have been where no other of the Host has been. No one else see's The Father of Lights like I do. I was there when the Stars first began. I heard the words; I heard the melodies used to tie it all together.

He asked me to make music, music that can build and create even sustain life. Oh not life like Light Father's, but melodies that live on after they are made. I was there as He hung these stars about Him. I was there when He set boundaries for the Realm. He paused, fully focused on the raging star about him, fear gone. He laughed as the seeming chaos flowed around him and he stood undamaged.

Lucifer looked at the raging inferno surrounding him. And looked at his garments as they reflected the shifts in light and scope, almost as bright as the very heart of the sun in which he stood.

"I am Lucifer!" He shouted to the elements around him as light kaleidoscoped off of him in a thousand shafts of light and reflection. He spun in a circle amidst the fire and watched as the star continued to rage. *Look at this! See I am the first created! I am strong, powerful, and unharmed by all that I survey! Who else but the Host and I can dwell in fire and flame! Who else can fly faster than light itself! The Light Father made me so and gave me gifts, to include leadership over the Host and power to build and create music and song.* He laughed; *I alone reflect His Glory and Majesty, I Light Bringer, no one else! And who is Gabriel? That he will take a message to these . . .* **Redeemed**. *Would it better that I Light Bringer go? After all I am the First. . .* He paused. He rose out of the flames and heat hovering amidst the glistening stars. His thoughts raced back to the Throne Room, *What am I to do?*

The Light Father said little at our last meeting and the Son said everything was fine. The music, worship, even the placing of the Host amidst the Heavens, all was fine He said . . . No that can't be right. No, He wouldn't need the Redeemed if all was well. He wouldn't send Gabriel soon to give message to them or need the Redeemed in our Realm or have any authority if all was well, Nor would he name any of HIS creation Redeemed! Redemption means there is fault! Who has this fault? Not I! Not Light Bringer. I was first among the Host! I reside over the Throne of God; I am the Realm's Musician and Director; there is no fault in me.

He stiffened as he caught a glimmer and more planets shown in the Realm. He raced back to the Realm just as swiftly as he had run from it!

He saw as he rushed headlong toward the growing spheres, the music the Father of Lights sang. It washed over all the planets and smaller satellites. And spread out further and further to the stars near where he was. *No, Father can't... No, no, no!*

He saw from a distance as a planet shown blue and green and its moon circle it and watched dumbfounded as the Host sang. . . . Holy, Holy, Holy is God Almighty!

Lucifer stopped near the Host and looked on as the ground began to form.

He snapped back to the present as he heard the cries from multiple places.

"You were going to destroy the Temple in three days and rebuild it; Save Yourself!"

I know they don't understand at all Father, but it doesn't pain me any less . . . He thought. He watched as more and more people milled by and most screamed at Him and threw dirt and spit at Him. In His eyes a great dark blood red cloud began to form behind the crowd with each cry. He could feel it, this growing hatred and malice . . . swelling, moving, breathing, almost a thing alive! Then came a cry to His right.

"If you are the Son of God . . . through ragged breaths... save Yourself and us!"

Jesus heard off to His left as at a distance, "Do you not fear God!" Deep inhale, voice as hollow as death itself, "We deserve punishment HE does not."

The other criminal railed on. His voice mixed with the crowd and the Pharisees.

"If you are the Christ, let God save Him! He saved others and let Him save Himself! If you are the Christ and King, come down off the Cross and we will believe and follow You!"

He closed His eyes and tried to breathe and push passed the agony in his body and heart. He knew that this was for a purpose, but it was not an easy thing He was enduring. If He had had more moisture in His body, He may have wept.

Jesus, the Son of God, opened His eyes and watched as a wave of darkness began at the edge of His sight and moved like a summer storm over the countryside. And He heard the thief say, "Remember me when you enter into Your Kingdom."

Jesus turned to him in the gathering twilight and spoke truthfully, kindly. . . "**Today**, you will be with me in Paradise."

"Father forgive them for they do not know what they do!" He shouted.

And Jesus watched the gathering blackness push back the light of the sun and flood His vision, and Golgotha, with darkness.

The Father of Lights tuned to the Son and spoke. "It has begun."

"I will call the Host. Prepare yourself; this will be difficult." The Father of Lights added. The Son noted the pain and hollowness of the Father's Words. War had come to the Realm and the release of Sin upon the Cosmos.

Blackness, deep, still, and unmoving, began to waiver. The darkness began to fold in on itself and the galaxies shivered as if cold. The Cosmos screamed, as it writhed and bucked in agony and torment, only to be silenced by the roar of hatred and tumult as the Host of Heaven and Lucifer's cohort collided!

The impact of power shook creation to its core and the concentric waves of destruction and tearing flowed out from its epicenter to claw and rip all in its path!

"To me! . . ." Michael and Gabriel shouted above the din of battle, "For the realm and Light Father!"

"For Light Bringer and the good of the Realm!" came the reply.

Another unearthly clash and the pillars in the Temple shook casting bits of gold falling to the street. And those walking the streets stumbled as the effects of the battle washed over everything.

Gabriel landed blow after blow against his adversary. And their effects seemed nothing to the rage filled enemy before him. Gabriel then grabbed him by the shoulders and with a mighty heave tossed him into a fast moving counter attack on his right.

"Michael we need help now! They are not stopping; we cannot hold this place!" He cried.

"We must; The Light Father said to face them and stop them!" Michael shouted dropping his rival with his sword. Michael looked around swiftly trying to find a better defensive position and beachhead from which the Host could stem this tide. The only place he could think of was the Temple and the Throne room. The very place they didn't want this to be brought too!

Michael the Archangel shouted over the constant sounds of sword and struggle "To the Temple steps, all of you!"

"You Clavis, you Marisus, and Donte cover the Temple doors, we may have to close ourselves behind its doors till Light Father decides if HE should step in or the Son!"

The wall of hatred and rage pressed against the beleaguered Host. On they fought a kaleidoscope of power and wings and sword and light! Yet, in spite of this the forces of Light Father seemed to give way, slow small steps at first, but still steps.

The ground heaved and buildings rattled. The melody of the Realm had ceased, buried amidst the cry of rage so large and deep, it was even felt through the walls and floors.

The Temple in the Realm was the greatest structure known. It was able to house easily the Host and even when The Light Father finished Creation - Mankind.

Michael looked on as more and more of the Host were being pushed back, retreating one step at a time. Gabriel to his right back peddled as a sword slash barely missed his right side. He slammed his fist into the face of the rage filled adversary momentarily stunning him. Time and again Gabriel found himself falling into a pattern. Sword slash, parry, block, slash, pummel strike and then a smash of fist into the opponents face. Yet, still he was edging back step-by-step almost moment-by-moment, *why? Why weren't they stopping; why hadn't The Light Fathers plan worked?? We can't continue this forever, even I am growing weary and tired!* Thoughts finished, he heard Michael cry, "Inside and close the doors quickly! No one fall behind, come now quickly, quickly!"

Seven Angels of the Host pushed the massive, gilded doors shut with a boom. The echo filled the Temple and the door frames shook. The din of battle muffled somewhat by the solid gold doors themselves.

"Michael this madness must **stop!**" Gabriel said gulping breath. "We cannot gain any headway against Lucifer and his allies." Gabriel's arm was shaking as he leaned heavily on it, hoping his added strength would somehow stop the continued onslaught of those attempting to push the door in.

"We must hold!" Michael shouted in anger. "Light Father said to hold and we shall!" His sword pommel shattered a small wash basin and table near the doors now being held closed by twelve angels. Its pieces stood as evidence of his frustration and anger.

The twelve angels looked as one at Michael and Gabriel imploringly, a deep sadness in their eyes, waiting, for what? Hope. . .

"I had to kill Jupiter . . ." he said in anguish. "He would not listen. He only raged at me and attacked! Light Bringer's Cohort cannot be reasoned with. I have tried. They mocked me and said I was blinded to what was really happening in the Realm and what The Light Father was trying to hide! When I asked what that was they said it would all be brought right, once Light Bringer was in place at the Temple and on the Throne until the Light Father was well again. . ."

Michael turned to his friend Gabriel and said softly, "We must do as Light Father asks; we must hold this line and Realm for HIS purposes and plan. We will not fail, or we will die in the attempt. But we must!"

"But Michael . . . these," looking at the rattling doors and frames, "were our brothers. . ."

The Son of God opened His eyes again in darkness momentarily disoriented by the inky blackness. *Oh yes, it's near time now*, He thought. His eyes panned the dimness and darkness around Him. Strangely He noted the crowd had fallen silent. Even the soldiers had stopped gambling and were looking at one another in stark fear. He could see in the darkness as they looked up into the heavens with no stars. And the demons of fear and paranoia were hard at work, causing fathers, mothers and children to cling to one another. *This was not how I wanted the Family to be,* He thought; *nor did I want this destructive loneliness and rejection this crowd carries.* He focused on a little boy shaking in this darkness totally alone off to the side. *He feels abandoned and his Father is only steps away, and his father is more concerned that he had broken his hoe than any comforting that would help him. Rejection will run deep in his life. If his father will not change, he will never be that artisan of cloth and color, nor Jerusalem will have the fashions he would make.* He turned his head more and saw one of the Roman Guard. *And this one,* He continued, *feels he is trapped by his father, since his father failed to make Senator, he is being forced on a path best left to others.*

The Son of God peered further into the darkness and found others hiding in terror of the night. He could hear the faint whispers of lies placed in their minds and hearts, over and over. He watched as the demons almost sensually brushed the minds, hearts, and souls of those in the crowd.

Fear has gained strength today. So has rejection and doubt. Self-loathing, self-hatred, narcissism, self-worth is sliding into the very pit. These were not made for this. Thankfully, when the task is finished, through My Redemptive work they can finally be free from all these things. And real life and hope and happiness can be found.

His thoughts ended as He saw a glimmer of light on the horizon and memories returned.

Light Father, the Supreme Ruler, God of all that was, is, and is to come, tensed. He saw the Realm around Him at war. He and the Son could feel the very fabric of life tearing and hear all of Creation groan as the two forces crashed upon one another as storm waves on a battered beach. In His heart He knew every step, every cry of hatred, every drop of life that ebbed from Host and Cohort alike. But the time was not yet, He knew, the one defining moment that locked the Universe into its course. He could alter it if He chose, but this was the path to restoration and hope.

"Son, do you see? Can you feel it? My heart aches . . . It will be soon." He spoke quietly. The Son looked at the Father of Lights and saw the pain, even agony in His eyes. *All we have done would be lost if my Father does all that His heart speaks. Yes, righteousness says mankind will falter and choose sin. Holiness then will cry for justice and payment for the sin. And through the great wounds in His . . . Our hearts, We will call on grace and mercy to point the way to freedom, redemption, hope and true life. And mankind will one day have Eternal life as it was meant to be. And we will have Creation back as we intended . . . though at such a cost, such a cost.*

Lucifer slammed into the angel before him with all the righteous fury he could muster! Again and again he pummeled him pushing deeper into the wall of light and bodies, edging closer to the doors of the Temple.

We must stop Light Father! He doesn't see the dangers. We have a perfect Realm and if mankind is to be part of it, surely we cannot have them come to us flawed. It would ruin everything! And what of Light Father Himself? He wants these Redeemed to walk freely in the Realm and have place. Why did He change things? He is not thinking clearly. I am sure and He is only doing this because He is not satisfied with what I have done. He thought. *But if we can get to the Throne room in the Temple we can fix that. I am sure He will listen and see reason. Are not the Host enough? Do we not serve faithfully and well? We are tireless worshipers and the music of course is brilliant. No, no - He is angry I am sure. And He is reacting out of that stress and fear . . . Fear?*

And what of this vast expanse of stars and now these planets ... what need do we have for them, except for these Redeemed. I truly do not understand, all the Father made and will make is perfect, or so He says. If what I understand of these Redeemed . . . they would not be and we would have to deal with them.

The Father of Lights Turned to the Son and Spoke. "The Host is falling back before Light Bringer and his horde. They fear, they question, and they even doubt why I, the Great I Am, has not stirred or moved to assist them or even stop this travesty." He paused, "My heart is filled with anguish, will they truly understand? This was never our intent to have Creation suffer for the choice of sin or not. No, He continued. Nor did we want anyone to doubt our promise, our Word, or character. As it stands later many of the Redeemed will struggle, not just with sin, but also with truly trusting us. Even though they may know in their mind they should; because of the lies and deception that follows Light Bringer to many it will be lost for a time. He is near the Temple now and the doors will not hold. The Host have done their duty, and have shown great love and honor to us. The moment of hope is almost passed. But I will stop this and allow per grace and mercy . . . Light Bringer's choice."

The doors of the Temple exploded inward and Lucifer and his horde raced toward the Throne of God.

"**Enough**." Was all that escaped the Father of Lights lips, a fraction of His true power embedded in the Word sent shockwaves throughout all of Creation itself and everything stopped.

Host and horde alike were stilled. No one moved or stirred, but paused waiting for the word from the Father of Lights. The Host had dropped their swords to their sides and released their opponents. The horde was still; yet straining against an unseen barrier, like an anxious beast set to run.

Lucifer flew to the steps near the Throne of God sword pointed at The Father of Lights and raged. "No! No it is not enough. Light Father you must stop or see our Realm destroyed. You must not allow these things to be. You . . . need but to rest. And you will see the truth. These parts of creation you make are wondrous. But is it not enough what we do have? Is it not wondrous to see the Host moving throughout all you survey and hearing your praise? What need have we for these **Redeemed**! Why will we have these "**broken**" among us? Why do we need flaws at all? How can they compare to us, your Host? We are strong, We are powerful; we are beautiful, and without defect are we not?"

Lucifer Continued, voice rising. "How can they equal us? What task can they do, that we cannot do better? How have we slipped from Your gaze, or not followed commands as dictated? Have our melodies been so terrible to Your ears as to move us aside to be . . . **replaced** by the "Flawed"? Can they stand among the stars as we? Can they walk through fire and cold as we? Can they look on suns like us? Or stand pure before you as we? No, no they cannot . . . they are less than even us. We have all obeyed! We all, especially I, followed every command and yet, we are being replaced. We are stepping aside for those less fortunate than us. What will they do? How have they captured Your heart against us? Has this Redeemed watched as You called into being stars, light, dark, sounds, music, melody, and even our Realm? Now along with Creation itself, we wait and we watch. Father of Lights, you need to step down and rest. Surely, you are not seeing things right. And until the time you are rested and well someone must hold this Realm together and continue with your requests. The Son too, must rest; even He has not been Himself. Surely, I could step in and hold the Realm till all are well. I am over the Throne of God and orchestrate the music of the Realm and the Host. I could assist You until that time as You feel you can return to your duties as Father of all."

The Father of Lights, Great I Am stood, His eyes filled with tears, deep in sorrow, He spoke gently and quietly. The Realm was still, awaiting His next words.

"Light Bringer, be it known, to all that hear My voice now: We never were dissatisfied with you. You were first among the Host, because We deemed it so. You were above the Throne, because you were created to be there. An honor and tribute to you and your heart and to Our Glory, we loved you then even as now. That position you hold just as the others was never intended to be used to dominate or control the Host or anyone. But those positions were to be a guide for those that would follow.

This would allow them to understand that everything, everything has worth and a place of honor in the Kingdom. From I the Father of Lights, to the atom that spins about that none can yet see! All of it reflects Our handiwork, Our fingerprint if you will, that gives Us glory but still has value beyond measure. Each of you, I could call by name, have great value, far beyond what you understand and see. Yet, you struggle so, due to lies and fear."

He looked directly at Lucifer; who still in defiance, had sword raised. The Father of Lights looked deep in his eyes and down into his heart. His countenance moved with his heart's pain. The Father knew already Light Bringer's choice, but grieved as He read it.

God continued. "This battle is ended. You will not fight one another any longer here in the Realm. There is a choice here for all. The choice brought to you is because of sin. The effects of sin that never should have been. But, out of mercy and grace, things can be made right. Contrary to what you have heard, I am not ill. Nor am I letting things in this Realm, or out of it, slip in any way. The need for the stars and planets are more than items of "ego" as you may have been told, but markers for those outside this Realm and for travel and wonder . . ."

Lucifer cringed inwardly at the last statement. *Yes, I said that is true. But is it really not ego? All we see is to be marked with Your hand is it? What of our own? All things bold and beautiful are to Your praise? The all Father is putting on quite a show.*

Speaking directly to Lucifer, the God of all Creation spoke "Lucifer, stop. Have you not heard? Have you not listened? Your place is above my Throne. You have been gifted with music and beauty to inspire all, not just in Our Realm. You are wrong to feel slighted or abused. These are lies that have caused sin to grow; you were never meant to bear the weight of the Universe. I alone as God do. I am the One; for many reasons, that can do so justly and in righteousness. You along with all Creation were to point and guide everything back to me, as examples of wonder and awe. I will ask you again, will you hear the truth and return to me and take your honored place, or have you decided otherwise?"

Light Bringer stopped, lowered his sword and straightened his garments. He caught the flashing hues of color as he smoothed out the wrinkles and tried to hide the sliced fabric.

"Light Father, true You are above all. There is none like You. All around us is evidence of Your might, power and glory. All this vast beauty and wonder of the Realm, this will be destroyed if You cannot see reason." He paused.

He spun a slow circle arms wide and continued, "This Realm is a small part of all Your work and it is truly wondrous! The stars, planets and Universe move with but a whisper from Your lips. And yet, I cannot but feel that we are missing a key element here. Why now, after so many millennia, is there need for Creation?

We the Host, sorry, Your Host would have outnumbered the stars themselves. We your Messengers strong, powerful and beauteous, help at every turn and whim.

Could it be that You Father, are fearful . . . of us? Could it be that You are afraid that we may decide to move beyond 'our place' as you say? I for one like things as they are. But, of course, you may have tired Yourself out from all that You have made and need rest. And you would not allow anyone else in the Realm, or out of it, to make any decisions, as we all know. It is a sad thing for someone so gifted and able, to have their resources unused or untapped. But that decision is yours and it is a loss of beauty and wonder all its own. I would have gladly assisted if I had been consulted. Of course, no one is as wise or knowledgeable as You. Therefore, sadly Creation would not be **perfect**. Why then, could not I as example create like You? Don't I create melodies and harmonies that live on after I speak? I could create wonders and beauty because I embody it. As for standing in your stead . . ." He sneered, ". . . I could be as the Most High, I was after all the first of the Host, why can I not watch over this great Realm in your stead while you rest Yourself . . .or is it that what you fear?" His words dripped now with disdain. "Yes! Yes that is the truth we all need to know now. This was never about my place above the Throne nor about the music, or the Host; You were afraid I might do better!" He laughed, cold and clear, continuing. "I have handled for millennia the Host and the music and many other things You called for. And now I see clearly, you were keeping me from my **rightful** place. You gave me beauty, even power and position, knowing one day I would seek it out to finally take my **true place**!"

"Then this decision to return as you have requested is beneath me." Turning to the Crowd, "And beneath them! You have led us well, but surely Your time is over. You are not yourself; You are weary and depressed and heart sick over Creation and the making of the Redeemed, as well you should be! The Great I Am has faltered and stumbled from His loftiness! No, I will not return. . . I will rule in your place. And we all shall build the Realm! And further Creation!" Raising his voice he toned "We shall build much and each of you will do wondrously! Under my benevolent guidance we shall expand this rule and show the Redeemed their true place! And nothing and no one will stop us! You, Father, have denied us this! To rule at your side and guide all with great wisdom and mercy, we, the great ones, the mighty ones, the Host! Isn't that fair and equal? All of us, together, under guidance of course, and that is what shall be soon." Some of the Host stirred and raised a cheer; others watched as Lucifer smiled, tears filled their eyes.

The Father of all the Universe spoke strong and clear. "We have heard you and have made a provision for what has transpired here today. You, Light Bringer have chosen to not accept the grace and mercy I offer you, nor its benefits. And also you of the Host have made a decision as well have you not?"

Rumblings of descent could be heard clearly now, a growing swell like a coming storm on a sea. And all Creation waited in mute silence, waiting on the Father of Lights next words.

"Light Bringer, Lucifer and all that choose to follow you from this Realm, you are judged and that rightly. You are cast from your place in this Realm to Earth, Sheol even the pit. For sin in your heart, along with pride, rebellion, and violence that dwells within you, so that all may see you and remember the cost of sin! You of the Host that have chosen a new king, will follow him to his new kingdom . . . it is done."

All of Creation and the Universe stood mute witness to the word spoken. The Word was not loud, nor long, forced, or even overwrought with emotion; it was just "**done**."

The Realm rippled; Creation trembled with the impact of Light Bringer and one third of the Host arrival on and in the earth below! A cry of agony was heard as the very fabric of Earth was changed to accommodate them.

Shock was evident on every face in the Realm as the Son surveyed the crowd. Then a deep sigh was heard throughout the entire Universe and Father of Lights returned to the Throne. He sat down again and turned to the Son and spoke.

"Woe to the Earth and Sea, because Satan has come down to you, having great wrath. . . You will need to be ready soon. And so must mankind."

Jesus, the Son of God, snapped back to the present and again found Himself in darkness. He had been expecting this moment and in His humanness, dreading it.

The darkness was now even more alive; if of course darkness lived. He began to feel deep in Himself the stirring subtle at first, yet it was growing. *So this is the beginning of real fear . . .* He thought.

He noticed the beginnings of the rapid heartbeat, blood pressure rising. And now the anxiety coupled with dread, and danger, threat, feeling of flight and rising anger intensified. He pushed up on the tortured heel again and gained a shallow breath, then another and another, finally leg muscle cramps began, and He lowered Himself back down. The Son of God heard laughter, the voice was familiar, it was Light Bringer's or Satan's, as he was thought of now by mortal men and angels. That sent a shockwave through His heart and soul unlike anything before. The laughter was not genuine or kind, or loving in any way. It held a malice and twisted hint of triumph which the owner thought genuine. The anxiety and fear grew in the heart of the Son of God. It seemed to move and shift with every beat of His aching, tortured heart, almost alive!

Little does he understand what takes place here. The Son of God thought. *He has missed the significance of what is done today, because of the lies and falsehoods he has told himself. He still feels he is right in what he does, that he can gain what was lost so long ago. And even triumph over man and Our plan to redeem mankind. He sees this Cross as the vehicle to end God's entire plan. He knows men's hearts, the want of sin and selfishness, and can easily manipulate their lives and actions to perceive great loss on their behalf and to turn still, hearts away from us and Redemption.* He groaned as He bore the wave upon wave of fear, then terror, building upon the generations past, present and future. The laughter increased growing in volume and strength. *He hopes to torture me worse and inflict deeper wounds upon me for the false slights and wrongdoings. His rage is such as to blind him from the better result that will come with My death. He sees an end and only an end.* The Son of God laughed in Himself and pushed up on His fragile heel. He could feel the weight of fear, anger, hatred, rejection, and self-loathing grow. And now the abandonment of millions, as anxiety, anguish of soul, regret, setting His soul to fever pitch, only to be denied the basic comfort of companionship and acceptance. He turned His heart toward Heaven; at least He still could commune with the Father! *Father, it's me your Son* pausing to gather His thoughts, *Is this how they feel every day? Even by those who say they are loved by Us? We never intended for the Family to be so broken or live so crushed and dying. They were to walk, whether in family or even individuals, in complete and total acceptance and peace, right?* He waited for the Father's response deep in His soul to feel the familiar touch of His heart that He knew and loved. Yet, there was silence and stillness as He waited.

He strained His ears to hear the familiar and welcome tones from Heaven, none came. He moved gaining another ragged breath and turned His face toward the darkened sky and heavens . . . waiting. Every fiber of His being now taut straining, looking, searching and hoping...however, all was met by cold, clear silence!

Even the shouts and jeers of the crowd and soldiers were stilled; He only heard His beating heart in His ears. *Where are you? Father, I can't see You or Your hand moving, nor Your mind or heart . . . did You hear my cry?* He grimaced inwardly, *that was **doubt!*** The Son of God shook as the realization dawned upon His soul; *I have been **abandoned!** I am alone. I have no one to help . . . even* He noticed the rage and laughter had ceased . . . *My enemy is silent.*

He pushed up again on the tortured heel and screamed with all His being at the darkness and lifeless sky. "**ELI, ELI, LAMA SABACHTHANI? Why my God have you forsaken Me!**" No one in the darkness of the hour saw the tears shed by the One and only Son of God. He hung in utter anguish and torment never before known or understood, yet, He did remember another time long, long ago it seemed. . .

CHAPTER 2

TINKER, TAILOR, SPY AND THE COST

The Son of God stepped down onto the cool lush Earth of the Garden. He could feel the thrum of life beneath His feet, and the tickle that the blades of grass made as He moved to the center of the Garden.

He was inspecting His work. He knew Creation was as He spoke or sang it, but some things, most things, need the personal touch and this garden was no different. He adjusted the color of a rose, somehow purple, didn't seem to fit. But the deep red would soon speak of great love. And the stem having thorns would speak more of the costliness of life, true life. He looked to the lush deep green of the grass, adjusted the height and tip, to ensure a gentle inviting touch. He wandered among the trees and shrubs and those He also inspected. Touching, changing, molding, sculpting, all was near readiness for the one, *no the couple,* that would live here.

The Son of God laughed. He laughed as the creation around Him responded to His touch. *All of Creation has Our fingerprint, from the stars to these flowers and lawn I tread upon, and soon mankind too.* He stopped and listened. The air carried music, even the gentle breeze, had a voice. The grass and flowers leaned in toward Him and the animals nearby came close, as he looked at each one in turn. He touched bear, deer, lion, and tiger, on they came, and they nuzzled the One Who held all in His hand. He turned and walked further into the Garden of God. *Man will call it that one day, and then be kept from it . . . by force, definitely not by Our choice, but his own. We must do it so the evil and sin will not touch Our Realm. But thankfully, it will not be for a while yet, but all too soon.* He thought.

He stood now in a clearing surrounded by trees of every type and size. Trees that would hold food, medicines and even shelter if handled correctly. The throng of Creation looked on as He turned back to them and spoke.

"The Father of Lights and I call on you to live; live with all that you are with joy and hope and point the way to the Kingdom that is, and to the Father of Lights." He looked on trying not to reveal the pain He felt.

"Soon, man will be among you, and he will need your help. He is young, younger even than your little ones. Share wisdom and this place in peace."

"There will come a time sooner than I would like, that will be hard on you, all of you. This very Earth upon which we now walk will ache for the choices he will make, and soon the peace you know will be shattered. But know, it is not permanent, and peace will again reign as now. But, you point the way to the Father and the kingdom . . . ALL of you, do this for The Father's Glory and man's hope." He moved deeper into the Garden of God and with the Master Builder's eye turned slowly, verifying that all was in readiness. And He could hear the calls of the birds, animals, chitter of insects, and the breeze in the trees whispering. . .

"Life, breath, peace, hope ... thank you for all you have done!"

The Son of God moved to a small brook that ended in a small pool of clear water shaded by pine trees. The trees stretched a half circle and flowed up a small hill to another copse of trees, mixed with oak, maple, gray birch and others. He could hear the gentle breeze whisper, branches rustled as He knelt by the pool. The scent of pine was soothing, as well as the carpet of pine nettles.

The Son of God closed His eyes and was still. Breathing deeply He reached out to touch Creation around him. **Peace**, *man will enjoy places like this one day. If he remembers, and stops I hope he will find us in places as these*, He thought. *The Father looks forward to times like these where there will be no distractions or worry just being and peace.*

He reached out His hand and touched the still pool. God's Son watched the ripple flow out from the contact and sparkle as the stray light strands touched the water. He cupped his hand and scooped out water pouring it into the pool watching as it shimmered. He put his hand again into the cool water and drew water to His mouth and swallowed.

Cool, clean, refreshing filled Hs heart. Sighing He stood and turned away from the pool to a patch of green not covered in nettles.

His hand brushed the green lawn and felt the Earth thrum from His touch. He smiled and paused, *everything is ready now, all is in place, but you.* He chuckled in His heart and continued; *too bad I couldn't solve sin's problem by waiting or not creating you. But truth to tell, you mean all to us and your presence in this place will fill our creation with such joy, laughter, excitement and yes, stress. See and future parents won't think we understand their struggle. I think it is time the world meets you my friend, loved by us and dear.*

The Son of God laid his hand upon the green lawn and wiped away the green carpet like a painter applying base to canvas. The rich brown Earth was surrounded by the green grass and sheltered by the shade of the trees. The Creator God began to hum and then He sang as He worked. All Creation heard the stir of melody, harmony, base line and structure. Birds alighted in the trees and curious animals had gathered to watch in silence.

His hands reached deep into the brown Earth and the ground became pliable and rolled as if it were liquid. The melody and music grew, and He formed a hand with all the correct digits and opposable thumb. And began to contour the wrist and forearm to the bicep, triceps, and shoulder. *The arms would be needed for balance and lifting, along with holding, working, protecting. The arms and hands could be used for many things, they needed to be strong, yet able to be gentle, to give comfort, and assurance.* He thought to Himself.

Creator God moved to the head and chest cavity and added the trunk and legs. *This Man is to be many things. So he will need to be physically strong and able; he will also need wisdom, tenderness, and be able to show mercy and kindness. He will need great knowledge and compassion to do as the Father of Light, the Spirit and I deem right.* The Son of God stopped. He reached for a small patch of ground and made two bumps in the ground. And turned back to the chest area of the man. He scooped up one small mound of dirt and with His other hand He opened the chest cavity. He looked at the rough pear shaped mound of Earth and paused.

I am sorry that you will bear the brunt of what is to come. The Son of God laughed, knowing full well that it would truly be Him that bore the brunt of what was to come. *But, you also will bear much and be so* *misunderstood. You will hold much and seem so empty and fragile, yet enable great things. The human heart would be man's receptacle of courage, joy, love, tenderness, compassion, dreams, songs, and bravery. And soon because of sin, deep sorrow and anguish, overrun with selfishness and death. Yet, thankfully, you can love one another, and **US** and live as you were meant too. In spite of your hearts bent to sin, We can be together and have a wonderful life and Eternity. You don't have to choose sin at all. There is that hope, albeit a small hope. I will do what must be done and with great joy! Know that at least . . .* God's Son thought tenderly, as He placed the heart in the Chest of the Man and also sealed the head that would house the man's vast intellect.

God's Son moved over the form He had made with great care; yet, the sculptor's skill flowed on as He hummed. The Divine Creator left no detail undone or unfished. Man and soon woman, would be the template for generations of humans that would fill the Earth. And the differences would only be superficial and skin deep. Their blood would flow the same, just His would soon on a dark and dreaded hill. But **His Blood** would redeem, where theirs could end their meager existence and short life, all because of sin and its death.

He stepped back from the form as the sun's light broke through the trees and washed it in a golden shaft of warmth. He reached down to the hand and wrist that was upturned and lifted. The rest of the form followed with ease and soon was upright and standing. He touched the cheek and molded it a little tighter and set the strong jaw and brushed away the soft nettles that clung to the hair, at this moment mud strands.

He made sure the legs and back were strong to bear great weight and to move and flow with equal stability and precision. *You will carry on this back many things, and many things you should not, but you will. Not that I or the Father of Lights like the idea, nor that want you to. All because of **Sin** that will weigh on you and destroy so many* The Son of God thought. *But not without hope. That you will have. I vow to you before you ever have life that My back will bear the greatest burden ever! So that you will never have too.* The Son of God cringed as His mind flashed to a day in the future and He heard a crack of whip and furrows of blood as they erupted from His back. He saw even now what He would face, all for love and mankind's sake. . .

The Creator and Sustainer of all things stood and wiped the Earth from His hands and walked around His creation. He with an artist eye covered the Creation from head-to-toe and made sure this was as it should be. This template for a whole race. A template for one He loved so dearly, and one that He would sacrifice so much for.

The Creator turned and saw Creation. Every type that walked on Earth, standing behind Him in the grove. Everyone has this curious look in their eye, and a voiceless question. And He knew what they were.

What is this one like? What is the name? What sound does it make? How will it be with little ones? He smiled. He needed to assure them that all was well. And that He as Creator would always be doing things for the good of all.

He spoke to them gently, "This is Adam. He is part of the Redeemed. He will be with us soon and watch over this Garden and you. He will have many questions, you and I together, will guide him. The time of sorrow is not yet, so you need not fear him or your little ones. I will be here as always too."

The Son of God turned back to the man before him; leaning close, He God, **breathed**.

The Creator and those encircling the grove stepped back. At first they heard a single clear note, then harmonies, bass, the music of Creation. .
.

And watched as the dirt and mud covered figure began to change. The changes were in time with the growing melody and song. With every beat and chord, they saw the mud and dirt of Earth melt away and leave clear smooth skin. The mud caked hair changed to strands of brown wavy curls and locks. The song of Creation rose and fell as it swirled around this figure, and finally fell silent as man stood before all.

The Son of God and Creation that was present could see a fire in his eyes. And from the tilt of His head with the intensity of tensed muscles, also a hint of fear, mixed with. . .*What am I seeing?* The Son thought, *fear, confusion, question. He was supposed to be in awe, wonder, joy, and hope, not this. .This must stop now.*

"**Adam** . . . He Paused. Gently again He spoke his name, **Adam**, I am *Your Father; No, no that's not right!* He thought with a chuckle, *that's someone else's line.*

"Created by God, you are part of this creation and part of My Universe. This is Eden, My Garden. You are to care for it and also the creatures that roam the land and sea. You will have authority over all. Except of course, Myself. And you will live here in love, joy, and peace. Do you understand?" The Son of God paused.

He turned as Creation melted back into the forest and trees. They will all come to Him soon, in their own time. "**Adam** walk with me." God said. He watched as Adam turned to face Him and moved in step with Him easily. *How soon it will be hard for you to walk with me,* He thought. *You were never intended to be anywhere else but here, at my side. And truthfully, you were to have me even closer still. Yet, that will come, but at such a high cost. But one I will gladly bear,* He Thought.

God the Son moved to a nearby clearing and stopped. The clearing was lush green and rimmed with trees. And off to the right a gentle brook rolled by. The Creator turned to Adam and spoke, "This is part of My Garden, Eden. I have a task for you at the moment. I need you to name your friends."

Adam looked confused. "God, Creator, You want me to name my friends?"

"Yes. I am sure you can do this. And this will be the first task you will complete for Me. Don't worry; you will do fine." God's Son grinned.

The Creator spoke one word. "**Come**" And one-by-one, all manner of creatures came from the wood. Adam sat down on the green lawn and waited.

I see wonder, and fear, but a healthy fear. One that will allow for protection and comfort. Not the terror earlier, He thought. *Oh, how much will be lost to that perversion that Satan and his horde's influence will cause; some would call it a condition.*

God's Son watched as Adam came face-to-face with a lion and its mate. *There! That's what I intended; there is wonder on his face mingled with excitement, awe, and joy!* His thoughts finished, "What will their name be Adam?" *I know full well what He will choose, but I must follow the plan.*

One-by-one two-by-two the animals flowed passed Adam, and he walked to the river where most of the fish had waited, on and on it flowed, the "**wonder**" God saw. . .never left his eyes.

The sun faded and twilight moved through the Garden casting red and other hues across the trees and plants. Creator God turned and spoke.

"You did well today Adam. I knew you could. Go and rest now, all of Creation needs to rest; it's been a long day for all of you."

"Alright, Creator I will," Adam said.

"Adam, you do know I love you . . . and I think you may call me by my name as well. You may find that I will soon have many names, but, Adonai is a favorite," the LORD said. "I must leave you for a time but I will return to you soon. Live and love well."

The Son of God turned from Adam and caught a brief smudge of darkness by a Hemlock tree. *I see you as well . . . **Liar,** He thought.*

The Word seemed to echo in the mind and heart of God's son as He breathed heavily. It seemed to grow in strength and intensity, even in volume until God in the flesh shocked awake amidst the ever present torture of the Cross!

Still He heard the word . . . liar, LIAR, **LIAR. . . LIAR . . . LIAR!** The crowd screamed! Then laughter.

*The Truth is this . . . I am the **TRUTH**, the **Way**, and **LIFE**. No one comes to the FATHER but through me. All of this work, all of Mankind's past and present, and future depends on defeating this **LIE**.* His thoughts continued.

*Lucifer is the Father of Lies. He was a Liar from the beginning. He even began believing, and will continue to believe them. He could have come back to the Realm and to **Us**. All of this, would not have been needed at all. But He questioned and took the lies as truth; then, even as now . . .* His thoughts faded as He traveled back to a place long ago.

The Son of God silently waited next to Adam; who at the moment, was still and staring into the flowing stream. He remained still and watched as the life of the Garden flowed around Adam. He saw as the birds darted overhead and sang to each other and to Him. As Creator, this warmed His heart. The trees and land was full of lush growth teeming with life. *This is His favorite place, by the stream of life and near the center of the Garden. The Tree of Life is near and the Tree of Knowledge. All these trees, here and throughout the Garden, have medicinal benefits.*

I'm not sure why mankind will choose pills over natural medicine, but sadly they will. And they will pay a high price for it . . . even more so than money. He thought.

I don't think He knows I am here. He is definitely deep in thought. There is an ache in his heart and soul. Yes, I knew this day would come, as with all men. His emotions and desires are conflicting and shaken.

"**Adam,**" He spoke his name as only God could. He then waited.

Adam Finally spoke and God's Son could hear the pain in his voice, tinged with loneliness.

"Adonai, Creator, I hurt, but am not sick. I ache, but I am not strained. I hunger, but am not in need of food. My heart aches and is sad, but I am surrounded on all sides by friends, beauty and wonder. I see the animals and fish, birds and even insects, **together** . . ." He paused, "with mates that were chosen for them. But Father, where is my mate?"

Man was made for intimacy and so was Creation. Intimacy, belonging, value, unconditional love. All of this We know and we want to share this with them and share life with them. The Creator thought. *But for many their battle with sin will hinder even the very basic things of relationship . . . especially intimacy. All because of a lie that they as individuals have no value or worth.*

"**That, Adam**, is a good Question. One that we can rectify shortly, because it isn't right that you are alone. And your mate will be many things to you. Valuable . . . things. More than you may understand at first," Adonai said. "But together there are more wonders than even your eyes have yet to see."

"Adam, I think you may want to rest now. And let your heart be at peace; do not worry, the Garden will be fine today. You need not labor and you may find that a good night sleep can solve many issues. I think when you wake from sleep, your answer may already be here. Know I love you, as does the Father and Spirit," God finished.

Adam rose from the ground and moved to his favorite resting place.

Creator God watched; as Adam walked to the small pine stand, near the pool and to the mat he had made to rest upon. As the last rays of sun cast themselves to Earth; they caught the water, sending flashes of gold against the deep evergreen branches. . And then Adam, the first man, fell asleep.

Now that you are asleep, the Creator thought, *We can help your heart dear one. I think you will be pleasantly surprised and comforted when I am finished. And the world may have a beauty it's never known, now and for future generations. She will be even more.*

The music began again, He knelt and began humming. The Creator touched Adam on his side and reached in and pulled a rib from his side. Gently He closed the skin, held the rib and shook His head. *There will be too many bad jokes about you and relationships when I finish Adam's mate. But, even bad humor makes a point.* His thoughts finished.

God's Son touched the ground and wiped away the lawn near Adam. He then pushed the rib into the malleable ground singing as He did. The song was a little different than Creation heard before. The song was lighter, brighter, and flowed sweetly. Then came a touch of sadness, tears, and tenderness. But in another moment it would soar melded with passion, protection and fierceness that is unequaled. *At least in human terms,* God thought.

God molded the hand, forearm and shoulder, more delicate and supple than Adam's. And then the trunk and legs. He took the hand and again stood His Creation up. He circled the figure and began to sing and weave melody and harmony.

The Master sculpture began the fine work of detail. His hands flowed over the head of the figure and the neck; blocks of mud fell away, revealing an elegance and beauty unseen before. As He worked the music never stopped. The face held tenderness and the eyes, a hint of mystery, and mischief, a gentle jaw and full inviting lips, that would display conversation, laughter, and warmth.

Next He molded the upper body for utility and a beauty all its own. And the smooth lines followed the hip, thigh and calve ending in delicate feet. He adjusted here and tucked there, sculpted and molded a sleekness and grace. *One thing I know she will attract attention wherever she goes. She is in no way intimidating like Adam, she is and will carry an air of compassion and empathy.*

He stepped back and looked over this new Creation, Adam's mate, helper, helpmeet, companion, lover, and friend. The figure held a regalness, dignity and beauty.

She will be the mother of nations; and yet, fiercely protect her home and family. Yes, quite unique indeed. God Finished. *Oh wait; she needs her crown and glory. There, you now are ready to meet Adam.* He had molded a covering that flowed down her shoulders and back, *your hair.*

God Breathed.

"Adam," God called, "wake up my friend and meet your mate."

The melody of Creation had faded and the morning sun shone into the small grove. The birds had just begun to sing and morning had arrived in the Garden.

He watched as Adam stretched and stood. Looking at the sunrise and he too caught the scent of wildflowers and honey. Another day, another piece of God's plan fulfilled.

Then He Heard Adam Gasp! He watched as Adam stood frozen. *Poor Adam,* He thought, *shock or awe? Wonder.* God laughed in His heart. Adam locked eyes with the figure before him. He took a tentative step in her direction and smiled.

"This is my mate? She will be called "woman," God heard him say. "Because she was taken from man." "Hello," Adam continued, "My Name is Adam. What is your name?"

The first woman spoke with assurance, "My name is Eve."

God watched in joy as the romance of the ages began in the Garden. He saw as Adam led her around to each of the animals, and pointed out the trees, shrubs, and birds. Just as Adam before her, wonder never left her eyes.

God left them near evening to enjoy the Garden and each other as intended.

The Father of Lights spoke to the Son, "You need to go to the Garden and help Adam. It has begun."

The Son looked down in despair as He watched Lucifer slink through the Garden and subtly speak to Eve. He knew what Satan would say. And it angered Him. *He couldn't even give them a month. His hatred over these perceived slights is strong and the lies he has come to believe as truth, push him farther and farther from any hope of redemption. Not that he sees any sin or wrong on his part. He sees only just, "Our blatant disregard for him and Our narcissistic drive to destroy his dreams and plans." He still would be God; created being though he is, sin has ravaged him so. If he would only repent.* The Son thought. *I will have to go down and soon pass judgment on this situation and also soon remove Our loved ones far away, and pass judgment on Creation, that never should have been. But; hope, still lives. And hope will win, carrying with it grace and mercy.*

The morning sun touched the Garden. Its light and warmth stirred Eve. She opened her eyes, stretched and stood. She passed her hands through her autumn colored main with ease. She looked for Adam, who was already somewhere in the Garden. She would find him she thought after something to eat! And headed deeper into the Garden. She grabbed a mango and enjoyed the sweet taste and aroma.

Then she saw the serpent. She had seen it in the Garden before. His scales reflecting light; in a kaleidoscope of color, and his voice smooth and clear.

"Did God really say, . . ." smoothly, "that you cannot eat from the trees of the Garden?" The Serpent paused.

Eve perked up "actually," she said with an air of confidence, "of all these trees in the Garden we can eat. But, the one in the center of the Garden we cannot eat nor touch. Lest we die."

God the Son stepped into the Garden unseen. He watched as the conversation continued, wishing he could step in and stop all of it. However, the plan He and The Father had set needed to be fulfilled. *I wish she had eyes as mine, she would not be standing here speaking to the Serpent. She would be crying to Adam to come and take his place and destroy this enemy and free Creation of its future chains.* He thought.

"**Really**, are you **Sure**?" the Serpent toned. "I think He knows that if you eat it, your eyes will be opened and you will be **just like God**. And you will know good and evil."

The Son watched painfully as Eve's struggle began. His eyes saw truth, and the inky blackness that permeated the Serpent and dripped from his skin. This was not the beautiful creature Eve saw, but Lucifer incarnate.

I want to stop this! But I mustn't. She must choose and so must Adam. Though I will handle Lucifer severely and justly. This must be allowed to finish its course, not that I am happy about it. He thought sadly.

Eve stopped and looked at the Tree of Knowledge. *I never told them not to touch it. I can hear her questions, how clever you are* **Lucifer**. *You want to hinder Our relationship even at the start,* He thought. He heard her thoughts . . . [*How did I get here? I don't remember coming to the Tree of Knowledge. It has good fruit, the branches are heavy with it. It is a beautiful tree. What did God really say? Why is it so hard to remember? I know my husband would be proud of me if I was smarter. And of course, if I am smarter I could do more things around the Garden and be of greater use to him. And of Couse, wisdom brings beauty right?]*

The Serpent stood still and watched like a hunter stalking prey. And a soft snicker began as Eve reached for the fruit on the closest branch. God Himself watched in dreaded silence, as her hand drew closer to the fruit and grasped it.

All of Creation held its collective breath; waiting, what would she choose? *Obedience? Or rebellion? Which will it be Eve, you haven't sinned yet, but the crossroads are here. Where is Adam? Your husband . . . I know there was not that much work to be done today. He will soon choose next. Will he stand or fall?* God thought.

Slowly, almost imperceptibly, the snicker became a giggle; then a pause. Only to be drowned out by laughter, not joyous, but terrible final evil laughter. Just then, Eve took a bite of the fruit.

The Son's heart saddened. And He waited see what Adam would choose, even though He knew. *She was Beautiful and wise, just as Adam was, how was it that she believed differently? I know why; because she questioned My purposes and My word and her value. Simple doubt caused disobedience and rebellion. Though they had help.* His thought ended as He watched Eve still.

Eve had squeezed her eyes closed tightly, expecting lightning or terrible, terrible death! Tentatively she opened her eyes, the fruit tasted sweet and cool. It was a refreshing taste. It felt warm, good and satisfying. Fear, dread, gave way to wonder. I am not dead just as the Serpent said. I must let Adam know and he too can eat of this fruit. What else has God not told us?

"Adam, Adam," she called.

"I am over here beloved!" Adam said.

God watched in silence as Adam turned to his wife and took from her hand the fruit of the tree. He did not question or pause, he took and ate.

Eve looked for the Serpent, but he was nowhere to be seen. She shrugged her shoulders and watched her husband finish the fruit.

God knew then the die had been cast, man had chosen sin and rebellion over love and grace. He would have to go the Cross, suffer and die to redeem His love, His dear ones.

God stood on a hill outside the Garden and listened. "Eve, what is this? We are naked. What has happened? How is this possible?" Adam said.

"I ate some fruit and now I am naked," she said.

"What fruit? Which one?" His voice rising.

"The same one you did," Eve countered.

"Which fruit, tell me?" He said.

"The Tree of Knowledge in the center of the Garden," Eve said.

"God will be here soon; we cannot be seen like this! We must do something **now**!" Adam spoke.

"We are not dead as the Serpent said, what else has God not told us?" she returned.

The Creator God of the Universe sighed deeply and slowly shook His head. *They don't understand; this was not a physical death but a spiritual death. We now will be separated because of **Sin** and the **Lies** spread by sin. Mankind will return to Us but only after Millennia of unnecessary hardships and pain. But for the sake of love and Our plan, redemption is possible and worth it.*

"Now, I must face Creation and judge it. And it breaks My heart to do so," God said.

"Adam, **Adam** . . . where are you?" Adonai called. *I know where you are. I know what you have done. Choices are made to the detriment of many. But another choice, to the blessing of all!* He thought, still moving through the Garden, to where they had both hidden themselves due to shame.

"I am Here Creator; I heard your step and voice and hid because I was naked," came Adam's sheepish voice from a lilac bush.

"Adam, who told you that you were naked? God paused. Have you eaten from the Tree of Knowledge that I told you not to eat of?"

The Creator waited. He knew what would come next, though He did not relish it.

Now; the blame game begins. One to the other and back again. No one taking responsibility for their actions or even repenting of the sin. His thoughts finished and Adam quickly spoke.

"The Woman you gave to be with me, gave of the Tree of Knowledge and I ate," The man said.

God turned to the woman, "What is this you have done?"

"The Serpent deceived me and I ate of the Tree," She said emphatically.

The Serpent was present now. *This is not the same Serpent I know, just the patsy that Satan deceived Eve with. He allowed it. And didn't warn her or Adam, so he also is to blame.* God thought.

"Because you have done this, you will be cursed now, and always, more than all cattle and beast of field. On your belly you will go all your days. I will make you the enemy of the woman and man, between her seed and yours. **HE** shall bruise you on the head, and you his heel." He said to the Serpent.

Turning to the woman God continued, "The pain of birth will greatly increase as you bear children and you will be desirous of your husband and of his place, but he will rule over you."

Finally, to the man, Adam, God spoke, "Because you listened to the voice of your wife; and ate from the Tree of Knowledge, I must now curse the ground. Because of this, both thorns and thistles will grow, and you will eat food by the sweat of your brow until you return to the Earth in death. Because you were taken from the ground as dust, to dust you will return."

God stood silent before them. *Sin must be paid for. Guilt borne by one who is innocent. I will bear that for them in the future, but I do this now as an example, that forgiveness comes at a high price. My sacrifice will wipe away all sin and guilt. But until that day, these sacrifices are but a shadow of the true price of sin's cost. And because He is like us, he must be moved from this Garden, lest he eat of the Tree of Life and live eternally evil, without conscience or regret.*

"Wait here," He said. "I will return."

The first man and woman huddled together in fear and anguish. Seeing for the first time God's holiness and righteous anger.

"I am sorry that you had to pay the price for man's foolishness; but know this sacrifice will teach them the preciousness of life, and the seriousness of sin." The Creator spoke over the two dead animals. The skins He created for them to wear felt awkward in His hands. *But, they must be covered. And they must know sin costs. The cost is more than they can understand.* His thoughts continued, *One day, they will truly understand.*

"**Cenehard,** come to me." God cried. And within moments, the angel stood before the Son of God.

"What is your command my King?" Cenehard said.

"I need you to stand at the entrance to Eden. Sword ready. Mankind cannot eat the fruit of the Tree of Life, **Ever**. The cost would be too great."

God Creator walked Adam and Eve to the edge of the Garden of God. He looked over His shoulder to the angel, Cenehard, blazing sword in hand. *This will be a lonely post for you my friend, but this will pass quickly, and man one day will return to paradise, not this Eden, but our very Realm and presence.* He thought.

He turned to the man and woman, speaking gently.

"Adam, Eve, do not return here. Only death awaits you. Though you have disobeyed My commands my love remains for you. I will hear you when you pray and call My Name. I will still watch over you. But we will not walk together in fellowship as before, for many lifetimes. But this is my promise to you . . . We will one day be together again. And you will be among the redeemed of God, and sin and pain, anguish and fear, will be no more. That I promise." God continued, "Be fruitful and multiply, have dominion over all this Earth and all that birds of the air and the beasts of the field, along with the seas and streams. Love one another."

CHAPTER 3:

BEGINNINGS

He snapped back to the present. Pain assaulted Him again. He pushed up to breathe once again. His body shook with the effort it took just to gather air in His lungs.

I don't know if I can finish this Father, He thought. *Oh, right, You can't hear me now. Not because you are deaf or weak but simply because this weight of* **sin** *and* **darkness** *is on me.*

Mankind was never to have borne this weight ever. They were not to struggle because of **SIN.** *Yes, struggle is involved to be men and women that were to rule. They were to rule over all the Earth and care for one another in peace.*

Living apart from the Father and I is hard enough; but having an enemy that plots and schemes, and commits all of his resources to find more ways to destroy and rob mankind of the blessings and gifts my father and I bestow. Robbing them of hope and peace, twisting their hearts, even against themselves . . . it seems this has always been the battle. My Father and I have been fighting the continued lies of the Enemy . . . bearing his mockery and arrogance, when just one plot succeeds. . .

In His mind the Son of God found Himself again in the Throne room of God the Father; and sadly, mankind's enemy.

"Light Father, it is I, Lucifer. . ." He smoothly toned, "You're long lost Son. You're second in command, helper and confidant . . ." He crooned, with evil twinkle in his eyes.

The Father spoke clear and strong. "Created one yes, not My confidant, nor anything else you have spewed from those lying lips."

"My, my, are we a bit tense, today all Father, . . .is the work of Redemption wearing upon you Ancient One. . . but of course, you are neither tired nor weary. You never tire of course, just us **lowly** creation." Lucifer spoke in smugness.

The Son of God stood. "What is it that you want Satan?" He said wearily.

"Oh, I am so sorry; did I not introduce myself correctly?? Or have you forgotten. Maybe just like you're Father, this **redemption** plan for those **humans** has worn out Your manners. I am Lucifer, the Morning Star. It is so sad to see just how far this place has fallen without me. No decorum or protocol just besmirchment of one's character."

"State your business or be silent Accuser." The Father of Lights said.

"Oh of course, forgive me, I do tend to prattle on about things. Seeing as I have very few to speak to, of any **adult nature**, your Creation included. But my report of the state of affairs, on this dustbowl of a world You've made and mankind's attempts at conquering it. It seems, that what I have said from the beginning is still true.

Your Creation, just does not have it in them to follow You successfully at all. It seems more and more are coming over to my side of things. I mean have seen how they treat one another and all this killing. Terrible, terrible . . . for something as simple as a woman or a few coins. . . that can be made easily. And the rampant disregard for the animals and everything. And what they do in daylight and dark . . . of course, I can't talk about that, decorum and all." He paused for effect.

Satan continued, "You seem to be losing control of all of this and those that you claim to be able to choose righteousness. They seem more times than not to do just that, not choose righteousness. But I again prattle . . ." he spit out. "So shall I wager with you for humor's sake as to how long these **humans** will survive in **my world**?" Satan Challenged.

"The world Lucifer, is not truly yours. I created it. It is mine. They may have been cheated out of what is truly theirs for now, but that will change. And you may find some that will choose righteousness over sin, but, I think mankind has had too much of your help I think. And if your influence was to diminish, man could yet choose good over evil." The Father of Lights sternly pointed out to Satan.

"If this is all you have to say be gone then," The Father of Lights paused.

"But look at all this **evil** . . . what does Your **righteousness** and **holiness** say **now** O' Great King!" Lucifer spat out. "I will destroy them **all**. That I promise; Your precious redeemed will pay the price of not following **me**...And the Realm will remain empty and barren of all that You have created. You will have **nothing!**" He screamed. "I, Lucifer have said it." And he disappeared in a cloud of darkness. The cloud dissipated and left a smudge on the gold floor of the Throne room.

The Son turned to the Father and said, "He does know, You are the One that gives him power for anything right??"

"No Son, I don't think he remembers anything but his hatred and lust for power, and that longing to rule." The Father spoke sadly.

"He doesn't even know he could return to us anymore. The sin in his heart has moved him beyond all reason and sense."

The Son turned to the Father again, sadness edged his voice, "What he said was true, sin must be punished. Just as the Garden. How do we proceed? Is there is no other way?"

"No Son, We must always offer light in darkness; hope for hopelessness, joy for sadness, peace for fear. He will always try to offer an easier, faster, less costly way to ours, only in the end to reveal his trap, when any hope has finally disappeared and their strength gone. He will promise much; yet, in truth, give little.

He always will give just enough truth, to catch some, but leave the whole truth behind. And He will always convince and lie to the redeemed that they are less than My spoken Word says or even revelation from prophets, or what angels state.

He will pose that question always, 'Did HE Truly say?' And sadly, that will be enough for most; they will wander far from their hope or calling, even the life I planned for them. The one that has them living and being to their fullest potential. The one where, in spite of **sin**, they have great joy, peace, and fulfillment. And finally come home to us in joy. And receive full reward."

The Father shook His head sadly, "And there will be those, that never understand OUR love for them, always infants, or young children in spirit. Never the men, or warriors bred for battle against a soon defeated foe. But for grace, but for mercy, but for forgiveness, but for redemption's work. These will find salvation hardest. Their unbelief or mistrust will hinder their growth, and even the receiving of what We have for them. They won't believe that they are forgiven **ever**. There will always be a piece of them, in doubt. But My Word will stand. They will be able to discern the truth and choose truth over lie. And then they will walk in their fullness. And that, Lucifer cannot let happen. He must reach them before any depth of life has taken place. And place in them that seed of doubt, fear, question, and mistrust. For many it will be those that they love the most, and wish to please. Their fathers, mothers, teachers, those that lead and guide during these forming years. How I **hate sin**! It is because of this that men die, needlessly. And that lives are shattered and broken, for what!? A little power, monetary gain, a small sphere of influence that dies with them. Their name briefly in lights, or misunderstood lust for love all because of what they have, not who they are! Mankind cannot see what they have lost. The Garden was no small thing. Their rebellion was not just momentary or brief, it sent waves upon waves of death where life should have ruled. Instead offering despair for hope. Blindness for true sight. And now to give their home to the one that it doesn't belong, angers me, to watch as My Creation and loved ones fall in death never meant for them. And for them to live in abject poverty because of some of Lucifer's lies. All these were to be rulers, conquerors, and princes and priests, as men and women of renown. Pointing to the grace and mercy of God through His great love for all men! Now, because of sin, I must punish them and hand to death souls that never should have died, or paid such a price for anything! But, this We knew. "

The Son looked into the Father of Lights eyes, there He saw passion for righteousness and all that is good, but also the need for sin's destruction. And He knew His plan.

"Father, they can't bear the cost of sin. That's why I must take their place. Will they see it? Will they see Our love for them and the hope in the Cross? I know judgment must fall but what of now; sin is great! The only one righteous is . . . Noah. What do We do? Do we start again?"

"You know Our plan; the only path available. In years to come, some will question what happens next. And speculate as to why a loving God would judge. And some will miss interpret the Covenant of God and the permanent sign in the heavens. Some will say that I, God the Father, could not punish. Unlike sin, I hurt to heal, not destroy. And one of the other many misunderstood signs will be after the rain. For some it will be a sign of freedom, others will see it for the truth it is. And see that it points to the heavens. Where We, God Ourselves, will bear the brunt of judgment on mankind's behalf never to destroy man totally again, which is another picture of redemption for all the world to see. This was God reaching down to mankind. Not to destroy, but to restore and give hope in a world so dark and confused. That world that is suffering in the throes of sin's power.

We must always bring to man's heart and mind the **choice**. Life or death, redemption or destruction, so they know we do love them. That We would save them and redeem them **At All Cost**." The Father of Lights finished.

The Son of God gasped for air and shot upright on the Cross. Where that ragged breath was met by waves of pain, threatening to steal this breath He worked hard to even take. His mind swam and cool darkness found Him again. Yet, amidst this pain, He could hear a heartbeat, as His memory raced on. . .

In His mind's eye He saw again the deluge and he could hear even in the Realm their cries. And in another flash, Noah bowed beside a simple altar and sacrifice. And over head the bow of Covenant glistening in the sun. The rainbow. . .

Then His mind raced to a great Tower and the world united as one. The mass of humanity saw it as mankind's greatest triumph! War defeated and peace brought to all, under one rule . . . only to find greed, lust for power, and man's attempt to reach God. To physically breach the Heavens and pass unhindered to the Realm. The memory rolled on as He faintly heard laughter in the distance. As God the Father scattered to the winds the now, fledgling nations of the world. He saw Lucifer laughing and clapping, man again had rebelled. And tried on his own, or so he thought to follow after God. To do what he was made to do conquer and rule. Coming to God was right, ruling was right too, but without the absence of sin; all of what man tried was tainted and full of death. And sin would forever separate man from the one that loved him most.

Other memories flashed, as history rolled on. This silent, hidden battle between truth and falsehood. A seeming battle the Father of Lights allowed to continue, knowing full well **He** could end it at any time. But the plan was set and the decrees of ages and times must be fulfilled.

God's Son remembered Abraham, from the quiet man in Ur, to the frightened man in Egypt that almost cost him his wife, and caused the Pharaoh of Egypt's house plagues because of God the Father's promise to protect him and make of him a great nation.

Heartache overwhelmed Him, as He saw again the flames and destruction of Sodom and Gomorrah. He heard the veiled laughter and glee, as the Accuser of mankind watched men die again trapped by sin's choice. His soul rang out again with mankind's hopelessness. Yet, His heart rose in joy. *When this day is done, man will truly be free!* He Thought.

Then there was Mount Moriah and Abraham and Isaac. God the Father had called to Abraham and had asked him to do something different. He saw the others on Earth striving with one another and saw the depth of their hungers, good and evil. And all, even Abraham had a hunger to be near God. Most did not know God the Father, or if they did they had forgotten, because of the ravages of sin and darkness. They only knew that someone, somewhere might help them and care for them. But also the subtle lie, that they needed to reach this God. And the only way was to . . . The list was manifold.

God the Son's anger grew, as He watched mankind strive to complete this list given to them by a **"Helpful friend."** God's expectation according to this list ranged from simple to grotesque. . . . All for the sole purpose of drawing near to God. Their heart cry bolstered by the possibility of being accepted by God or God's . . . only to find disappointment and emptiness. Strength and hope failing; they turned back from the "Grand Quest." And embraced a colder, harsher, and more deadly master. Such guilt, shame, empty promise, and then death.

And all the while Satan watched and waited. Gleefully he would mark down the souls he had raised to worldly height and laugh as they comet-like crashed in despair and death at the end. Lucifer would then proclaim to the Heavens and all the Realm, another loss for the cause of righteousness.

Thus the seeming endless war raged on with no apparent end in sight.

Yet, as the Son of God's memory raced on, He knew the Realm and God the Father's plan never ceased its work, even when hopelessness was seemingly the evident outcome. His heart soared as He remembered the "God Moments" that men and women would speak of throughout time. Those moments that overwhelmingly showed God was alive and well, and righteousness had not fled the heart of man.

The war of good against evil did not exclusively reside in the Middle East, but ranged far and wide, over all the Earth. God the Father even was working in the nations that "knew not God."

The primary goal of Lucifer, the Father of Lies, was the complete and total destruction of anything God the Father of Lights built for good. Thus, nation after nation, country after country, city upon city, town upon town, people, and individuals were all subject to his ardor and hate.

And yet, a simple thread throughout history subtly wove in and out of events large and small to show those who would notice the Father of Lights handiwork and plan.

Thus, it was so when in the Mediterranean that Rome began to grow. Battles fought, nation subjugated, provinces captured and navies were built. Armies had heard of the fierceness of "The Legion" and its Soldiers. And they feared what would become of their very lives, let alone their homes and lands.

The Son of God's memory paused on one man, the Centurion Perseus Quintis Nerva. He smiled inwardly as He remembered the events prior to His coming to Earth. . .

Perseus Quintis Nerva stood, head bowed in the early morning sun, shining through the window that overlooked the main Temple square. He had a decision to make; in military terms an easy one, but his heart blanched at the politics of it all.

Why does this "Puppet" Herod ask me such things? He thought, *He makes my job all the more difficult. Not only am I in the eyes of Rome already, but now if I am not careful, I would have a start of a rebellion on my hands. . .and the last man to fail to solve the problem I replaced.* He shook his head. He tilted his face upward and soaked in the morning warmth of the sun. *Funny, somehow I find fighting an enemy in the field far easier.*

*But he asks that the Hebrews come en-masse to the Temple and have sacrifice for the "sins" and do not want our security or Temple Guard, in the Temple. They say it's an affront to their God and He would not be pleased. How many other nations have I heard that same message, only to find it was a hidden gathering, for rebellion or riot. I don't understand these Hebrews; they say their God is different than mine. They say that Mars, Jupiter and the like are nothing, just figments and imaginings of a man's heart hoping for redemption. **Redemption** from what? I do my duty as Centurion and Commander, a soldier not a politician. A man of honor and integrity. I have served with distinction and courage. I was praised in the Senate and Proconsul, even saw the Emperor . . . to be stationed here, in the desert.*

My family has power in Rome, but not enough to keep me from the ire of someone. He laughed, *maybe it was the Hebrew's God that put me here. I guess I need to have talk with Him one day.*

He turned from the window and stepped to the table. He moved the chair out and sat. He looked down at the map laid out on one side of the table showing all of Jerusalem and its streets. Buildings were marked and specific cross streets. And he looked at the unsealed letter from Herod "the Great" as he called himself. He shook his head again, as his eyes looked from there to the map.

So many narrow and broken streets, we would be hard pressed to effectively overwhelm an enemy with force. We will just have to change our tact and hopefully, maybe. . . He laughed. *We can get help from their God.* He thought.

He reached down and pulled parchment from its holder and took his pen and inkwell to begin his letter to Herod in answer to the "King's request." His hand was steady and even, the words flowing from the pen, should have been a poet's, and Herod did like flowery speeches. After he finished, he waited for the ink to dry and re-read what was written.

It read as follows:

From the Legion Hero of Bellum Cantabricum, I Centurion Perseus Quintis Nerva,

> Give sanction to your peoples' gathering to pay homage and supplication to your God YHWH. I do so in hopes that your people and your God know of Rome's benevolence and care

for those under its watch and guidance. I, of course, know that you, Great Herod, also honor your God and would not in your haste or religious fervor allow your people to incite or influence the Temple or its patrons to cause incident. Because I know you are Rome's friend and confidant, and would not see any more strife between your people and mine. And of course, it would be sad that such a day would be marred by some poor chosen word, or action.

I have little knowledge of your God, but if it would help Rome and our stay here, I also would gladly attend if it's appropriate.

Sincerely, Centurion Perseus Quintis Nerva

May your "Day of Atonement" be accepted in your God's sight.

Hopefully, this will be enough. He thought. *Then again, if he is as ruthless as stories say . . . We may yet have issue.*

"**Marcus**, Marcus come here please." He called to the door.

The Commander of the horde stepped in, suited in full armor, sweat already flowing from his brow. The smile on the big man's face showed joy. He stopped and saluted before Perseus' table.

"Yes, Centurion, What is your command?"

He stated crisply. His Eyes never left the standard prominently displayed behind and to the left of Perseus.

Perseus chuckled, "So Marcus, which of the new recruits have you tortured so early in the day? And do I need a replacement?"

Marcus Aquila gave a stricken look to his superior and friend and said, "No one is dead, yet. But Leone Crassius, will not doze on watch again. Once he wakes up of course."

"Oh, I am sure he will not repeat that mistake, ever. Water? Drink and listen; I would like to hear your voice on this matter," Perseus said.

The Commander turned from the Table and went to the wash basin and washed his hands and face. He took a fine linen towel from its place

57

and dried himself. From the pitcher of water nearby he filled a cup and drank all of it and refilled it again.

Turning to his friend, the Centurion, he moved to the table. And waited for his friend to speak. His voice was calm, even and rich.

"From the Legion Hero of Bellum Cantabricum, I Centurion Perseus Quintis Nerva,

> Give sanction to your peoples gathering to pay homage and supplication to your God YHWH. I do so in hopes that your people and your God, know of Rome's benevolence and care for those under its watch and guidance. I, of course know that you, Great Herod, also honor your God and would not in your haste or religious fervor allow your people to incite or influence the Temple or its patrons to cause incident. Because I know you are Rome's friend and confidant, and would not see any more strife between your people and mine. And of course, it would be sad that such a day would be marred by some poor chosen word, or action. I have little knowledge of your God, but if it would help Rome and our stay here, I also would gladly attend if it's appropriate.

> Sincerely, Centurion Perseus Quintis Nerva

> May your "Day of Atonement" be accepted in your God's sight."

Perseus stopped and looked to his commander.

He waited knowing that he would get a clear ungarnished answer or thought. Inwardly he smiled, he fights the same . . . honest true effort. He looked to his commander.

"Centurion," he said, "I for one do not trust this one who names himself King or Great. I know Rome has placed him in charge over the district, but in my heart, I don't see truth. I would not cater to him as you. I would station men there and tell him it is a security matter and he should be thankful we are here to hold order of the rabble that comes thru this city to worship this God. But, you are wiser and more knowledgeable than I that is why you are Centurion and my commander. Why ask me at all?" Marcus finished.

"I ask you Commander because you hide nothing. You see clearly and you do not fence with a situation; you look clearly and find ways to overcome it. And right now I need to see clearly, so I can answer this request and keep Rome and my honor, along with keeping the Hebrews happy and satisfied. I would rather face an enemy I know than this arena of snakes," Perseus remarked.

"Well then Centurion, may I say, most **snakes** become harmless . . . **if**, you **remove** the head." He chuckled. "I do not envy you, or this placating of egos and soothing of pride. I prefer a more direct and definitive approach." His voice trailed off.

"True my friend, I myself feel the same. But I fear, Rome would not accept my solution to the Hebrew situation, since their "*king*" might lose his place or worse. But, who am I, to disagree with the Emperor's wishes. He knows more than I, or so they say. And it would be inconvenient to go and have to explain things to him directly."

"And," Marcus said, "I would **hate** to have to **train** another Centurion."

They both erupted in laughter at this. . .

"Why . . . the . . . **insolence** of that **Roman dog!**" Herod screamed as his fine crystal goblet shattered against the wall, staining the marble facade with red wine. Herod the "Great" was up off his throne in fury and he threw the penned scroll into the warming Basin near his throne.

"Who does he think he is that he presumes to "Favor" me with my request! I am the King and the overseer of this district, by **Rome's own hand!** And he proceeds to "allow me" to worship. And to then threaten . . . I shall have his **head!**" Herod absently watched as the coals began to burn the silken rug near the basin he kicked over in his fury. "You there, bring another basin and clean this up!" He said as he stalked out of his throne room to his private room.

Years flashed past, as the Son of God struggled again to breathe. *These moments are almost lasting an eternity and I know of that. Oh to see the Throne room again and the Host . . . and My Father . . .* His thoughts raced to that one day thirty- three years before, or was it a little earlier. . .

The Son of God felt a nudge in His soul and turned to the Father of Lights. He saw in His eyes all the ages of time and a love none, not even He could fathom, and He was God the Father's Son. He spoke, "Yes, **Father. . .**"

"Son, **its time**." The Father spoke, His heart edged in sadness. He rose from the Throne and met His Son. All of Heaven and the Realm stopped. Angels were prostrate on the golden street, even the Elders had stopped the cry of Holy, Holy, Holy, and Heaven's music was stilled. All eyes were fixed upon God the Father and the Son. Every heart held awe, wonder, respect, and yes, even anticipation. For they all knew that this was the beginning of the Father's plan. The plan set from before time and space, and even sin. The liberation and redemption of man's soul and the joy that it would bring to the Realm and all of Creation. The Restoration. The Reclamation.

The Father looked into the Son's eyes and spoke clearly, arm's length as if gauging His son's feelings and attitude. "Son, you do know, I love you. . ."

"Yes, Father, that I know well."

The Father pulled His Son close and held the embrace. The Father of Lights heart raced to through the ages to a small sand colored house.

In it were father, mother and a young woman. The young woman dark of hair, bright of eye, plain simple beauty. She was singing, as she swept and danced with her broom. The Father had searched in a moment, all the hearts and minds of the women of Israel. In hers, He found tenderness, compassion, love, yet a fierce hunger to follow after Yahweh and a spark of true courage that would be brought to a wildfire on a dreadful day. He saw an unflagging drive to complete dreams given.

She was dreamer this Mary. She dreamed of Yahweh's glory and promise of a great nation and His righteousness throughout all the Earth. And of course, the normal dreams, a boy to fall in love with, a handsome husband, a family of honor and prestige, all the things of life. Most of the other women held many of the same things in their hearts . . . but, none were willing to let **HIM** lead them or follow, after the way was pointed out.

Why Mary, she had a tender and contrite heart. And He knew, although it would hurt her deeply, that she would follow **HIS** plan without fail. And her husband Joseph would as well. But of course, He wouldn't put it in Joseph's heart; yet, there was time still to hold His Son.

"Son, I will miss you. . ." The Father of Lights spoke holding the embrace.

"I know Father . . . The Son of God voiced, "But it must be."

"Yes . . . The Father paused ". . . but it will seem so long. Know this then, I love you."

The Son of God broke the embrace and looked deeply into the eyes of His Father. The words spoken next would reverberate in the Father of Lights heart always.

"Father, that . . ." spoke the Son with a smile, "I know always."

"Dante, **DANTE**! Lucifer Prince and Power of the Air cried. He stood in his place musing as always when Dante knelt head bowed. He waited in silence. He knew.

His Sovereign would speak soon. And it would not do to rush him, he was in one of his moods again. Dante noted; those moods, were more frequent lately. And he valued his head more than pointing things out to his leader.

"Ah there you are Dante; I need you to gather information for me. And I need it done quickly, quietly." The enemy of man's souls said.

"At once my Liege, what do you wish me to do?" Dante replied.

"I know that **crafty** All Father is up to **something**; I can feel it. And I need to know of it so I can devise a plan to thwart it and destroy any hope of success, like I always do."

"Of Course, as always, but what should I look for, if I may ask?" Came the simple reply.

"Dante, you know of course, the All Fathers weakness for these **humans**, and his hope of **redemption**? Satan spoke. "There is a stirring I feel, a working on the All Father's part, but I do not know what it is. And I must know to thwart it and bring about ours goals, our victory . . . So that the Realm and Universe, will once again have order."

"Yes, sir, I will spread the word and even go myself. Dante paused, in your wisdom sir, any thoughts as to where to start?"

"Oh, you flatter me, I think you know already. Look to Nazareth," Satan said.

"At Once! " Dante spoke as He flew off.

"I do not believe my eyes. I see the portends, but I still cannot believe it." Abdi-ill-Ba-Alum said. He turned to others gathered in the hall of seeing at Akkad. "This is an important thing. I am sure the King would want to know."

"Yes, of course . . . but the real question is would he allow us to travel?" Muranu said. His eyes sparkling in the flickering lamplight. He turned to window and felt the breeze upon his face. "We have searched long for this."

Naram the youngest of the group studied the map of the stars. And the other notes scrawled upon scrolls spread wide upon the bench. He had been here it seemed for days learning and watching. This was his place, the Hall of Seeing. He was to learn how to heal through herbs, roots, and flowers. And to watch the night sky and discern the future, Naram was of a long line of seers. His grand Father, Aldu, had been in a line of succession that stretched back hundreds of years. It seemed as long as they had recorded history, his family, was a seer. And so was Grand Seer Abdi- Ba alum.

"This points to the final fulfilment of Belshazzar, Daniel of the Hebrews Prophecy. He said there would come one who would be a Light and Rule as King. He would bring hope to the nations, among other things. And as you know, we seek Daniel's God and worship Him, at least some of us still do."

He moved from the bench to the window beside Muranu. Muranu was silent, but gazing at the stars. They had known each other most their lives. They had entered the Seeing Hall together as young men at their appointed time. He shook his head at the thought of the forty years that had passed.

"Oh for the strength and energy of youth, what we could do with it, we could do more than turn lead to gold." Abdi laughed and looked to his friend who still stood silent gazing at the heavens. "Muranu, what is it brother . . . what do you see, why are you silent and still?"

"Abdi, this King that comes, the Anointed to rule, we knew His days and arrival. But we do not know the place. It will be difficult." Muranu spoke calmly.

"That seems no different than a hundred other prophecies when have found. But why are you troubled, Muranu?"

"Because, Grand Seer, this one sent by Daniel's God is cut off. And nothing else is said from Daniel's visions. And the words from these other would be prophets make no sense. He is cut off and there the hope ends. Or so these signs and portends point in these scrolls." His eyes flashed, as he turned from the window to the workbench and table. "I would have thought that Daniel's God, would have had more power than this, to allow His chosen to be cut off." He said angrily.

Muranu paced to the other side of the large table and grabbed a scroll. He held it up to display it to the others and continued. "This, this was the scroll of the Reign of King Nebuchadnezzar the First, and this tells of Daniel's God touching our King of ages past and turning him into a beast for seven years! And then at the King's cry of repentance, he was a man again! And what of the parting of the Red Sea? The rivers of blood, plagues, the fall of Jericho . . . the passion in his eyes and voice rose to a cry of frustration! And then what, what do we see. . . death! Not the reign of hope, or of Daniel's God building. How did Daniel write of it . . . his Kingdom! Nothing, nothing and the hearts of men are unchanged and sick! Why would Daniel write of an Anointed Ruler, and other of their Prophets . . .? A Son will be born to you . . . only to have it end! No, I cannot believe this God I learned of would just let things pass and drop from His hand." Muranu finished.

Abdi touched his friends shoulder and spoke evenly. "No one ever said seeing was easy, nor welcome. We see much; and can change so little, except it seems this God of Daniel's. And I know of your hearts frustration, I too had those questions I would ask of . . . what was His name. . . Yahweh?"

Naram spoke quietly, "If he is a King; and He is in the midst of enemies, is it not our mandate to help Him? I know I am not a true Seer yet, but couldn't we go and help . . . somehow? Or we could send Him help, gold, incense, myrrh and other things, if our King permits. . ." his voice trailed off.

"Naram speaks truth. I will not command this, but I will go and help this King of Daniel. Because if His GOD can change our King's heart, this GOD can do anything." Abdi said.

CHAPTER 4

HOPE

The cart creaked as Joseph stopped in front of the gate. He grabbed the yoke and pulled back hard. He walked in front of the ox and pushed against the animal's nose. "Stop now, Bertram. Just stop, I said." He turned his head from the following dust cloud. The morning breeze carried the dust and sand right where he now stood. He coughed and moved to the bell by the gate. Sweat began to bead on his forehead. *It's not even the fourth hour yet and I'm already sweating.* He thought. *Father better pay me extra for this delivery; how else am I to prepare for my future? This Roman needed the new table for his guests to eat at. I hope he likes it. I worked hard to finish it on time. Father did say he may try and talk us down in final price, but we shall see.*

He looked up and saw the master of the house and servants walking to the gate. He and his father had met him at the shop a week ago. They had also haggled with them over pricing and work. He seemed nice enough for a Roman!

"Ah Joseph, you bring my table! How is your father? I thought he might be here at delivery." The master said.

"I apologize on behalf of my father, Centurion. He also had a delivery at another house. And he begged me to ask your pardon." Joseph said.

"Oh no, there is no need for an apology; I quite understand. I am glad that business is growing for you all. I still say your father should allow me to use my contacts in Rome to help his business. His work is solid and well done. Beautiful in fact. It's a shame he was reluctant on that point," Perseus said.

"Well, Centurion. . ." Joseph began.

"Perseus, Please." He interrupted.

"Perseus, we are rather a small carpentry shop, and being that small, I would never have time for anything else." Joseph finished.

"True, very true, I suppose you are right. A young man needs to do many things before he settles down and starts a family." Perseus chuckled.

"A family sir, are you sure you have not been speaking to my father without my knowledge?" Joseph said.

The Centurion wrapped his arm around Joseph's neck and moved him toward the house. Motioning to the servants, who dutifully began unloading the table. "Now, Joseph, what would give you that idea. Come, I have your payment in the house, come and take water as well, it's going to be another warm day." The voices faded as they entered the house.

The Son of God's mind raced on further, to another day. . .

Mary just finished weeding the small wheat terrace. She turned and stood. She laughed and walked to the well nearby. She reached up and began to lower the small bucket into the well. *I don't know how we do it. This terrace is barely enough to feed me, and yet, mother seems to be able to stretch things. It must be YHWH's doing. He did say he would bless us if we obeyed his voice. But, then again, it has been quite some time since He has spoken to the tribes. The tribe fathers argue that YHWH has forsaken us to the Romans. Even though they say the scrolls speak of a Deliverer. I have heard such stories for so long, but YHWH must be doing something because we are not destroyed.* She thought. *And there has always been a judge, prophet or King to lead our people. Oh, to walk as our forefathers did, with real words from YHWH, not these paid priests that tell lies. And how can they charge so much to sacrifice? I think they are just after coin, not worship of YHWH! I wonder what YHWH will do?? Is He judging us now through the Romans like in Ages past?? OH, Help us O'LORD . . . .* Her thoughts ended.

She turned from the cup at the well and picked up the hoe. Then a bright flash and a word, "Mary, fear not . . . You are highly favored of God."

Startled she dropped the hoe and stepped back involuntarily. She stood silent and transfixed as her visitor continued.

"The LORD is with you, you will conceive in your womb and bear a son and call him Jesus. He will be great and called the Son of the Most High. And the Lord God will give Him the Throne of David, His father, and He will reign over the House of Jacob forever. His Kingdom shall have no end."

Mary couldn't believe her ears, or her eyes. *Who was this man? And why was he even speaking to her? Where did he come from? I don't understand. I must be overwhelmed by the sun. It must be the heat. This man called me by name. . .*

She found her voice and slowly lowered her hand from shielding her eyes.

"How can this be? Since I am a virgin?" she said plainly.

"Mary, the LORD will overshadow you. So that which is born in you will be of the Holy Spirit. And He will be called the Son of the Most High, The Son of God. . . ."

Her visitor waited. *Is this happening? This is an angel of God! I'm not dead.* She thought.

An Angel here, is speaking to me? YHWH is speaking to me a young woman. How can this be happening? I am not a leader in the tribe nor even a father of a house? This has got to be the effects of the sun. She hesitated again. She was frozen unable to move. And saw this man in shimmering pure white waiting. She even noticed the wry expression on his face. The one that says, *"Have you caught up with me yet?"*

Ok, how did the prophets handle things when YHWH or angels spoke to them? She continued thinking. *I do not know why he is speaking to me, but I must answer him anyway. I know our tradition speaks of a woman bearing a Child of Promise . . . but YHWH's Son?*

"May it be as you have said. Your servant hears." She heard her voice say. Then the man in glistening clothes spoke again. His deep baritone voice resonated through her frame.

"Even your relative Elizabeth, who was barren, is in her sixth month as God said. Nothing is impossible with God." And in a flash the angel of God departed.

The warm sun still touched her face; she could hear the breeze softly touch the wheat terrace and the song bird's melody, but it was some time before Mary stirred due to the angel's message and its magnitude. *I am only young. Not even a full woman; yet, YHWH says I will bear a son? . . . HIS Son . . . I saw an angel and lived! He spoke to me, and I answered . . . Oh Mary, what have you got yourself into I wonder . . .* her thoughts slowly ended. She thought, as she moved mutely to the house and the smell of dinner.

Joseph pushed Bertram to the water trough and used his dust cover to wipe the sweat from his brow. Bertram greedily drank and then turned to the fodder and began to eat as Joseph turned and looked at the worn out cart. *I still don't think this will be enough for the bride price, or much less the start of a home, when we need to replace the cart for deliveries.* He sighed. *I guess I will not be rich in a day, or year . . . this may take a while. But, I know in the end, Mary will be worth all the work.* He chuckled in his heart. *Now if I can find the courage to ask her when the time is right. I wonder what she would say now if she only knew. Her family is known in Nazareth and her father is a good man. Her mother is kind and Mary is so much like her, but who am I kidding, I doubt she even knows my name. I mean there was that wedding feast a few months ago. And my father and hers were speaking, I assume it was business. I heard her laughter, bright and clear, come from a small table and a group of young maidens and friends. And then she smiled, when she looked at me well . . . that is one day I won't forget. I still can't believe I made that mess. I wonder if dad had to replace that rug or not.* His Thoughts ended as he walked into the front of the shop and dropped the coin bag on the table where the ledger was. His father, Micah, was still cutting a few planks with the saw. He could smell the sawdust, and mixed with the heat and sun, brought fresh cedar to his senses.

"Father, I have delivered the table to the Centurion, as you asked. Are you sure you haven't been speaking to him about my future plans without my Knowledge?" He said.

Micah chuckled and stopped cutting the planks he was working on. He lifted his eyes to those of his son and said, "Joseph, son, I know the Centurion is a very perceptive man.

He would not be where he is today, if it was not so. And besides son, it does not take a father's **extreme** wisdom . . . He paused for effect, to see that Mary has won your heart, even before your love for her is known to her. But in truth, no I have not. Your secret is safe with me."

"How did you know?" Joseph asked.

"Son, I may be older than you, but I too loved once. And have never regretted it, though your mother may think differently." He laughed as he finished.

"Now come help finish these planks so we can eat. Your mother's kitchen is smelling wonderful." He said, as Joseph came around the table to his father's side.

Joseph stood transfixed by the stars overhead. After dinner this was his favorite thing to do, up on the small roof of the carpentry shop. He could see most of the neighborhood he ran through in his younger days. Now that he had reached that age, he didn't run much anymore. But worked and saved. But the stars captured his heart almost as much as Mary did. And tonight was no different. They shone as jewels on black tapestry, bright and clear, close enough it seemed to reach out and take them from the sky. *The sky seems to stretch on forever.* He thought. *I wonder what YHW sees when HE looks at the sky. Or is it like King David said, "What is man that you are mindful of Him. . ." YHW looks; the Scrolls say, from the Heavens, do we bring him joy? Or anger.*

I know He has been silent, father says for years. No prophet or King, just . . . servitude to the **Romans.**

YHW, Perseus, the Centurion seems good. Not a harsh man, it is too bad he cannot know you. Rome would never allow it. The Caesar would squash him and us. I wonder, can you hear me? Or am I too small, too insignificant . . . probably for Mary too I suppose. He turned from the bright stars and made his way down to the house in silence.

*Joseph was so unsure of himself then, and he fretted needlessly about Mary. If he had only known; then again, they almost didn't marry. . .*The Son of God remembered as His thoughts raced on.

"What are **saying** . . . Mary?! What are you going on about?" Joseph stammered.

The carpenter shop smelled of cedar shavings and heat. The sun had found the lattice above and was shooting shafts of gold and green to the floor below.

Mary's voice carried wonder and awe as she spoke to Joseph, her eyes sparkled as much as her black hair. He had never seen her look more alive and beautiful; he was glad to know he would have this one, to be his own.

She began barley able to contain her excitement. "I saw an angel today. I was working on the terrace garden and I saw an angel." She paused.

Joseph sat stunned . . . a look of wry humor on his face and spoke with a chuckle. "I am sure that little Leah would thank you for that. . ."

"No, Joseph, not Benjamin's daughter, but really an angel." She emphatically stated.

"You saw an angel, really. And did he tell you why it has been so hot lately and little rain? Or maybe this angel brought my tax money. . ." He mocked.

"Joseph! Why do mock me so? Is it so unbelievable that YHWH would send an angel to me?" She said truly hurt.

"No, Mary, but I had understood that YHWH speaks only to prophets or Priests, or family fathers. Joseph paused. Then again, I am surprised He is speaking at all."

"Joseph, how can you say that? Don't you fear God? I would hate to see you punished for speaking against YHWH."

"At this moment Mary we YHWH's Beloved, are the only ones being punished. That's why the Romans are here. We have displeased YHWH enough for Him to put us into bondage and trial. No, I do not fear YHWH's judgment and his punishment. So many have turned from the Law and mixed with others and fallen into the trap of false worship; truly, they have forsaken Him.

His Covenant to Abraham, King David and our forefathers talks of punishment for our disobedience. I am not surprised. I guess I am more weary of things, hoping somehow things will change. The Scrolls talk of many things. However, most it talks of a Deliverer and establishing YHWH'S Kingdom on the Earth. I want that; Israel needs that. Our families need that. But, in all my years, I have not seen any signs of a Deliverer or God moving. How can we know?" Joseph finished.

Mary moved closer to the bench Joseph was resting against, and looked intently at him and shared, "Joseph, Could YHWH bring the Deliverer through a woman in our age? I know what the angel said to me, but it seems so crazy. To think that God would overshadow someone and then they would bare this child. God's Son. I couldn't believe my ears. And this angel was hard to look at; he was so bright and fearsome. But he said that I was favored among women. . ."

Joseph's eyes twinkled with his voice as he replied, "I know I favor you over most women, but then again, that's just me." He finished dodging as she swatted at him. "Joseph! I am being serious!" He quickly grabbed her shoulders and pulled her close and kissed her and let her go to finish. "So am I." He stepped back to the bench and began sanding a chair with ornate flowers carved into the back and the slats of the chair itself. "Mary I would love to finish this stirring conversation with you, but Father will have my head if I don't have this finished by the time he returns, so we may stain it." He finished.

She looked upon Joseph with a wry grin on her face and said in a mocking contempt, "Well, is that just like a man, kiss a girl and toss her aside for something else!" She turned her back to him waiting. Eyes closed, she listened, focused on any movement or noise. And was rewarded by the touch of strong hands and arms wrapped around her and warmth at her back, and a soft clear voice in her ear.

"Unfortunately Mary, this is all you will be able to receive from me at the moment," holding her tighter. "But, don't think I am not keeping track of what I owe you. You will receive payment at due time. And no matter how much I wish the time was here, we do have tradition to uphold and our ages. But, I will not hurry things, I want to offer more, so . . . more, takes more time, sadly. But what a day of reckoning that will be." He released her and spoke clearly

"And I will enjoy making the payments. But I must first finish my chores and save for the future"

"Who's future Joseph . . .?" Mary Paused. She turned to him smiling, looking into his eyes again. She finished with, "Do you have someone in mind? And paused. "Anyone I would know?"

"I have a feeling, Mary, you know more than you let on. And if you must know . . . yes." But again tradition must be upheld and followed. We of course wouldn't want to miss YHWH's blessing." He spoke.

Mary smiled shyly and said, "Okay, Joseph, You may keep me in suspense. But know this, one cannot wait forever, and it would be a shame for you to miss out on the opportunity of a lifetime." She turned again and headed for the door. She smiled to herself, as she heard Joseph say through the closing door, "I don't think either of us will miss that opportunity, dear heart."

Opportunity of a lifetime she had said. YHWH, He thought, *the years I have to wait seem long. Can I do as you and tradition states? Does she really love me? I can only guess. Because YHWH, it seems you send angels to young non–engaged girls, not men of dreams any more. So, I can't expect any warnings or guidance ahead of time. I thought the Priests said you were a romantic. . . That Love was who You were. I know it's only two years away that I should have the money for the marriage price, but sometimes, tradition is more difficult to follow than your heart. I would marry her in the spring if I knew the city wouldn't end up in an uproar because I didn't wait the appropriate time.* His thoughts ended as he moved back to sanding the chair. And the slow monotony of what his life had become … every day ordinary, dreamless work but he knew, that was tradition as well. To work well and hard and to be solid in his job. Dependable and faithful they called it. And unshakeable in purpose. *I am faithful, dependable, and solid. I will make a great husband and provider for my family,* rang in in his thoughts, as the sandpaper sung in his ears and time marched on to evening.

And with each stroke of paper on wood, sawdust and Joseph's life seemed to ebb away, a life of no great significance or meaning. And then came the subtle whisper of thought one he had grown used to. One that he had hoped would fade and disappear with age. Maturity and wisdom are part and parcel of life they say. But, this, this was something else entirely.

"**Cirilion** the Master needs an update" . . . the demon paused. "Is he responding to the doubts placed in his mind?" Dante whispered. "Ahh, yes, Dante, but as you know with these humans, some days it is slower than others. I think when Joseph finds her pregnant, he will toss her away like trash. Heartbroken, he will then go on to the nearest cow available. He will have children and the All Father's dream will be wiped away easily and we will have mastery again and forever!" Cirilion crooned.

"See that he does." Dante spoke, "I would hate to have to assign someone else to the task of destroying hope in Joseph. These creations the All Father has made are tedious and cumbersome. Though easily moved to stubbornness, envy, jealousy, and even outright hatred. **Certainly,** he Mocked, the **epitome** of Creation. Laughing he continued, "Don't let up for one moment, and make sure the pressure is on to please his earthly father more and more. We build strife between the two. They must be competitive and centered on themselves. Even brush the wife, mother aside. She cannot speak to him of real love or sacrifice, nor the father. He must be singled out and bear all this on his own heart. See to it that his friends mock his family life and trade. He must not marry **her**. It was fortunate that our Master had been watching that devious All Father closely. He even invited Light Bringer to the Throne Room to report again. Can you believe it? I am beginning to understand how the Master says the "All Father" is not himself or well. He is supposedly all wise, all knowing, all powerful, and yet, trusts in these creations. And He stakes all on their following His commands . . . It is better that like us, we are to go, to do, and to obey! At least we know where we stand with the Master." Dante finished. He turned from Cirilion and spoke as he faded out of sight in a dark splotch ". . . Work well and you will be rewarded. . ."

Joseph continued, pressure, stroke, pressure, sawdust life. Drudgery and mundane. Then door of the shop opened and he heard his Father say, "**Joseph**, Joseph we need to talk about the chairs again. Did you make that other delivery? . . ." His voice faded as the stroke of sand paper continued in Joseph's ears.

Mary danced as she swept, humming a tune. She saw in her mind the wedding day. All the families were there. The hall was full. And flowers were everywhere; the scent of gardenias, lilies and wild roses, and music, laughter, joy amidst the laborious occupation of Rome. . . *One day we will be together, you and I, after this is but a memory!* She spun and hit the jar with the broom. The small jar cracked and oil leaked out on the ground. Her mother and cried out, "**Mary**, what are you doing?"

"**WHAT!** . . . Oh mother, I am so sorry. I didn't mean to break the jar. . ."

"It is fine honey. I will take care of it. We will be fine; I'm sure." She finished.

"I don't think so, that's a day's wage now, and that was to last till the end of the week. What were you thinking? Oil is expensive and now I must replace it. **Honestly**, sometimes I think there is no thought in you but celebration. How can you make a good wife acting this way!" Her Father chided. "**Rueben!**" Hannah interrupted.

Mary dropped the broom and ran out the front door in tears. Hannah slapped Rueben and finished. "Now look what you've done! You need to speak with your daughter; you've broken her heart over what? A few pieces of silver, we have more than enough." Hannah turned her back and said under her breath, "Sometimes, I think you only dream of more money, not her happiness or mine. . ."

Sufficiently chided, he squared his shoulders and walked into the bright afternoon sun to face its heat and his daughter. He looked one last time over his shoulder toward Hannah, his wife who conveniently was busy picking up the jar, and catching the leaking oil. *I know what she said was true,* he thought with a heavy audible sigh, *but the **Law** and the **prophets** never told us how to raise a young woman soon to be married. I have no idea how to do this; I am, it seems, constantly at war with myself and the need to be tender to all in this house. I have many times wondered how **YHWH** does it. **HE** can judge rightly and yet, be tender to those in pain who are hurting. All I know is how to work hard and be forceful in business. . . .**YHWH,** can I ask Your help? **Now this Moment**, to rescue my daughter's heart like you rescued us from Egypt? To have her and I triumph together in this. . .* His thoughts faded as the heat from the sun and the sound of his daughter's tears met his ears. He shaded his eyes, as he walked to the small terrace garden and the shaking form of his daughter.

He stood silent slightly behind his daughter. He reached slowly for her shoulder and touched her. Mary's shaking ceased, and he softly spoke.

"**Mary**," Rueben paused, sighed deeply again and continued, "Mary, can you forgive an old man his words and foolishness? I was wrong to chide you for what was an accident and of no real cause for anger. I again say I am sorry to you. Will you forgive?" He waited, he waited for the tirade that should have been his and the wrath of a wounded heart.

The silence stretched on, no words just tears. He knew she would answer, should answer him. His mind raced to the idea of a disapproving customer and the need to soothe and placate, but luckily he didn't speak. He knew that if he was silent, things, even this, would work out. And he knew that he would need to offer a soothing gift to her and her mother. Not because they didn't deserve the gift, but that he had again proven his words could either win the heart or destroy life.

I understand YHWH knows all, but I wonder if it is true, that He makes no mistakes. I mean no disrespect YHWH, but I see no good coming from this, nor do I see joy anywhere for my family because my words come quick. The Priests say you make no mistake, but cannot abide foolish words. Sorry then, the words in my house, they were foolish. Forgive me please. I just hope my wife and daughter will as well.

His thoughts ended as the tears stopped and a small voice was heard.

"Abba, oh Abba, I am so sorry for breaking the jar. I know money is hard to come by and I was foolish. I was day dreaming of Joseph and marriage; I am so sorry." Every word bit into his heart as she spoke it. He knew in all truth, he was at fault not her.

"Mary, you were not at fault. Least of all for dreaming of better days than these. No, I was wrong even to mention it. I reacted and wasn't thinking at all. I was the wrong doer here. Again, I want to apologize to you and beg your forgiveness." He ended in a broken voice.

He again waited. She had turned to him now, but she was looking at the ground. She was at war with herself. He could see the turmoil. She wanted to rail at him; yet, he knew she was holding her tongue out of respect and honor. And that made his pain all more serious and costly. How could he make this right? What could he say? He had no Idea. He did the only thing he knew. And the only thing he loved the most.

Gently, and slowly, he tilted her head up and wiped the tears from her face and looked into her eyes. *These are not the eyes of that little girl I knew so long ago, nor of the child I watched grow. These are the eyes of a woman that has been hurt and longs for hope. Can I give her that? Or is that simply YHW's place.* He paused. *Regardless, I know what I must do. And I will shrink from it. I will be her father, until YHW deems it time, and then I will be the dutiful grandfather and patriarch of the house. And hopefully, not so harsh then. And maybe just maybe, my wife will forgive her husband his mistake.*

He pulled her close and wrapped his arms around her and held her until the tears from both of them died. Darkness and stars shone, when they went back into the house.

Moonlight and stars lit the room as he lay still. All the noises of night met his ears. He felt the gentle breeze and listened to Hannah as she slept. The stars it seemed, were brighter and closer than he Remembered. And the moon shown bright and full through the window. He heard the crickets chirp and the local animals settling in for the night in the stalls nearby.

YHWH, he thought, *I had forgotten how beautiful nights could be. And the wonders of what you have made. Is this the same moon King David saw as he kept sheep. Or our father, Abraham, as he moved to the land of Canaan? Silly of me to question, but it somehow was lost on me today. I am thankful, even in spite of Rome. We have seen nations come and go, but You are there always. The Priests say we should not question You at all, or bring our desires to You. I would be free from Rome if I had but the choice. You did promise a Kingdom. And a forever Kingdom, actually. I hope it comes soon because the Romans are trouble. Yes, in spite of what the Priests say, we did this to ourselves; we are our own worst enemy. Sometimes YHWH, I think of King David. And I remember his life. You took him from a shepherd to the palace. Do you know that it inspired me to have my business? Oh yes, I forget, You know already. You have never failed Israel. We turned from you often it seems, but you never failed. And just when it was darkest, it seems, You sent a Deliverer. I hope Your Deliverer comes soon. I am ready to be free again, and Yes, YHWH, thank you for my daughter and reconciling us. You have given me much and I thank you. I only hope my wife will not hold this over me too long.*

He turned back to look at Hannah, she still seemed to be resting. And the light of the moon caught the silver in her hair. *She is still beautiful, though we are not as young as we once were. You gave me YHW a beautiful wife. And a wise one, though I know I don't admit it enough.* He gently reached to move the lock of sliver and took in her beauty. She opened her eyes and looked into his. Smiling she said, "You did well today Ruben. And I am proud of you." Smiling still she said, "Now hold me and let's get some sleep". He smiled and for once, he didn't argue with his wife. Soon, stillness reigned in the house, as the stars and moon looked on.

The carpenter shop was hot, as always, but a bit more vocal this day.
. .

"What do you mean Beniah only gave you **30 Shekels** for the stool;
it should have been 60. And we had to alter it **twice**!" Micah roared.
Joseph stood head down.

"I know I did the sanding and stain, remember? But he said
something about not being able to do more since the tax. I did remind
him of the agreement, but that's all he gave. He complained of the
Romans." Joseph added quietly.

"We **ALL** have to deal with these Roman dogs!" Micah cried as he
threw the hammer at the bench barely missing the newly stained
tabletop.

"Son, how can we do business like this! I barely can put food on the
table as it is. And to teach you this business and prepare you for
betrothal. . ." His frustrated voice trailed off.

"I am truly sorry Father. I am sorry I didn't get your price! I am sorry
I am not the Son you wanted. I am sorry I don't have the head for
business as you. I am just sorry. . ." Joseph's voice trailed off as he left
the shop storming out to the street and sun.

*What am I supposed to do now? My father's angry and I cannot do
as he wishes. I am sure I will pay for the mistake. And Beniah, he said
that was all he had. And he had to pay so much in taxes to the Romans.
I certainly didn't see anything missing from his house. He is older than
Father, and he has never been struggling that I can tell. Surely, he has
a benefactor in Rome! I know Father made a mistake in not accepting
Perseus' offer. I for one will never make that mistake! I will do whatever
is necessary for my family. I will not hesitate to care for my wife and
family. What am I thinking, I will be surprised if I marry at all. Mother
says not to worry, that this stress will pass. But I don't see how. All I do
is wrong! Nothing makes Father happy!* He stopped his angry thoughts
for a moment to dodge a small child and leaned heavily on the building
near him. The heat and the sun and dust did little to change the mood.
He stood and wiped the dust from his tunic and walked further, oblivious
to the market place and it bright calls for meats, treats. and wonders. He
looked at the stalls as he passed, nothing and no one appealed to him. It
was as if he was looking from the outside in. People pushed by him, and
spoke to him, but he never really saw them. His answers were automatic

and plain. "Good day" or "shalom" but nothing reached his heart. He found a fruit vendor and purchased a small batch of figs and walked to a small wall and hopped up and sat legs dangling down to eat a fig, watching the people pass by.

The market place was in full swing now. Vendors of foods, clothing, products were touting their wares as the "best in all of Jerusalem," or wherever they were from.

The market place usually held his attention and fascinated him. It was a window to the world. A place of magic and wonder . . . he Chuckled . . . *not really*. But it spoke of places and things never seen or done. He longed to see more of the world and have a place in it. *But now,* he thought, *I wonder if I ever will. I mean, honestly look at how Father reacted. He was truly angry for me not getting 30 shekels. What was I supposed to do anyway? Beniah was my Father's friend. He should have been out asking instead of me. I am just a boy, ok, not according to tradition anyways. I am seventeen now. And going nowhere . . .* he shook his head. He also ate another fig. It was sweet and full, and reminded him of his mother's pies. And all she made, he loved the smell of the house as she cooked. *Oh the lamb and the herbs. Or the stew, that was wonderful. I sure hope Mary can cook. I would hate to think she was all beauty and no talent.* He laughed out loud again. *If she ever says yes. I know years ago she hinted at it. But, it has been a while since I have seen her and spoken to her. Yeah, I remember the Betrothal Ceremony and all that was said. But that was a years ago and with coming of the Romans. I doubt marriages will even be allowed. It is bad enough we have to do everything they say. I really don't like their ways. And I know YHWH isn't happy either. But I am not a father or tribe leader yet. And God hasn't fulfilled His promise of a Deliverer, yet. It's been what five or six generations? And we still are under Rome's heel. And the High Priests say nothing. They are to hear from God, but nothing changes. The poor are still poor. The rich are richer . . . and the rest wait to see what will happen. No one, not even Father moves. He just gets up and works in the shop and sells and comes home, and does it all over again. Day-after-day, month-after-month He is steady and consistent. That's what I thought I was. I thought that was what he wanted. He told me that he was to give me the business after I become married or older.* He shook his head again. *Now I doubt I will ever see Mary or betrothal. And of course Mother does nothing. She sides with him. I know it. She disapproves too I know.*

Cirilion smiled as his whisper finally laid the seed of doubt in his Heart. He would see this task through and gain favor with the Master. He would then be able to leave this cursed place and be among his kind again. He could put up with a few more months of the sights and smells to gain victory for the Kingdom. Unheard by Joseph or anyone around him. . . Cirilion spoke, "**Now** for His **supposed friends** and **mother**," he Hissed.

Joseph continued to watch the crowds come and go. Then as the daylight dimmed, he saw the stalls close and the crowd thin, he turned for home. And he felt that there would not be joy, nor would it have brought any joy because he knew a battle awaited, one he was sure to lose.

Twilight was beginning when he found the outer door of the house. He smelled the dinner his mother had prepared and his stomach growled. He steeled himself for the tirade that would be his, his father would surely let him know how displeased he was with him "running off today when work was to be done." His hand was reaching for the latch when his mother opened the door and jumped at seeing him. And then she grabbed him and steered him from the door, as she closed it quickly behind her. She held her finger to her lips silencing him. He waited as she led him off to the side of the house with no window, and spoke in a whisper.

"Joseph, Joseph where have you been? I was worried **sick!** Your father was none too pleased about your disappearance either. He has paced the shop like a tiger. He chased more customers away than usual. What **happened** to you two?" She said.

Joseph straightened and smoothed his hair and tunic. And then looked his mother in the eyes and spoke, "He and I had issue with Beniah's payment. I didn't get the amount he had asked me to. He was angry and anyway, He should have gone not me!"

Hannah spoke, "Now Joseph, you know you're father when it comes to money . . . He was just as worried as I was. You just left! You just left. How? Why?"

"I can't do anything right! As it is I can never make him happy. Nor you. You are not happy. But then again, you always side with him **anyways!**" He blurted out. Unsure of where that thought came from, but it felt right. "And how in the world am I to have a wife or a future, with all this going on! The Romans taxing everyone and money is harder and harder to come by! No matter what I do! I work hard and sand like he says. I stain like he says, but **no**! I miss 30 shekels and **wham**! I am sure he wants Thomas as a son and not me!"

Hannah grabbed her son by the shoulders and spoke harshly "Now you just stop! I will have none of that! He loves you Joseph! You are his son, not some beggar or customer. You are the firstborn. Thomas is a neighborhood boy, who has nothing and no one. He helps him because it is right to do. No other reason. He holds you to more standard because you are his son. As is right! But, even in this, his love for you is deep. Can't you see?"

Joseph stood still and she could see muscles tense and anger behind his eyes.

"He was angry not that you lost 30 shekels, but that he could not do more." She spoke plainly.

"What do you mean Mother? He couldn't do more?" Joseph waited.

"Your father; yes, **your father**," she said with added emphasis, "got all he needed for the year months ago. We have no need. In fact, we have extra. And all of that was to be put aside for you and your betrothal and house after marriage. You have been working for years on your own income for the future. Didn't you know? Didn't he tell you?"

Joseph stared blankly at his mother. He couldn't believe his ears. His heart said, *It couldn't be true. All those words, the anger. He couldn't believe it. And she always sides with him, she was giving up opulence for him? Really?* He thought in dreadful Silence.

"Mother, you are saying that most of each year, I was already working for my own house and future?" he said quietly. "Yes, yes you have. All those long night's sanding and staining were to guarantee your home with Mary and a good life. All of that was your doing. Your father, wanted you to have better than he did. And to make sure you understood the value of doing the work, good solid work like him, and what it would do for you. Not just as a business man or a home . . . but as a man. To know you can do something well. Great enough in fact that others would pay you to do work for them. Good money and to stand proud in that accomplishment. He wanted you to grow up. Not become bitter at the work or hardness of the work." "Mother I. . ." he stopped.

"Son, listen, it is more than birth that makes a man. Being a man carries with it responsibility. Responsibility, honor, courage, persistence and great compassion." She paused. "I know this sound s funny coming from a woman, speaking on what it is to be a man, but all of it is true. He really was not angry at you for the 30 shekels you didn't get. Yes, he had hoped you would fight for the full amount, but, what moved him more, was your compassion. That you would offer to take what they had because of the trouble Rome has placed on us and the strain on Israel and our country. That you would sacrifice to help others. That is something YHWH would have you do always." She finished.

"Oh Mother, I have been so wrong." He hung his head and tears shook his body.

She quickly grabbed her son and squeezed him tight. Allowing his tears to wet her neck and tunic as he shook in silent sobs. Soon they stopped. And she lifted his eyes to hers. And wiped them with a cloth and smiled. "Don't you think it's time we ate, I for one am hungry. And I cooked it!" She laughed.

Cirilion stood in shock as mother and son walked arm and arm to the door and through it. He saw Micah's Face; hoping that the seed of failure about his son's sale would breed anger, which died as Micah himself rushed to the boy and scooped him up in his arms and held him close. Cirilion's face was a mask of confusion and then rage, as he realized that his plan had failed.

"This makes no sense; I planted the idea of more money for the work in Micah's mind. . ." He said, "His heart is joyful at work and making money. Surely, this idea of more, was something he would have liked. And of course, when Joseph went to Beniah's House and heard of the Roman extra tax . . . knowing his father, and Joseph's **need** to make him proud, surely that should have caused Joseph to demand the full amount! How could I have gotten it wrong? **No**. No I didn't misread him. I was successful in planting the seeds of doubt, of lust for more money, for more standing with his father! And I nurtured the resentment of his Mother siding with his Father. I **heard their speech**. I heard **his tone**. I know I was right! How could I be wrong? How could I have misinterpreted his actions?"

Then like a slow sunrise, it dawned on Cirilion, he would have to give an account to the Master. Now there, he said is a real problem. I have to explain how I failed to Light Bringer. He will not be pleased at all. I may be in for a bit of trouble. Well, I guess I have to go back and face the music. He laughed. But, I don't have to rush now do I? He faded in a wash of black.

Joseph stood in the shop with his father Micah. His Father already busy marking out the wood for the next order and making sure it was marked correctly. The lamp light cast shadows along the wall of tools and the moonlight shown through the lattice and the dust from the day.

"Father, **Abba**, why didn't you tell me what you were doing? I would have reacted differently I think." He said wiping down the chair he had stained and dusted. "Son, I didn't say anything to you because I know what I thought; when my father gave me advice or attempted to guide me. You need to know you are your own man. I am your father yes, and I may have wisdom you may need. But there comes a time, when you need to begin to stand on your own. You know the Law. You know shat YHWH says to us as a people and a family. You do good work. And I as your Father am proud. But, Son, every man, woman, child, must seek YHWH on their own. Yes, yes, offer the sacrifices, yes follow the Law and Prophets. But each house itself must seek after his heart and guidance. And you . . . Yes, YOU Joseph, must decide, to follow YHWH or not. I cannot tell you even as a father, though I would like too, which way to choose. YHWH calls each father, each tribe, and each nation to Himself to follow and be blessed, or to be left outside of the blessing. You see faith in YHWH, is not just a Hebrew thing or if they would Roman, every man must choose. If I forced you, would faith be your own? But If I failed to tell you, I would go against what YHWH intended. Because forcing you is wrong, not telling you is even worse. But the worst truly is when you act out, live life, thinking it's yours, but not truly possessing it for yourself."

Joseph stopped and listened as his father continued, "All the Prophets had to choose. Even King David had to choose. Oh yes, he was great among the Kings, but, what did he say to the Prophet Nathan and to YHWH Himself? After Bathsheba and Uriah? Create in me a clean heart, O' God, and renew a steadfast spirit within me. Do not cast me away from Your presence and do not take Your Holy Spirit from me. Restore to me the joy of Your salvation . . . This was a call to YHWH personally, and that is what faith is to be for every person. Yes, nations can follow Him, tribes and people, but, we ourselves must choose. He asks us to choose. Remember the Prophet and Father, Moses? When he was at Moab and YHWH Himself spoke through him? . . . I call Heaven and Earth to witness against you today, that I have set before you life and death, the blessing and the curse. So choose life in order that you may live, you and your descendants . . .

This life; Joseph, son, all these traditions, remind us to choose. To choose life with YHWH. To Choose His Law, His Blessing, why? For life yes. For blessings yes, for protection, yes, for our needs as a nation, but more so, to walk and live and breathe as YHWH intended. Not only as free men, but free in our hearts, souls, and IN All that we are. . Free, truly free.

And it was so, when Father Adam, was at Creation, then even when Father Abraham was first called out of UR. YHWH made covenant with Abraham. He was to choose to follow and walk before YHWH in all things. He spoke to YHWH face to face. And as promised YHWH blessed him and kept him. But you know all of this. Why do I prattle on so." Micah finished.

"It's okay Abba, I still like to hear you tell it. And to know you still believe." Joseph said.

"Son, do you still believe also?" Micah Countered. He was still marking the cuts for the piece they were going to make. He paused waiting on his son. Even in the dim light now of the lamps, he could sense struggle. But he waited to hear his son, and his answer.

CHAPTER 5

BETHLEHEM, ANGELS, SHEPHERDS, EGYPT

Christ's thoughts raced back to the Heavens before the darkness, before the pain and coming death. Back to the other most tearful moment in His life.

The Heavens and the Realm rang with song. His heart even amidst the suffering, found a small sliver of hope. He remembered His home in Heaven. It was bittersweet because, with all his humanness, He wanted to return there. Yet, He still fought to stay. His heart, He knew, was straining and fighting for every bit of life it could grab. And slowly failing. . . He also knew the great despair of longing again. And truly never returning there in His present state. Yet, He heard His Father's voice again. And though it cut Him deep, He relished the sound and remembered. . .

His Father, the Father of Lights, turned to Him and spoke. "Son; it is time. The years and days have been fulfilled. We cannot delay anymore. This must be done."

"I understand Father."

"Holy Spirit," the Son said, "Is all in readiness? Are things in place?"

"Yes, it is. You will find everything in place. Though maybe not to Your liking I would think. But We have agreed that this must take place. There truly is no other way." The Spirit of God chuckled, "I have delivered allot of babies, but not one such as You." Smiling. "Ah, well. . ." the Father of Lights said, "at least I don't have to change the diapers. . ." the Realm shook with His laughter. Soon the Son laughed deep full and strong. "It is going to be different for a while. But; I am glad to do it." Father; all those generations, nations, and people. . . So many will miss it."

"Yes, they will," He said sadly. "But, those that don't will be filled to overflowing with joy and eventually true peace. And We will have accomplished the redemption of man and Creation. And restoration of all We have made. To have again those We love, to lavish on and to show wonders they will spend forever talking about . . . to Our great joy and peace. To be forever together. And never again separated or torn apart from **US**. That I will be as before **the Jehovah Shalom**. Where nothing is broken or missing ever again.

The Father of Lights Looked on His Son and continued. "You understand that when You step from this Realm to Earth, you will have to lay aside Your true power and rely on the Holy Spirit to assist you. Not unlike what our children will need to do to truly live and walk with **Us**. I will still be with You for a time. And in that small moment, you may lose hope, but remember My love. And that it will never depart from You. Many generations will find My love difficult, even to accept, when they struggle or succumb to sin. Many will not understand the truth of it all, until in their lifetime years later. But the joy of lavishing on them and being with them, will overshadow the questions and fears. And many when they truly understand My love for them and what I have done for them, will run again into my arms and embrace, even at this distance. How I long for the days to be completed faster. But, this must be." The Father sighed as He finished.

The Holy Spirit turned to them both and spoke, "I am sure that once our children hold in their hands our Word, they will draw near. Sadly though, many will be misguided or ignorant of what our Word holds. And of course; when the Son walks the Earth, because of Lightbringer's lies, He will have to work at showing them and even explaining to them the truth. But He will accomplish what We have planned. Though in His human frailty, it will be doubly hard, but it can be done."

"Father, many don't 'even believe I exist. Oh, they recognize my role in Creation, but as for the role I have in the Believers life, miracles, provision or anything else. . " His voice trailed off as the Son of God finished. "We may yet find some who truly walk in faith as We intended. And I will do so on the Earth as an example. Even in the writings of our Word, show it. But you are right. The lies of the Enemy have so permeated the promises, many will find it hard to stay in faith. Oh, no not for salvation sake, but more for the Covenant and full promises, as Son's and Daughter's. But there will be some and they will shine as examples of faith. Even some, more than the Prophets and teachers." The Son said.

"But now, We move together in this. We agree that the Son must step down to Earth again wrapped in flesh to accomplish what Our love and holiness demands. Now remember, the Host still doesn't understand our plan, but they will assist in all things. Of Course; Light bringer, Satan, will obviously try and stop Our plan and cause chaos or harm". The Holy Spirit Finished.

"And just so you know; I may **embellish things a bit**, I know its **man's redemption, salvation and Creation's restoration** at stake, but I am sending My Son to Earth and they need to know it. I will not do less for **You** than for them. . ."the Father chuckled.

The Son of God remembered that night well. He of all people would remember the sending to Mary. *The transfer of Almighty God to a house of flesh. A very small, small house.* He thought. It was a wonder now looking from His humanness to think that all that God was, is, and ever will be, wrapped in a house, so fragile and small. But; in reality, He relished the idea, to bear God's great love, ***Our love,*** He thought, *to Earth, and walk again among Creation and live a sinless, perfect life, and bear sin's burden and punishment, to free all creation from slavery and sin's grasp. But that was what? Thirty-three years ago. A man's life, part of a generation of men, how will they see it? Will they understand? Will it make a difference to them? I know the Father, Spirit and I made this plan, and it will be fulfilled. But I can understand even more, man's questions and fears. The fears and questions they were to never have.* He finished.

The Son of God chuckled to Himself, as He remembered more. . .

At first there was Heaven; the Realm as He God knew it, then a darkness and a feeling of movement. Then a flash of light. He knew that Holy Spirit had touched Mary. And He knew that He was now God in Flesh . . . Oh, just the beginnings; He had time to go and grow, but His mission was started.

He could hear music, feel warmth and joy, to include, hope, awe and even a bit of fear.

He felt her move and dance. And He heard her voice. And it soothed His human heart. *Is this what they miss? Do they know* the Son thought, *that every life born on Earth has God's spark? That Light of life and God's own fingerprint? That even in the womb, they give glory to God? And His heart rejoices. . .Oh, how the Enemy has lied . . .If they could only see what happens at that moment of life. . .He thought. How it would change who they believe they are and how much they are valued by God. I know it's true; some feel that children born from sin or other situations are somehow tainted and less. But, the truth as hard as it is, is that every life has God's spark of life and is of fathomless value and beauty. The Enemy lies so naturally; destroying hope or value in life's situations. Even those My Father and the Spirit and I change for good. And those futures coming still. Many because of sin's cost and effects, will be deemed less. Until; they find hope in Me and new life through this Cross. One day, people will be loved as intended, valued as intended, and restored to what I intended them to be.*

He watched as God and the process began. *My Birth of course; is a bit different than men's, but man will touch the egg and God gives the Light of Life at this moment and life begins. But many will doubt what is true because of the Lies of the Enemy. He of course will lie about how they came to be.* The Son of God chuckled to Himself. *He will lie even about the age of the Earth and the things We placed upon it. Out of his hatred of man and God; even the lie that they were from lower creation. And that they were not given the "Spark of God" or the fingerprint of God.* He watched as the cells split and began to form a new life. Soon the embryo and More. *Even now; amidst this pain and death; I remember the heartbeat. Her heartbeat; and the feelings of wonder and Awe. Other children may or may not remember. But; they will find comfort and hope resting against their Mothers neck, hearing and feeling that heartbeat, once again.*

The Son of God's mind and heart raced to that glorious night. A Night never again to be seen or heard. This was to be the night that He would begin to walk the Earth and bear the Honor and Glory of The Father of Lights and begin to fulfill the plan they had mapped out to the ultimate end of total and complete redemption.

He remembered as He experienced the growth in the womb. And how His fingers and toes were formed and the lungs breathing and gaining Nutrients from food and the process. *He remembered Mary's voice. Her singing and even the sadness. The sadness of the struggle between faith and reality.*

The Trinity knew that she and Joseph would bear scorn and laughter, even the disowning of their community to complete their task and fulfill their part of the plan. Joseph though seemingly silent and astute; he had great compassion. And Mary great Faith and a seeming unshakeable trust . . . almost.

God the Father knew; as did all of Us, that When I spoke those words "and a sword will pierce your own soul—to the end that thoughts from many hearts may be revealed." It devastated Mary, as it would any mother. She was a kind, compassionate, loving and God honoring mother. She had heard God's promise and had lived with the knowledge that one day I would pay the cost of man's redemption. She truly didn't understand but, she believed God, and followed with all of her heart. She knew of the Covenant Promise that a Messiah, Savior, would rescue Israel, but didn't truly know it was the redemption of all of Creation and mankind together. That this one act I will soon complete, will forever change all of Creation. And restore what the Father and We intended at Creation. And even more, that We no longer need walk beside man, but We can walk in man. And fellowship closer than ever before. And still lavish on them all the gifts and wonders that we intended. Now and forever. His thoughts ended as pain shot through His broken frame. And He gasped for breath again, struggling to continue the process. . .

Not only was the Son of God bearing all sin and its struggle . . . He was longing for relief. Relief from as Paul in the future would say ". . . the wages of sin. . ." and even more so . . . greater separation soon to become reality.

He remembered Joseph and Mary; and the rocky road to a stable. . . He saw all of it; unlike mankind, who cannot see everything in the womb. Of course; they can feel, hear, react, but not like God. He chuckled that He had unique perspective.

Joseph held tightly to the reins. He stumbled a bit over the rough pathway. Normally, he wouldn't move at night. Most nights it was too dark, even in starlight. And most times, the caravans wouldn't move from the fires till morning because of thieves and robbers. But; this time, things were different. He knew Mary was having a rough time of it.

It's not like I know how she feels; being with child and all. He chuckled to Himself. *I know man things . . . to be rough and tumble, and to defend my family from danger . . .* He paused in thought. *. . .my Family,* He smiled ruefully, *Wow how does that even make sense. We were betrothed and promised to each other; by our families and the community, but then YHWH stepped in. And now Mary is carrying YHWH'S Son, the Promised Messiah, and I and she are to watch over Him and care for Him? How can I say my family? When YHWH certainly already had plans. Maybe I should say we; Mary and I, are part of His family. That's almost too much for me even to think of. We care for the Messiah. Why Us? Why now?*

As He moved along the rough roadway, it seemed he could see more of the road, as it was getting brighter and clearer. He chuckled *I am sure YHWH would not want me to injure His Son! Thank you for the light YHWH.* His thoughts continued, *Now if you could make it a bit warmer. I am okay in my cloak, but I am sure Mary is not as warm as I.*

The roadway was quiet. Not even small creatures seemed to be about. And the clops of the donkey's hoofs and his steps seemed even louder in the night. He moved on in sure steps, attempting to lead the animal around the rough parts of what stood for a roadway in the country. He looked back at Mary. She smiled down at him and bore the travel quietly.

I don't know how she does it. Joseph's thoughts continued. *I know I struggled with what tradition and the community says is right, and even what the Rabbi's and Priests say. We were betrothed and she was already with child . . . I can hear the Priest's voice still. . .* "Now Remember Joseph, your father Micah and Mary's father, Reuben, have setup the Mohar and the documents have been stamped. You are now officially betrothed. . . Please; do not in any way, shame your father or clan by doing anything ***foolish*. . .*" Abram Simeon emphasized gruffly. "This is a serious matter, and in spite of what you may hear, betrothal is permanent except for infidelity or serious reasons. And I would hate to think that your lack of control or Miriam's would cause such insult to the community. Like Benjamin of Nun. That boy has caused more harm than good." The Elder Priest spoke from Joseph's memory.

I still can't believe YHWH sent and an angel to change my mind. Those were hard days. I had so many conflicting feelings and conflicting thoughts. . . Do I do as the community says? Do I follow the Law only?

I dearly loved and love Mary, but i could not comprehend that she had not been unfaithful. She had tried to explain all those days. His heart sank, as he remembered the pain he felt and the anger and frustration of all that had happened.

"Mary do you think me a fool?? He glared at the young woman standing before him. Anger rising, hurt welling, and frustration building. . . He waited for a response, as his mind reeled from her message.

The workshop was dimming because of the oncoming evening. And the added shadows added to the gloom descending upon Joseph's heart. And in a far corner **Cirilion** *thought,* *This has got to work. The Master said I had one last chance to Thwart All Father and stop Man's Hope . . .* **Cirilion** smiled evilly as he whispered in Joseph's ear . . . *She was unfaithful to you Joseph. She was to remain pure and clean before YHWH and the Community. She doesn't love you. If she did, she would not be with child. And O' what of the family's honor? How will Micah react to this situation and what will he think of you?? You can't even control your future bride! And she will shame you all if this gets out! How can a woman truly know God sent an angel? He speaks to Prophets and Priests, not women and certainly not unfaithful ones!* The whispers continued unhindered. *.You need to do something and do it now! You need to stop this whole thing. Besides, how do you really know that this child is of God? And not some urge or local fling? Has YHWH spoken before to women? Or through women?? Surely, HE couldn't be. . .* He Paused. *I have to be careful, If I push too much, he will see the flaw. If I wait, I may yet have victory. . .* Cirilion waited now silent.

"Mary," he continued, "my heart is torn. I love you so much and yet, this is what I see. You tell me an angel of God spoke to you and said that a child will be born in you by the Holy Spirit of God! How would you think YHWH would stoop so low as to bear a child in you. To a betrothed woman, YHWH would be breaking His own Law!"

I know," he continued, "I may not be the handsomest or wealthiest of Israel. Nor of Nazareth, but I am an honest, hardworking man. True to my word. And I have been true to you. I have waited and been pure for you." He ended quietly.

He remembered her sobbing and shaking visibly at his words and accusations. He had wounded her deeply and the hurt, fear, and anger made everything worse. Especially, when Mary spoke softly. . .

"Joseph, isn't it every woman of Israel's dream to bear the Messiah as the Prophet Isaiah proclaimed. . . Therefore the Lord Himself will give you a sign: Behold, the virgin will conceive and give birth to a Son, and she will name Him Emmanuel. He will eat curds and honey at the time He knows enough to refuse evil and choose good. . ." she paused.

Joseph's anger rose again. He spit the words bitterly. "How can you in your state even think to speak of the Prophet or his words??" He spun back to her with his heart full of righteous anger. . .

YHWH speaks to Prophets and through angels yes. But not wayward women or young maidens that cannot control themselves."

"I have been with no one! I have saved myself for you as the Law demands!" she screamed. She dropped her hand to her belly and whispered. . This, this is YHWH's doing as the angel said. She hesitated, then finished. "I am on my own now. But I will bear this alone as it seems YHWH has spoken to me. Even my relative, Elizabeth, is with child miraculously . . . YHWH does as He chooses, Law or not, Prophets or not."

She turned from Joseph and rushed into the night from the workshop. Joseph heard the door close and the darkness and silence enveloped him, as the lantern slowly dimmed and went out.

Joseph came into the house weary and worn. He moved stiffly to the washing bin and pitcher. He smelled the soaps and took a towel. His mother would smack him good if he didn't clean up. Yes, he was his own man now, but he still was in his father's house and his mother's rules. And sometimes her rules were worse than working for his father.

He absently washed his hands in the basin. He half-filled the basin with water; the soap and water felt warm to his skin as he lathered. Then, he washed and wiped rotely, as his mind and heart were struggling to find peace after the days news.

He could smell the finished dinner at the table and hear his mother humming and fussing over fixing the evening meal.

Joseph laughed as he heard a slap and, "Get your hands out of the desert Micah!"

He smiled as he heard his father's reply . . . "But dear heart, it is just so good I cannot wait!" his father said in earnest. His mother finished with laughter.

"Well Micah, as anyone can see with your robes, someone has not stopped you from eating desert first, instead of the meal!" Their laughter filled the house. And yet, it did little to alleviate the tension and hurt in Joseph's heart and soul.

Joseph ate quietly and finished dinner. He then moved to the rooftop and solitude. He walked to the edge wall of the roof and looked over the city. The stars were bright as usual and the light smell of jasmine and orchid on the light breeze was a comfort. Joseph stood stock still, eyes closed and silent, drinking in the breeze and noises of the night. The gentle evening breeze kissed his cheek and the its fragrance filled him with hope.

And Boy do I need hope tonight. He thought. *What am I to do? I have followed the Law as YHWH demands. And I have been faithful as YHWH demands. And it seems Mary has not. Though I don't understand why she would lie to me. She has never before. And I doubt at this day and time that it is some prank or Joke. I thought I could trust her. I thought I had found the one wife I should marry.*

But if what she says is true, that she is with Child, Priest Simeon will lump me in with Benjamin of Nun and I may find it impossible to marry anyone. And even have a business as Father has intended. And If I lose what little business I do have, how can I even think to raise a family.

*Ok, YHWH, what am I to do? Oh I know the Priests may say come talk with me and will seek YHWH'S answer! Since you did **this** . . . what do you say?? I really do need an answer.* His thoughts stopped, as he heard his father's step behind him.

He felt his father's hand on his shoulder and heard his father's voice.

"Joseph, **Son**, You were awfully quiet at dinner. And didn't seem yourself. Can I help you somehow? I can be a good listener, really." Micah finished waiting.

It was a long time before Joseph spoke, with quiet tones. Micah waited silent.

"Father, ***Abba***, what do you do when you have a hard decision to make?" Joseph said

"Decisions are never really easy; in spite of what the Law, Prophets and Priests say." He sat on the walls edge looking out over the city beside Joseph and continued.

"I don't know if this will help. But If I have all the facts and see as much as I am able, usually I can come up with an answer. One that solves my problem and even keeps your mother happy and satisfied. And most times YHWH seems to not have issue with it. As for the Priests . . . well, they are a breed all their own. And they seem to have their own agenda. And sadly, not YHWH'S in some cases." He finished.

"Father, Abba," Joseph hesitated, "You know I love Mary right?" he asked.

"Yes, son I do."

"I don't know what to do." Joseph continued.

"Is she well Joseph or does she need something. . ." Micah asked.

"That is the question *Abba*, she seems fine; but I am not so sure of some of her choices. . ." Joseph's voice tailed off.

Micah chuckled lightly. "You may find son, women's choice can change by the minute, and not make sense to we mere men."

"Father, you have said in business you must find a balance, in meeting your needs and the customers right?"

"Yes that's true." Micah continued. "But Mary is not a customer; she is, and should be much more."

"Oh I know that Father," Joseph interjected. "But I am not sure how to resolve the issue I have found out about today."

Micah looked at his son's silhouette against the starlit sky and moon glow.

He waited debating his next step as a father and even as a friend. His Son was a man now, betrothed and soon to be married. And he didn't want to intrude or force his son's answer or decision. He knew his son was carrying a weight, but didn't want to rush him or cause him to make a rash decision.

"Well son, if it helps, I will keep this in confidence. You are the man of your house. If I can be of help, I will try."

"Father; what do you know of the Law?? Not in sacrifices, but, faithfulness, to the marriage?" Joseph finished.

Micah waited in Silence. Joseph sat stone still. And then turned to his father, face obscured in the dimness.

"Mary came by the Shop a few days ago and started out with some crazy story and . . ." Joseph's words rolled out like water ". . . And something about an angel and YHWH and . . ." He stopped. Micah could hear the tremor in his son's voice and even the anguish. He listened to the heavy breathing and could almost feel his son's struggle to speak. Finally, Joseph began again.

"She said . . . **She said**, she was met by an Angel . . ," he said voice breaking, "and His Message, that she was to have a child and it would be a Child of God. God's Son. And that this Child would be of the Holy Spirit. . ." He stopped trying to keep his voice steady. "And then she said she was pregnant by God. . ." Joseph finished and began weeping. "What do I do?"

Micah slid closer to his son and wrapped his arm around his shoulders and pulled him tight against his side, sitting silently by his son, as his godly son wept in the dark.

Joseph was brought back to the present by the braying of Jerum, his donkey.

"I know, I **know Jerum**, Bethlehem is not too much farther. And Yes, I know Mary is cold too. Come on – watch the rocks Jerum. Soon, we will sleep, soon." Joseph finished laughing.

Joseph's thought raced to that night long ago it seemed. *I know what my father said. But, how can I divorce Mary, we haven't been married long at all. And I know he said he could handle the community and Priest's snubs, he had done it before. He said the Law states – Known adultery is death. And then of course the shame to Mary's family and ours.* His thoughts were a jumbled mess. Just like his bed from all the tossing and turning. *Well if I don't sleep soon I should just get up and work on those bowls for Thomas Judah. Boy, how do I get myself into these things . . .* His thoughts ended.

Joseph sat bolt upright as light filled the room. He rubbed his eyes trying to see into the pulsating light near his bed. *Am I dreaming? Or am I awake?* His thoughts raced, *what's going on?* Then the light coalesced into a large man in glowing clothes and . . . . *This can't be right*, he thought, *are those wings? I must be seeing things.*

Joseph filled with fear, didn't dare move or speak. *Is this really an angel of God! From all the stories from my father and the Priests, meeting an angel was not always good. And it cost the person something, even his life!* His eyes stung from the brightness and then the room shook, as the angel spoke with a strong deep voice.

"Joseph, son of David, do not be afraid to take Mary home as your wife. For, what is conceived in her, is of the Holy Ghost.. . She will give birth to a Son, and you are to give Him the name Jesus. For He will save His people from their sins."

Then, the angel left in a flash of light!

He awoke stunned. *Was this real? Did I see and angel and live?* He thought. He began to laugh and his worries faded and his heart changed. He could feel the rush of joy from deep inside. He was in shock and awe; he had never felt like this before and *what was it the Priests said . . .If YHWH ever speaks to you, you obey Him. The Law said to shun her and divorce her and I was ready to do so . . . Though quietly. I must follow the Law that's what YHWH wants*. The joy had become intense and the laughter louder.

Well, he spoke to room, **YHWH** changed his mind again and now . . . **Now**. He leaped from his Bed! Grabbed his clothes and cloak and moved the workshop.

No sense in sleeping now! I don't have to hide the child or even divorce her! YHWH has done it. He quieted my fears and zealousness. His thoughts stopped

As he began to talk to himself aloud and to the empty shop, he moved the bench where the bowls sat waiting for sanding and sealing. "YHWH is real! His works are true. Just as I have been taught. But what will the Priests say? Are they right? Is the Law right? Or did it change just now? No the Law is the Law and it must be followed; until YHWH," he laughed louder and stronger, "tells you different by His angel."

The joyous memory faded as he caught himself laughing, as he led Jerum the donkey on the worn path to Bethlehem.

Mary looked down from her perch on Jerum's back and asked.

"Why are you happy, my husband?" she said eyes twinkling.

"Just remembering, Mary, how foolish I had been."

"*Foolish?* You.. . never!"

They laughed loud and strong and the night resounded with their joy!

She smiled, she could see the lights of Bethlehem and hear the music of harps and singing.

She looked down, and placed a hand on her belly. She shook her head, *in me,* she thought, *is of the Most High!?*

Mary, held and cherished these things in her heart. She then dimly heard the voice of Joseph.

"We will soon be in Bethlehem.. . Then, we may rest."

The donkey brayed in the night, almost as if to agree, that it had been a hard ordeal. They moved off down the hill to the city.

Amidst the pain and struggling breath the Son of God remembered. *I felt every touch, heard every word and felt everything. If parents only knew of what We have given when We give life. The Father knows that life fully, completely, and has great plans for the Child. Whether Boy or Girl, He gives them life and calls them to know Him. But, sin, still active in man's heart destroys many and destroys life. Most never see their great potential or the fulfillment of God's plan because evil lives, not by the Father's choice. But, to be just and righteous, HE must give choice to Choose love over hate, peace over fear, and so much more.*

The night was cold and crisp. He heard the soft clop of the donkey's hooves, the wisps of breath from his leading of Jerum. The constant chill about his shoulders and hands. . . Joseph knew if he was cold, Mary would have it worse by far. He needed to hurry and find shelter.

She was quietly riding on Jerum's back and she smiled down from her perch and said, "It will be good to rest in Bethlehem."

"Yes, Mary it will. It will be good to rest. Soon, soon we will be there." Joseph finished.

Minutes faded to an hour.

"There Mary, see the lights of Bethlehem." He saw the lights as they entered the city. He heard the music and heard the singing and rejoicing. He was a bit overwhelmed by the crowd's, but he pushed on.

I am sure that Inn is on this street . . . Then again, it has been a while, months since I have been here. I could be mistaken. He paused, as a group of people moved passed. He moved down further through group after group. Some were huddled around a small fire. Others moved with celebration and laughter, while others still staggered by drink.

Well, at least we can celebrate a little, he thought, as he and Jerum's burden turned a corner, finding a familiar street with even more lights. *There it is. . . . Benhadad's Inn; I knew it! I am glad we are here. Hopefully, he will have room. And we can Rest.* He stopped and tied Jerum to the post and turned to help Mary from the donkey's back.

Mary said quietly, "It will be good to rest after this hard travel."

"Yes, it will Mary," Joseph said and swatted Jerum's Rump who brayed. And Joseph continued, "And I bet it will be good for you Eh Jerum, since you carried all the weight!" Laughing he dodged Mary's swat. "Oh Joseph," he pulled her close as she said, "You will get yours!" Holding her tighter he said, "I hope so."

He helped Mary up the steps to the door and he hit the door with the flat of his hand hard to try and overcome the noise coming from inside. He hit the door again even harder, glancing back at Mary and hoping he would get a response before she fell from exhaustion.

Suddenly, the door opened flooding the street will light and noise! Before Joseph stood the Inn Keeper. Gruffly, he yelled above the din. "Yes, yes what do you want!" Benhadad Bartholomew finished.

Fighting to be heard Joseph cried, "We need a room. We are here for the Census!"

"So is half the country! I am full; there is no more room!" Benhadad answered.

"But there must be something! Joseph Pleaded, "My wife is with Child!"

The Inn Keeper looked on, obviously frustrated, and spoke again, "Again, I say I am full!"

But in that same moment His wife slapped him on the shoulder and said, "Nonsense! Can't you see she is **with child**; Benhadad Bartholomew, I swear you have the understanding of a rock!" she finished.

"But where can they go? All the rooms are filled." He implored his wife. "I know, but she needs to be out of the cold and in a warm place. . ." His wife began. "Let me think. . . Let me think." Moments passed then, "I have it! They can bed down in the stables only for tonight and once a patron leaves, they can have a warm room. And we have lots of blankets and the stable can bear a fire." She finished.

Joseph knowing Mary, slowly, turned to her. And looked into her eyes. *She has borne so much how can I ask this of her. But what can I do? This is as far as she can endure.*

Mary nodded. Joseph turned back to the Inn Keeper and his wife. Who promptly said, "I am so sorry dear, but we will fix this in the morning, The stable is in the back. We built a room and put fencing around it. You should be warm in the back corner and once I get you the blankets and warm drink . . ." She said as she moved off, turned, and spoke to her husband, "**Benhadad!** Don't just stand there like a cedar of Lebanon, show them how to get to the stable! Help them get settled. I will be out with blankets and warm drink! **Now move**. . ."

The Inn Keeper, knowing he had lost all hope of keeping his dignity, moved quietly through door to the street and toward the back alley toward the stable. Joseph led Mary on Jerum not far behind.

The Son of God heard His Father's voice again and remembered. He drew comfort from His Father's voice and the memory. . .

The Voice of God the Father of Lights thundered! "Michael! Take some of the host and watch over Bethlehem! My Son is soon to be born!"

The Father of Lights chuckled. "We need to celebrate! I have already called to the world with the star and I know the Wise Men have seen it. And some even follow it now. They will arrive later! The world needs to know My Son and the Reason for His birth. However, the Kings of the Earth do not hear or see. Who would? This is for everyone! For every nation, tongue, and tribe for now and always until the world itself is rebuilt and restored. For all of humanity until the time of restoration and We are reunited in holiness and righteousness! Well, We call to the ones who will truly hear. . ." He finished.

Michael, the Archangel, smiled. He knew the reason for the birth, but truly understanding it, was quite another matter. He raised a mighty arm, and thousands flocked to his side! The heavens shook with their shouts!

The Father of Lights spoke again. And the heavens shook again!

"Remember, the evil one may try and harm Him. Watch closely! See he does not appear. Then tell of His coming. For **He** is my **Son**."

The shout of victory arose! And thousands streaked to Earth, to guard the Son of God!

And in a dim corner of the sky, Satan shook. The knowledge of the angels guarding Jesus would change the plan, only slightly.

Joseph and Mary had settled in the back corner of the stable. To their left, there were stalls for whatever the need. Horses, donkeys, even a camel. The far wall had other pens for a pair cows and a ewe sheep and lamb. It was enclosed enough by the doorway to hold the heat of the fire and animals. The hay smelt warm and the chill of night was gone. Mary rested quietly on a small parcel of hay and blankets.

Joseph stoked the fire and looked at the lodgings. . "*Well,* he thought, *I am Sorry YHWH I could do no better for your Son. I wanted to even do more for my wife Mary. But this is all I can do. And with the Census and the crowds . . .* He paused, *I am surprised we were not outside the city, as we have been traveling. I hope I am doing well. I have no Idea how to be a father or husband to anyone . . . let alone YHWH's Son.*

Joseph took note that he would need more firewood. More than likely, this would be a long night indeed. The chill, for now was gone, but he knew it would grow colder. He also knew Mary, being with child, could not endure much more.

Joseph moved outside the stable and began the hunt for wood, sticks, even thatch to burn in order keep the stable warm and cozy. He was a carpenter and knew what wood burned the best, however the wood was somewhat sparse here in Bethlehem. He was also concerned that he would go too far from Mary and Jerum, which would not be safe.

Somehow he scrounged up a small armful and headed back. The breeze was chilly and light; he glanced up at the stars, they seemed closer somehow. He felt that he could almost touch them. And one in particular seemed closest of all. This star was brighter than even any other in the night sky.

The stars shone like jewels on velvet and the chilled breeze from the hillside told of coming cold. But the shepherds had been here before. They knew how to make a fire and bed down the sheep for the night. Laughter and conversation could be heard over the crackle of the fire and the light bleating of the sheep in the hillside pen.

It was the youngest's turn to watch overnight. He sat staff and sling near at hand in front of the doorway to the sheep pen. The doorway was one carved into the hillside. It wasn't as big as those in the cities, but it was enough to keep the sheep safely and easily protected.

"Go on Reuben, back in to the pen!"

He pushed on the little head and tried to spin the body, to head it in the right direction.¬ but, this one was stubborn, and fought against the shepherd.

"Come Reuben, in the pen with you! Come now," he spoke softly, almost conspiritively. .you are making me look bad. *And in front of Ben and the others too.* The little sheep cried and turned back. **Finally**, he sighed, *I can watch in* **peace!** *. . . Then again, there are the* **wolves!** His thoughts ended, He held tighter to his staff.

Joseph was awakened by a cry! One of pain! He sat up quickly and lit the lantern.

"Mary, are you well!?"

"It . . . it. . .is **time!**? **MY husband!"**

She cried out again, as those words carried on the night wind.

She was to have her child, tonight! Joseph thought fearfully.

The other members of the stable took little notice of the events. They continued to munch, whinny, or honk, as they were made to do. And Joseph . . . helped as best he could.

The sky over the stables was lit by it seemed a single star! And it glowed brightly against the bright backdrop of night. The star, at least now, was not a sun. It was an angel! Watching over the young life soon to be born.

The others in the heavenly host, raced to the hillside, to tell the news! The Angel Gabriel, broke through the night. And stood in the heavens, glistening as a bright flame!

The shepherds, brought out of slumber by the brightness, shook in utter fear! Jonathan, still at the pen, couldn't believe his eyes!

There in the sky! A . . . angel of God! And we still live! How can this be!? I must tell Ben!

He scrambled to the main fire, now dying in ashes. Only to find them all awake, shaking, and pointing, trying to understand the vision and visitation!

"Ben, Ben! Do you **see**!" cried the boy.

He stopped next to Ben who was kneeling now, eyes closed and shaking. He said only "yes" and began to pray. Why, Jonathan did not know.

But then, the angel spoke . . . the voice booming, **"Do not fear! I bring you good news! And that, of great joy! For all people! Today in the City of David, a Savior is born. He is Christ the Lord! This will be a sign to you, you will find the baby, wrapped in cloths and lying in a manger."**

The shepherds stood unable to speak for the magnitude of the message. They hardly could believe, that here in Bethlehem, there was their . . . Savior! But, this was an angel, so . . . **so what to do!?**

Those words hung in the air; then the heavenly host, sang. The night echoed in joyous praise! Unheard or unequaled before!

The whole Earth seemed alive with the praise of Jehovah God!

Ben stood slowly, looking at the others. Almost hoping he was the only one to see the sight. Jonathan then took his arm and spoke, "Did you see that? Let's go and see, what the Angel said!"

Ben looked down at the youth, shaking his head. He spoke softly and with sadness, "Jonathan, I do not think it is **our** place."

"But, **Ben** . . . why not!?" The question was edged in tearfulness.

He looked into the boy's eyes, as tears were welling. The boy spoke again.

"Didn't the angel say it was for **all people?** . . And are we, not **people!?"**

"Yes, son, you are right."

He looked at the others; they smiled." **We go to Bethlehem!**"

Jonathan closed the door to the small pen. And moved down the hillside following his father, Benjamin, and the other shepherds. He was full excitement and wonder.

The sky above the stables was almost as bright as noonday! Yet, no one in the stables seemed to take notice, and the surrounding village suddenly was still. Still, as in anticipation of some great event, or happening.

Mary held her charge tenderly. And somewhat fearfully. *This the* **Messiah,** she thought, *I must be very,* **very careful***.*

The Son of God held onto that moment. Though still in great pain and struggling to breathe, He smelt the stables. He remembered the warmth and the light of the angel overhead.

I remember. I was so tightly wrapped I could not move. And yes, her voice soothed me. But even then, I knew why, I was there. She pulled me to her neck, I heard her heartbeat and voice again. And of course the animals all making noise as well. The Father of Lights said the animals would recognize me, even though Creation was long ago. And seemingly, at least, for men far away. I felt her love and Joseph's. He was doubly nervous; He chuckled, *not only because he too knew I was the Messiah, but he also was a new father or guardian. He was charged with watching over Me. They both were . . . But how could they know. They never dreamed of the life and miracles they would be a part of. They would be heartbroken, as I, the firstborn, would carry the honor of My Father. To a rugged, horrible, and violent Cross! I would buy back the Father's most precious possession, all mankind, and even Creation itself. However, that was the plan.*

His thoughts continued. *Lightbringer, Satan, thought he had Our plans beaten, he didn't know it, but even he fulfilled Scripture.*

The Son of God strained to push Himself up on the bruised and painful heal. He gulped the air and relaxed again into the semi-permanent place of pain. His eyes were dimming and the thrum blood was loud in His ears, so He closed His eyes and tried again to shut out the   noise,   screams   of   hatred,   and Satan's evil laughter. . .

He went back to that night to recapture some joy . . . but even amidst this pain….Suddenly, in His mind's eye, He was back there again … God in Man, the God Man, tightly wrapped and hearing Mary sing.

The memory brought joy in this dark moment. *I think even the animals quieted, as she sung and hummed. I felt she was nervous and a little afraid, she was a new mother. Somehow she moved from awe to motherhood in those hours . . . but when the shepherds came, she was reminded, and so was I.*

The angel waited above the stable. He was to keep watch. He could call the others in moments. He knew of the rebellion day and Light Father's words. When he cast Lightbringer, Satan to Earth, he would be vigilant over the Son of God. He looked on at the couple and the Son.

He saw the shepherds search the streets for the stables and saw their awe and wonder, as they found Mary, Joseph and the babe.

Ben and his fellow shepherds walked slowly to the entrance of the stables. Peering in, they saw Joseph and Mary resting on the hay and blankets the Inn Keeper had furnished, as they sat quietly near the fire.

"Hello, we are sorry to disturb you. We were told our Savior and Messiah would be in a stable and a trough in Bethlehem." Ben spoke in quiet tones.

Joseph got up and moved to Ben motioning them into the stable. And Mary just then placed the babe in the trough, padded with hay and a small blanket.

"My name is Benjamin bar Judah, of the Hills." Joseph heard and watched as the introductions continued.

"My son, Jonathan, and the rest can introduce themselves." Ben finished. "We came to see our Messiah and Savior. The angels surprised us!" He laughed. "No Terrified Us! I have never seen an angel, so huge, bigger than a man of the Roman Guard."

"Is it appropriate for us to be here? We were surprised that this message was given to US," he continued. You know what people think of Us. . ." Ben stopped.

The Son of God remembered the look of awe, as one-by-one, they approached His cradle. He laughed in is heart, *Yes, I suppose it was. Light Father, Father God was trying even then to make a point. That God Himself came down, not with fanfare or great extravagance, though He couldn't leave out the angels; He just couldn't, but that love would go to any means to reach its goal. And love . . . what did Paul say? Love is patient, love is kind. And more. My Father wanted people to know He was near, and loved them greatly. And that this was the beginning of His Promise and as He told the angel to say . . . this hope, Savior and Messiah, was for everyone anywhere. And to prove the point*

... a trough, shepherds, those weren't things associated with wealth, power, or even royalty.

His Memory shifted to the small shepherd boy Jonathan. He came and stopped and knelt by His cradle. He remembered his eyes filled with tears and his heart full of wonder, that **he** a shepherd boy was looking at **the Savior, the Messiah**. But more that God had sent them an angel, **them,** who were no one, the least.

He saw his tears as the boy gently touched His small hand and quickly spun away and hid in the back of the crowd. *He was called by my Father; He heard, and understood. Though there was no need for fear, but this does happen when God shows up. He became a follower of Mine,* Jesus thought. *He is here by the Cross with John and the others.*

He remembered how each of the shepherds told the story of the angel's message, the Host shouting praise and the Promise. He also remembered the small crowd gathered around the stable. The Inn Keeper afraid of reprisal, the shepherds, and patrons. The shepherds went all throughout Bethlehem telling any who would listen of the story. Soon, the shepherds left Bethlehem, and returned to the hillside shouting praise to God in great Joy!

And Mary, he thought, *how her heart rose with joy and pride, as any mother, when told of great things of her Son and for Him. Her faith grew, her hope, joy, even her assurance, that she had heard God the Father's call and obeyed. And Joseph too. Mary held all of this deep in her heart.*

The Son of God thoughts raced to another day.

"Joseph, there are so many people, and I thought the Priest would have stopped us from the circumcision," Mary said.

"No Mary, Jesus is a Son of Israel, and it's the proper thing to do." Joseph answered. "Besides, it was time to see Jerusalem again and gather food, and other things. I needed to get some new tools. And now that He has been circumcised He has standing in Israel. He can learn the Torah and do as YHWH has chosen."

Jesus remembered the shout of joy, as Simeon made his way to the couple. And Mary's shock! Joseph was ready to defend them both. The old man moved in sure even steps. And his Tallit moved with the same rhythm. Simeon stopped and spoke to them both.

"I am sorry if I frightened you. I meant no fear. But I have been promised by YHWH, that I would see The Messiah, His Salvation and All of Israel's . . . May I hold the child?" He paused holding out weathered hands. Mary glanced quickly at Joseph.

Who spoke up, "Who are you, who speaks of YHWH and His Promise?"

"I am Simeon; and an old man promised by YHWH," He paused, "not to die until I saw the Messiah. May I hold the Child?" he asked.

"His name is Jesus, Yeshua," Joseph said. He looked to Mary, who handed him to the elder. He looked intently at Jesus, tears formed in his eyes. . . He looked heavenward and said allowed. . . **"Now, Lord, You are letting Your bondservant depart in peace, according to Your word; For my eyes have seen Your salvation, Which You have prepared in the presence of all the peoples: A light for revelation for the Gentiles, And the glory of Your people Israel."**

Joseph and Mary were stunned, even speechless.

And as Simeon handed Jesus back to his mother he continued. . .

"Behold, this Child is appointed for the fall and rise of many in Israel, and as a sign to be opposed—and a sword will pierce your own soul—to the end that thoughts from many hearts may be revealed."

"Thank you." He said, "May YHWH Bless and keep you and make His face shine upon you and give you peace - as He has me." Simeon turned, and quietly was lost in the crowd.

Mary and Joseph's eyes met and turned to the baby Jesus in quiet amazement and awe. The people around had stopped. They all had heard Simeon's word and prophecy. For prophecy it was. And nearby Anna the Prophetess spoke to any who would hear the Promise of God's redemption and mankind's salvation. Joseph turned to one of the men nearby and asked, "Who is **she**?"

The man replied, **"That,** with a grin, is Anna the Prophetess; she serves here day and night, fasting and in prayer. She is eighty-four. I wish I had her energy."

And Mary and Joseph left the Temple more in awe, if that were possible, and headed back to Bethlehem.

The Son of God winched in pain; and gritted His teeth against the flair up. *Maybe its pain! My mind seems muddled. It seems I have forgotten* **something**. *I did try to be a good child. My childhood, at points, seem a blur.* **Oh Yes!** *I can't forget that visit of the Seer's and the Wise Men: Abdi-ill-Ba-alum, Muranu, and Naram, the youngest of the group. They came to the house when I was a few years older. I remember times when Joseph and Mary were concerned, but not like this . . . it was during Herod the First's reign and the great mourning of Israel.*

"Muranu, my friend is all in readiness??" Abdi –ill-Ba-alum asked. He pulled his heavy cloak tighter about his shoulders and moved to his appointed charger. A white Arabian he called "Swift." He mounted and looked over the group and long line of pack animals and some servants.

Muranu smiled and said, "Yes, Abdi, we have forgotten nothing. Though, with all of **this** . . ." Pointing to the caravan, "it may take us years!"

Abdi-ill-Ba-alum straightened in the saddle and spoke loud enough for all to hear.

"You have served this Kingdom well. Our King and yours has called us to journey to honor Belteshazzar's, Daniel's, King, that he spoke of in his book. It is said, "Belteshazzar could see with His God's help." In honor of His God we will honor him in the midst of enemies, so prepare yourselves. This coming King was promised to set nations free. And you all have heard and read of Belteshazzar Daniel. The King will be in need and we would honor him with gifts of benefit. And if need be, bravery for the King, just as we would for ours!" He paused, looking to the Heavens. "This is our quest and *That* . . ." pointing to the brightest star in the sky, "Is our guide! We Go!" He shouted.

They certainly did just that. And they were Wise Men. His memory jumped to the time in Bethlehem. He could see the small house and smell the bread. *Oh, how wonderful it was and the fruits with the laughter and joy!* The memories swelled His heart, yet gave no relief for the constant agony in His body and the slow death playing out for all to see.

"I cannot go on another day!" Naram groaned. "I guess I am not Seer worthy! Day and night we have followed your star Grand Seer Abdi, and found no King, nor Kingdom!"

"Calm yourself Naram. Muranu and I have not made a mistake. Sometimes finding answers and fulfillment of hidden Word or Promise . . . is not easy, nor safe. Belteshazzar's God spoke and wrote through him, a Promise and Hope. His God told him to write it out." Abdi Paused, "Yes, we have traveled far and faced many dangers." And he chuckled, "Seeming toil of chore. But the Star is still in the sky. It still goes before us; urging us on, in spite of weariness, fear, or hardship! We must continue. And you have reached a point where most stop Naram. Many go no farther to find their needed answers, nor their greatest treasure . . . So no, you're learning as a Seer is not finished, but truly beginning."

Muranu leaned over from his saddle and spoke quietly. "Is that how you kept me going Abdi, Grand Speeches?" Abdi –ill-Ba-alum laughed shaking his head. "Oh no, you, I kept you believing that food was the fuel of wisdom, ha-ha; how do you think I got as heavy as I am!" The Night resounded in laughter.

The morning light caught the dew and caused the land and plants to sparkle.

Muranu stretched the road weariness for his body and spoke to all that could hear. Looking up at the Bright Morning Star; the King's Star he said.

"I have looked and re-read the Scrolls and Belteshazzar's writings. We are going the right way; we will stop at Jerusalem, and speak with the King there. He surely will know where to find the coming King! And this journey of months and weeks will be over. And then we can go home again." He finished taking a bit of meat from the servant.

"Jerusalem? Didn't Belteshazzar speak of Bethlehem?" Naram said.

Muranu spoke is surprise, "Oh Naram, ha ha, you have been paying attention!"

He continued. "We go to Jerusalem to ask passage through the countryside. And the freedom to worship. Some Kings and countries can be dangerous," hmph he scoffed, "and more yet need to be placated."

Little did they know how true his statement would be. The Son of God groaned in pain. His mind struggling to stay focused and complete

His task. *There were dangerous and deadly Kings in places of power. And some had help they couldn't or chose not see. . . .*

The night time entry to Herod the First's palace held no fear for the demon, **Dante**; the human guards couldn't see him if he chose. He had an appointment with Herod that he could not miss. He was on a mission for his sovereign Lucifer. He looked down at Herod's sleeping body caught in a dream. He smiled evilly, *If I do this right; it will be a nightmare for Light Father's Son!* He thought, as he leaned down to whisper in Herod's ear. Dante watched as Herod turned over to his left side. He also heard a groan. ***Time to sow more seeds of fear and paranoia. This will push the dream's intensity and he will react as we plan. This is not going to be hard at all.***

Muranu stopped his horse and wiped his face with his riding towel. He looked back at the Grand Seer Abdi ill Ba Alum. Who at that moment was wiping the sweat from his brow and looking weary too.

"Abdi, old friend, we have passed Palmyra, and I believe we will soon be in Damascus, so we may water and rest the horses and the caravan. Soon, very soon we will stop. And then we will see Jerusalem and find the new King." He finished.

"It will be good to stop. And get a good meal too." Abdi said.

"What's wrong with our meals?" Naram spoke up. Both Muranu and Abdi spoke as one humorously "Oh, no nothing . . . nothing at all!" Laughing.

Dante chuckled as he watched Herod. ***What does he call himself? Oh Yes! The Great! He will be great alright. He will be greatly stressed and fearful when I am done. Night three of the tension and fear grows. I sure hope I am rewarded in a good manner.*** The whispers and Herod's tossing continued.

*Oh to **Rest** and be at **Peace**, as the Magi were. They strived hard to reach their goal, but were able to rest in relative peace. I will not have peace till this is finished. And the Earth and mankind is redeemed. And Father will have peace with man once my sacrifice is finished. Then We wait for those who will come and find hope from hopelessness and deliverance from fear,* The Son of God thought.

"Finally, there it is; there it is Jerusalem - The house of Peace. The place of Abraham, Moses, David the King and Solomon. We must find an inn and rest! Let us wash ourselves and go to the King and find the promised new King." Abdi-ill- Ba-Alum proclaimed.

The moon over Jerusalem shown bright in the sky, as the caravan was finally tucked away in the stables, rooms, and warm Beds. Their Journey almost at an end.

Seer Muranu came back into the rooms they had paid for in Jerusalem. The Grand Seer felt the great tension in his friend and colleague even from a distance. He waited, as he knew his friend would speak soon enough.

Muranu slapped the dust and dirt from his clothes; his voice, the tension radiant, as he spoke.

"Abi, Grand Seer, this makes no sense at all!" he spoke angrily. The Seer still waited in silence.

"We have seen the signs. In the Scrolls and in the sky! And even found the times and days to bring us here!" he paused to throw his tunic shawl on the nearby couch. His voice just as tense as his body. "But no one! No one . . . has heard of the new King that was born to rule the Jews!" he stopped. Hands flexing. The Gran Seer watched as the frustration slowly bled away to calm. He spoke clearly and calmly as Naram looked on.

"Muranu, brother, peace. You have asked about this in the market and booths of the city? And within the gate?" he finished.

Muranu wiped the stress from his forehead and finished, "Yes, at each of those places. And the answer was the same."

He moved to the table where Seer Ba Alum was sitting.

"For such a wondrous city, Belteshazzar spoke about, they live in ignorance of a baby King. Only of Herod, the Great, and Romans. Local Births of friends and family. No Kingly proclamations or edicts. Nothing, absolutely nothing of a new King!" he threw his hands up in frustration again. "How could we be wrong?? What did we miss?"

The Grand Seer took his wineskin, drank its contents, and set it on the table. He was lost in thought, as minutes passed. He looked Muranu in the eyes and spoke.

"Muranu, we missed nothing. The King is near." Abi held up his hand to forego the start of his objection. "Do you remember the Scrolls and their message?" Again, he held up his hand. Muranu waited.

"You, yourself said He would be born and grow, then would be cut off. Would not Belteshazzar's God YHWH want to see HIS plan fulfilled? Would HE not protect this Child against the future to fulfill it? What does your military mind tell you? Would you not hide the announcement and truth, so that victory would come to you or the promise complete?" he finished.

"So what do we do now?" Muranu said.

Abdi Chuckled. "Believe it or not, we go to the reigning King in Jerusalem. He would know. And from what I understand, we may not be helping the new King After all."

Herod Tetrarch drank more of his wine, as he lounged on his couch watching the dancers and jugglers entertain his patrons. There was laughter and music, but there was a tightness in his gut as he looked over the room. Questioning each one and what he saw in his heart.

Dante smiled hidden from men's view. His eyes sparkled, as Herod's eyes lit up each one. And *Yes, O Great One, each of these, has more than enough reason to bear you ill or want your power and money. You must watch closely, be vigilant, look for the plots and snakes in the bushes and palace!* **Dante** whispered.

Herod's thoughts were broken by a servant as he spoke in his Ear. "King Herod, a message from the city and gate guards for you. A caravan of Magi arrived yesterday. . ." His voice trailed off as Herod took the paper.

The note said, **"My King, from Gate Guard Philemon, yesterday at late hour a caravan came into the city and found lodging. We watched them as you wanted quietly. But today, one of their number wandered the streets and asked questions. Questions about a "New King that was born. One to rule the Jews."** A knot of fear and dread began to build in the pit of his stomach, as he read on. **"I remember the cleansing you did of your enemies; I was there. Could we have missed some one? For I know of none other that would be able to be called King. . . Even by Rome."**

Herod sat up and tossed the crumpled note into the fire, and the dread grew to fever pitch. He stood to his feet, raising his voice. "Leave my presence all of you! Leave I say! I must rest. Come back tomorrow!" He turned to the Court Guard. "See they All Leave, **Now**!" He paused. "I may need the Guard shortly. See it done."

"Yes, my King," they moved to clear the room, as Herod moved swiftly down the colonnade to his private rooms.

Herod the first entered his rooms in a whirlwind. The room was lit always and the heating brazier was still glowing red. He sank roughly into his favorite chair. **Dante,** still on assignment, smiled as Herod sank into the chair. Even Dante could see the tension on his face. He knew his seeds had taken root. He watched in glee, as his hands opened and closed in stress. He looked on as the would be ruler reached for his goblet to drink his favorite wine.

Empty! How can this be empty! I have told these lazy useless servants to keep it full and as much as possible cold! His angry thoughts ended as he threw the goblet against the far wall.

"Selena! Selena, attend at once!" He bellowed.

Dante leaned close to Herod's ear and began to whisper and weave more doubts and scenarios with intrigue.

Dante spoke so only Herod could hear. And each word, or lie rather, and questions, reverberated in his mind and heart. ***It is happening again.*** Herod heard, thinking the thoughts were his own . . . ***Just as at the start. I knew what I had to do to secure my place here in Israel and Rome. I took the opportunity and made much of it. And I knew my family and those opposed to me. I have hundreds of ears and eyes. How?? How could I have missed this? A new King?*** Dante paused, as there was a gentle rap on the door. Selena carried a cold pitcher of wine into the room on the plater and set it beside Herod on his table. She knelt and bowed to the ground. And then slowly got up, and backed out of the room.

Dante noticed his whispers had the desired effect; Herod had barely noticed or acknowledged the servants in their entry, or exit. **Dante** smiled as the web of darkness grew. He circled Herod's chair as a predator would, whispering, probing … flaw or weakness, hunger, desire … circling as bird of prey to strike.

Dante continued. *Who are these Magi? From where do they come? And Why . . .* He Paused. *Why would they ask about a new born King? Here, In Jerusalem? What do they know that I do not? Could it be that I have forgotten someone to remove long ago, or is this a test from Rome, even from my enemies? With all my informants, how could this have been missed? And who will pay for it.* Dante stopped, just as Herod's thoughts did.

"Jacob Simon! Come here1" Herod bellowed. "Guards! Guards!" Herod waited.

He could hear the heavy footfalls of his Palace Guard, as they responded to his call. He almost laughed, as they burst into the room armed for battle.

The Chief Guard, Jacob Simon, moved to his side leaning in said, "You called O' King! Are you well?"

"No, not in the Least! I could have died before my precious Guard came to my rescue!" he said with dripping sarcasm.

"But Sir, we were clearing the palace as ordered. . ." Jacob began in Protest. . .

"It doesn't matter," Herod said with a wave of his hand. "I need you to go and shake the merchants, vendors, and harlots. And find out everything about these new arrivals, The Magi. The one's who spoke about a King!"

"But it is late evening O' King, all the market is closed. All, but the Harlots." Jacob said.

"I do not care the hour." Herod growled, "I will not be put to a disadvantage here in my own city or my own country by some heathen magicians!!" He got up from his chair and warmed his hands on brazier. He continued, "I have been challenged in my own city. I will not rest until I have answers. So, neither will they, nor my eyes and ears, or anyone in this city. Now leave me and get it done!"

Herod stood staring into the fire of brazier long after the sounds of the guards exit died on the night breeze.

The tension and fear were melting away as Herod soaked in his private bath. The servants had already left breads and cheeses. and the wine helped as well. He didn't want to use the large Roman bath in the court, it was early and cool. But he used that mostly for the other parties he held. He grabbed more dates and figs, and enjoyed the rays streaming in from the widows and lattice.

He heard the gentle padding of Selena's feet and felt her kneeling presence at his back.

"There is a message, O' King, the guards deemed it urgent, I beg forgiveness." She spoke in a whisper.

"There is no need to fear Selena, you have done no wrong, but they may have. . ." He turned and took the message from her small hand and read it. "You may go and eat . . . I may need you soon."

He watched, as she backed away from the bath and headed to her rooms and small cook area.

He looked again at the message:

Sire, we have done as you have asked. We have scoured the city. And the only thing we could find is that the Magi were from the East. And are preparing to ask for an audience from you. We told them to come to the Reception Hall and await you.

Signed: The Palace Guard

Well it seems fortune and cunning have yielded a catch. Maybe, it will be a catch that may profit all. Or at least me, he thought as he moved the steps and his bed chambers.

Grand Seer Abdi-ill-Ba-Alum leaned upon the staff, as all the others shifted uneasily. He again straightened his robes and looked again at the crate of fruit cakes they had prepared. He chuckled to himself, as the others jumped at the announcing trumpets and watched as the Palace Guard marched Herod to his seat in the reception room.

Sad, from all the things written in our Books of Belteshazzar's home, and all the talks Nebuchadnezzar had with him. He said his people were different. Not given to opulence or greed, This must be one, who does not know his God. I have seen thousands like this man. I must tread carefully. And we must be careful of what we seek and not endanger the new King. His thoughts ended.

The Court Guard Captain stepped forward and cried, "All here, know now Herod the King will hear your pleas and complaints and serve justice according to the law and his great wisdom!"

Herod stood, straightened his robes and eyed the growing crowd. Many he recognized and most he did not. Then his eyes caught the robes of the Magi. *Why are they in the back? If they are officials or important, why are they in with the rabble.* He thought.

He motioned to the Guard and whispered to him; and he then stepped from the throne to the court, moving with even steps to the back corner. And to the Magi.

The Grand Seer Abdi spoke in a harsh whisper to his friends. "Ah, now we come to it. He has seen us, mind yourselves, follow my instruction, and be watchful. We do not know if this is an honorable man or not. Nor do we know if he truly knows the God YHWH, as Belteshazzar, Daniel's God."

He stood tall and held tight to his staff, as the others braced for battle. It was true they didn't know Herod. But there had been rumors. . .

"I am Jacob Simon, Court Guard." he started. "Please forgive me, you are in the wrong place. You were to be first to be heard. I did not realize your importance. You are emissaries from the East and Seer's by your dress?" he paused, waiting.

"Yes, we are. But We did not want to disturb his Majesty with our coming. But we do seek answers to some questions if he would give us an ear." Abdi finished politely.

"Follow me , and your names. . ."

"His name is Muranu, Senior Seer, he will speak for us. Though I am Abdi-ill-Ba-Alum, and Naram, our acolyte."

The Guard moved them through the crowd to the steps of the Dais. And Waited. The Guard knelt and waited. He counted the seconds till Herod would speak. This was the way of things; to set guest and criminals on edge, and drive home the reality of whose presence they were in.

"Rise Captain, and who are these with you?" Herod intoned smoothly.

"O' King, these are emissaries from the East, Seer's. Senior Seer Muranu Sir and his colleagues." He finished.

"Ah, visitors to our great city. Welcome, and how can the King of Judea be of service to you?" Herod crooned.

Muranu stepped forward, bowed and began.

"We O' King, come with simple questions; that one of your great wisdom, though we feign to ask, must have answers for. We, my colleagues and I, are seeking the new born King. He is to be ruler of the Jews. Spoken of by one of your country, you know as Daniel, we as Belteshazzar. I know we ask much, but word of your greatness and benevolence has reached our country and we are to come to worship Him and bring gifts to Him and you." Muranu stepped back to Abdi's side and waited.

Herod rose from his throne and spoke to Muranu, "A King? A new born King?" He moved to the left on the Dias, hands clasped behind his back in thought. "To rule the Jews, you say. You have come to worship Him? And give Him gifts?" He crossed back and forth across the Dias. As he spoke, he stopped, then turned again to Muranu and the waiting crowd.

"I know of no, new born King. As for ruling the Jews, I know I do and Rome. I am sorry, but, I don't have your answers, but I promise to have our scribes and searchers find answers for you." He said wearily.

Muranu stepped forward again and motioned for Naram to take the crate of fruit cakes to the steps and leave it.

"We thank you O'King. Any help would be most gracious. Please take this small token of exotic fruit cakes baked from our country and enjoy them. These are the best in our land and they give great strength and endurance to those that eat. We hope you enjoy them."

"I accept your gift and thank you as well. If you still want answers, may I have you return to these chambers soon. I will send a guard to bring you if I find answers."

"We will O' King." Muranu finished and they turned as one and walked from the chamber.

Finally, I can leave this place. The rabble has been quieted. Though I found it hard to focus, with those Magi here in the city. And they still hold mystery. I will have to get the scribes here tonight and charge them to find answers. So, I know what next steps are needed. His thoughts ended.

"Guards, clear the room. I must eat. Captain attend me." He said.

Jacob moved to the Dais and waited. "Bring all the Scribes to my chambers, all of them. Have them bring their scrolls and their precious Urim and Thummim. Not that I expect YHWH to answer. But I must find what they are talking about and secure this throne. I will not have it taken from me, especially after all the work I have done, to keep it." Herod Finished.

"At once Sir," Herod watched as the Captain moved away. He rose and walked out of the chamber toward his private rooms and food.

"Open the gate! Open the gate! By order of the Guard!" Jacob Simon called. As he pounded on the gate of the Scribe's school door. He waited as he heard shouting and shuffling behind the door. As the door opened, light and the head Scribe stepped before him.

"What is the meaning of this! We are in rest. What do you want?" clearly angry.

"I am here by order of King Herod. He demands audience and for you to bring your scrolls and the Urim and Thummim, that he would find answers to his questions. . ."

"Since when has Herod wanted to hear from us, or YHWH. Did he lose his golden goblet given him by Rome??" The head Scribe interrupted.

"No. But I know a head scribe that might lose something if he and all the Scribes are not at the audience chambers in one hour." Jacob Simon countered.

"I see." The head scribe paused. "We will be there." He finished, as the door closed and bolted.

Herod paced like a caged tiger on dais in the audience chamber. He knew if he were to remain in power, things must be done. And he must watch for any treachery or even slight that would reveal his enemy and how to defeat this "new born King."

Dante watched and planned. Over the last days he had seeded dreams and fears in Herod's Mind. And since Herod was prone to power and paranoia, it made his job all the more simple.

Herod heard his guard's steps and other voices coming to the chamber. *Good, they know their place, and know who holds the power. Now to try and find answers and somehow keep this from Rome or turn it to my advantage that I saved them from a coup or insurrection.* He thought

The braziers were lit and sconces were lit around the walls by the servants. Light grew and evening shadows were gone. He could see the scribes and student faces now. Some marked with concern others. Rightful Awe. He waited, as tables were brought the scrolls and papyrus was laid out. Finally, he spoke from his seat on the Dais.

"Thank you all for coming on such short notice. I have need of your great wisdom. My questions will be simple; and your answers could greatly be rewarded." He crooned.

Shiloh Bar Judah did not hide the contempt from his voice as he spoke to Herod.

"We scribes and those of the school are always ready to give answer . . . If the one asking is truly seeking."

Herod waited a few breaths, and choosing his words carefully, he never voiced them. He heard the outer gate slam open and more guards and voices approached his chambers. . .

"What is this!" The High Priest Bellowed. "Your guards tear me from my bed and demanded I and my fellow Priests come here at such late hour. For questions?" He said.

Joshua, his Lieutenant of the Palace Guard interjected.

"I apologize O' King, for my tardiness. But it seems the High Priest Aristobulus was in a private time of prayer with a Jewess and needed to dress. I and the other priests had to wait."

Herod stood and smoothed his robes and said, "Well, now that we are all here." Eyes resting on his brother-in-law. "And properly attired, I have questions that need answers. And I need them tonight."

He looked at each group in turn as he spoke. "It has come to my attention that there is a new born King, here in Israel. How did I know, or find out? I heard from foreigners and seers! They claim to want to worship Him and have gifts for Him. And it seems no one in this Chamber knew anything about it! You have all made me look the fool! And I will not forget it. I need to know who this King is and where he is, so I might deal with Him. And you may just save your necks as well."

Shiloh Bar Judah spoke, "So, this is what has caused Jerusalem such chaos and fear, a new King. You do know, YHWH sets up and takes down. Even you should understand that. If this is why we were roused from our rest. Then, you are in more need than you know."

"I need answers! Not lectures from book-bound simpletons!" Herod Answered. Dante whispered into his ear. He continued, "Guards see to it no one leaves until I have what I need." Herod turned to a servant and said, "Bring the Food."

"Now, can we begin . . .?" He spoke to the room.

How like Squabbling hens and roosters they sound. Herod Thought. *But even in this they battle each other. As always; just as now, vying for position and power. Not unlike Kings and generals. I would have hoped it would not be this long to have some answer. How many hours has it been?*

Dante continued the whispers as Herod waited and watched. ***See, they think they better than you. They surround themselves with as much pomp and circumstance as any. They are fearful of you. And their own ideas of the Prophets and our leaders cause division and conflict. Controlling them will be easy. A word here. Denarii there. Gift, a bauble. All will make them pliable. But, if these Magi and Seers are right . . . They will have to be dealt with.***

Herod stretched and stood. And spoke to the room again. . .

"Is there anything yet you can say? Is there nothing you can find? Or are you here just to eat my food and drink my wine?"

The Priests and scribes fell silent, though their eyes said it all. Dante leaned in unnoticed, unseen whispering. ***Do they know something or is it make-believe? Aren't these the wise ones of Jerusalem? Of Israel? It's been hours. Are they not supposed to know their own writings?***

Shiloh Bar Judah and High Priest Aristobulus together approached the Dias. And Shiloh spoke so the room could hear.

"We O' King, the High Priest and I, have come to a consensus. We have searched from Moses to Isaiah, and even to Micah. Moses promised Israel a Deliverer. Even from Adam's time. But, Prophet Isaiah speaks of this ruler, King, Messiah and Micah." He Paused. "We have no name, but we do have a place. Bethlehem. A small town not far away. Though we know of it; we are not convinced of what he meant. There are parts that to us are unclear."

The High Priest Aristobulus read aloud, **"But you, Bethlehem Ephrathah, though you are small among the clans of Judah, out of you will come for me One who will be ruler over Israel, whose origins are from of Old, from ancient times."**

The High Priest continued. "The Scrolls mention YHWH would bring a ruler. That is easy enough. But, origins of Old? Ancient times? That is the confusing part. How old? Ancient times makes no sense. This part could be from something long ago. Maybe Daniel as they said." He finished.

Herod Held up a hand and interrupted his Brother-in-law Priest. "Bethlehem. You are sure. Bethlehem. A new King there? And none of you knew."

"But O' King, we knew of it," He stammered. "But the time could be anytime. No others Scrolls give when. It could be now or when Rome is dust." Aristobulus finished

"Thank you all. I have the answers I have sought. You may go. I will send my Guards with you to safely take you back."

He turned to the Captain of the Guard. "Clear the room. Quickly, take them back and dim this hall and meet me in my chambers when it is accomplished."

Herod left the hall for his private room.

Dante was not far behind, preparing the whispers to kill the Son of God.

The Son of God coughed blood. He pushed up on the bruised heel and breathed as best He could. His eyesight was dimming. He knew his heart was laboring. And He couldn't begin to describe the pain. It wasn't just parts. But the whole. He looked out on John and the others. *Soon,* He thought, *this hurtful part will be over for you all. And then you will find great joy. And so much more. But this is the start.*

Again He remembered

Herod stared into the brazier's flames and began his plans Dante's whispered that melded into his thoughts, as he whispered them. Herod began to voice them. . .

"If I am not careful, I will lose my throne. I will lose all I have worked for. And these scribes and my fool Brother-in-Law Priest may yet be a bigger problem. Though I am sure he could be removed easily." He emptied his goblet and poured more in.

"These Magi, if what the Scrolls, and they say is true, I must deal with this new King. Oh, but I cannot be overly obvious in my intent. If they saw what my wise council did not- [He laughed.] Surely they would see other intentions. But, maybe, just maybe … if I suggest that I too would worship with them, I might be able to end this quickly and quietly. Every man has his price, yes? Maybe they do. Or at worst, the baby's father does." His words died on the wind as a knock came to his door.

"Yes."

"It is I, the Captain of the Guard, as requested."

"Come in Jacob, come in. Has everything been done as I asked?"

"Yes, Sir," Jacob Paused. "Now what?"

"I have only one more thing for you to do. And I know it is late. But I need you to find the Magi if you can. If they haven't left. And bring them here. Take a few guards and make sure they get here safely if you find them. Hurry." He said.

"Grand Seer and Seer Muranu, it is Captain of the Guard; I have word from Herod. Please open the door, Jacob Simon waited.

Muranu opened the door; rubbing sleep from his eyes, "Yes."

"Oh, good. Forgive the late hour, but we were sent to bring you to Herod in the audience hall. We were told to let you know we have answers, and he felt it important that you come privately, without all the pomp of protocol," Jacob finished.

"Oh, oh … of course Muranu stammered; we will need a few moments to ready ourselves. Can you wait? I am sorry, though these rooms are good, they do not have the room as our regular rooms do in our country."

"We understand. We will be here ready to escort you to the hall when you are ready."

The Captain of the Guard turned from the closed door and spoke to the escort.

"We must get them to Herod quietly. No one interferes and no one sees. Do you understand me?" He said.

The streets they traveled were still. Only the noise of boots and breathing could be heard as they made their way to the audience hall. When the group reached the gate entrance Abdi stopped Muranu whispering

"We must be doubly careful now. This could be nothing, but an audience at night normally bodes ill. Be watchful."

"Yes, my friend, that goes for you to Naram." Who grimly nodded.

The Captain of the Guard was met by his Lieutenant, Joshua.

"I am sorry Captain, but King Herod, felt it best to meet with the Seers privately in his chambers. This way." Lighting his lamp, the Lieutenant led the way to the private rooms. The group followed in his wake.

Dante whispered again in Herod's ear. . .

You must walk carefully. They must not suspect anything. You are a King and a diplomat. You were chosen by Rome and Power. Sometimes," Dante crooned, ***"feigning weakness and gentleness garners what we need. And then we can deal with this . . . King. And keep things as they are.***

Herod turned to the knock on the door and the tables with the Scrolls, as Jacob Simon and the Magi entered the room. He could see their concern and wariness.

Dante Whispered. ***Time for the magic; set them at ease, strive to sound genuine.***

"Ah, Seers, I am glad you have come. I have fulfilled my promise and found your answer. Though I don't know the Kings name, I do know however know his location. It is Bethlehem." He said.

Muranu waited, still hesitant. "You are sure?" He finished.

"Yes, yes, come in please. Forgive my manners. Bring food and drink Selena!" He cried.

Herod continued. "I am sure that soon the weariness of your travels will be diminished and our food, along with our city will have strengthened you. So, now you can go in joy to find this King." Herod ushered them to the Scrolls. "See for yourselves. One of our country beside Daniel and Isaiah, Micah also spoke of it."

The Grand Seer Abdi-Ill-Ba-Alum moved to the Scrolls and read.

"I find it interesting that no one spoke of the star."

"Star?"

"Yes, King Herod. We had writings and Scrolls as well. But; the greatest was the sign in the heavens. We have followed it all these months. A star in the Heavens brighter than any other. A "Kings Star" if you will."

"I see. There was some such mention in the area, of a star years ago. And a host of angels, some said by. . . of all things shepherds. But we found nothing. No other heavenly signs or wonders. So, life moved on. I wish I was as confident as you."

Dante Whispered, *Lie, Now*. . .

"I grow weary of the crown." He said as moved to his goblet and grabbed a fig.

"Yes, yes I know, it's hard to believe one could tire of responsibility, duty, and honor. But; with all the infighting here. Oh, I know you haven't seen it, the Priests and Pharisees, and Scribes, all scrambling for scraps of power and influence. And not to mention Rome." He moved to his chair and sat heavily.

"I would gladly give it up to find rest. Peace. Even quiet." He chuckled

"We have to fulfill a promise to our King. We were sent to assist him and help anyway we could." Naram chimed in. He didn't notice the harsh look of both the Senior Magi.

"Oh, then good. I am glad I found what you needed." Herod said clapping his hands.

"I have it!" He said with a smile. "You go and find Him. And send word of His location in Bethlehem and I will come and worship Him with you; and I will bring the elders and Priests, as well. And bring Him gifts as is His due."

"Of course, we will send you word, O' King." The Grand Seer finished.

"If it please you O' King, we would ask your leave that we might prepare for our trip tomorrow. And once we have found Him, we will send word to you by messenger, or ourselves here." Muranu said.

"Of course, of course. I look forward to joining you. And meeting this new King. Captain, see they return to their rooms safely. And thank you Great Magi for offering me the opportunity to be finally at rest."

Herod's speech ended, and he sat serenely on his chair with a smile. He held the smile until the gate door closed in the outer court.

Now, all I must do is wait. And this would-be King will be removed. And as I said I may rest. He thought and Dante smiled.

"Naram! How could you!" Muranu shouted in their rooms. You have threatened all we are trying to accomplish!"

"Easy Muranu, we may yet snatch victory from defeat." Abdi smiled. "Now we know for sure this King is in grave danger. Still, we may fulfill our task and bring hope yet."

The caravan stood ready again. This time it was easier to see. The day was bright and clear. Their mounts snorted and pawed the ground anxious to be moving again.

"We go. Be wary, watchful, and ready to defend our journey and this new King. His enemies are many. And we have only met a few. Be brave and true." Muranu said.

"Look there, the star! In the sky! Just as before. And we are nearing Bethlehem. I cannot believe it. Just as the other night, it points the way." Naram said. He turned to the Grand Seer, as Abdi said, "We saw true those long months ago. And we knew it was Belteshazzar's God that showed us those writings and signs. He spoke from the Heavens calling to us, as He does to all men. I sense like Belteshazzar, that He is a good, faithful, powerful God. Who wants good for His people and I believe the world."

The Son of God was in the house again. He could smell the cook fire and the scents of the flowers. He heard her voice again singing as she cooked. He even heard the soft scrape against wood as his father quietly worked in the corner.

He saw their faces. He watched his father's ruff hands, as they worked the planer to smooth an edge on a chair leg. The room was aglow with firelight, lamps, and music. Warmth and love. *Almost like home. One day I will be there again.* He thought.

He heard again the knock on the door. And watched His father stop and set the planer and leg on the floor, then move to the door. He wasn't a big man as a Roman, but he covered the door sufficiently. And then He heard again their voices.

"We beg forgiveness for the hour. I am Grand Seer Abdi-ill-Ba-Alum from the East and my company. We have come to see the new King. The one who would rule the Jews." He said simply. Jesus saw his father's stunned look and Mary's concern.

He saw his father welcome them in. He noticed the robes and trappings of Kings. Like David of Old or Solomon. He heard the leader tell the others to wait outside.

The house seemed even smaller as the men stood holding boxes and other gifts. His father offered them to come closer with a wave of his hand.

Jesus looked into their faces. He remembered that look. The same look of the shepherd from the hillside and what else? Wonder. He knew why they were here. He knew the reason. He smiled and He watched as one-by-one, they placed their boxes on the floor and worshipped. They were almost prostrate. Again, they looked at him in wonder. And then turned to His father and mother, and spoke with joy.

"We have come far to find Him. And we were charged to worship Him as Daniel and others spoke. YHWH, Daniel's great God Who loves always and calls from even His heaven to men. We bring you and Him these gifts. Please do not refuse. This one frankincense because he is God, and god is worthy of worship. The next is gold for His Kingship and defense against enemies. And lastly the Myrrh to anoint Him in His death and fragrant mourning. I know this is a happy, and sad time all at once for you," he said to his father and mother.

"And now," the Grand Seer spoke directly to him. "And to you, O' King, we give these gifts as your due. And we look for Your Kingdom, and as Your own people write . . . Your reign will be forever and ever. We wish you well and long life O' King. We stand ready protect you as need arises."

He watched as his father walked slowly to his side and picked him up in his arms. Turning to the strangers, the Seers, to the Magi he said, "We thank you for these gifts. Mary and I, we truly thank you. But sometimes it is still a wonder that YHWH chose us to care for His Son." After a short pause he continued. "We welcome you to stay for as long as you need. But the house is small and you may have to camp outside if your group is large. We can go to market in the morning and get food for all. And we can fellowship as YHWH intends. I for one would like to hear the story of how YHWH called to you. We both were called by His angels." His father finished.

The Seers and the Magi moved close and looked into His eyes, and even touched His face. He remembered each one as men of wisdom and knowledge, also men of faith. He knew what was in their hearts because Light Father God spoke to Him.

Grand Seer Abdi-ill-Ba-Alum spoke, "We will stay here, outside and we will share our food with you. It is the least we can do for the King. And yes, the stories we can tell." He smiled and moved to the door.

Jesus walked with Joseph to the door and watched as the group moved to a small patch of green across the Street and began unpacking. Joseph called to Jesus, "Close the door Son, please. And come and eat, your mother has made my favorite!"   Jesus closed the door and came to the table.

Jesus, Joseph, and Mary listened intently to Muranu's Story.

"We had found Daniel's scrolls and all that he, and Nebuchadnezzar, had spoken about and written. And as our custom dictates, we went to the roof of our rooms to see the stars and their wonders. We had our tools to observe and note changes in the sky, temperature, and wind. Grand Seer Abdi; the grumpy one at the time, he is old you know," he said chuckling, "had missed his dinner and was hungry. So, we sent a servant to get fruits."

He paused, as he watched the sparks from the fire rise on the night breeze. The weather was clear; there were no storms or rain. The stars were bright as diamonds. I was at the corner of the roof and Abdi walked to me chewing a fig. "Wondrous is it not. . ."

"Oh, good, you're calm again. Finally eating are we?"

"Well it seems eating and living are of special interest lately. I am not as young as I was."

"Muranu, was there to be a moon tonight?"

"No, why?"

"Look there." He told me as he pointed and I did. That was when we first saw it. A star brighter than the rest. In the north part of the sky. O' no not the North Star. But Brighter than any around it. We watched then for months. We searched the records of Omens and Talismans, as well as other written events. You see when the Great Nebuchadnezzar met your God YHWH, one of our Kings, and he was a changed man. And after, we used our understanding to make sure there was no weather to explain it, Omen, or curse even. We sought the Scrolls in the great library and began to see if any event like it had happened before.

We read the account of Daniel and our King. So, we looked deeper into Daniel and His God. And his writings. After much study and the star growing in brightness, we thought to look for more evidence. We were moved by all that Daniel and others had written; enough so, that we asked our King to allow us to search for Him and help Him if we could. That is our purpose in our country. And so we wanted to meet your new King."

"I have found YHWH to be a God of wonder and miracles," Joseph said. "And that He speaks to His people. I was spoken to by an angel to go ahead and take Mary as my wife." He laughed.

"And I was told by another angel that I, the Mary before you, would bear YHWH's Son and name Him, Jesus. She quoted the angels words again by heart. . . **The LORD is with you. You will conceive in your womb and bear a Son and call Him Jesus. He will be great and called the Son of the Most High. And the Lord God will give Him the Throne of David, his father, and He will reign over the House of Jacob forever. And His Kingdom will have no end."**

"I was shocked to think that I would be a vessel fit for Him to use, even though many young maidens wish they could be the one. Why was

I chosen? I don't know. But I gladly took on YHWH'S Son's care." She smiled and hugged Jesus close.

"As did I," Joseph said quietly.

"Then we were not wrong in coming to see Him, nor the gifts. Though Daniel said He would be cut off?" Muranu questioned softly. "I am not sure how an eternal Kingdom can be if the King is dead."

"Oh, and there were shepherds that came and told us that a host of angels were in the sky praising God when He was born. The awe and sheer power they must have felt," she paused. "We, of course, were busy at the time." She laughed as she finished.

"Well, I know it is late, and I am sure mother and Son should be resting," Abdi said in his most grandfatherly tone. And I also am not as young as I used to be. I will bid you good night." He rose and walked toward his tent.

"Yes," Joseph said, "good night Seer. And yes, we all need sleep." He turned to Muranu and finished. "I am amazed at YHWH. He is loving, kind, full of righteousness and justice, but so willing to forgive."

He took Mary by the hand and began to walk to the house. "Isn't it wonderful to see others being spoken to by YHWH??"

"Yes, Joseph, it gives me peace. I often wondered if we were alone in all of this. In spite of the Scrolls and Torah. Peace." Mary Finished.

"Captain of the Guard! Captain! Come at Once!" Herod bellowed. He could hear the footfalls in the hall and saw the door swing wide and Jacob enter, sword ready.

"Yes, O' King I am here."

"Good. Any news from Bethlehem and the Seers? It has been a week." Herod asked.

"None Sire. No one has seen them and no word has reached my ears or anyone's. Nothing has been reported." The Captain said.

Dante whispered harshly. *. . . **There you see; those foreigners mocked you and lied to you. They have dealt treacherously. Are you sure the Priests and Scribes didn't help them in any way? Your plan is stopped! You will be replaced by a new King!***

"No!" He cried. "Those treacherous, Magi! They will pay. I swear it!"

Herod's mind raced. How can I stop this King?? How, How? Wait. . . Dante whispered eagerly. . . ***This is a new born King? A baby . . . Well, there seems to be only one option and one solution. Since we cannot find the family directly. . . We will remove the problem as any King would.***

"Jacob, take as many guards as possible and go to Bethlehem. Kill every child two years and under! I will not stand idly by and watch my throne destroyed, nor my kingdom attacked from within! I will take care of Rome; I can mark it as preventative actions against riots and insurrections. Now go. And don't return until it is done." Herod Finished.

"Yes, O' King." Jacob walked out the door in silence.

He was outside the eternal King's house and the tent was flooded by light! And there stood an angel, as Joseph and Mary, had described. When he spoke the ground shook.

"Abdi-ill-Ba-Alum, Muranu, Naram: Listen to Me. Herod of Judea is angry and is not pleased with you. I warn you. Do not go home by the way you have come. Go home another way in safety." He awoke to dawn shaking.

"Muranu, Naram, attend me. Come quickly!" Abdi called.

"It seems Daniel's God has spoken. We will not return to Herod or send word of the Child King. We will follow another route home in peace." The Gran Seer said.

Muranu and Naram nodded and together added "We both had the same dream. The same angel, all of us. We will obey the angel's word. Though, what will become of the Child King?"

"I think YHWH, Daniel's God will care for Him. I do not think He needs us. Let us go. It will be good to be home. Though, I will never forget this King or Daniel's God." Abdi finished.

The night was dark and the stars shone in the Heavens, only dimmed by torches. The group looked down on the small town of Bethlehem.

The Captain of the Guard spoke quietly to his men. "Remember, we are here to do a job by the King's order. And it will be done. It must be done. He is the King."

Bethlehem only heard marching feet and doors smashing, and then . . . screams of terror . . . and the cries of dying children.

Door after door. House after house. Crash! Splintered doors. . . "by order of the King of Judea! All children two years and under must die!" "No, no not my baby!" Echoed through all of Bethlehem that night. Weeping lasted more than the night that day.

Another Scripture fulfilled;, the Son of God remembered in anguish and pain. **This is what the Lord says: "a voice is heard in Ramah, lamenting and bitter weeping. Rachel is weeping for her children; she refuses to be comforted for her children, because they are no more."**

Joseph, Jesus, and Mary lay quiet in their small tent along the road. Joseph and his family rested quietly and in safety.

Well, that was something! Not long after the Magi and Seers, who shows up but another angel in a dream to tell me to take the family to Egypt. And that I am to stay there until Herod dies. So more Scripture can be fulfilled. **When Israel was a youth I loved him, and out of Egypt I called my Son.** *Funny, YHWH did that with Moses, and now. . . Jesus.* Joseph's thoughts ended in sweet sleep.

CHAPTER 6

PASSOVER, PRIESTS, AND PROUD PARENTS

"Jesus, come help open the shutters in the shop!" Joseph called, as opened the window and the morning light shown in.

"Yes, Father, I am coming."

Joseph smiled; he breathed deep and continued, "Ahh, another wonderful day in Nazareth, eh Jesus. We have a beautiful day to work by."

Jesus moved to the other shutters and opened them. Opening the door of the shop, he then stepped outside. He felt the sun on his face and smelled the flowers. He felt the breeze softly sweep across his face. He was glad to help in the shop. He was twelve. He would be learning some of his father's trade, and he found he had a knack for building.

"Father," Jesus said, "I do not know where you get weather information. Because for the last years you have said the same thing, whether it is raining or not."

Joseph laughed along with Jesus and finished. "Well, it is always good to work, and of course, your mother agrees."

"Father, I honestly think she wants to keep you from under her feet or out of her hair." The shop resounded in laughter.

Joseph then finished, "True, son very, very true."

Joseph walked to the bench and sat, looking at his latest project. He had gotten a message from the Centurion in Jerusalem. The message **said, "I Perseus Quintis Nerva, send you greetings and hope you are well. I am in need of your talent for a few chairs and tables for the barracks. I remember your father's work and I hear yours is as**

good. We will send soldiers and a cart to retrieve them when finished. Sadly, I cannot bring this to you in person. Duty demands my focus be on Jerusalem and not good friends.

Signed: Perseus, Centurion"

"Well, soon it will be time to go to Jerusalem to celebrate Passover. I had hoped to be done with the Centurion's order. I am amazed though, that he remembered me. I was just a boy not much older than you." Joseph picked up and chair and set it on the floor. He dusted the seat and sat on it, testing it. He then stepped on the rung and then the seat.

Jesus watched, as his father, Joseph, jumped and brought his weight down upon the seat. He watched Joseph's face. There was trepidation, as he tested each part. His face exuded joy when nothing broke or cracked.

"I know I must look foolish, as I test these. But these are for burly, brute Romans. Most of them will sit on these with armor and sword. Sadly, they should have iron chairs, or something else to help in situations. But I have not learned in my years all I could. I remember the wonders of Egypt and all that YHWH did for us while there. Your mother is looking forward to this trip. We may yet see Elizabeth and John. And I am sure she would want to see Rueben, her father. And her mother."

Joseph turned to Jesus in mock concern, "And you young man better behave! I wouldn't want you to have too much fun on this trip with the Passover being serious."

"Of course, Father." Jesus said dutiful tone ending in laughter. "I will strive to be a good boy."

"Good, good," Joseph laughed. "Now that we have settled, let's go eat."

Joseph tightened down the pack on Jerum and turned and called to Mary and Jesus.

"It is time to start the trip. We are to meet Benasher at the crossroad. We will be joining his caravan. He has a cart, so the young ones can ride and not tire from the journey."

"Coming father, I have the basket with food. Should I carry it, or add it to Jerum's pack?" Jesus asked.

"Tie it to his pack. I am going to make sure the shop is locked up and that the notice is plain to see. You know how the Roman's don't read."

Joseph returned to find Jesus and Mary waiting beside Jerum grinning. He paused, looked all around and checked his robes and then said, "What? What have I missed? What are you two up to?"

"Why would we be up to anything my dear Joseph?" Mary said.

"Nothing Father, nothing at all." Jesus said.

"Oh good, I thought I had forgotten something." Joseph said relieved.

"Well, you didn't but, I have a gift for you. Here." Jesus said.

Joseph took from Jesus the offered gift. A small figure with a staff.

"Son what is this? Why?" Joseph looked at the great detail. Clearly, days of work.

"I carved it when I was able. I see you like that when I hear of the shepherds story and the angels. I see you leading Jerum and I thought you might like it." Jesus finished.

"It is beautiful. Son thank you." Joseph said hugging Jesus. "I will cherish it. And it shows great talent." He paused a breath. "And I knew you would be a great carpenter."

"I just wanted you to have it. And know I love you." Jesus said.

"I know son; I do know and I thank you."

Joseph took Jerum's reign and said, "And now we are off to Jerusalem and Passover!"

Jesus walked beside Jerum and his father in the morning sun. It was warm, but not hot like summer. The scent of spring was carried on the breeze, as they moved along the route to Jerusalem. As he walked he saw more and more families join them on the roadway. Some he knew from Nazareth, and some business men and travelers in route to places even beyond Jerusalem.

The camp fire was crackling and the food cooking. Jesus looked at the stars overhead and turned to Joseph and asked.

"Father, I look at the heavens and sometimes I feel small. But, I am filled with awe that YHWH made them and all that we see. What do you see when you look?"

"Me? I loved to look. As a boy, I would wonder if YHWH really heard me when I prayed. I felt just like King David and also felt small like you. I wonder too. Why, YHWH chose us. And that he sees men and loves them, also wanting good for them. Many, even here, may not know YHWH as He would want, but He pursues them just the same. And for Israel, He offers covenant. I see YHWH as all that He promised. Though, we all have a hard time seeing it sometimes. Chuckling, "Believing it, don't we Mary?" He finished.

"Yes, my husband we do," she laughed.

Talk could be heard around many fires that night on the road. And Jesus watched and listened to story after story. Some of joy, excitement, sadness. But tales just the same of YHWH'S care, provision, protection, and power.

The Damascus Gate was alive with people, animals and Romans, as well. And the stone covered road leading to the gate was filling fast. Jesus looked behind and saw even more people now behind them.

"Father, I don't remember it being this busy last Passover."

"Me neither, Son. Maybe since the Romans, people are more afraid, or they find some peace in the midst of our troubles. And Passover does that. That's not all we have it for. We will be through the gate soon and on our way. I am sure of it." Joseph glanced at Mary and smiled.

Jesus could see the Temple up ahead and turned to Joseph. "Are we going to see Elizabeth and John?"

"We may. And we have the lamb. I was surprised it was so quiet this trip."

"Maybe it knows about Passover. And the price." *I know I do*. Jesus thought.

"Maybe, but YHWH has said blood must atone for sins. And this is to remind us that YHWH keeps His promise and protects us. And always will. And once we have done our part of the cleansing, family will come and we will eat and remember what YHWH has done." Joseph finished.

"Wasn't the Passover good this year Mary?" Joseph said. "And seeing your father and mother," he chuckled, "and even John. I tell you the boys can sure be a handful."

"Yes, it was. And definitely yes to being a handful! I just don't understand. I guess I would have thought God's Son would be less human. But what do I know. We have seen more of YHWH in our life time thus far than most prophets." Mary finished.

"Where is Jesus, by the way?"

"I haven't seen Him. But I am sure he is somewhere in this group. Probably with the other youngsters, or keeping an eye on the animals. You know how He likes the outdoors and exploring." Joseph finished.

Mary looked at Joseph and spoke in earnest, "There are times Joseph that He goes into the hills and prays, even on the roof. He seems to come back different when He does. Oh not anything bad, but . . . even better."

"Well, you know what the Priests would say . . . That time in prayer is never wasted. And I have no reason to complain. He works hard in the shop and His work is tremendous." Joseph said. He took Mary's hand and said, "I am sure he is fine. He is a good Son. And I doubt YHWH would let anything happen to Him. Least of all without His permission. I am sure when we stop for the night, He will show up."

"Okay, I will be patient and wait and try not to worry. He was sent by YHWH after all."

The night was cool and the gentle breeze carried the scent of orchids to the campfire. And as always, the group of fires help conversation and laughter. The old men regaled the younger with tales of long ago and the younger attempted to be heard.

Joseph placed more kindling and what stood for firewood on the road onto the fire. He watched, as it sparked and popped. He sat warming his hands and Mary spoke.

"Joseph, Jesus is not here. And it is late. Where could he be?"

"I will speak to the group in the morning and see if anyone knows anything. I am sure Elizabeth, Zechariah, or John know where He is. And if He is not here, we can go back. The weather is good and I am sure we will find Him. All those passing our group said nothing of troubles. And even at twelve Jesus is able to protect Himself. We will make a decision in the morning. Be at peace Mary."

"Be at peace you say . . . How can I be at peace when. . ." Mary mumbled.

"Zechariah, Zechariah," Joseph started, "have you seen Jesus? He is not with the group."

"No, I have not. But maybe John has seen Him. He is with his mother burying the fire and gathering our things," Zechariah said, as he tightened the straps on the bedrolls and positioned them on the back of the donkey.

Joseph moved through the small knot of people to where he had seen John and Elizabeth. As he did, he caught sight of Benasher who was filling his cart and speaking with the men nearby.

"Shalom Benasher, I hope you are well." Joseph started.

"Well, bah, I come to Jerusalem for Passover and hope for blessing and I seem to lose more than I make!" Laughing he continued, "Shalom Joseph, what can I do for you this good day?"

"I know this is not as important as your profits, or lack thereof, but possibly have you seen my Son, Jesus? He was not at the campfire last night and we assumed He was somewhere in the group and He is not here. Zechariah, Elizabeth and even John haven't seen Him."

"No. I have not seen Him today. And I did not see Him yesterday when we began the trip home."

"I thank you. Mary and I will head back and see if He is in Jerusalem. Blessings on you Benasher."

"Blessings on you Joseph. May the road be clear and you travel swift."

Joseph came to Mary by Jerum and their belongings. She looked at Joseph hopeful.

"Well, Mary, it seems Jesus was not with the group, nor among our friends or family. We will go back to Jerusalem and see."

Worry creased Mary's face as she said, "Okay, I don't understand; this is not like Jesus. Let us go."

"We are going back to find Jesus. We will try and catch up soon." Joseph said, as he hugged Zechariah and Elizabeth.

"I am sure he is fine Joseph. I will ask YHWH to guide your steps and watch over you as you go."

"It is good I have a Priest in the family for sure answers to prayer."
He laughed.

"And don't you forget it!" Zechariah answered, "But I think YHWH
is closer to you than you would admit."

Joseph paused looking at Mary who smiled. "Yes, yes, that is true.
Sometimes, I forget."

Joseph, Mary and Jerum turned to begin the trek back to Jerusalem
as the Benasher and his caravan moved to Nazareth.

Jesus remembered the outer court and the teachers sitting and
conversing. *What a few days that was.* He grimaced, as pain lanced from
his heel to neck. He pushed up again for breath and tried to relax just for
a moment. *That doesn't work does it; they certainly designed this as a
most painful and constant slow way to die. Soon it will be over and all
of mankind will be free from sin and be able to have what he lost so long
ago.*

Jesus moved in sure steps as He made his way through the throngs
of people and the animals being led to sacrifice. He paused at the
Beautiful Gate and looked at the people bustling about, with the sounds
of snippets of conversation and Priests crying out, like vendors at a
Bazar.

"Perfect unblemished lamb-certified by the High Priest only . . ."

"What do you mean my lamb is not fit to be part of the sacrifice. . ."

*Father, do they not see? This Temple in all its glory is nothing.
Compared to what Adam had at the beginning. As for these sacrifices,
if they only knew. But they will. However, they have at least tried to
follow what you set down through Moses; although, not perfectly. And
they have not truly made this a House of Prayer yet either.* He thought,
as He moved through the women's court and entered the gate near the
altar.

He moved through the crowd and watched as the sacrifices on the
altar continued.

The Priest hand's raised prayed to YHWH and called for forgiveness,
blessing, and even the protection of the family nearby. And just as they
cleared off that animal another met the altar. A seeming parade of oxen,

ram, lamb, doves, blood, death, and YHWH'S blink. Then it all started again.

_Son__, He heard the father in his heart, **do you see? They work hard on the outward appearance, but where is their heart? Where is the walking with Me? The fellowship and intimacy as we had with Adam before? I blink at these offerings now until the One true sacrifice is made. I must, or I would destroy all we have made. Many may never know why I blink. Why all these years I have waited. So, that all mankind can be free from sin and death. I am glad that You hear Me and that You will be the One sacrifice . . . The only true sacrifice._**

Jesus turned from the altar and walked toward the Priest's court and the seated group of men. He saw the robes and trappings. He heard more of the conversations, as He approached. He stopped and waited to be seen by a nearby Priest.

"Shalom to you young man, what may this Priest of YHWH do for you today?"

"Shalom, I am Jesus. My family and I came for Passover. I wanted to see more of the Temple and talk with you all. I remember from Moses and others how the tabernacle and even King Solomon's temple was done. And how YHWH longs to be with his chosen Israel." Jesus finished.

"True, YHWH does want to be near His chosen. But without the sacrifice, we sadly," the Priest paused, "cannot come close enough."

"Is it alright that I sit with you all and ask questions?"

"Yes, yes you can. What do you say gentlemen, can this young man learn from us today?"

"Certainly, it will be a break from the regular babble we hear!" The Priest said laughing.

"Babble? What babble. . ." The oldest Priest said. "We only hear from YHWH. Don't you know?"

And another, "Or until the price is right."

"Well, Jesus, what questions do you have?" The old Priest started.

"Well Mary, we are back in Jerusalem. It is late, so we need to find an inn. We will start looking for Jesus in the morning." Joseph said.

"But we must find Him!"

"Mary, I know you are worried, but Jesus is old enough to look out for Himself. We will find Him and soon go home. Who knows, He could be staying at the inn. I need to tie Jerum up."

The night was cool and quiet as Joseph and Mary slept. Though Mary didn't sleep peacefully because of her worries. However, she did finally sleep.

The next day Joseph said, "Mary, stay here in the inn. Maybe Jesus will come and I will look at some of our business customers and places we have gone together, he and I. Please do not worry. I will find Him. As Zechariah said, "He was asking YHWH to guide my steps. I am sure He will."

"Yes, Joseph, I will wait here. But I do not like it."

The oldest Priest in the group said, "What is your answer when we ask 'how are we to love YHWH (God)?' "

Jesus smiled at Benjamin of Shimel. **Hear, O' Israel! The Lord is our God; the Lord is one! You shall love the Lord your God with all your heart and with all your soul and with all your might. These words, which I am commanding you today, shall be on your heart. You shall teach them diligently to your sons and shall talk of them when you sit in your house and when you walk by the way and when you lie down and when you rise up. You shall bind them as a sign on your hand and they shall be as frontals on your forehead. You shall write them on the doorposts of your house and on your gates."**

Benjamin answered, "Ahh … I see some one reads and knows some things. Good answer."

He looked at the other Priests and asked them. "Who has a question for Jesus?"

"I do," one of the Priests said.

Jesus waited patiently, as they prepared the question. The conversation back and forth continued and the day moved on.

"Where could Jesus be! We have looked everywhere! Joseph we went to the inn and for two days now, we hear nothing! We ask at all of your business customers and they have not seen Him! What are we to do?? What will YHWH do? He is His Son!" Mary said frantically

"Mary, Mary, **MARY!**" Joseph said grabbing her shoulders and pulling her into an embrace. "We will find Him and YHWH will do as He has always done. Care and protect His chosen people and children, even the missing ones. I am sure of it. We will rest again tonight. . ."

"How can I rest knowing Jesus is out there somewhere, possibly cold and hungry or worse." She cried.

"He is soon a young man and He can handle a few days away from us. Who knows, He could have gone fishing in the Jordan by now." Joseph chuckled. "He is fine. I am sure."

The inn was quiet and still; all of the patrons were asleep, but one. And she turned to the window and whispered to the heavens. . .

"YHWH God, I love my Son, Your Son. Can you watch over Him and keep Him? I know He was given to us by You. But I do not want to fail as a guardian, nor a mother. And if I fail, I wonder what You will do? For you are Almighty and I am not. I know it is foolish, but I am a woman. And You know we were made to love deeply and truly. So, Your Son has my heart and I do not want to lose my Son, or Yours." She finished. And finally fell asleep peacefully.

*****

The morning as was bright and clear as Joseph and Mary left the inn. It had been three days and no word of Jesus and no one in that part of Jerusalem had seen Him.

"Well, we have waited and asked. No one has seen Him. All my customers have not seen Him. And He has not come to this inn, or the others I inquired at. So, we must search again, but where?" He thought aloud.

Mary looked at Joseph worriedly, as he finished strapping the bedding and other items to Jerum's back. He calmly walked around Jerum to Mary and said, "We will go to the Temple. We can pray and see if anyone there has seen Him. And if He is not there, we will go home. And if He is at home we will be happy. But He may not like the work I will give Him for running away."

Joseph and Mary moved up the street toward the Temple. It wasn't as busy as when the Passover had been. But the street was bustling. The vendors were on the way to their spaces. And those in need of sacrifice, and even priestly advice, were all moving toward the Temple.

Joseph tensed, as he passed by the Roman guards near the gate. He still had a hard time seeing Romans near the Temple. But he would search just the same and find Jesus and go home.

He held Mary's hand as they passed through the Beautiful Gate to the Court of Women.

She is still as beautiful as the day I spoke to her at the first. And I am so glad I did. And I thank you YHWH for guiding me by Your angels to follow through and finish our marriage. His thoughts continued. *YHWH, I ask could you help us find Jesus? I know it is a little thing for you, but Mary is afraid, as any mother would be, and I am worried as well. I know that I was put in charge to guard Your Son. Please, please help us.*

Joseph and Mary moved through the crowd and looked for Jesus amidst the people of the open court on their right. There was few people there, but it still looked busy. They saw no sign of Him. They moved off through the worshipers and others to the left of the entrance, and again no sign of Jesus.

Joseph glanced at Mary, and even he could see the growing concern, which would escalate quickly to desperation if they could not find Him quickly. They moved to the other side through the crowd and came near the Treasury

Joseph saw the Treasury entrance and the Temple guard and also caught the raised voices. And pulled Mary away quickly.

Anger and trouble at the Treasury not really a surprise, but we will steer clear. YHWH wants us to give out of the purity of heart and love for Him. Not pressure, or as it seems greed. I never knew that the Temple would be like a business. His thoughts ended.

"Mary, this never ceases to amaze me. I have been here year- after-year. And it seems the altar is perpetually offering sacrifice and the Priests seem to never tire. But I wonder at the heart of the people? Do they understand why they sacrifice? Oh, I know YHWH commands it;

that we may walk with Him and be in Covenant, but I even wonder if we mean it. To really be near to YHWH God."

"Joseph, doesn't YHWH know your heart and mine? Does HE not see what we do? He told Moses to establish this, so we follow. Is that not what we are to do?"

Joseph and Mary moved on to the Court of the Priests and the hope of finding Jesus somewhere in the Temple, or at the least have them seek YHWH God to find Him, and end this struggle.

People, people even here in the Court of the Priests. And The Priests are busy; I sure hope they have time to pray for us, or even use the Urim and Thummim to find Jesus. His thoughts ended as he moved to a small knot of Priests in a heated discussion

"That was a fine answer Jesus. You must make your parents proud." Benjamin of Shimel said.

"And speaking of parents. . ." Jesus began as He rose.

Joseph spoke to the group, "Shalom, we have come for our Son."

The elder Priest, Benjamin, answered, "Shalom to you. You must be very proud of your Son. . . "

"Joseph."

"Ah, Joseph. . .As I was saying, you should be proud. Your Son has much knowledge and understanding. And made our days here a joy to search the Scriptures and learn one from another."

Mary took Jesus by the arm and spoke with concern. "Son, why have you treated us this way? Your father and I have been anxiously looking for you!"

Jesus looked her in the eye and spoke clearly and evenly.

"Why is it that you were looking for Me? Did you not know that I had to be in My Father's House? And about MY Father's Business."

The elder Priest Benjamin cut the silence and tension after seeing their bewilderment and confusion.

"We were glad to sit with Him. And He was a good Son and one that YHWH would be proud of. He will be a blessing to your house and your name I am sure. Let me bless you. . . The Lord bless you, and keep you; the Lord make His face shine on you, and be gracious to you; The Lord lift up His countenance on you, and give you peace. Shalom, house of Joseph and may you see the favor of God." He finished.

Jesus heard then from Heaven by the Spirit, ***Son, Go with them and do as they ask. And listen for My voice. Your time will come soon. But for all to be fulfilled. Go and be a good Son and grow.***

I will go Father. I will do as you ask. Even after all they have seen, they don't understand. I will do as you say. His thoughts ended.

"I am sorry Father, please forgive, let us go home." Joseph hugged his son with Mary.

"Yes, let's go home," and they moved together toward the gate and Nazareth.

Mary held onto these things in her heart. Proud that Jesus was a good Son, noting in her heart the Priest's words. And the words rang in her ears. . . .**One that YHWH would be proud of** . . . She was glad that they had found Him. Her anxiousness and anger lessened, as she walked toward the gate and home.

   ***

CHAPTER 7

BAPTISM, CONVERSATION AND TEMPTATION

The time I stayed with Mary and Joseph was not easy. It was tough. Even it seemed to obey my Father in Heaven; during my growing years from a young man to an adult. Being a teenager is never easy and my emotions were all over the place. Listening to my parents, even my heavenly Father, was difficult, and even cleaning my room was a challenge. People often think that I was the perfect child, and I guess I was, but I lived through all that young people did then and in the years to come. I was a normal kid, teenager, and young adult. I am grateful that the writers of the Bible left some things out, such as my voice and some awkwardness, but I was every bit as human as my neighbors. The writers were kind and maybe it was the Father, but I look back on those years of simple obedience and hard work, even with the tears and joys of friends and family, knowing that I touched every area of what it was to be totally human, and yet, God too. Thankfully, the writers were able to transition from chapter-to-chapter with a single line, and I did too.

And Jesus kept increasing in wisdom and stature, and in favor with God and men.

As I grew; I found God calling. I heard His Voice and felt His presence by the Holy Spirit. And it wasn't much different than what my future brothers and sisters would know. But still; day-after-day, it was a simple, honest life, and obedience.

Though I knew God then as now, there came a point that God Himself, had set to begin My destiny and calling. And yes, just as My birth, God celebrated with great joy. However, I had to leave my place and seek my cousin, John.

He too had a destiny and calling that God the Father had set. I know it had made Zechariah, Elizabeth, and others nervous or skeptical. But even I knew we would meet one day and the plan the Father had set down before the ages began, would begin. I had to be set apart . . . just as John. And I was. His thoughts ended and He remembered.

Jesus walked the road to the spot where John was said to be baptizing. He looked at the crowd near the Jordan and its muddy banks and slim palm trees. The water made life spring forth in this desert outside of Jerusalem. The Jordan was almost the same color as the mud. But, the mud had grown because of the crowds, the hundreds milling around and being baptized by John. There, curious onlookers, and skeptics alike, came to see what many had said was a mad man, a looney and worse. Even the elite, the Priests, some in prayer he noted. Others stood in judgement over the people looking to return to God. He could hear his voice strong, clear, and sure. . .

"I am the voice of one calling out in the wilderness, 'Prepare the way of the Lord, Make His paths straight! Repent, for the Kingdom of Heaven is at hand. Produce fruit consistent with repentance; and do not assume that you can say to yourselves, 'We have Abraham as our Father.' 'For I tell you that God is able, from these stones, to raise up children for Abraham. And the axe is already laid at the root of the trees; therefore, every tree that does not bear good fruit is being cut down and thrown into the fire."

He watched from a distance, as the religious leaders scoffed and grumbled. And more people moved to the water's edge and stepped in to be near John. Jesus smiled as He watched. Time and again, John would smile and take a hand and move a bit from the shore. He spoke to them and then as he did, they would go into the water backward signifying death and come up out of the water to new life. He watched as more came from the countryside and sought out John. The crowd around the Jordan grew.

He moved quietly and unnoticed to a nearby palm and sat. Jesus watched as John spoke, shared, and baptized. The air was warm and a gentle breeze carried the song of birds.

John paused, looking at the crowd and Jesus heard his words again. . . "I am the voice of one calling out in the wilderness, 'Prepare the way of the Lord, Make His paths straight! Repent, for the Kingdom of Heaven is at hand."

Jesus looked on as the crowds began to thin. The religious leaders were conversing in a tight knot nearby. They held an air of superiority and disdain. *I guess you leaders of Israel cannot believe that a man not dressed as you, nor in the Priesthood, can hear from God YHWH. You hold power, wealth, and position. But you are blind, poor, and naked. The Father calls to hearts that would obey, believe and follow after Him to do the works of Righteousness. But your hearts are far from God . . . one Day Paul will pen the verse. . . "Treacherous, reckless, conceited, lovers of pleasure rather than lovers of God, holding to a form of godliness, although they have denied its power, avoid such people as these."*

His thoughts continued. *You were to be the leaders and the guides. To bring God's people, My people, to the Father. And turn men's hearts from wickedness to holiness, to true repentance.*

Jesus stood and moved toward John and the Jordan. The crowds had thinned, and only a few remained. But the religious leaders still stood nearby. He moved to the edge of the muddy Jordan. He heard the song of the birds and felt the breeze, as he took in the fragrant smell of flowers. He then stepped in the Jordan, and moved towards John.

John spoke to Jesus quietly, "I have the need to be baptized by You. Why are You coming to me?"

"Allow Me, so that righteousness and the Scriptures can be fulfilled."

Jesus looked intently at John and smiled. He Remembered that day when Elizabeth spoke to Mary and his leaping in the womb. He remembered His love for God and His call. He knew John would hear from God and obey Him in all He asked. But He also knew the impact John would have and was having here and now calling a wayward nation home again.

John took Jesus by the hand and stepped further out into the Jordan. John turned to the crowd and religious leaders and spoke in a loud voice.

"Behold, the Lamb of God who takes away the sin of the world! I spoke of Him that would come, who was before me, this same one, who would be revealed to Israel. The One who is mightier than I and the One whose straps of His sandals I am not fit to untie. He will baptize you with the Holy Spirit and Fire."

John plunged Jesus beneath the water and pulled him up.

"I did not recognize Him, but He who sent me to baptize in water said to me, 'He upon whom you see the Spirit descending and remaining upon Him, this is the One who baptizes in the Holy Spirit.' And I myself have seen, and have testified that this is the Son of God."

And they saw the Heavens part and as promised the Holy Spirit of God descended as a Dove and rested upon Jesus. Jesus remained still, praying in quietness. And they all heard the voice of God from Heaven say, "This is My beloved Son, in whom I am well pleased."

Jesus opened His eyes, smiled at John, and hugged him. Jesus then turned and walked out of the Jordan.

Jesus walked straight form the Jordan towards the wilderness and desert. He seemed to be moved and urged by the Spirit of God to leave the Jordan, and go where the Father and Holy Spirit guided Him.

Son, it is time for you to confront the Adversary, Lightbringer; You must be tested just as my children and nation will be tested. Lightbringer believes he will triumph; and the redemption of man and even creation will fail and he will rule it all. He heard the Father and felt the move in His Spirit.

Father in heaven, I hear You. I will obey and do as You ask. Does he not know, You are the One who allows anything in Heaven, or on Earth? In all things, you are God. Jesus thought.

Go into the wilderness nearby to pray and fast. Prepare your heart, mind, and soul. Know that I am near and I will guide You. The Holy Spirit, as You know, will guide You as well. Listen for my Voice and the Spirit's moving. You know Lightbringer is full of hatred, bitterness, envy . . . he is still seeking to kill, steal, and destroy. Be watchful and ready.

Jesus moved on as He began His journey into the wilderness; and the battle He soon knew He would face.

He felt the heat of the sun on his back and a breeze carried the smell of flowers, and the birds' song ended, as He moved further into the wilderness. The rough and rocky ground was a burnt umber; and somehow the weeds still grew in the heat. He remembered what creation had wrought. As Almighty God He saw the destruction caused by sin and death. *And Adam's poor choice of caretaker. How is it that they could not see, or was it that they chose not to see? He made the choice and it cost more than he understood. But we will bring things to right. I know I have set aside my rights and privileges to walk as men do to fulfill the plan.*

I doubt Lightbringer-Satan will flinch at the sight of Me anymore. But the Father in Heaven is right. I have the Spirit of God and the Word of God. We will do what We must. His thoughts ended, as He climbed over the crest of a hill and looked out at the rock ledges and canyon ways ahead. *Desolation and emptiness await . . . Well, at least there is scrub brush to make a fire if needed.*

He moved off the hill and moved to the pathway before Him. The pathway became a canyon and the sun's heat was dimmed, as was the brightness of the day. He pushed on and moved further into the crags and rock walls.

I guess I better find a good place to stop for the night and the wild animals should shy from the fire. He thought. *Oh Father, You know I really miss having them come by and stay with me. I miss how it was.*

Yes, Son so do I. But soon man's redemption will be complete and then when it is time, Creation will be as well. But not yet. . . .I am truly sorry.

"I understand Father. And I will do as You have asked. It seems so different, not having You there to turn to in the Throne room. But it is still nice to hear You and know Your voice and the Holy Spirit's." He finished and He paused to listen to the echo of His voice in the canyon. Smiling, Jesus continued walking and talking.

"It's a good thing we are in the wilderness Father, I wouldn't want anyone to think I was crazy!" He laughed. "But, they also thought Noah was crazy about that Flood, right? . . . I am glad this won't take one hundred and twenty years to complete. And thankfully, now, we won't have to wipe the slate clean or have such loss of life."

It breaks My heart to think of it still. People don't understand. Nor, do the believers understand that I know everything. I remember all things. I truly cannot forget. I choose to forgive and show mercy.

Before now, I overlooked things because of the sacrifices. All those sacrifices were to point people to a need of a Savior, and a way to wipe sin away. But now that You are here as We planned, We can actually change men's hearts, minds, and souls. After the redemption all of mankind, they will be able to choose righteousness . . . and do as they should.

"Yes; but it will be hard. Lightbringer-Lucifer, will still lie and seek to steal, kill, and destroy. And men are weak if the Holy Spirit does not assist them. I am glad they will have You for a helper. But too many now, and in the future, will say You were only for a time. Or that only special people can be filled with You. They forget the examples in Your Word Father, like David, Samson, and more."

Jesus walked out of the small canyon and found a small patch of grass and a small indention in the nearby hill. Not a cave, but adequate shelter from the sun and rain. There was also a small spring. "I think this will do." Jesus laughed.

He raised His eyes to Heaven and spoke, "Thank you Father," laughing, "You didn't just put this here, right?" Looking at the rough grass and small scrub brush near the spring. He bent down and scooped water in His hand. The water was cool and clean.

Oh, no… Though I could have, You know. But what good would it have done when You are to be tested. To have the Teacher skew the test. I asked You to fast and pray. You will do so, just as your future brothers and sisters will. You will learn My voice and the Spirit's to be able to hear Our call and move. You will need this. . . And so will they, more than they know. But, many will deny that I, or the Spirit, speak after the Word of God is completed and printed. Whether by miracle or voice, sadly some will not believe the Holy Spirit is real, nor His love either.

"I think I will make a fire and pray. Father, what will it be like for them? They have never seen You. Nor for some, never heard Your voice, or even felt the move of the Holy Spirit. Even today with John. . . people were **surprised** that you spoke at all. Or that they could hear You. Does sin do so much that it deadens ears, makes eyes blind, and hearts cold?"

Yes, yes it does.

Jesus went nearby and pulled some scrub brush and found some small branches. It wouldn't be a bonfire but, a good start. He could search more after He filled His water bag and started the fire.

Better hurry, the sun is setting and I don't want to trip in the dark. And the night life will soon be moving around. He paused. *And the fire is a must; its gonna be chilly tonight. And I want to keep warm and enjoy things. This is going to be interesting. But it will be nice to spend time in the Spirit's and Father's presence. . . However long it is. . .* His thoughts ended.

Minutes later Jesus sat in front of a solid fire with His water bag nearby, He soaked in the heat.

"Well, now that everything is prepared. I can pray and fellowship as you wanted Father." He spoke aloud.

"So, Father, Holy Spirit, how do We begin? It seems strange to pray. I mean, We used to know each other's thoughts but spoke aloud for the angel's sake. And now, I am to pray as they will. I know You promised that I could fellowship with You and that You will be there, along with the Spirit. But what of them? My brethren? Those now and later. Will they be able to have constant fellowship as We used to? Or will things get in the way? I am sure Lucifer will not let that stand. He will do all to distract and hinder . . . to continue to steal, kill and destroy. Father, I am going to need to teach them how to maintain their fellowship and how to hear the Spirit. But if sin blinds, deafens, and hinders . . . they will have to work harder. And depending on what they hear, or are taught, it may be virtually impossible to know You or the Spirit of God. I guess I will pray now as they would. Hopefully, they will find that intimacy as You and I share. But Adam **feared** you, didn't **trust** anymore. I hope it is not the same for the future ones. How sad that would be. Father, they would be afraid of the very One who loves them the most. Not to mention how the Spirit wants to help, or as We will reveal to dwell in them."

Son, this is why sin must be destroyed. And the works of the Devil, Satan, Lightbringer. This is why You are here. To live as they will fully, and show by the Spirit's power they can overcome the enemy and sin and walk in real freedom and hope. They won't know the joy it is for Us . . .Just to hear their voice and to fellowship with them. However limited that may become. Fear, doubt, and deceit are his weapons. But most will find The Way. Most will have fellowship and walk in freedom. They can also teach others. And soon, they will be home and all will be right.

Jesus bowed his head and prayed aloud. . . "Our Father who art in Heaven, hallowed be thy Name. . . ."

*****

Jesus opened His eyes, as He finished praying and saw the dying embers of the fire. He felt the chilly breeze gently touching Him. He looked up at the blanket of stars shining from the heavens. And spoke to the Father again aloud.

"They definitely look different from here, Father. Not like in Our Realm. And it may be this body, but they do seem brighter. The stars stirs me and call me closer to You. And maybe it shows the right perspective. That you Father are extravagant in all You do. You and I made a Universe and placed those we love in it. To show wonders and signs, and to call all men back to Ourselves. We just wanted them to share in all We made. And for them to know our love and care always. But again, because of sin, they don't believe it and find it hard to believe. I am going to build the fire closer to the rock indention and lie down for the night. I will see you in the morning Father."

I will be here, even after You close Your eyes. And yes, I will be here in the morning. Remember Solomon's words? The Lord's acts of mercy indeed do not end, for His compassions do not fail. They are new every morning. Great is Your faithfulness. This is always true. Even when they don't believe or feel they merit it. No one does. It is just our love and mercy. Our character that is shown, no matter what. And what kind of God, or God of Love would I be if . . . kindness, mercy, grace, and more would stop? I would stop being Me. And If I stop anything. . . I want to stop sin. Not just for man's sake, but even for My own sake, to end this war. End man's destruction and make all things right again. For all those being born and those who will be born, it will take time. Even beyond these days. But it must be done. And We must continue to show forgiveness, mercy, and grace first. Then judgement, only after all other avenues are used up. Good night Son. Sleep well and know I love You.

"Good Night Father." Jesus said as He laid down on the ground and wrapped Himself in His cloak. The fire burned steady at His back. Far enough away that He would not be cold, but would keep wolves and others away.

Then the whispers started. Just loud enough to distract. Whispers that He could not find the source of. Whispers in the night and impressions. Though no one else was there. He rolled back and faced the rock wall and closed His eyes.

"Father, I commit myself to you. You promised peace for those you love, even sweet sleep." Jesus spoke aloud.

He doesn't love you. . . He didn't really tell you to come out here. . . You are not hearing God's voice. . . . You are not the Son of God. . . You are a Charlatan . . . the voices whispered.

****

Jesus, God's Son, snapped awake, as He began gasping. He pushed up on the tortured heal trying to push past the ever present pain in His body and limbs. *I must have passed out. I am not surprised. With all the blood loss and pain. At least it was good to remember the time of fasting with the Father. It was joy those forty days until. . .* His thoughts turned back to that other day. . .And His test.

****

Jesus woke in a chill. He turned to the now dead fire and the morning sun. The heat from the sun on His face warmed Him some. But He really needed to get the fire going again, so He could warm Himself. He stood somewhat stiffly and stretched.

He startled the deer and the rock rabbit looking on from the spring as He stood. And then the smaller animals slowly made their way to the spring for the morning drink.

"Good Morning to you all. You may drink freely. I however, must start a fire, so I can warm up a bit, though I know the sun will be warm soon. I will not bother you. I will warn you in advance that the brown bear will be by soon and try and drink. He is big, but is gentle. How do I know you say? I asked him. So you need not run away. He isn't hunting today."

Moving off into the small amount of brush nearby, He grabbed more dead branches and scrub brush to burn. Soon, the fire was lit and the animals left the spring to forage.

Jesus was feeling warmer now. His stomach grumbled loudly and long. He felt hungry.

Well, I guess forty days and nights without food is important. I guess I better soon forage myself. Maybe the bear will let me share his berries. . . laughing to Himself, His thoughts finished, *probably not. And I did want to speak with the Father anyway, to see what I am to do today.*

Jesus watched as a black-crimson smudge appeared nearby and it coalesced into Lightbringer-Lucifer. Jesus stood and waited. *So now comes the test,* He thought, *just when a man would be weakest and most vulnerable. No wonder the Father wanted fellowship and fasting,* He thought. *This is the first morning there have been no whispers or dreams.*

Lightbringer-Lucifer moved with predatory grace. His raiment reflecting the sun with crimson and gold flashes. He moved toward Jesus and the fire.

"Ah, what a *beautiful morning,* is it not? The sun is **shining** and the air is **fresh** and **clean**, though I am surprised this place hasn't fallen apart from the Light Father's neglect." He spoke in feigned wonder. "Then again, it seems Your Father has done it again. **Tsk, Tsk, Tsk** . . . . Favoritism, again! **What**? Of course, He wouldn't allow His Son to truly rough it. I mean look around . . ." he said with arms outstretched. . . "A **spri**n**g** and small **hovel** for you sleep in, out of the weather . . ." almost as generous as that **stable** . . . *hmmmmm*. So, much for a Father's Love . . ." he crooned mockingly. "He has provided Your water and lodging, even His sunshine. Generous, Generous," He scoffed. "I am sure you had beg for it. Really at his age, it is just sad, sad, sad . . . Oh my! You look thinner? Have you lost weight?" Lucifer looked at the ground slowly shaking his head ". . . Such *neglect*, His own Son," he said with mock concern . . . "Oh that's right. . . forty days and nights fasting. Why? Tell me. . .You can tell me why. Did He forget? Has His vaunted power slipped? Oh. . ." Lucifer grinned. "Oh, I am sure after all this time You might be hungry. . ." His voice dripped. "Oh, I truly understand. You are hungry I am sure. Why He wanted you not to eat. That seems foolish to me. But who am I. I am just a lowly servant cast from my place due to jealousy." Lucifer paused. He leaned in closer to Jesus and whispered, "If, You are the Son of God. . ." chuckling, "just speak the Word and these stones will be bread for You . . . surely, it would be okay. I mean you have a need. . ." his voice faded.

Jesus, unmoved spoke clearly, and with confidence. "It is written . . . Man will not live by bread alone . . . but by every Word that comes from the mouth of God."

My Father does all things for a reason. Nothing is done on a whim. These forty days and nights were to remind the nation of their wandering, and His care for them. He is Jehovah Jireh, the Provider, and more. I wish the elders of Israel could see this now. But that knowledge will come in time. And as for My eating, I set aside My rights to be obedient and walk in the Spirit, as my brothers and sisters will have to. His thoughts ended.

Lucifer bowed with grand flourish and pomp. "Oh, of course, true, true. You can do as You choose. I for one never go hungry, nor do I let those around me go without." He lied smoothly.

"Well, with that out of the way. . . let's go on a little trip shall we!"

In a moment Jesus saw the Temple Mount and its fortified walls, shinning in the morning sun. Golden rays played across the stones and flowed down into the Kidron Valley. The morning dew reflected on the grass and trees. The valley near the Temple Mount was full of glistening date trees, pomegranate, fig and olive; it was a truly beautiful sight. The flowers and plants sent an aroma of joy to His heart.

His stomach tightened, as Lucifer coalesced again on the Temple parapet. Jesus' memory flashed back to the Throne Room of God. And how often He would have spoken with Him. Jesus remembered Lucifer had dwelt above the Throne, as guard and glory reflector, and the music he designed. He was magnificent to behold; now however, the crimson and black blotches he reflected destroyed the beauty before him. And his voice so smooth and soothing, belayed the hatred and disdain of what He and the Father had created. And now for those whom He would die for.

"Ahh, the Temple." Lucifer laughed. "Oh, not anything like it was in the realm. By far not as beautiful. And the music… definitely not anything like the realms. Sadly, these humans cannot carry a tune at all. It sounds more like screeches to me. But I guess your Father likes listening to crows." "Jesus. . ." he crooned, "come see..."

Jesus moved to the parapet and looked out upon the Kidron Valley bathed in sunlight. Truly beautiful. The wash of color, the sounds of birds, and scent of flowers, the warmth of the sun on His face. He cherished the moment and held it in His heart.

Lucifer stood on the top of the parapet and spoke to Jesus again. As he motioned for Jesus to join him.

"Oh, is the Son of God, afraid?? He scoffed, "Come closer, you can trust me. . ."

Jesus didn't move. Suddenly Lucifer disappeared from the parapet and grabbed Jesus and held him on the parapet's edge overlooking the Kidron Valley hundreds of feet below.

"Ohh," Lucifer laughed, "watch that last step! It's a big one!"

Jesus looked at His feet, mere inches from the edge and the drop to the valley floor.

"Well, this is a problem." Lucifer, paused mid-sentence and held his chin as if in thought, "Ohh, not to worry. I mean . . . Since. . . If you are the Son of God, throw yourself off! Doesn't your Father promise . . . that He gave orders to the angels about you? That they would catch You and bear You up, so that you wouldn't even trip over a stone??" Lucifer continued. "I mean wouldn't it be easier to get everyone's attention?? I mean if You do intend to redeem man. . . . just get their attention. That would work, right?" he finished.

Jesus unmoved and unafraid spoke clearly.

"The Scriptures do say also, 'You shall not put your God to the test.' "

He wanted me not to obey the Father. To bypass the Cross. for fame and fortune? Even to shorten My assignment which would have destroyed our plans. My sacrifice would be in vain. It would not fulfill the Covenant, nor truly offer hope if they cannot do as I have. They would not walk in the Spirit's power, either. His thoughts ended.

"Ok, since you have refused my offers and slighted me again, I myself must be gracious of course!" He lied. "Come with me."

The next thing Jesus saw was a vast mountaintop. The sun was bright and sky clear. And again Lucifer coalesced beside him. He looked pityingly at Jesus. And spoke as a parent to a child.

"I am so sorry; I am sure you are tired by now. And All these decisions; and the traveling. Obviously, Your choices have been made out hunger and depravation. So, I hope this will be quick, so that you can eat. I need You to focus, can you do that?" He crooned and waved his hand in grand flourish.

And as Jesus looked on, scenes appeared before Him.

He saw nations, cities, towns, industry and gold, jewels and vast armies. one after another, in seemingly ceaseless display of human accomplishment, power, and wealth. Lucifer stood silent. As nation after nation was displayed and their goods and prosperity. The tableau froze. The only thing heard was the wind.

Jesus waited. There was no dread, no fear now, no hint of question. In His spirit rose righteousness, authority, and power. Pure, clear, truth. . . But He waited for what He knew would come.

"I am sure me bringing you here has intrigued you. But, You shouldn't be surprised. After all, **all of this is mine;** after Your human failed at his job. I told the Light Father that this would be a mistake! But, oh no, no one listens. Oh, I understand His love for His Creation. But this is what happens when You put lesser beings in charge! But, I being gracious and kind, have an offer for You. . . Think of it, You could restore the kingdoms of the world and rule in power and glory . . . with hardly any effort at all. I am sure the Light Father would be ecstatic and overjoyed at the return of His petty kingdoms, though He might strain Himself taking care of things . . . this all could be Yours. And it is mine to give . . ." His voice trailed off.

"It's a simple thing really. . . fall down now and worship me. Worship me. Simple and all this will be yours."

Jesus spoke with full authority and power.

"Go, Satan. It is written – 'You shall worship the LORD your God! And Serve Him only!' "

The air reverberated with power and the mountaintop and Lucifer were gone. And He found Himself near the cold fire and spring. The morning sun glistened and the birds sang. The air was filled with the scent of flowers. Angels came and surrounded Him.

"Michael, Cenehard, Gabriel - how nice of you to come. It has been quite a while." Jesus said with a smile.

"Yes it has," Michael said, "and we brought food and drink, including our companionship."

Michael turned to Jesus and said, "Majesty, after being by Yourself this long, and the trial. . . would it be okay to hug You? We have seen men find comfort in it."

"Of Course, You can. I would have hugged you anyway. I miss you all. You are home to me. Thank you for coming." Jesus finished.

"Well, truthfully . . ." Cenehard broke in, "Light Father told us to! Though we have missed you as well." He finished. Jesus looked to the Heavens and smiled. And said, "Thank You Father. Thank you." He closed His eyes, breathed deeply, and enjoyed the moment. *Home. Family. One day,* He thought. *We all will be together forever! What a day that will be.*

"Here, let me start a fire. . ." Jesus said.

And Satan/Lucifer waited for a more opportune time. . .

CHAPTER 8

WATER, WINE AND CLEANSING THE TEMPLE

You know Father, I liked the sea . . . Oh yeah, right now You can't hear me. It was always calming to me. And most people find the sea, lakes, and oceans that way. But, as a place to work, it is a rough place as I learned from Peter, James, John, and their father, Zebedee. Well, we will see how great fishers of men they become. I remember when we began learning together . . . Jesus thought as He remembered another day. . .

Jesus moved along the edge of the Sea of Galilee. He felt the breeze and saw the fishing boats out on the water. He marveled at the cloudless sky. *Well, it is quiet for the moment. But anything around the sea can change quickly. I wonder if Zebedee and his sons are out on the water now.* His thoughts ended, as He shielded His eyes and peered at the boats on the water. *I don't recognize any of them. Then again, I am new to which boat is whose,* he laughed. *Think of it, the Creator of the world I walk on, and I can't tell James' boat from Simon's.*

He turned and continued walking up the seaside and noticed a boat pulled to shore with men tending to their nets. As He got nearer, Jesus could hear loud voices and laughter.

"I tried to explain to the Roman guard that he paid too much for his fish. But the vendor told him it was a Musht. So, he gave him the coins and the man gave him a Kinneret. He paid full price for one Kinneret." Laughter erupted, as they mended their nets.

"Well, at least someone made money. And I am sure the Roman didn't know the difference."

Everyone looked up as Jesus came into view. "Shalom, and what can we do for you today?" Simon said, as the laughter died down.

"I am sure Simon that this man will do fine without our help. My father, Zebedee, needs these nets fixed and since you lost our bet fishing last night. . ." James started.

"Shalom to you all. My name is Yeshua/Jesus. I was admiring the lake and your boats."

"Oh, admiring the lake and boats, eh? It certainly wasn't Simon's boat; his was empty." John exploded in laughter.

"I fished well; they weren't there. I promise you." Simon assured them all.

"Yes, Yeshua you say, what can **we** do for you? Pay no attention to these thieves and pirates, Do you need a boat? I can rent it to you easily, if you do." Simon said smoothly.

Jesus laughed. "Pirates and thieves. Hmm, maybe I need to watch myself, and my coin purse." He continued. "No actually, I don't need a boat yet. But I overheard what happened to the Roman. Do you think YHWH would approve?" He said to all.

Jesus noticed the shock on their faces and continued.

"Doesn't the Torah say . . . treat a stranger as one of your own? Because you were strangers in Egypt, so says the Lord?"

Jesus watched as each man shifted where he sat. Finally, and not surprising to Jesus, Simon spoke again.

"I tried to tell him; truly I did. But Romans . . . and some fisherman don't listen. Simon continued. "Are you a Rabbi? Or Priest, today is not a Synagogue day."

"Of a sort, I am from Nazareth and I was walking by the direction of my Father and He said to walk by the sea and talk to the men fishing." Jesus offered.

"Oh, Your Father. Does He know Zebedee, my father?" James said.

"My Father knows lots of people. And I am a carpenter's son. So I am doing as My Father suggested. And am just reminding you of what you already know. And I know that can be hard sometimes." Jesus finished.

"Are you sure you are not a Rabbi or Priest? You sound a lot like one." John said.

"I am not; though My Father, would tell you otherwise. I have spoken often with the Priests in Jerusalem. And want to share what I know and help my brothers and sisters follow after YHWH."

"You are sure you are not a Priest?" Simon stated again.

"No, Simon, how can I help you with your nets. . ." Jesus offered.

"Well . . ." Peter, and the Sons of Zebedee smiled, "let us show you."

****

Jesus returned to the present as His body shook in pain. *Father, I know you can't hear Me right now, the darkness is great. This is truly hard to do . . . I am struggling. But I know it must be done and completed for men to be free!* He pushed up again on His tortured heel and tried to breathe. Pulling in air and the burnt desert smell.

I remember the days by the shore and mending the nets. They wondered why I would walk the shore and help them. Friendships began, teaching happened, and they found friendship. And slowly they came to know Me and trust Me.

I heard from My mother then; Mary, about a wedding, and found I had been invited to attend and bring guests. . . Jesus remembered.

Jesus sat in the wedding feast in Cana. Bright melodies flowed through out the room and outside. Laughter and joy met His ears. *Well there is quite a crowd. Not sure why I was invited. But, the Mohar has been done and the Ketubah contract signed, now the celebration. I am not so sure these seven day weddings are a good thing, or not.* He laughed to Himself. *I am sure those that follow us in the future may find it too strenuous. But, the Father said to attend. And so I shall. Plus, my mother, has somehow placed herself in this wedding. This is the third day and it seems to be going strong.*

Jesus moved to the Huppah canopy and the dancing around it. He watched as the bride and groom laughed, and moved with the music and their companions. Simon and the others were nearby. He moved toward them.

Simon spoke loudly above the music. "This is quite a feast." Chuckling, "I guess Jesus/Yeshua has some connections." He finished.

"There you go, thinking with your stomach. . ." James interjected. "But you are right. This is some wedding. And isn't that Mary there too. His mother?"

"Yes," Jesus said, "that is. I am not sure how, but she somehow has become part of all this. I think most Jewish moms have more power than they let on. Certainly, my backside remembers the switch," laughing.

"But do you know, this is a good thing; this was to be a picture of YHWH'S care and love. "Moses showed it at Rephidim. And King Solomon. "He has brought me to his banquet hall, and his banner over me is love." He promised to be our God and care for us. He was, is and will be our protection, as He was with Moses and our God that loves, as with Solomon and more. That's why there is the Huppah and all the other parts. YHWH is in Covenant with Israel and all men."

"All Men? . . . Even the Romans?"

"Yes, even them." Jesus finished.

Mary Moved to where Jesus stood with His guests. Jesus saw her coming toward Him with purpose. He whispered to the men, "Here comes my Centurion, on a mission it seems. . ." laughing.

"Jesus/Yeshua can I speak with you?" Mary said pulling Him away from Simon and the others.

"Yes, of course. What's wrong Mother, you seems upset?"

She leaned in close and spoke in hushed tones. "They are out of wine."

"Woman, Mother, What does this have to do with Me? It isn't yet time. . ."

Mary turned to the servants and said, "Whatever He says to you do." The servants waited, as Mary moved away to another part of the celebration. Jesus closed His eyes and prayed. He saw the six pots used for ceremonial cleansing and turned to the servants.

"Fill the pots with water." They moved off to do so. And Simon and the others looked on.

It seems fitting to use these pots. And they should be more than enough. Soon they won't need these ceremonies and things to be clean or fellowship with us. And new wine will flow. Oh, not the wine of drink. . . But of the Holy Spirit and Our fellowship. Think of it. No need for the washing or sacrifice. Just My Blood sacrifice, and faith. They will be clean and stay clean because of that and the very Word of God. His thoughts ended as the head servant came back minutes later and said, "The pots are full."

"Good. Now go take a pitcher to the headwaiter."

The servant looked at Jesus and raised an eyebrow but said nothing. He moved to the first ceremonial pot and drew out the pitcher. Then he moved to find the headwaiter and fulfill his task.

Simon and the others that had come with Jesus moved toward Him and waited. Jesus stood quietly as they whispered one to another.

Father, it seemed a good thing to show Your provision, protection, goodness, power and yes, even honoring of our parents here. I thank You for what You have done, His thoughts ended, as the headwaiter came toward Him. The head servant smiling, and the headwaiter spoke aloud for all to hear, "I told the bridegroom usually they give out the best wine at the beginning of these weddings, but he and his family saved it till the end. I don't know where this came from!"

The head servant walked past Jesus smiling and said, "From these sir," showing him the ceremonial pots.

Jesus sat again at the table with Simon, James, and John Zebedee. They took looked at Jesus and at the ceremonial pots, wondering how it all could have happened.

Jesus went from there to Capernaum by the sea and stayed there some days. His Disciples and His mother stayed there as well.

****

Son, it is time to begin. Leave Nazareth and go to Capernaum to stay there. Speak the Word and call Israel back to Me. Show forth My goodness, grace, mercy and Our love for all men. Jesus heard from the Father.

"I will. And it seems that John's work is almost at an end. They told me he had been arrested by Herod Antipas. Watch over him Father, as I know you will." Jesus said aloud.

Jesus, the Son of God, returned to the present. He pushed up on His heel and again tried to fill His tortured lungs with air, as He attempted to look around at the crowd still milling at the Cross.

So many times I wanted to shout at you and wished I could force belief or force your eyes open. But that was this human flesh. Not God's plan. The Father longed to return everything to all that was. But sin had captured all and drove men even closer to death, and Lucifer/Lightbringer, reveled in destruction and death. He did not flinch at his actions, but in hatred for Us and man, aided the process. He killed, destroyed, and stole, trapping all and celebrating his triumphs, even up until today. The Father charged me to speak the Word, so I did.

When Jesus went to Galilee and found the Synagogue, He began teaching and preaching the gospel of God.

After a day of teaching, Jesus was walking the shore of Galilee and saw Simon, Andrew, and the brothers, Zebedee, working the nets again. He walked to them as He always had. They looked up and waited.

"Follow me and I will make you fishers of men." Jesus spoke with authority. Simon looked at Andrew and the Sons of Zebedee. He paused holding his net. He looked to the other men nearby and held out his net, then moved to where Jesus stood.

Jesus could see the question in their eyes, even the trepidation of leaving a business and life they knew. James and John's father looked up smiled and kept working, as Jesus and the group moved away.

Father, I guess I need to find the rest. And begin in earnest. He thought.

So as Jesus walked Galilee, He looked for Phillip at Bethsaida. After Finding Him, He said, "Follow Me."

Phillip left Jesus and found Nathanael and said, "We have found the Messiah . . . Jesus of Nazareth."

Nathanael scoffed "Nothing good comes from Nazareth."

"Come and see," Phillip finished.

Jesus looked up from where He was sitting and said, "Look an Israelite that has no deceit," just as Nathanael approached.

"Do I know you?"

Jesus finished, "Before Phillip called you to come here I saw you under the fig tree."

"Teacher, You are the Son of God, the Messiah and King of Israel."
Jesus chuckled, "Because I told you I saw you under the fig tree, you
believe? Greater things you will see. You will even see the Heavens
opened and even angels assisting me."

Jesus left Capernaum and headed to Jerusalem for the Passover. Jesus
thought back to the trips on the road.

*I feel different this time. I have traveled to Passover often, as I am
commanded to. My father, Joseph, and Mary may be already there.
Maybe I will see them. If not, I can visit them later,* He thought, as He
moved along the road.

Jesus noted the crowds, as He moved toward Jerusalem and the
Temple. He moved easily through the crowd and entered the Temple
grounds. He thought back to how big this all was; as a young man, now,
he found nothing had changed. The Temple still was huge. The
sacrifices still continued. The crowds filled the courts. And the money
changers and vendors still take advantage of the people. He walked by
the pens where sheep, calves, and goats waited. He even heard the dove
vendors calling out prices for two doves, and other deals. Jesus stopped
at a vendor and saw the simple cords to guide the animals to offering.
He looked at the vendor and asked for three and paid the price.

Jesus moved off to a quiet corner of the Temple; but still in view of
the vendors and animals and the altar. He looked on, as He began tying
the three ends into a knot, intertwining the cords. Now He had a small
end He could grip. And then three cords with knots on the end.

Father in Heaven, do you see? Nothing has changed since I was a
boy. Are they truly here to worship, or just to make coin? I know You
hear everything and see everything.

*Yes, Son, I do. Many have forgotten what it is to worship at all.
Once Your sacrifice is made and the Law and Prophets fulfilled,
worship can begin again. With not just My overlooking sin in that
sense, Your sacrifice will be enough to restore communion as We
wanted. But this . . . this. . . This Temple will almost not be needed.
And it will become again a House of Prayer. And remember My Word,
through the Prophets. . . For zeal for Your house has consumed me,
And the reproaches of those who reproach You have fallen on me.*

Jesus looked at the homemade whip in His hand. He felt the ruff rope
against His hands and fingers. *This is nothing like the Father would*

want. He would have wanted men to choose to worship freely and deep from their hearts. But this, this is mercantile, business, and thievery. And the Priests claim righteousness and holiness; yet, take bribes and gifts to curry favor with officials, and even the Romans. And it seems no one truly seeks to honor God, at least, in leadership. Again He paused.

Deep in His heart and soul Jesus felt the move of the Spirit. This time it was not a direction to walk, or encouragement. But He felt a flood of power and authority, not unlike during the temptation. He stood and felt the rhythm of His heartbeat and looked out on the Temple, and the changers … all busy. Yet, no one was in prayer or worship of God. In His whole being He heard and felt the call ***to Cleanse My Temple, it is to be a House of Prayer. .***

Jesus breathed deeply and moved with purpose to the first table and flipped the table and used the whip on the vendors and shouted, "For zeal for Your house has consumed me, and the reproaches of those who reproach You have fallen on me. It is written, 'My House is to be a House of Prayer!' "

As He moved from table to table, His strength never wavered, nor did His determination. He watched as the animals and people moved out of His way and the whip. Again and again, He turned the tables and forced the vendors to run. Again and again, He shouted the words, "For zeal for Your house has consumed me, and the reproaches of those who reproach You have fallen on me. It is written, 'My House is to be a House of Prayer!' "

The Temple guards and Priests looked on, stunned by the growing crowd of people following after Jesus and repeating His cry. Not one touched coin or ware. The Temple sacrifice almost stopped. And Jesus moved to the Beautiful Gate and moved toward Capernaum.

CHAPTER 9

NICODEMUS, WOMAN AND A WELL, FREEDOM

With My Father's call to all men to worship and turn from sin; I had to cleanse the Temple, even though it might not last to fulfill Scripture and honor My Father. It had to be done. Though, men's hearts are not totally open yet. I was told to come to Jerusalem again. But the Spirit, nor my Father; has told me yet, where to go. The night is quiet and Jerusalem is seemly still. His thoughts ended,

Maybe I should go to the Synagogue pinnacle and look at the stars and moon. I certainly could use the quiet after the noise of the Temple. He moved quietly up the street to the Temple Mount and moved past the Temple and Roman guards almost unnoticed. He moved in sure steps to the pinnacle and area where the Shofar was blown. He looked out over the Kidron Valley and the night sky.

The stars shown as jewels against the velvet sky. The moon cast its white light upon the valley landscape and trees of Solomon's Garden. The birds still called and the breeze was gentle. *Peaceful, truly peaceful. Not like the Test.* He chuckled to Himself. *No, not like the test.*

Jesus thoughts ended as He heard the sound of sandal steps approaching Him. He continued to drink in His surroundings as he waited for a voice He knew would speak.

"Rabbi;" a deep baritone voice spoke, "Rabbi . . . I."

Jesus turned to a Priest of the Pharisees. Still in his official garb, and glancing about as if searching for something. Jesus waited. ***Son, this is Nicodemus. He has a question. . . You need to answer him.***

Okay, Father I will. I wondered when You would bring the person to me since I did not know where to go. He thought.

"Rabbi, we know You have come from God, as a Teacher. Because no one can do what you do, without God's blessing and power."

Jesus spoke to Nicodemus' question unvoiced. "Truly, unless a person is born again, he cannot even see the Kingdom of God."

Nicodemus looked stunned. Then replied. "How can a person be born again? Certainly, He cannot enter the womb again? Can he?"

"Truly, I tell you, unless one born of water and the Spirit of God, he cannot enter God's Kingdom. That born of the flesh is flesh and of the Spirit, Spirit." Jesus answered.

"Why are you amazed at this? When I said you must be born again? Just like the wind blows where it chooses and you hear its sound, but you cannot see where it is going, but you see the effects, so are they that born of the Spirit." Jesus finished.

Nicodemus shook his head and looked at Jesus. Nicodemus searched the face of Jesus for answers he could not face.

Nicodemus finished, "How can this be?"

The moon's light reflected off his garments and showed the lines of age on his face and his confusion.

Jesus looked Nicodemus in the eyes and spoke plainly.

"You are a teacher of Israel, and yet, you do not know this or understand it?" Jesus continued, "Men testify and speak about what they know. And you accept their word. But you do not accept My word. Since I have told you these things and you do not believe me, how can I tell you of heavenly things and have you believe?" Jesus continued. "No one has entered Heaven. But one came from heaven, the Son of Man. And Just like Moses lifted the serpent on a pole in the wilderness, so must the Son of Man be lifted up. . . So that any who believe in Him will have Eternal life."

Jesus saw in Nicodemus eyes and facial expression he had garnered the reference. But was struggling with the implications of His message. *How can you marry the two? I wonder Nicodemus. The truth of a Messiah and what it would mean to the broken priesthood. And a forgiveness, without limit or reason to boast in works.*

Jesus spoke to Nicodemus in compassion and tenderness. Knowing he soon would live it out. . .

"God loved the world so much that He sent His One and only Son, that anyone who believes in Him, will not perish but have Eternal life. You see God did not send His Son into the world to condemn the world, but to save the world through Him. And the one who believes will not be judged. But the one who doesn't believe is already judged because he does not believe in the name of the One and only Son of God. This is God's judgement that Light has come into the world, but men loved darkness more than the Light, because their deeds were evil. And those that do evil hate the Light, because they will be brought to Light and exposed. But the one who practices the truth, comes to the Light and his deeds are proved by God."

Jesus watched as Nicodemus turned and walked toward the street and into the night.

I hope you can understand Nicodemus. This is different than what they know now. And my charge to preach the Word of God and His Kingdom grate against this priesthood and its works. Jesus thoughts continued. *Father God, will they see? Will they understand? How the Law has pointed to Your Messiah and His death and resurrection? And what they will and can become through genuine, simple, faith.*

Jesus moved away from Jerusalem, toward Capernaum, and rest.

******

The next day Jesus and His followers went to Judea and He was baptizing and spent time with His followers. There they found John there also baptizing. Those that were there asked about "purification" and sought answers.

John's disciples came to him and said, "Jesus, the One you spoke about is also baptizing and people are coming to Him. Should we be concerned?"

John responded simply. "You know as I had said, 'I am not the Christ, but I was sent before Him to testify.' Just like the groomsman rejoices in the groom having a bride, and hearing his voice, so do I. He must increase and I decrease. Since he came from Heaven and is above all, no one seems to believe His Word. But God has shown that what He says is true and sealed him with the Spirit without measure and has given all things into His hand. He who believes in the Son has Eternal life, but those that disobey the Son, God's wrath abides on them."

Jesus heard from the Father while He was on the road. *Son, You need to go Samaria; there is someone you need to speak to. And you also know the Pharisees are concerned that You are baptizing more people than John. But we knew this would happen.*

Okay Father, I will. I will speak to whomever You send Me. This is like what my future brothers and sisters will do. Hopefully, they will hear and obey You as well. Because this I know at the least, all people are precious to You and You love them so.

Jesus stopped by a well close to Jacob's well, near the city of Sychar, as evening was coming on. He brushed off the dust of the road and sat down, as the other followers went to buy food and drink because of the travel.

Jesus watched as a woman made her way toward Him and the well that He leaned on. She carried the water pots in the traditional manner. He could see the wear on her garments. And the tattered clothing. This was the best this woman had. And she bore the water pots with grace.

She came to the well and Jesus. She set down the pots and was beginning to lower the bucket down. When Jesus spoke.

"May I have a drink?"

So Father this is the one I should speak to? Jesus thought **Yes Son.** *But Father, You know they believe that they are the "Keepers of the Law and Torah." That because of Joseph and our History, we are at odds.* **Yes, Son, at odds and yet, both nations, both peoples in need of a Messiah and hope. You will see.**

Jesus looked into her eyes and saw more than tiredness and labor. He saw the truth; life had been hard for her. And she was almost at her end. Her faith wanted to see YHWH'S blessing and provision, and care, and yet . . .

"Sir, You are Jew. And You know I am a Samaritan, and a woman; how can you ask me for a drink?"

"If you understood the gift of God and Who was asking for a drink of water, you yourself would have asked Him and He would give you living water."

The woman laughed and said, "You do not even have a way to draw water. And it is a deep well. How can you get living water? You do not look greater than our father, Jacob, who drank from here and watered all he had. Are You?"

Jesus smiled. "Everyone who drinks this water will be thirsty again. But, anyone who drinks of the water I give . . . it will spring up within them to Eternal life, and they will not thirst again."

Jesus watched as the woman thought on what she had heard. He could see the struggle to understand and even the years of pain and hardship. She thought she had found a way to ease her life with less pain, less struggle. So she spoke, "Sir, **please**. . ." Jesus heard her anguish and pain. He knew. "Give me this water, **please**," barely a whisper, "so I will never be thirsty, or have to draw water from this place anymore."

Jesus knew there was more. He paused and then said, "Go and bring back you husband . . ."

She knew she had been caught. And answered, "I don't have a husband."

Jesus spoke tenderly, "You are right you do not have a husband; though, you have had five. And the one live with is not your husband."

She changed the subject quickly. "It seems to me You are prophet. Our fathers worshiped here and yet, you people, say that in Jerusalem is the place where everyone should worship."

"Woman there is a time coming when no one on this mountain, or in Jerusalem, will worship the Father. You do not understand. The time has come that true worshippers will worship the Father in Spirit and Truth. And they are the ones the Father seeks. God YHWH is Spirit. And those that worship must worship Him in Spirit and in Truth."

She jumped in, "I know the Messiah is coming, and when Christ, God's chosen comes, He will tell us all things."

Jesus said, "I am He."

She left everything and went toward town. Leaving Jesus still at the well.

As she entered the city, she moved the men at the gate and said loudly, "Come and see a man who told me everything I had done . . . This isn't Christ the Messiah is it?" Curious, some men followed her, and called to others to follow. Many left the city and headed toward the well and Jesus.

Jesus looked on as Simon urged him to eat and the others too.

"I am fine. I have food that you do not know about." James said, "Okay, who slipped back here and gave Him food before us?"

Jesus stopped them and said, "My food is doing the Father's will. The fields are white for harvest. And the reaper is gathering wages to Eternal life. And you are sharing in it."

Many people from the town came and asked Jesus to stay. And more of them believed. Not just because of the woman's word . . . They told her and Jesus, "We believe; not because of what the woman said. But because we have heard for ourselves. And now we know He is the Savior of the world." He stayed there two days teaching and sharing.

Son, You need to go to Galilee and enter the Synagogues. Teach and fulfill the Word of God. And of course there will be people I want you to meet. And show my mercy, grace, and even forgiveness too.

Jesus was filled with the Holy Spirit and moved in the Spirit's Power.

Okay Father, I will go. I will do as you ask. Jesus thought as He left Samaria and headed down the dusty road to Galilee. He came to a Synagogue in Galilee and began to teach. Day-after-day He spoke and taught in the Synagogue. And word that He was teaching spread.

He moved from there to. . .

Nazareth! I missed this place. There were good memories here. I would love to walk the city again. But, My Father has given me a mission. And I must fulfill it. So, off to the Synagogue I go. I know it's what YHWH has commanded we do. And now with My mission, this is just normal now. As it should be. Coming to the House of God. Being in God's Presence. Learning and Growing in His Word, hearing and obeying His voice. . .walking with God. He thought as He entered the Synagogue. He knew it was the Sabbath and He stood to read. The attendant in the Synagogue handed him the book of the Prophet Isaiah.

Jesus looked at the worn papyrus and felt the weight of it. *Isaiah.* His thoughts flooded back to Isaiah's vision. . . *Do you remember that Father? He said . . . he saw you. And he saw Your glory and heard the Seraphim cry of Heaven . . . I miss that. But, I will now fulfill your Word.*

Jesus turned in the book to the passage and began to read aloud

"The Spirit of the Lord is upon Me, because He anointed Me to preach the Gospel to the poor. He has sent Me to proclaim release to the captives, and recovery of sight to the blind, To set free those who are oppressed, to proclaim the favorable year of the Lord."

He gently closed the book. He then handed the book to the attendant and sat down. He could feel every eye was locked on Him and they were waiting . . . waiting for His Word. His message. . . . and Jesus knew . . . some of the people said, "How did he get so wise? How can He do these miracles? That is Joseph's Son, right? Isn't He brothers with James, Joses, Judas and Simon? And His sisters?" They were smiling and thinking to themselves, "He is a good speaker, kind and gracious."

"Today this Scripture is fulfilled." Jesus Paused.

Continuing Jesus said, "I am sure you would say You are just a carpenter's son, or do here, in Nazareth, what You did in Capernaum. But the truth is truly, a Prophet is not welcome in his hometown. Just like in Elijah's day. There were many widows in Elijah's day. When the rain did not fall for three and a half years. And of course, a famine hit the land. But the Prophet was sent to none of them. But he was sent to Zarephath, of Sidon. And he was sent to Naaman the Syrian to cleanse his leprosy . . ." They took offense at him.

Jesus watched as the tenor of the Synagogue change. He knew what would come when they realized His message. And what was next. . . The whole Synagogue was filled with rage! They rushed Him and grabbed Him. Then they moved Him out of the city to the edge of the hill on which it stood, as they were planning to throw him off!

Jesus stopped and He watched as the crowd, roared passed and He went on his way.

Jesus left there and was headed to Galilee. Jesus was surprised at His reception. But He also knew they did not believe Him as the Samaritans had. They only believed because of the miracles they had seen and heard.

There was an official of Herod Antipas who had heard Jesus was in Cana of Galilee, where He had turned the water to wine. He had traveled two days on the road. And was desperate to see Jesus. The official searched and searched. Finally, he found Jesus as He left the Synagogue where he had been teaching.

Jesus saw the official stop and get down from his horse, and call out to Him.

"Jesus, I beg you . . . could you come down to my house and heal my son? He is at the point of death!" Jesus watched as desperation washed across his face. He saw the dust and dirt from the road and his weariness. The official wore the robes of Herod Antipas office.

Jesus responded aloud. "So unless you people see signs and wonders, you just will not believe. . ."

"Please, sir, he is at the point of death. . ." He begged.

"Go your way; your son lives." Jesus replied. Jesus watched, as he quickly got back on his horse and turned and headed for the road to Capernaum. He watched as the official urged his mount into a gallop.

Father, is their trust and belief in you so fragile because of sin. That unless, for the next moment, if they do not see Your work or hand . . . that all is lost? Jesus thought. Jesus moved on and He knew what the official would find. His son healed. Jesus smiled, knowing that soon the man's servants would meet him on the road. . .

He said He was healed. And I was to go my way, the official thought as he pushed his mount faster. He felt the wind on his face. And felt every pounding of the horses hoof cut into his hope. He had left his son and home out of desperation and fear. He loved his son. He was precious to him. And the doctors he had sought could do nothing, even though he was of the Court of Herod Antipas. *What is the point of having money and power, when you are powerless against sickness or disease? Or even death . . . I don't want to think about it.* The road seemed to stretch endlessly as minutes became hours. He soon saw the familiar turn of the road where he would stop and water the horse. And he was filled with dread.

I don't understand there is my carriage and two servants . . . He thought . . . *No. . .*

He stopped and caught the eye of one of his servants. They moved toward him. The dread he had felt became a knot, as he watched his servants rush toward him. He saw the joy on their faces and heard it in their shout.

"Master, your son lives! Your son is well!" they cried as the knelt before him. Stunned, the official couldn't speak. They again repeated news. He grabbed one by the shoulders and lifted him to his feet and looked into his eyes. "What, what did you say?" He whispered.

The servant broke protocol and embraced him and repeated. "Sir, your son, your son is alive."

The official leaned heavy on the servant, as relief flooded over him. The other servant grabbed his arm and supported him with his body. They stood in place as their Master attempted to steady himself. Both now supporting him.

"When?" He said. "When did this happen? . . . I saw you and for a moment, I feared the worst. . ." "

He was healed about one in the afternoon," the servant said.

The official straightened and cleared the dust form his clothes and raised his head, looking at his servants he said. "We must head home quickly. We must tell everyone in the house! That was the time Jesus of Nazareth told me to go my way because my son was healed. He did as He said. He is the Messiah. We must tell all the house."

The servants took the reins of his horse and they watered them. The official got into the carriage and they rode off toward their home in joy.

****

Jesus went to Capernaum and He began to teach at the Synagogue. Jesus knew what the people in the Synagogue were thinking. What is this? He speaks with authority, like He knows for certain. He does not speak like the Scribes or Priests. He was going to continue, but he heard and saw a dark smudge surrounding the man speaking. . .

"Why are you here . . .? Jesus of Nazareth? Have you come to destroy us? We know who You are. . . You are the Holy One of God!" The hollow voice cried.

"Be quiet and come out of Him, now." Jesus spoke authoritatively.

Jesus watched as the demon threw the man to the floor and he convulsed and was still then left unharmed.

A murmur rose throughout the Synagogue. And He heard them say almost in one voice, "Amazing! What new teaching, He even commands demons and they obey him."

Word of this spread throughout all of the districts and the surrounding Area. As they left the Synagogue, Jesus and the disciples followed Simon and Andrew to their house.

Jesus saw the mixture of hope and concern on Simon's face, as He said, "Jesus, my mother-in-law is sick and has a fever." He could sense the trepidation and hesitation to even have asked. But he had asked.

So Jesus walked from the room to where she lay in bed. He reached out taking her hand. He smiled and gently lifted her out of the bed and she stood on her feet. Astonishment filled her as she held His hand and looked into His eyes. She was whole again. No sickness or fever. No weakness or lack. Jesus let go of her hand. He smiled again.

She moved off to the cooking area and began to prepare food and brought them something to drink. Jesus overhead her say, "Forgive the mess of my house. I am sure you must be hungry. I will make you something."

"I know I am," Jesus smiled.

As evening fell and the last rays of the sunset faded, Jesus heard the Father: ***Son, prepare Yourself. There are many here in need. And they need your help. Show them My love, grace and mercy.*** *I will Father God.* He smiled. *I am sure news of what happened today in the Synagogue and here in this house has spread,* He thought. Jesus heard a knock at the door. And Simon went to answer it.

So it begins, Jesus thought.

"Jesus . . . um. . ." Simon said stunned. "It looks as if the whole city is at this door. What do we do?"

Jesus looked at Simon in sympathy and smiled as He spoke. "We Simon, help them."

Jesus stepped to the doorway. He saw the crowd and their pain. And He spoke gently but in authority. "Those sick come here."

Simon and the other disciples stood outside the door on either side and looked on. They watched as minutes became hours. Sickness and disease cured. Demons fled in silence. Peoples hearts and lives restored. Simon leaned heavy against the door and sighed as the last of the crowd had dispersed. Jesus was drinking at the table and no one spoke until Simon said, "I think we need to rest."

Jesus awoke. The house was still and quiet. He listened, eyes closed trying to gauge the time by the sounds He heard. There were no birds yet and the sun had not risen yet either. Jesus got up from the mat and took his cloak, and headed to the door of the house. He moved as quietly as possible. The night lamps were sputtering, as their oil was almost gone.

As he moved past the other mats and the table, He froze because of noise. He wasn't sure what He heard. He waited, still and then He heard it again. To his ears it was a mix between a low growl and the huff a dog might make. He hadn't heard it when he first stood by the mat they had for Him. But again He heard it.

His eyes had adjusted to the dim light of the house and the night lamps flickering. He saw Andrew and some of the others that had come with him and he moved past them closer to the door. And again He heard the noise . . . He froze.

Son, Come, pray and fellowship. After last night you need time away. And I want to tell you what I plan, He heard the Father say. *Ok, I will Father,* He responded, *but I might be delayed. It seems the only door to the house is blocked by a large animal or dog.* He heard the sound again. His ears filled with a low growl and long huff. Just then, a night lamp nearby, sputtered to weak life and He finally understood.

It was Peter! The big man had placed his mat by the door. Probably, to make sure no one else would try to enter. *And He is very protective Father. I will meet with you shortly if I can reach the door. I will have to step over him. I would hate to wake him or anyone. But I will try.* Jesus responded.

Jesus stretched and stepped gingerly over the sleeping man; the snore erupted. Peter rolled toward him! Somehow, Jesus pushed the door open, turned and quietly closed it again. Jesus looked up and saw the stars, smiling and responded to the Father.

I have made it past the obstacle without waking anyone, He laughed to Himself. *Though I don't think I would have woken anyone else, not with that noise. I am surprised that they are all still asleep.*

Jesus moved in sure steps through the street and the early morning to meet with His Heavenly Father. He looked forward to the communion and the familiar presence of both the Holy Spirit and the Father. His smile grew, as he thought of the time with both of them. *It's not like You are not with me every day and hour, but these times of prayer and fellowship are different somehow.* He thought.

"Where could He have gone? Did anyone see Him leave?" Simon said.

Andrew jabbed his brother in the stomach and said, "None of us did, you were the one guarding the door!" He laughed. "I barely got any sleep because of your snoring. It was worse than a day of fishing!" he ended

Peter gave his brother an exasperated look. "I sometimes nap when the fish don't bite, but that's rare!" He insisted.

"Of course," the others said grinning.

"We have to find him, and make sure he is okay." Peter looked out the window at the growing crowd. "And people have come by to meet Jesus. And the streets are filling. And you know how the Priests get angry with Him." He finished.

"Well, let us finish eating at least." Someone said.

****

Jesus leaned against the fig tree enjoying its fruit and saw Simon and the others top the hill outside Cana.

"Good afternoon . . ." Jesus said with a smile. "Good to see you all awake. Did you all sleep well? There was a growling I heard earlier." He laughed.

"Funny," Simon said snidely.

"You should know," He continued, "that **we** were worried about You. And came looking for You. Along with most of the town. We had to push our way past the house door to even make it this far!" Peter finished.

Jesus jumped up and dusted off His robes and dropped the few pieces on the ground. He stretched and looked into the sun and said, "Anyone Hungry? These figs are sweet. Well. . ." He looked at all of them in turn and finished. "We need to go to the towns nearby, so I can share my message. That's why I came in first place."

"I hope you are up for this Peter," Andrew whispered. "It looks like another whirlwind tour of the Synagogues and setting people free from demons again. Who knows, you might lose that belly," he said laughing. As he jogged to catch Jesus.

****

As Jesus walked along the road He noticed a figure moving toward Him. He knew in a moment the figure was a leper. He saw the man attempting to decide if he should step off the road into the ruff brush, and lie down, or hide. He saw the ragged clothes that would barely keep one warm in late afternoon, much less the night time wilderness.

Jesus watched as he moved closer. Jesus saw the matted hair, the wild eyes, the anxiousness of his movement. And his fear and desperation. He stumbled, only a step or two, then he froze.

*He knows he's been **seen**. He knows what the Law **demands**; and yet, he dares to hope. Hope that he might this day be clean. That today, he could begin to feel a part of life again and have a place among the people. That finally, after all these days and years, he would find Joy again, and true hope again. Even peace again. And find YHWH God's blessing again. And find that YHWH God truly had not forsaken him. And that he could live again, even to never be alone again or fear again. This was not what the Law was meant for; the Law was to show all men their need, not to tear lives apart. Nor make sin's ravages evidence to keep or throw away YHWH God's Creation, or glory that all men bare. And the Priests lord it over many; Priests that have fine dress, yet darkness in their heart.*

Jesus watched as the man glanced quickly around and hobbled to him. Shrinking in fear and dread, he knelt before Jesus, and in a shaking voice, tried to speak.

"Jesus/Yeshua," he pleaded. Barely raising his eyes up at all. "Please Jesus. Yeshua, if you are willing. If you are willing; you, can make me clean." He pleaded.

Jesus felt compassion rise from the very core of His being. He could not deny this son of Israel, nor His Father's Creation, to bear this any longer. He knew what He must do.

"**I AM** willing. Be cleansed." Jesus spoke. And He watched as the leprosy was wiped clean. And his body and strength restored. He watched as the cleansing astounded the man. He watched as the man ran desperate hands over his body, arms, and legs. He watched as truth dawned.

"Thank you." The man whispered. Inwardly Jesus smiled and joy filled Him. But He looked the man in the eye and said sternly.

"Listen to me. Do not say a word to anyone. No one. But go to the Priests and offer the sacrifice for cleansing, as Moses commanded as a testimony to them. Now go."

The man turned and moved off to do as Jesus had asked. *I am not so sure my rebuke worked.* Jesus laughed. *I don't think he is going to be quiet about anything, Father.* Jesus thought.

No Son, definitely not. But I am glad You were here to change his life and give the nation Priests, any who can see, what We intended for all men. To truly cleanse men from sin. And Your sacrifice will do just that . . . if they believe and receive it. The Father responded.

****

CHAPTER 10

JESUS SPOKE HEALING, THE CENTURION, A MISSING CEILING AND MORE

Jesus had gone to Jerusalem for a feast of the Jews. And He was passing by the Sheep Gate and the pool. They called it Bethesda. He moved into one of the five porticos. He saw multitudes of people. He saw many blind, sick, lame, and withered people. And then saw the one His Father told Him of. He moved further in and saw and smelt the sickness and disease. It was tangible and heavy. *These people need doctors, healers, and medicines. He shook His head. These are now the forgotten and the castaways, literally the refuse of the city. Why don't the Priests call upon My Father? Do miracles have to be done by prophets alone? Or angels alone? This all is the result of sin and disobedience. Adam chose and they are paying the price.*

Jesus moved to the sick man who He knew had been this way for thirty-eight years ill, paralyzed. He looked at him and spoke kindly. "Do you want to get well?"

The man turned his head and spoke to Jesus plainly

"I have no help. No one will carry me to the pool. So, that when the waters are stirred, I have to attempt to move myself. And by that time, others make it into the waters before me."

Jesus said, "Get up. Pick up your mat and walk."

For the briefest of moments, he stared at Jesus, questioning. *Did He really just tell me to get up and walk? I have been here a long time. Does He know that?*

He felt the surge of life through his body. Jesus hadn't moved, but continued to look at him in earnest. The man felt what? Strength? Power? Life? He had almost forgotten what it was to even have energy to think, breathe, and be.

The man turned his hips, astounded that he could actually move! He placed both feet flat on the ground and pushed off the mat with his arms! He stood. *How long had it been?* He was standing. He had strength in his legs. *No pain or weakness,* he stood. He flexed his hands, and arms. *They had worked before, but were stronger now. He felt youthful.* Slowly, he bent and took the edges of his mat and lifted, straightening. *There is no weakness in anything!* He thought. *I am moving. I am healed and strong. I can now go home and live again.*

He began to move with mat through the crowd. Those around him stared at first. Then he heard the voices. They were indignant and condescending. He heard then as from a distance. "What are you doing?"—"It is not right for you to carry your mat today!"—"It's the Sabbath! Do you not know?"

Finally, the man stopped and turned to those questioning and said, "Look a man told me to get up and take my mat and walk."

"Who told you?" they said.

He looked back the way he came and did not see anyone but the sick and hurting. He did not see Jesus anywhere. The people were shocked.

Minutes later Jesus walked up to the man and spoke. "Now that you are well. Sin no more."

The man left Jesus and found those that were indignant with Him. He told them that it was Jesus who had told Him to take up his mat and walk. They were angry.

Not long after this, Jesus heard that John had been put in prison.

Jesus found Himself teaching near the Sea of Galilee. And the crowd was increasing and pushing Him toward the water. He turned and saw Simon, along with the Sons of Zebedee, mending their nets. He called to Simon Peter and got into his boat.

"Simon can you move us a little from the shore?"

Simon complied, though Jesus could sense his weariness. Now that he was far enough from the shore, so that everyone could hear, easily,

He taught the crowd. And Simon Peter mended their nets and listened too.

Son, its time you called Simon and the others to follow You full Time. But I know they may hesitate, so We will show them they need not be afraid. He heard the Father say. *Okay Father, I will. Though Simon and the others are tired. I will do as you say.* Jesus thought.

"Simon, put out into the deep water, and drop your nets for a catch." Jesus said.

Simon hung his head. He struggled not to let his frustration show, and spoke, "Master . . ." he said in exasperation. "We worked all night. And we caught nothing." He held out his hand almost as a plea. His head fell again. Exhaustion and weariness were a weight upon his shoulders. But he found his voice. "But, I will do as you say," he said with resignation. Jesus sat in his place, as Simon Peter unfurled the sail and moved farther out. Jesus saw the weariness in his movements. And heard the frustration in his words to Andrew. Jesus watched, as he walked to the nets he had repaired and threw them out upon the water. Jesus knew Simon Peter was at the end. Jesus smiled and waited for what would come.

Simon looked out on the sea. It was smooth as glass. Rarely was it ever so smooth. This was a place where storms erupted in moments. And many times; if you were not careful, very careful, destruction and loss came swiftly.

Jesus sat where He had taught from, smiling. Simon Peter was confused. Then the boat tilted. Simon reacted as any fisherman would. He grabbed the nearest line and steadied himself. The water was still like glass. *Why would the boat tilt? The nets are in still water.* He thought. Then he moved to the side of the boat that the nets were out on.

Simon was stunned. And fear began to rise as the boat tilted more. He looked out at the net. It had expanded to its full. And it was pulling the boat down!

"Andrew! Call out to the Brothers Zebedee, have them come along side! Hurry!"

Jesus didn't move. Simon looked at Him. Jesus was still in his teaching spot. Simon Peter looked on as James and John pulled their boats alongside Peter's.

"Simon, Simon, what's all the noise! I thought we were done for day!" They said in unison. "My boat is sinking! I need help! I need you to help! My nets are almost at the breaking point!" Simon said urgently.

"Okay, we will load our boat as well. John, toss our nets if we need to," James said.

Minutes later both boats were full and overflowing with fish and their nets as well. Simon Peter fell at Jesus' feet in utter amazement and fear, crying out.

"Lord, Lord go away from me!" He said in tears, "I am a sinful man!"

Jesus raised Simon Peter to his feet and said, "Do not be afraid. Now you will catch men alive. You will be fishers of men." Soon they brought the boats to shore. And Immediately, Simon Peter and the others left everything, and followed Jesus.

    ****

Centurion Perseus Quintis Nerva came to Jesus at Capernaum. He had heard of Jesus and the miracles that Jesus did. He had spoken with the Jewish elders about Him. And about his servant. And they came with him to Jesus.

Jesus stopped what He was doing, as He saw the Centurion and the elders approaching. Jesus watched as he walked toward Him. He walked in confidence and strength with his helmet under his right arm. His centurion's cloak gathered at a broach at the neckline. The rest fell down off his left shoulder. The sun glinted off the breast plate and his greaves. Jesus caught sight of the swords held by belts and other pieces.

He looks as if he is coming to meet a dignitary or emperor. I know they are hard men, but there is something about his eyes. I don't know if I am more surprised that he is coming to Me, or that the elders are with him. I guess we will soon see. Jesus thought.

Perseus knelt before Jesus with head bowed. He placed the helmet on the ground and was silent.

Jesus waited quietly for him to speak.

Centurion Perseus Quintis Nerva's smooth baritone broke the silence.

"**Lord**. . . Jesus, my dearest and most faithful servant lies at home near death, paralyzed. There was an accident. He has served me for many years and he is almost like a son to me. I hesitated to come before you because I know your kindred hate Romans. And I have done all I could and Rome too. I spoke to the elders that came here with me and they said that I should come and ask. I ask for my servant's sake. And yes, myself because he is dear to me. Will you heal him?"

Jesus looked from Perseus to the elders. They stepped up and said to him.

"He is worthy for You to grant him this; for he loves our nation. He alone built our Synagogue."

Jesus looked from the elders to Perseus. Compassion flooded Him. He looked at the Centurion and said, "Yes, I will go back with you and heal your Servant."

Centurion Perseus Quintis Nerva stood and looked to Jesus with tears welling in his eyes. Jesus watched as his eyes found a spot near his feet and he spoke with emotion. "No. . . No I am not worthy for You to enter my house. Say the word and my servant will be healed." Jesus marveled. The Centurion cleared his throat and spoke in authority.

"I am someone in authority. And under it, I have soldiers I command and servants, as well. I say to one soldier, "Go here and do this thing. And they do. I call my servants and they come. And they do as I ask."

Jesus truly amazed, interrupted him, and said, "I tell you all the truth, I have not found anyone with this great faith in all of Israel. **Go**. Just as you have believed it will be done."

Then Centurion and the elders of his city left Jesus and returned home. ***I am sure you know his servant is healed. Joy will come to that house.*** God the Father spoke to Jesus. *Yes, I know. If only Abraham's children believed as he, or understood. This would change everything. I hope my brothers and sisters in the future will have it.* Jesus thought back.

Jesus returned to Capernaum and his home.

****

Jesus awoke to the sounds of the sea in the distance. He looked out a window to west and saw the fertile fields of Gennesaret and people. Crowds of people were already outside his home. *Well Father, it seems my day is already started for Me. I ask you to strengthen Me by the Spirit and enable me to do as you wish today.* Jesus thought.

Well, You have drawn quite a crowd. And yes, I am here and the Spirit will strengthen you. His Father said. ***Oh, and don't cook them breakfast,*** as He laughed. *Really Holy Spirit, I only burnt My meal once. And you didn't even eat it. Gabriel and Michael did.* Jesus grinned

Jesus moved to where they would hear Him best and sat down. He noted in the crowd were Pharisees and teachers of the Law from every corner of Galilee and the surrounding area, as well. *They have been here for days. Some to truly learn, most to try and find fault and accuse Me. And with a crowd this size I am sure someone will say something.* Jesus thought to Himself.

He sat down and began to teach. And as the minutes became hours, the crowd also grew. Jesus noted that the area all around his house and the door was taken. He thought to Himself, *Ah again, no room in the inn, and its getting more full if that's even possible.* He looked on as movement caught His eye. He could see the back of crowd turn and say something to someone. The response moved from one side of the crowd to the other. Almost in a slow wave. He noted it was so tightly packed with people that he doubted if anyone could approach the door or Him. Simon Peter would be happy.

As the minutes passed, Jesus noted the dust catching the sunlight filtering through the windows. It sparkled and danced. He spoke uninterrupted. And He heard a faint scrape. And noticed that the dust was increasing. He stopped speaking. And waited listening.

The crowd was looking intently at Him, expecting more. But he remained quiet. He heard muffled voices and more scraping and now even a deep cracking, as more dust fell from the ceiling.

As Jesus waited, a larger piece of the ceiling tile fell, and shattered in front of Him. Now bathed in sunlight and dust, Jesus looked up and so did the crowd. Jesus smiled to Himself and spoke to the Father. *It seems Father, I now have a new skylight. Is that what it is called?* ***Oh it will be . . . and it may increase your property value.*** Jesus heard the humor in the Father's response.

Jesus watched as the hole in His roof, the *skylight* increased. Soon it was wide enough for a table to fit through. The sunlight was soon blocked by a mat and a person being let down before Jesus. He looked up at the men on the roof. Everyone, tunic less, even some bare chested. *They lowered Him Down with all they had.* Jesus thought. The Holy Spirit filled Him. He saw the man's friend's faith. So, Jesus waited until the man was in full view of all the crowd and the Pharisees.

Jesus then said, "Son, take courage, your sins are forgiven."

The teachers of the Law and Pharisees all thought and spoke among themselves. "This man blasphemes; only God can forgive sins. . ."

Jesus knew what they were thinking and saying among themselves. And continued. "Why are you struggling in your hearts and minds? What is the reason?" He paused. "I ask you which is easier? To say your sins are forgiven, or get up and take your mat and go home?" The man was still and all the people were quiet.

Jesus stood arms wide and finished. "But so that **you** know the Son of Man has authority on the Earth to forgive sins as well . . . He turned to the man on the mat and said with authority. "**I** tell you, **Get Up. Pick up your Mat** and **Go Home**."

The crowd and the Priests were awestruck and silent. Jesus waited still and quiet. Then in a wave of praise, as one they cried out. "We have never seen anything like this! That YHWH God would give this authority to men."

Jesus remained where he was head bowed. *I hope you were glorified Father. I am not sure they understand or see. They have lost so much.* Jesus thoughts finished.

****

After Jesus taught again at the seaside. He was moving from there and saw Levi, son of Alphaeus (Matthew), in his tax booth. Jesus spoke in authority and said, "Follow me." And Matthew got up, left everything and followed Jesus.

Not long after Jesus was at the table in Matthew's House. Matthew wanted to throw a feast in Jesus' honor. And there were many tax collectors and others that were irreligious and frowned upon by people.

Some of the Pharisee's and Scribes were there as well and they complained to the disciples and said, "Why is Jesus eating with tax collectors and sinners, or worse?"

Jesus turned to them and said, "The sick indeed need a physician, not the healthy. I haven't come to call the righteous, but sinners to repentance. But go and learn what this means. I desire compassion, and not sacrifice."

****

It was the Sabbath and Jesus entered the Synagogue. And He saw the Pharisees and Scribes there too. The Spirit of God showed Him a man in their midst, his right hand was deformed, withered and useless. The Pharisees and Scribes were trying to trap Him, so they could accuse Him of breaking the Sabbath.

And they spoke smugly, "Is it lawful to heal on the Sabbath?"

Jesus knowing it was to trap Him said, "I will ask you a question, 'If anyone you had a sheep or oxen and it fell into a ditch on the Sabbath, would you not grab it by the horns and pull it out?"

Jesus surveyed the crowd; they all were still and silent. He called to the man. "Come here to me." Jesus saw his fear. And then his confusion, even trepidation.

"You ask if it is right to do these things, is not this man more valuable than sheep or an ox?" Jesus scanned the crowd again. Still silence. No one moved or spoke a word. He looked at each man in turn with anger. Not one word, not a sound, grieved at their hardness of heart.

He turned to the man and said, "Stretch out your hand." In fear the man did. And immediately it was completely whole, healed, and fully useful.

Jesus left there and went to the mountain to pray. And the Priests and Scribes conferred together how they could best destroy Him.

*****

Jesus arrived at the mountain and was preparing to pray. Jesus was weary and worn. And not a little disappointed with the religious leaders and their lack.

Father, I am weary. More and more people come to Me seeking. Seeking not only the immediate needs of healing, food, shelter, and restoration. But it seems they are slowly turning in faith. He stopped, dropped to His knees and bowed His head. *The Priests and Scribes were supposed to help your people. They were to store up supplies and even feed the poor. The whole nation was to have done so. Now, they rob and steal from your people. They even destroy the sacrifice. Those I confronted in the Synagogue were angrier that I healed on the Sabbath, than the fact of healing one of your children. Why? Is their heart so dark and callous now, that even these miracles don't sway them? Father, they were to point all to you and their need of forgiveness and salvation.* Jesus thoughts ended.

Son, I am glad you came to the mountain to pray. Yes, I know I have watched them strive for holiness and be filled with pride when they thought it accomplished. And yet, they take bribes and steal just as anyone could. This is why We must continue. This is why You must finish what We have started at all cost. And now we need to discuss the next steps and the disciples as a Memorial to the Sons of Israel. And you are right, it is hard to minister with a crowd at your back. But I am not surprised at all. When the Spirit is working He draws men to You. And therefore, as you see, the great crowds. And when your future brothers and sisters allow, they may find it is the same. Miracles follow your message. And the Spirit calls to men's hearts.

Jesus looked to Heaven and spoke aloud. "I am glad I am here. You have seen those around Me. And know their hearts. You know best. And the choices are not easy. Some . . . well, are unique. This may take some time, Father." He chuckled.

Jesus rose to His feet. The night seemed to have flown by and now the morning light reflected the dew, setting the hillside alive with bits of liquid crystal. He moved down the slope to the base of the hill. And He was met by those following Him.

He looked at each person in turn, some were there to truly follow Him and believe his message. Others He knew where there just for the food, healing, and some handouts. He scanned the crowd for the Priests and Scribe. He shook His head sadly. *Not one. None of your Priests have chosen yet Father. But I must choose twelve in honor of the nation and the future Church.* His thoughts ended.

"I am going up the Mount again. I will call those to come up. The rest wait here. Please." Jesus turned and climbed the hill.

One-by-one Jesus called out their names and they walked up the mount to Him and sat with Him.

"Simon, Peter, and Andrew." "James and John." "Phillip" "Bartholomew, Matthew, Thomas, James of Alphaeus, Simon, Judas, and Judas Iscariot."

Jesus looked at the Twelve and spoke with authority. "You will be with me now till the end, and you will go out and preach the Word, cast out demons, heal the sick, cleanse the lepers, and more."

He moved a bit higher on the hill and sat again. And the said to the Twelve. "Since you are here, I need to share with you what it is to follow after Me and be a disciple, or even a follower. Because I hold you all to the higher standard than just the Law or tradition." He paused

Jesus looked out on the hillside as more people came and sat. His followers and the Twelve sat, and it seemed more came by the moment. *So many People. Many truly hungry for God and more. And The Twelve are anxious to learn now and follow me truly. Here I go Father; be glorified.* He thought. And He opened his mouth and spoke with authority.

"Prosperous, happy, fortunate, are the poor in spirit, for theirs is the Kingdom of Heaven. And those who mourn, for they shall be comforted. The same for the gentle, for they shall inherit the Earth. And those who hunger, and thirst for righteousness, for they shall be satisfied. The merciful, for they shall receive mercy. The pure in heart, for they shall see God. The peacemakers, for they shall be called Sons of God. And those who have been persecuted for the sake of righteousness, theirs is the Kingdom of Heaven. And when people insult you and persecute you, and falsely say all kinds of evil against you, because of Me, rejoice and be glad, for your reward in Heaven is great. They treated the prophets the same who were before you. . . ." Jesus paused. He noticed the crowd had grown. And He continued. "You need to be the salt of the Earth; salt preserves. But if it is used up; it is only good to be thrown out, and trampled by men because it cannot be made salted again. You are to be the light of the world. And you know a city on hill, cannot be hid. Why would you put a lamp under a basket? You put light on a stand so it lights all around itself and gives light to all those in the house. You need to let your light so shine before men; that they would see it and glorify God in Heaven. But do not believe even for a moment that I have come to abolish the Law or what the Prophets have spoken. I came to fulfil the Law. And not one letter or stroke of the pen, will pass away until all of it has been accomplished and fulfilled. Whoever disregards even the smallest of these commands will be least in the Kingdom of Heaven, but whoever keeps them, even teaches them will be great. But I tell you truthfully, unless your righteousness surpasses and exceeds that of the Scribes and Pharisees . . . You will not enter the Kingdom of Heaven."

Jesus continued, "You have heard that our forefathers and men of Old were told, 'Do not commit murder. And if they do, they will answer to the Court.' But I tell you that when you are angry with your brother you are guilty. And even when you say you are no good. Or say you are a fool. It is enough that you are in danger of the fires of Hell. So it is better for you to leave your offering at the altar because you know your brother has something against you. Go and reconcile, first to your brother or those you have wronged. And then finish your offering. Or when you go to the Court of Law; if anything can be resolved do it. So that you will not be handed over to the judge for punishment and thrown into prison. Because you know they will not release anyone till everything has been paid for, down to the penny.' "

"And again, 'You were told do not commit adultery.' But truthfully anyone who lusts after a woman, has already committed the act in heart. It would be better if what you see with your eye causes you to stumble, to take it out and throw it away. Or if what you hold in your right hand causes you to stumble, cut it off and throw it away. So that there is less to go into Hell. You were told that if you send your wife away, to give a certificate of divorce. But I say, only if she is unfaithful and because it was allowed by Moses, because of your hard hearts. And again do not make false promises that you will never fulfill. But fulfill you vows before God. And do not swear, or take an Oath by Heaven because it is God's Throne, or the Earth because it is His footstool. Or even Jerusalem because it is the city of the Great King. Also not by your head because you cannot make one hair turn to black or white. But your promises should be yes and do it. Or no and do that. Anything else, is evil and wrong. You have heard it said an eye for an eye. And tooth for tooth. But I tell you do not fight an evil person if possible. If a person slaps you on the cheek turn the other also. Even if someone wants to sue you for your tunic and shirt, go above and beyond. Or if you are asked to walk a great distance go beyond that too. If someone asks something of you, or wishes to borrow from you in need, do not turn them away if you can help."

"I know you have heard it said, 'Love your neighbor and hate your enemy.' But I say to you truthfully, love your enemies and pray for those that persecute you, and you will show yourselves as Sons of God. Why? Because He causes the sun to shine on those that are evil, and those that are good. He causes the rain to fall on the righteous and the unrighteous. If you love and show love only to those that love you, what good is it? What reward is it? You greet your brothers and speak well to them. The tax collectors and Gentiles do those things. Be perfect as your Father in Heaven is perfect."

Jesus continued, "Whatever you do, do not do it to be seen of men. Because if it is your reward in Heaven is Lost. And if you give, or help a poor person, do not blow a trumpet, or make an announcement like the hypocrites in the Synagogues. Do it quietly, secretly, because your Father in Heaven sees it and will reward you. And when you are praying, go to your inner closet and close the door and pray. Your Father in Heaven sees in secret and will reward you. Do not use needless repetition as the Gentiles do. Remember, Your Father knows what you have need of before you even ask. Pray like this for example: **Our Heavenly Father, Holy and Revered is your Name. May your Kingdom be established and Your will Accomplished. Here on Earth just as it is in Heaven itself. Thank you for we know you will give us our daily bread. Thank you that you forgive our debts. Just as we should forgive those that owe us. Thank you that you will not cause us to be tempted or oppressed. Thank you for protecting us against the evil one and his plans. Your Kingdom, Your Power, and Glory is forever.** Remember to forgive others, as Your Heavenly Father has forgiven you.

Jesus continued, "Now, when fasting, do not put on a gloomy face like hypocrites do. Or neglect your appearance like them, to show people you fast. That is their reward. But you should anoint your head, wash your face, so that no one will know but your Father in Heaven. And He sees this and will reward you. Do not live your life to store up treasure here because it is better to store it in Heaven, where moths or rust cannot destroy it or thieves cannot steal it. Remember where your heart truly is, so is your treasure. Your eyes, are the light for your body. So if your eyes are clear, you, are full of light. But if your eyes are dark or you are blind, you will be full of darkness. And if all you have is darkness, how great is that darkness! Remember no one can serve two masters. Because in truth he will love one, and hate the other. And be fully devoted to one, and not the other. You truly cannot serve god and riches."

"Do not worry about what you will eat or drink or what you will wear. Life is more than food and clothes. Remember the birds; they do not plant crops or put crops into barns; yet, your Heavenly Father feeds them. You are worth so much more. How does worrying help you? Does it add even one hour to your life? Are you worried about your clothes? Remember the lilies of the field and how they grow; they do not work, and yet, even Solomon in all his glory and finery was not clothed like them. So if God, your Heavenly Father, clothes even the grass that withers and dies, and then is tossed in the fire. Will He not clothe you? You of small faith. So stop worrying about what you will eat or what you will wear, the Gentiles eagerly struggle with these things. Do you not realize your Heavenly Father knows you need these things? Seek His Kingdom first and His righteousness and all of these things will be yours. Do not worry about tomorrow. Tomorrow will handle itself. Everyday has enough trouble on its own."

Do not judge hypocritically or harshly, but with compassion, so that you will be judged the same way. The same standard you use will be used against you. Why do you point out the speck in your brothers eye, but have a log in your own? How can you say to your brother, let me help you take out that speck, with a log in your own? Hypocrite, first take out the log in your own eye, so then you clearly see and help your brother. Do not give what is of value to people who do not care. Because they will not be grateful and then turn on you. So in prayer, ask the Father, ask, seek, and knock. For everyone who asks receives, and he who seeks finds, and to him who knocks it will be opened. What Father here if His Son asks for bread, would you give him a rock? Or maybe a fish? Would you give him a snake instead? If you fathers being earthly know how to care for your children, don't you think your Heavenly Father will give you good things? So, if you treat others as you want to be treated, you fulfill the Law and Prophets. Enter through the narrow gate. Because broad is the gate and wide is the path to destruction and many go that way. But the way to life is narrow and few find it."

"Watch out for false prophets and teachers; many come looking like sheep, but are truly ravenous wolves. You will be able to tell by the fruit they grow. Can you get grapes from thorn bushes? Or gigs from thistles? A good tree produces good fruit. A bad tree produces bad fruit. A tree cannot produce good and bad fruit. It is one or the other. And if a tree produces bad fruit it is cut and thrown into the fire. So look at the fruit."

Not everyone who cries Lord, Lord will enter Heaven. The person that does the will of My Father in Heaven will. Many will say, 'Did we not prophesy in Your Name or cast out demons or do great miracles in your Name?' I will reply, 'I never knew you depart from Me you who practice Lawlessness.' But if anyone who hears and acts on My words will be considered a wise man. Like one who built his house on the Rock. The rain fell, floods came, winds blew and slammed against the house, but it did not move. Because it was built on the Rock. But the one who does not will be like a foolish man, who built his house on sand. The rain fell, floods came, winds blew and slammed against the house, and the house fell and great was its fall." Jesus finished speaking and all people were amazed at what He taught and that He taught with authority, unlike the Scribes.

CHAPTER 11

THE WIDOW, THE WEEPING WOMAN, THE MAN IN GADARENES

Son, I need you to go to the city of Nain. There is something I need You to do. He heard the Father.

Okay Father. I will.

Jesus traveled toward the city of Nain. He and His disciples were followed by a big crowd. Jesus was almost to the city gate when He met a funeral procession.

This is her. She is a widow. And that is her only son. She has no one else to care for her.

He saw the widow woman and He saw the body that was being carried to the tomb. He saw the crowd of mourners weeping, following her. He was moved with compassion by the Spirit.

He moved to the procession. He came alongside the men carrying the wrapped body. He said, "Wait."

Jesus turned to the widow and said, "Do not weep."

They stopped and looked at Him. Shocked that anyone would stop the funeral and mourning process. He touched the coffin and they stopped completely.

Then Jesus spoke with authority, **"Son, young man, I say arise."**

The young man sat up. Still covered in cloths, he began to pull them away and began to speak. "What is happening? Why am I here?"

Jesus helped the young man down and presented him to his mother.

Jesus saw in the mother's eyes shock, fear, disbelief, and the first glimmer of hope that this was happening that he was there, standing there, alive! That this was real. This was no vison or dream. Tentatively she reached for him. She touched his cheek, and arms, shoulders, chest, stunned. The mother's hands verified that this was tangible reality! The young man smiled and reached for her hand and held it. And then pulled her into a fierce embrace as both their sorrows, and rapturous joy exploded! Their tears flowed and kisses, as they embraced each other. The mourners Jesus saw held that same shock, fear, and incomprehensible joy over the last moments. Then slowly, a giggle, laughter, as joy overtook everyone's sorrow. The mourners were gone. Death had lost, mourning was replaced by joy! And joy became shouting! Everyone cried out, almost in one voice.

"A Great Prophet has shown up among us! God has visited His people!"

The news of the event spread throughout all of Judea and all of the surrounding districts.

****

Jesus was asked by Simon, a Pharisee, to come and dine with him. He agreed. And came to Simon's house. The house was large and well lit. And Jesus noted. *Good sturdy furniture.* He had taken note of it, remembering His time working with Joseph. He was at the table and was reclining. Jesus was looking around the room, noting other prominent religious leaders, and even some city officials. *Well, I have moved up I guess from that feeding trough, huh Father. . . Though, sometimes, I think back on those days, and I have good memories. Not so much of Egypt though,* He thought grinning. He took a drink of water and felt a drop, and then more, on His feet. As He looked, there kneeling at His feet, weeping, was a woman, even He knew, by her attire. *She weeps. Father, her wounds run deep. Rejected by many; abused much, but still longing for love, care, acceptance, and more. Father, do you see? I know You do. . . She now is trying to dry my feet with her hair. Now she is kissing My feet. And anointing them with the vial of perfume.*

The Simon who had asked Jesus to dine was shocked and thought to himself, *if this man is really a prophet, I am not sure He would allow her to touch Him, since she is a sinner.*

Jesus knew what He thought. And turned to Him and said, "Simon, I have something to say to you. And I need to know your answer."

Simon looked at Jesus and said, "Teacher, tell me and I will tell you."

"A money lender had two people that owed him money. One, he owed five hundred denarii, and the other just fifty. And both were unable to pay off the debt. So, he graciously, forgave them both their debt. Simon, which would love him more?" Simon thought for a few moments. Jesus could see him weigh answers between, the teaching of the Law and his mentors, and even, Jesus's notoriety. Soon, he turned to Jesus and said, "I suppose; the one that he forgave the greater debt."

Jesus looked at him and answered, "You judged correctly." And Jesus turned to the woman and said to Simon, "Simon, do you see this woman? *The one you called a sinner,* He thought, "I entered your house here. You gave me no water for my feet. But she from the time she entered has not stopped wetting My feet with her tears, and wiping them with her hair. You gave Me no kiss, but she has not ceased in kissing My feet. You did not anoint My head with oil. But she anointed My feet with perfume. So for these very reasons, I tell you this: her sins, which are many, have been forgiven because she loved much. But he who is forgiven for little loves little." And He turned to the woman, speaking in authority, **"Your sins have been Forgiven."** Jesus knew their thoughts. *Who is this man, who even forgives sins?* Then Jesus finished, **"Your faith has saved you. Go in Peace."**

****

Not long after these events, John the Baptist in prison at Herod's Palace called two of his disciples and said to them, "Ask the Lord Jesus . . . Are you the One we are expecting? Or should we look for someone else?" The disciples left the prison and went to find Jesus. Jesus was in the area of Tyre and Sidon when the men sent from John found Him. Jesus, as always it seemed, even to Him, was surrounded by people in need. And the men coming His way were no different. Jesus could see the anxiousness of the men and the concern of an important errand. Jesus waited quietly, as they began to speak.

"Shalom Yeshua/Jesus, John the Baptist sent us to you." One said. He glanced at the other and continued, "John wanted to know these things. Are You the expected One? Or do we look for someone else?"

The disciple finished. Jesus smiled and turned to the crowd. He called the sick, oppressed, and blind forward. The men watched as He touched all that came to Him. Jesus touched those that were sick and they were made well. He touched men's blind eyes and they saw. He cast out demons and healed the afflicted. The lame walked and the dead were raised up. The men stood by watching, as minutes became hours.

Jesus turned to the men and said, "go and tell john these things. And all that you have seen and heard. The blind receive their sight; the lame walk; the deaf hear; the dead are made alive, and the poor hear the good news of the gospel. Happy, fortunate, prosperous is he who is not offended by Me."

Jesus paused. He watched as John's disciples went their way. Then He turned to the crowd and began to talk of John.

"What were you looking for in that wilderness? Possibly a reed shaken by the wind? Or maybe a man in fine clothing that lives in a palace? Or better a prophet? He was and more. He was written about and the message was this: Behold I send a messenger before You. He will prepare the way for You."

I tell you truthfully, of those born of women, there is no one greater than John. But understand, even the least in God's Kingdom is greater than him."

When All the people heard this, the tax collectors and sinners, acknowledged that God was righteous because they heard from John their need of repentance, but the Pharisees and Scribes, did not. Nor, did they repent.

Son, You need to go across the lake. There is someone on the other side that needs You. And things may get rough. He heard the Father.

That evening Jesus turned to His disciples and said, "Let us go to the other side; there is a need." Jesus turned back to the crowd and dismissed them. Simon and the others helped Him into the boat. The sea was quiet and the breeze was gentle. He moved to the back of the boat and sat down. Simon and the others set sail and they moved toward the other shore. And some followed in their boats.

Jesus felt the breeze on His face and the gentle rock of the boat on the water. Jesus yawned. *Father, it looks like we are headed to the other* side as requested. And if I am not careful, this boat ride may put me to sleep. **Go ahead and rest, your disciples can get you to the other side.**

Jesus looked at Simon and the others calmly watching the sails, as they moved and glided across the lake. The night was cool and the rhythm of boat made it easy to close His eyes. They had helped many and ministered to many. *So why not,* He thought.

He could hear Simon and Andrew laughing and others recounting the events of today. And He heard the wonder in their voice as they spoke. Jesus settled in and soon was asleep.

Simon spoke to Andrew after seeing Jesus asleep. "Well, seems **someone** is tired. Well, we'll wake Him when we get to shore. Gonna be **smooth sailing** tonight." He finished.

"Yeah, just make sure you are pointed to the **other** shore, brother." Andrew laughed.

"I will have you know it was the **fog** that caused that turn around, not my skill as a helmsman, Andrew." Simon answered credulously.

"**Suure**, brother." Andrew replied, as Simon heard snickers from the rest.

Andrew minutes later grabbed Simon by the arm and whispered harshly. "I don't like this at all Simon. I don't like the feel of it."

"Well, you and I know the lake can be fickle. We shouldn't worry too much; it's just a little choppy." He answered feeling the wind pickup.

Simon raised his voice to James, John, and Andrew, as the waves grew larger and the rain began to pelt them. "Tie that sheet line down. And watch that it doesn't tear!" Simon looked up as rain slapped his face. "Terrific!" He said sarcastically and rolling his eyes. "Now we have a squall." He looked back through the heavy rain and saw Jesus still asleep. Simon shook his head and spoke with even more shocked sarcasm. "How can He **sleep** with this **rain** and waves! Oh that's right, Rabbi's and Carpenter's never have to work in squalls." He finished as the others tied the sail to the mast and pulled the oars free of their storage.

Simon almost lost his footing and hit the boat's side, but grabbed the anchor line. The anchor was at least as heavy as two men; still, it barely kept him in the boat. The storm was worsening. The waves began to swell. Just then, he looked up and saw James almost go over because of a wave. Andrew had grabbed his Tunic hard, and leaned back. And the others were holding to the boat's rail. Everyone was fighting to stay in the boat.

"Simon, **Simon!** Wake Jesus now!" John shouted. "This storm is not lessening and I for one don't want anyone sleeping that could help, or if we are to die, everyone should face it as a man!"

Jesus was rudely awakened by angry voices and vigorous shaking and water! Cold water! And the crash of waves over the sides of the boat. Jesus was still shaken and groggy; the water and rain temporarily blinded Him. James, John, Simon, and the others shouted, "Lord! Don't you care! We are going die! Save us!"

"Why are you afraid? Do you still have no faith?"

Jesus stood and spoke in power and authority. **"Wind cease. Waves still. Rain cease."**

Suddenly, it was silent. No Sound, no rain, no wind, no waves … absolute stillness. Simon and the others looked on dumbfounded. Each in turn looked at each other. And all around them there was stillness and quiet. Then they all looked at Jesus. Together they whispered, "What kind of Man is this? That the wind and waves obey Him?"

Simon coughed, wiping his rain soaked hair out of his eyes, as he grabbed an oar. John, Andrew, and James took on oars as well. Soon oars in the water, they moved closer to the shore and the Gadarenes.

Son, as I told you the one who has a need is nearby. And the need is great. The Father said.

Jesus waited until the boat was pulled to shore and then got out. *So, this is the area of the Gadarenes. Well, I have heard stories, but the Father says there is someone with great need.*

Jesus walked on the shore and began to move up a hill, suddenly He noticed a man running toward Him. Jesus stopped, as the man drew closer He saw his wild hair and grime covered body. He saw the scars on his arms and legs, and most of his body. He also saw he was completely naked. Jesus waited. He could see the black smudge of darkness following along with him like a ghost image, or like eyes having double vision with blurred edges.

The man was big and lean, but the evidence of his ordeal had stolen strength and vitality from him. He moved, hunched over, as if under a great weight. The man knelt before Jesus and shouted, **"What business do we have with each other, Jesus, Son of the Most High God? I beg you not to torment me?"** The raw, guttural, grating voice finished.

Jesus could see the bruises and scars of attempted capture, or worse still, the effects of broken chains and beatings, self-inflicted, or otherwise. *So the rumors are true. Night and day they say he runs among the tombs and screams. He is seized by demons often and is thrown against jagged rocks. He also cuts himself because he is forced to. He has no power or control. He is a helpless puppet and slave to the demons every whim and sadistic torture. No Power, no voice, no strength, no hope, no peace. Not even silence. Only the ceaseless echo of voices in his mind and ears. Driving him on and on. No rest. They say no one can hold him. No chain, no shackles. Well that will change soon.* Jesus thought.

Jesus spoke with power and authority. **"What is your name?"**

"Legion." Jesus heard the multitude of voice echoes. **"Do not send us to the abyss."** He looked from Jesus to the hillside nearby him. And said **"There, there, them, them."** Jesus looked and a herd of pigs was on the hillside. A great herd of 2,000.

Jesus spoke **"Go."** And the legion left the man who fell to the ground unharmed. The legion then entered the herd of pigs. Jesus watched as the herd let out an eerie tortured cry, as one, raced down the hillside to the lake, and drowned.

Jesus looked up on the hill and saw the herdsman. As they ran in terror over the hill, toward the city. When the townspeople heard the story told them by the herdsman, they went out to find Jesus.

Jesus watched as the city council and elders came toward Him. They were followed by the herdsman. Everyone one of them . . . terrified and anxious. And as Jesus waited, more and more people followed; they came from the countryside to see what had happened.

Jesus was seated with the man who was fully clothed and free of the demons. He was talking to Jesus and his disciples.

A great crowd stood in front of Jesus and the man that was freed of the demons. They knew him and they saw him clothed and whole. Jesus sat quietly, as the herdsman again recounted to all those around the events as they knew them. The man also remained quiet.

Jesus could see the anxiousness of the men and leaders. And the air of fear grew. Jesus surveyed the crowd. He saw, as each person and elder recognized the man and their shock at the man now fully clothed and quiet. *I wonder how long they had watched him be otherwise. The whole city knows of him. And it seems the whole countryside. But why are they afraid? Shouldn't they rejoice? Their fear and terror is over. There is no more need of worry or anything. People can travel this way again. And the city can thrive again. Father, what is it? Why are they still afraid??* Jesus thought

One of the elders of the city moved closer to Jesus. And said, "You need to leave."

Jesus looked into his eyes and noted fear yes, but more than that, He noted *rejection.* He looked at the crowd and all the elders, and *knew . . . Father, they want no part of this. They have seen the miracle and they want nothing to do with it, nothing. They don't even want to acknowledge it. They see this man changed, whole, and they want nothing of it.*

Son, the lies of the enemy/Lightbringer/Satan are so strong with some. He blinds them to even reality. I love all men and I seek their redemption and wholeness. But if they make that choice, to tell me no, and I know it is final, I honor it. Hell will be full of those making that same choice. Men's salvation just as the Lucifer's/Lightbringer/Satan, rejection . . . Is honored. This is their choice, though my heart breaks. And I chase, work, seek, and cry out to them, till that final moment, where the choice cannot be changed. That is why you are here. Why again You must be the sacrifice, they cannot, but You can. And You being God, as pure, holy, and fully man without sin can make that sacrifice; then redemption will be complete and finished.

The elder spoke again. This time he was joined by the herdsman and people of the city. "Sir, You need to leave. Please leave here." Jesus responded. "You are sure? You truly want me to go?"

The elder seemed to stand straighter and with effort repeated, "Yes, we elders and those of the city, and this area, ask You to leave."

The man that was freed and looked on in shock. He looked at each one in turn. What met him was hard, cold faces, determined to remove Jesus and him, as well. He turned to Jesus. And spoke in earnest, "Take me with You. I want to follow You, please, after all you have done. Can I not follow?" He pleaded with Jesus.

Jesus looked into his eyes and spoke tenderly. "Go back to your house and your family. And tell of the great things God has done for you."

The man nodded sadly, then hugged Jesus. He began to walk away, as Jesus and the disciples got into the boat. Jesus heard the Father.

Son, just so you know, he will go home. And he will do as you asked and more. I see him sharing throughout all of Decapolis and more. Jesus felt the Father's joy.

****

And as Jesus returned to Capernaum and home. There was a great crowd waiting on the shore. The crowd that had waited, welcomed him. So Jesus stayed at the shore with the boat and the disciples.

Jesus watched as an official of the Synagogue approached. His name, Jesus knew was Jairus. He fell at his feet, weeping.

Jesus saw his anguish and heard Jairus through the sobs. "Jesus, my little daughter, my **only** daughter, is near death. I beg you, **please**, please come and lay your hands on her, that she will get well and live. And not die!"

Jesus got up and said to the official, "I will go with you."

Jesus began walking with Jairus and the disciples. Soon Jesus found he was surrounded, as the crowd pressed closer and closer in on Him. Jesus almost had to push people to move.

At that very moment, in the crowd, barely able to move herself, was a woman. She had seen the Synagogue official kneel before Jesus. She was frightened. Jesus was her only hope now. She had battled for days in her heart over this choice. She knew according to Law she should not be in public. But what choice did she have. She pushed against the people in front of her and moved a step closer to Jesus than before. *This is almost like an ocean,* she thought, as the crowd moved as one to the official's house. Determined she pushed harder, as she could see Him, closer now. And the crowd shifted a little, and she caught sight of his chlamys, (or cloak), and prayer shawl with tzitzit (fringes). She could almost reach Him now. But the crowd surged and moved. She was so close now. *Fear, dread; and what? Excitement,* she felt. *Just a bit father. Oh YHWH help me! I can't go on without . . . Help!* The crowd shifted again. She grabbed in desperation and caught a part of His prayer shawl.

Her mind raced back to the days of anguish, fear, and hopelessness. She heard the doctor's voice and his proclamation of her doom and her hopes of death. "I am sorry, truly sorry. There is nothing more we can do. And you have spent your husband's fortune to find a cure! We have done all we know. **I am truly sorry**." The doctor's words echoed in her mind. And then her days of battling the decision. *I need help and no one can help me! Not the **doctor's**, or seems even the Priests, though **YHWH knows**. He can heal. And He promised healing for His people. Who was that new Prophet? Jesus/Yeshua of Nazareth? He is said to do miracles. But who am I? I cannot even go in public. He would never come to Me, or My house. But **maybe**, if I can get to Him. **YHWH** knows my heart and I am sure I can be forgiven for breaking the Law to get the healing I need. I must find a way! **I must!***

She grabbed the tzitzit. And her heart rang with, ***if I can just touch, even, just His clothes, I can be healed!*** And Jesus, at that moment felt healing power flow out from Him and said, "Who touched me?"

The disciples near said, "Jesus, look around You, You see this crowd. Yet, You asked, who touched me?"

The woman stopped. She knew the moment she had touched His clothes, she was completely, totally healed. Jesus turned. Looking into her eyes, she stepped closer in tears trembling and fell at His feet. Jesus looked at her and she began to speak. "I touched you. I had no other choice. All my husband's money and mine is gone. And for twelve years, I have sought to find a cure for my illness. The doctors can find no cure. The Priests have no answer and I had no hope until now. I know I have broken the Law, as Jairus may tell you. But I have no one to help anymore. I am sorry. I will leave," she said.

Jesus looked at her and said gently, "**Daughter**, your **faith** has made you whole. Go in peace."

They moved on to Jairus's house. Jesus saw the front door open and another official move toward them. He glanced at Jairus and saw recognition dawn on his face. The new official spoke quietly, 'Jairus, there is no need for you to bother the Teacher any longer." The man grabbed Jairus's shoulders and finished. "I am sorry Jairus; your daughter is dead." Jairus heartbroken, began to slump. But Jesus turned to Jairus speaking with authority, "Do not be afraid. But believe."

Jesus saw and heard the loud commotion of their weeping and mourning. They moved inside. And Jesus spoke again with authority. "What is all this noise? She is not dead, but she is asleep." The whole room mocked and laughed for they had seen her die. However, Jesus told the mourners and the mockers to leave. Once they were sent from the house, only His disciples, and Jairus and his wife remained. Jesus walked into the room where Jairus's daughter was. He said with authority "child arise" and he took her hand and she stood and came out of the room where she was lying.

"Get her something to eat." Jairus and his wife hugged their daughter fiercely and wept for joy. Simon Peter, James, and John rejoiced. "Do not tell anyone."

Jesus was returning to His house in Capernaum. And as He was going He heard two men crying out. "Son of David, have mercy on us! Son of David have mercy on us!" as they followed Him to His door. Jesus walked to His door and went inside and sat down. Jesus took a deep breath and the men entered His house. He could see they were blind.

He said, "Gentlemen, do you believe I am able to do this?"

"Yes," they said in unison.

Jesus stood and moved them, then touched their eyes. Jesus spoke with authority, "It will be done according to your faith."

Immediately they could see.

"Now, both of you, tell no one." Jesus said sternly and they left Jesus' home.

Jesus heard the Father, *You know they are even now, telling everyone*. Jesus thought He heard the Father chuckle.

Jesus walked outside His house and looked out on to the lake. *Father, these last few days have been full. Thank you all for Your guidance and help. Those blind men We healed, you are right, they will not be quiet. And most I asked not to tell, didn't listen. It will be nice when I don't have to concern Myself anymore with it. But I will do as you have asked. Thank you for hearing and listening Father.*

Son, I understand, We planned these things to cover all aspects of the redemption and salvation of men. We didn't want them to turn to You just because of the miracles, but see You and recognize You for who you are. They were to take the prophet's messages and the Law and see the hope. See a Messiah, Savior, Redeemer, Friend, and more. One day faith will be the only reason. Men will repent of their sin truly and turn back to Us, and be redeemed and made whole. And all the works of the Devil will be destroyed; men will be no longer bound, or bowed by sin, sickness, disease or Satan's killing, stealing, or destroying.

And speaking of the Devil's/Lightbringer's, Satan's work. . . Jesus heard light knock on the door. And He went back inside and opened the door.

Jesus looked at the small group outside his door. As Jesus looked again, He saw the smudge of blackness and ghost image of darkness on the man. The people with him, fearful at best, with pleading eyes, said, "Can you help him? He cannot speak. And we know of no one else that could help."

Jesus turned and closed His door and walked out to the front of His house. He was met by an even bigger crowd. Jesus sighed. He looked at the man and Jesus said, "I will help." He spoke with authority, "**Come out**."

Jesus waited quietly. The man looked at him, stunned, unsure, questioning. The people that had brought him waited too. They too were looking to see what, if anything, would change.

Then the crowd and the man's friends heard. "Well, am I okay? How do I know I am free of this bondage . . .?"

Jesus smiled and his friends smiled. They even began to laugh, as the amazed crowd all around was heard to say, "We have never seen anything like this in all of Israel!"

And again Jesus looked over the all the crowd and had compassion on them. He shook his head and breathed deep, as He knew another day of healing and deliverance had begun.

He spoke softly to the Father, as He watched the man laughing, crying, and hugging those near him.

"Father, they are all like frightened, injured, broken sheep with no shepherd or one to care for them. How much they have truly lost." He finished.

****

Jesus was at Capernaum with the Twelve that he had sent out with authority; they had returned. He was going to hear a report of all that happened, when Jesus heard a knock at the door. He opened the door and He found disciples of John. They were asking to speak with Him. He brought them inside and sat down. Everyone waited to hear what John's disciples would say.

One of the men said, "Jesus, I bear bad news. It is hard, even for me, to say it. But I need to tell You all that has happened. I will try to make clear everything." Jesus listened, as he continued, obviously overwrought with emotion.

"As you know, Herod Tetrarch, liked to listen to John. Though sometimes John had said he was confused, or perplexed by what he had heard. He would often speak with Herod. But this time, it was different. John told Herod what he was doing was wrong. And that he did not have a right to have Herodias as his wife. And as you know, for his wife's sake, Herod put him in prison at Machaerus. And for the most part, John was content. And Herod would bring him out and they would talk.

Then, one day, his birthday actually. He was throwing a great party, and everyone was there. And Salome entertained with dancing.

Now Herod was afraid of John. And he knew the people believed him to be a prophet, as you know. And he kept him alive and safe because he wanted to ensure his reign and Rome's favor."

The disciple paused. Clearly overcome by the message and situation. Jesus waited and listened along with the Twelve.

He found his voice again after a few minutes and continued.

"Whether it was Herod's choice or not and I think not. Salome had danced so that Herod was heard to say, "I will give you anything, even to half of my kingdom." He was fighting to keep his voice from breaking, as he continued.

"They say she thanked Herod and she rushed out of the party to find her mother, Herodias, who even John knew. She hated him for more, than just pointing out their sin. She hated him and was looking to destroy him. But Herod, worried maybe, over causing rebellion or preventing one, had tucked him away again. It was told us by a servant that had overheard Salome and Herodias speaking that Herodias told Salome. "Ask for the head of John on a silver platter." So, she went to Herod and gave her answer.

And of course, Herod, in spite of his feelings for John, gave the order."

He was weeping now. Jesus touched him. After a few moments, he finished.

"We, at least, were able to take his body and put him into a tomb. I am sorry Jesus to tell you of his death."

Jesus stood and looked at all those in the room in turn. He bowed his head and was silent. They all waited to see what Jesus would do. Jesus spoke to everyone there.

"We need to go away. We need to go to a secluded place and rest. We ourselves, and you, as well," looking at the disciples of John.

Jesus continued. "We will head toward Bethsaida and possibly find a quiet spot. Maybe not too far from there."

So they all got into a boat and began the trip across the lake toward Bethsaida. Soon they found a quiet spot and began to mourn, and attempt to rest.

The Twelve gave their report about all that had happened. Marveling at the miracles and things done by the Spirit's power, Jesus went up the mountain and sat down with His disciples. He began to rest. He looked out from there and saw people coming from everywhere toward Him.

He moved down the hill. Jesus again was moved with compassion and began to teach and heal all who were sick and in need. Minutes turned into hours, as Jesus tirelessly spoke and healed.

Jesus finished His speaking and healing of those around Him. He took a few moments to stop, breathe, and look upon the great sea of people. As far as Jesus could see, there were people. In the distance He saw the Sea of Galilee and the reflection of the late afternoon sun. ***Son,*** He heard Father say, ***You have met many needs today. And fulfilled Isaiah's words fully. But, not every need has been met. Look there are men, women, and children here. You have healed bodies and souls. But they need to know I can provide for both spiritual hunger, and physical as well. I am, I was, and will always be Jehovah Jireh. We have healed things that men may never see with earthly eyes. But they need to eat.***

So, what am I to do? He thought. ***Have the Twelve feed them, as a testimony to the nation and the one I am going to borrow from. This may surprise the Twelve,*** the Father finished.

"Phillip come here!" Jesus smiled. And Phillip rushed to Him, as the others followed. Simon Peter and the others were looking concerned, as Jesus turned to Phillip and said, "Do you see the people? Where can we go and buy bread that they may eat?"

Phillip looked over the crowd and said sheepishly, "Even if we had more than 200 denarii, that would only be a morsel for those here. I do not know."

"It is late; we need to send them away, so they can go into the towns; and buy food, and find lodging." The twelve agreed.

Jesus looked at them each in turn and said "you; give them something to eat."

"What do we have? How can we feed this many?" They agreed together.

Jesus said, "Go and look." *Father, have they forgotten what you did already? They told of how even demons were subject to them, and how you cared for them. I am sorry Father that they don't see.* His thoughts finished,

So the Twelve went out into the sea of people, to look. A little later Andrew, Simon Peter's brother said, "I found a lad; he has five barley loaves and two fish. But what are they among so many?"

Jesus held up His hand and said to the Twelve. "Make the people sit in groups of fifty."

Jesus watched as the Twelve moved among the people and they began seating everyone. After a time they were fully seated, as Jesus looked at them. He laughed to Himself, smiling. *Father, there are five thousand men, women, and children. You aren't worried are you?* **No Son,** He knew the Father laughed**, I will be fine. I hope that the nation, the Twelve and these here, understand what We show. I am. I do provide and more**. Jesus smiled again, then He looked to Heaven and blessed the loaves and the fish.

Jesus broke the bread and fish, as He moved among the people giving the food away. Jesus continued to walk among the crowd and pass out food. And many asked for more. Jesus looked at them and never turned them away. After a long while, all of them had been satisfied, Jesus also sat and ate, alongside the Twelve. They too were satisfied.

Jesus stood and said to them, "Gather up in baskets all that is left. Lose nothing. Now go!" He watched as the Twelve gathered the baskets and moved among crowd again. The lad who had offered his lunch came to Jesus. Jesus smiled and thanked him.

"Do not worry, son, you gave to the Father, and He will take care of you, I promise. You will see." Jesus finished. The lad smiled and said, "I was glad I gave it. My mother taught me to share. But it was more fun to see that you helped feed all these people with it."

Simon Peter and the Twelve came back breathing heavy. And said, "We did as you asked. I have no idea what we will do with it . . . But there are twelve baskets full. And nothing is on the ground or lost."

Jesus smiled at the lad, hugged him and said, "I believe we need to give you back the lunch the Father borrowed."

The boy laughed. "Wow! I am not sure what my mom will do with twelve baskets! She didn't think I would finish what I had."

Jesus laughed with everyone.

Jesus spoke to crowd and all who would hear.

"If you want to truly follow Me you must first deny yourself, and take up your cross daily, and then follow Me. If anyone wishes to save his life, he will lose it. But whoever loses his life, for my sake, will save it and find it. How does it profit you to gain all that the world has, yet lose or forfeit your very soul? You see, if you are ashamed of Me and My words, the Son of Man will be ashamed when He comes in glory with the Father and the angels. There are those here that will not taste death, till they see the Kingdom of God.

Jesus heard those around him say, "This is the prophet that was foretold to come into this world."

Jesus went up the hill and the Twelve followed. He sat down and asked them, "Who do the people think I am?" He waited for the Twelve to respond. He could see concern and question on each face. And even hesitation to speak.

Finally, some said, "John the Baptist, Elijah, or one of the other prophets that has risen again." Jesus smiled and waited looking at each one in turn.

"Okay, but who do **you**, believe I am?" He waited quietly, as the question registered on every heart and mind. Again Jesus saw question, concern, and hesitation. It was Simon Peter who broke the awkward silence of the moment with, "You are the **Messiah**, the **Son** of the living God."

Jesus smiled and said, "Yes, Peter **I am**. And the Father revealed it to you. But, do not tell anyone because I must go through many trials and be rejected by all the elders, chief priests and Scribes. And be killed and be raised the third day."

Jesus looked at each of them in turn. He saw their shock, confusion, and worry. But they were quiet and did not respond to what was said.

Jesus broke the silence. "I need you all to go to the other side, while I send the crowd away. And then I am going up farther to pray," Jesus said. The Twelve, in extreme reluctance, began to move. They moved down the hill, toward shore and the boat.

Jesus moved down the hill with them and began speaking to crowd. "It is late and much has been done today, you need to rest. Go home and rest, please."

The great sea of people didn't move at first. Then, one by one, or small groups, they moved to their boats. Some began the trek into town, or took the paths, that earlier brought them to Jesus. More and more people came by on their way back home. They said to Jesus, "You are the prophet. You have done great things here! Surely, You should be our King!" a large group said.

Father, do you hear? And attempt to change our plan. Lightbringer/Lucifer/Satan was subtle this time. **Yes, though you are the King rightly, it is not according to our plan. It would not accomplish what is needed.** The Father finished.

Jesus responded, "No, it is not because of the truth that you want me to be King, but because you were fed. Go home."

After all the people had left, Jesus turned and headed back up the hill to pray. "Father, I need time with you and Spirit. More decisions need to be made."

Jesus knelt and prayed. He poured out His heart to the Father and Spirit. And the communion was sweet.

Father he said, "After a day like today, this is nice to be with You and the Spirit. To know Your presence and hear Your voices, I am being refreshed. I hope that My future brothers and sisters can find this too. Communion. Father, I hope they can learn this, and grasp it. Because without You, they can do nothing. Spirit of God you will be busy I am sure, soon. I hope they will understand and know it is their right as Your children, to abide with you and commune with You, walking everyday with you."

Yes, the Father said. **They need to know these things, but. . . if they can't hear or don't know, their life with Us will be bland and more work than needed, and some may make preferences into law, and walking in the Spirit, drudgery.**

"Well, let's hope that doesn't happen often." Jesus continued praying and talking with Father.

****

CHAPTER 12

WALKING ON WATER, FEED THE HUNGRY, HEALING WITH COMPASSION

"Simon! James! John!" Andrew shouted. "We are getting nowhere!" as a wave bounced the boat backwards.

Simon Peter pulled with all he had on the oar, and it gave only a little. He remembered the wind and waves had begun lightly as they left the shore. But soon the wind was strong enough that they barely made it one mile off shore. And they had to pull the sail in. Now, it was even worse, and that was hours ago.

Thomas chimed in, "The only thing I got is sick, and stuck in this tub!" as it bounced to the side.

"Hey, it's a good boat! We got it cheap!" Matthew cried

"Why is it lately that whenever we get into a boat, we have trouble?? Tell me that will you!" James Alpheus shouted sardonically.

"We are fisherman! We have worked this lake for years! It shouldn't be this hard!" James shouted.

"Oh really! Don't forget **HE** said, 'Go to the other side!' " Nathaniel said with sarcasm, as Bartholomew strained at the oar and said, "Go to the other side! He says, huh, **right!**"

"You have got to be kidding me! We have only gone 4 miles in this wind!" John shouted.

Thaddeus said. "Somebody else can row! I can't do this anymore!"

The boat rocked hard and was pushed to the left by a swell. Then it dropped four feet, as the other wave troughed. Moments turned to minutes, hours it seemed days. The waves and wind were relentless. And there were no signs of it letting up.

Jesus came down off the mountain and could see in the distance a boat, **their** boat still battling the waves and wind. "Father," Jesus said, "It's late. They should have been farther along than this. What do you want Me to do?" Jesus waited for the Father's response.

Jesus felt the wind on His face and saw the waves crash on shore. He looked to Heaven and still heard nothing. But the waves in the distance and the wind rushing past Him.

"Okay, no advice?" He waited again.

"Okay, I am just going to head across the lake. And I won't interfere if you are testing them. But if it's Lightbringer, I will." Jesus finished. He tightened His belt and checked His sandals and made sure his prayer shawl would not blow away and stepped toward the shore. As He stepped out onto the rough wave tossed lake, all around Him, He saw wave after wave … big swells and small swells. And with each step, the waves smoothed out in front of Him, as He walked. However, on both sides, the waves continued. "So, Father, this is interesting, I know you are allowing the wind and rough sea. And I also know, there must be a purpose. Do you want to share it with Me?"

He looked ahead, beyond the swells of rough water now, some waist high, or more, and saw the boat in the distance. He could see the Twelve and their rowing. Jesus could see the strain on each face and muscle.

Maybe, I should just pass by them and meet them on shore. Right Father? He thought. *Or Not? Which will it be??*

Jesus kept walking steadily and was able to see more clearly, even though the lake spray sometimes got in the way. *Well, at least the moon is out and I have a clear path. But I wonder, what I look like with all this wind and spray. . .* He thought. Then it happened!

He saw Andrew holding onto the mast and heard him cry "**Look!** . . . On the water, it's a **ghost!** Look all of you!" He heard echoes on the water, "What! A Ghost? How can there be. We're going to die!"

Quickly Jesus cried, "Do not be afraid! It is I, Jesus/Yeshua!" He moved closer to the boat.

While He was still yards from the boat, and as the boat was tossing, He heard Simon Peter shout, "Lord, if it is **You**, tell me to come to you on the water!" And Jesus spoke in authority, **"Come to Me."** And Peter dropped his oar and stood. The boat was still moving. But Simon worked his way to the rail. Then he climbed over.

Jesus watched, as Simon Peter's feet touched the water and the waves where he stepped flattened. He saw astonishment and shock on Simon Peter's face. Peter stepped again; the water in front of him smoothed out. But the lake around him still bore evidence to the wind and its gusts.

Well, Father, what do you think? Boldness? Faith? Courage? Stubbornness? Jesus thought.

Jesus watched, as Peter took another step and another. He could see Peter's face, smiling, and he was wide-eyed in wonder at standing on the water! Jesus stepped closer and closer . . . and then He watched as Peter's wonderment stopped! He watched as the adrenalin and the faith of the moment began to fade and human reality, reason, broke into his mind.

Jesus saw Simon Peter lose focus on His Words and promise. Simon Peter looked to his left and saw the wave swell, and felt the wind rushing past. And then He looked right and saw another swell and saw the effects of the wind and the saw the spray! Simon Peter then paused. Simon Peter, in that briefest of moments, feared! Doubt, had found a place in his heart! And doubt brought with it, greater fear, and disbelief! And Jesus watched as He began to drop into the water and the waves on either side slammed against him! He saw stark terror in Simon Peter's eyes, as the water was at his waist in a moment! And Simon Peter cried out! "Lord! Save me!" in desperation.

Jesus was there in a moment! He extended His hand, grasping Simon Peter's hand and lifted! Jesus looked into Simon Peter's eyes. And the moment froze! Jesus spoke, as Simon Peter steadied himself, and relief flooded his being!

"Why did you lose faith Simon? Why is it so little?" Jesus finished. And they walked three steps, and got into the boat. And The Twelve welcomed them gladly. The wind and waves stopped! Everything was still! They looked around and found they were already at the shore! Astonishment dawned on every face! And they all fell down and worshipped Jesus! And said as one. "You truly are the Son of God!"

****

The Son of God returned to the present and pain! Jesus repeated the pattern again, push up on the one heel, and grab what little breath He could! There was little relief now. And His breathing was labored.

The events are coming even faster now! As death closes in, with each beat of My heart and pain! My being hurts! But there will be no relief until the fulfillment of God's commands is not yet! If only, like those in Gennesaret, I would . . . He raced back to that day!

They had come, He and the disciples, to the area of Gennesaret. The word had gotten out to the whole region that He was there. Jesus watched as people from everywhere ran and brought pallets with people on them. Jesus marveled, as He walked throughout the area and taught. Everywhere He stepped foot in the cities, villages, the countryside, even in the market places, there were pallets of the sick. The Men that brought them begged Jesus just to let them touch the fringe of His shawl, and everyone who did was healed, completely cured.

****

Son, Your calling is to the children of Israel first, but there are some that are in need that are not. Go to the area of Tyre and Sidon. Work needs to be done there. And then go to Decapolis and to Capernaum again.

Okay Father, I will. Jesus thought.

Jesus and the Twelve began the trek to the area of Tyre. He was glad to be away from Galilee and the cities for a while. And He was glad to look on the other sea for a while. Maybe rest after He did what the Father wanted, of course. He remembered the time of Joshua and the Tribe of Asher. And the tribes on that side of the Jordan. It would be nice to look out on a true sea.

Jesus entered the house near the sea hoping that since it was paid for discreetly, that maybe, just maybe, no one would know. And He could possibly have a day or two of quiet rest, even though the Father had given Him a task.

The morning was clear and bright. The waves gently touched the sand and the Twelve were out looking for a fishing spot. He laughed. "You can take a man from Galilee, but . . . wait that's not right!"

Well Father, we are here. I hope we can rest a bit. But, if not, We will begin. I will go out soon and share with the people. The Tribe of Asher was here once. I hope there is a Synagogue. He thought.

A Canaanite woman, a Syrophoenician, heard that Jesus was in the house. She came and cried out to Jesus, "Have Mercy on me! Lord, Son of David. . . Please, please help my daughter! She is cruelly possessed; can You help her and heal her?"

Jesus didn't say a word. He saw her fear, and He saw her anguish and desperation. But He said nothing.

She left Him and she ran to the Twelve, and asked them to help, pleading! Sometime later the Twelve came to Jesus.

"We need you to send that woman away! She keeps asking for her daughter to be healed!" one of the Twelve said.

And another chimed in, "She won't leave us alone!"

Again; Jesus heard her cry. And she repeated her plea! "**Please**," sobbing, **please!** Help my daughter! She is helpless, powerless!"

Jesus looked at her, and finally spoke. "I have been called to the children of Israel. And it is not right to give to dogs and strangers what is the children's bread."

She fell at his feet again, "Lord," weeping, "that is true. But even dogs; eat the crumbs that fall from their master's table!"

"Woman, your faith is great! And Because of your answer, go home now, your daughter is free! The demon gone."

*****

Jesus left there and went to the area of Sidon and all throughout the region, even to Decapolis, teaching and healing people. And He began to return to Galilee and Capernaum. As always, Jesus noted that He was followed by a large crowd. Some people brought a man to Him who was deaf and could not speak clearly. They begged Jesus to lay His hands on him. "Our friend," Jesus heard, "is deaf. And he cannot speak, nor be understood. Can you heal him?"

Jesus looked at the man. He could see concern and confusion, even embarrassment. So, Jesus took him by the hand and found a place away from the crowd and noise. He looked to Heaven and sighed deeply.

Father, I couldn't even hide away. And the people came from everywhere. I helped the woman, and I will help this man as well. He looks as if he's ashamed because of coming to Me, almost as if he is a burden. That's not what is true. You want people to come to You. You want to heal and make whole. Jesus thought.

Jesus cupped the man's face in His hands and looked into his eyes. He held him like that a minute or two. Then He took His hands away and stuck a finger in each ear and spit on His finger, touched His tongue and spoke in authority, **"Ephphatha, Be opened!"** All at once the man could hear and speak clearly.

"Since you can hear me now, don't tell anyone. You can return to your friends."

After the man had left. ***Son,*** the Father started.

"I know, I know, they aren't keeping quiet." Jesus said. They both laughed. And it was proclaimed throughout the region of Jesus - **He has done all things well! He can cause the deaf to hear and mute to speak!**

And Jesus again was at Bethsaida where He taught the people. And after a few days of teaching, He turned to the Twelve and said, "I cannot let these people go away hungry! All of them have stayed here for at least 3 days. And some have traveled a long way to stay here. My Spirit cries out for compassion. And if I let them go . . . many will faint on the way home or worse. But where can we find bread enough for them?" He looked at the Disciples and they said, "Where can we find enough Bread?"

Jesus asked, "How much Bread do we have?"

One of the Twelve said, "Seven Loaves."

Jesus asked again. "Any fish?" *Father, it seems silly to me to have to ask fisherman if we have fish.* He thought.

"We have a few small ones," another said.

"Have them sit down and you will distribute the food." He said to the Twelve. Jesus looked to Heaven and blessed the bread and the fish. Then He began to break off pieces and have the Twelve pass them out. And so the Twelve passed out the bread and fish until everyone was full and satisfied. Jesus told them again, "Gather up the leftovers in the baskets." The Twelve did so. And they had seven baskets full.

Even as Jesus finished this the Pharisees came out to Him and began to argue with Him and ask for a sign from Heaven to test Him! He stopped and said nothing for a few moments. *Father, why do they look for a sign! When will they just believe!* He thought. "No, Jesus responded. "No sign will be given this generation!" He moved off into the boat and left the area. And as they were crossing the lake to the other side Jesus spoke to them. "Beware the leaven of the Pharisees and Herod."

The Twelve were nervous and anxious because they only had one loaf of bread. And they whispered to one another.

"Peter was supposed to get bread." "No, no it was James." "What! I wasn't. Phillip was!" "Wait! Judas has the purse, he was supposed to!"

Jesus said to them all. "Why are whispering among yourselves, because you don't have more bread? Do you not understand? Are your hearts so hard? Do your eyes not see? Or your ears not hear? Do you Remember when I fed the five thousand? He paused looking at each one. How many baskets full of leftovers did you gather from it?"

"Twelve." They all said sheepishly.

Jesus nodded, "Yes, yes you did. And now . . . from the feeding and breaking of bread for the four thousand?"

"Seven." The Twelve said weakly.

Jesus looked at them in turn. Leaning against the mast. "Do you still, not understand?"

Soon after at Bethsaida another group brought Jesus a blind man. And of course the crowd of onlookers was large. Again Jesus took the blind man by the hand out of the village and away from the crowd. Jesus spit in the man's eyes and laid His hands on him. And He asked the man, "What do you see?"

The man blinked and turned his head. He looked around. "I see," he paused, "I see, people tall as trees walking around." So Jesus touched him again and laid His hands on him. And the man could see clearly and well.

"Now that you are healed. Go home. Do not even go back into the village." Jesus said.

****

As Jesus and the Twelve were walking on the Sabbath through the lower city, they saw a man that was blind. Jesus saw the place of the alms cup and his worn clothes. *His place here in Jerusalem has been established. This street is along a main thoroughfare. You never intended Father, that anyone not see, move, or live. You wanted men to thrive; and yet, sin has killed stolen and destroyed more than they know.* He Thought.

Yes, Son, He heard the Father, ***Men were to live with Us. They were to truly care for the Earth, and all that is in it. And if anything else was needed, to come to Us and ask. So they may truly live in peace with no sickness, no disease, or struggle. Adam cost them more than they understand, or could believe.***

As Jesus paused and looked at the blind man, one of the Twelve, asked, "Rabbi, who sinned, that this man is blind? He looks like it has been from birth? Did he? Or his parents?"

Jesus looked at the man and then the disciples. And said, "Neither. He didn't sin, nor his parents. He was blind that the glory and power of God would be shown here, in Jerusalem, and beyond, as a testimony to the Scribes, Pharisees and Elders. And as testimony to the nation of Israel. We must work while it is day and do the works of the Father because there will be a day coming where no one can work any longer. And a day when night falls, and no one can work at night. While also I am here, I am the light of the world."

Jesus bent down and spit on the ground. He then made a small amount of mud. He scooped up the mud in His hand. He walked to the blind man who felt the nearness of someone. He felt the man flinch and held up his hands for protection. Jesus touched his shoulder. Peace flooded the man. And then Jesus put the mud on his eyes. Without a word Jesus finished. And then He said, "Now, go and wash your eyes in the pool of Silaom and see."

So, Jesus and the Twelve raised him to his feet and pointed him in the direction of the pool. He made his way to the pool. He heard the familiar sound of the street and he remembered how many steps to the corner, and then how many steps to the other street.

I don't understand. How is what this man has done going to help me? He heard water. He heard people milling around. And asked.

"Shalom, can any tell me, if this is the pool of Silaom?"

"Yes, this is it, why?" A gruff voice said.

"I was told to wash my eyes. Can you guide me to the pool?"

"Why do I. . ." He heard a slap! Then a woman's voice. "Of course, my husband will guide you!"

The man in the gruff voice said, "Here, let me help you. Here you go! The edge is here. And the basin is directly in front of you. The fountain washes the basin well, so there is no need to worry about the little dirt I see."

The blind man felt the edge and stopped. "Thank you sir, thank you. That is two people today that helped me."

"You are welcome."

He heard the man step away and heard the woman's voice. "Now, was that so hard? I am proud of you, that you helped. Now, let's finish at the market." The blind man smiled as he heard the man respond. "My money purse is almost empty. . ."

"Well, Jesus, said to wash. So here I go." The blind man said.

The man felt the cool water, as his hands broke its surface. He cupped his hands and splashed the water over his face. And felt the mud and dirt dropped off into the pool.

His eyes were closed. His thoughts raced.

I know He told me to wash. But I thought for sure that He was there to rob me. And when He came close, I was worried. So many over the years have robbed me, and even threatened me. But He touched my shoulder and I was flooded with peace. I wasn't sure how mud on my eyes would help me. All these years, darkness. The doctors could do nothing; and the Priest and Scribes, they claimed there was sin. And YHWH was angry with me for something I had done. Well, I guess the moment of truth is here. His thoughts finished.

He washed his face again and felt cool water, and heard the splash, as it fell back into the pool.

I guess I need to open my eyes and see like He said. Wash and see! His thoughts ended, as he slowly opened his eyes. He slowly, hesitantly, opened his eyes. The battle in his mind and heart raged. *All these years he had lived in darkness and it was familiar, comfortable, even expected. His human heart struggled with the possible change. He wasn't sure if he had faith or not. After all the years of Priests and Scribes with their disdain or disapproval. Even the disdain of people around him. And if he did see as promised, what would he do now? He has lived so many years by the alms of people. He wouldn't know what to do. What could he do? He never learned a trade. He wasn't good with animals. He laughed aloud, so even being a lowly shepherd was not really a possibility. His hands and legs were strong, but he wasn't trained for anything. One thing at a time. Just like walking in darkness, he had to do one thing at a time.*

He stood **stunned**! The light and sound mixed and he saw the fountain and pool clearly. His eyes didn't hurt. They weren't blurry or anything! He saw! He looked into the pool and saw the ripples the fountain made and his reflection! *So this is me?* His hands touched his face. He saw the reflection do the same. *Well, my hair is a mess and the beard. . . Well I definitely need to get cleaned up! It seems the folks that had helped me in the past really didn't care. I guess I need to go to my spot and get my cup, and clear out. I wonder what the people and those that know me will say.* He thought.

The healed man walked slowly back to where he would sit and ask for alms. The street was crowded and noisy as usual. But it was strange to him. There was brightness everywhere. Colors and people! He heard the voices and conversations just a bit quieter now. He walked with a steady gate and with ease. He looked at the vendors on the street. *That face does not fit the voice!* He laughed. *And these others. . . Ahh, they might!* Joy grew in his heart. He walked past more people and saw the fabrics and smelled the flowers. He turned a corner and found his spot. He then saw the cup. He knelt down; he closed his eyes, and reached for the cup. He ran his fingers over the surface of the cup. It felt normal. He opened his eyes. He looked at the side of the building where he would sit. He tentatively, touched the wall. He saw that the brick had sweat stains and a small indention where he leaned and sat. He turned and sat, leaning against the building again, eyes closed. *Yes,* he thought *this is my place. All these years. And now. . . What will I do?* He opened his eyes and stood. Still holding his cup, he heard the same people pass by and say, "Where is the blind beggar? That man looks like him." "I don't think it's him, but it might be his twin!" Someone stopped and said, "Sir, where is the blind man? He's always at this spot. He's been there for years?"

He straightened and said, "I am he."

People began to gather now; neighbors and even strangers. "Wait. . . You can see? How can you see?" someone said. "For years you were blind."

"Yes, yes I was, it was me." He answered again. Again, they asked the question, "How is that possible? If you are him, no one could help him. He was blind since birth."

"Yes, I was. You see the Man named Jesus made mud and spread it on my eyes. And told me to go to the Pool of Siloam and wash my eyes. So, I did as He asked. And now I can see!" He finished.

The few people had become a crowd, and they asked, "Where is this, Jesus?"

"I don't know," he answered.

The men of the crowd looked at one another, and took him by the arm and said, "We are taking you to the Priests! You could have been cheating us all these years, if it is you! The Priests and Scribes will know!"

"But I have told you all I know! Why would I lie? Don't you recognize my voice? I haven't changed clothes yet. Though I need some better ones." He urged. But no one listened.

They moved as one to the Temple and they walked the steps to the area of the Priests and stopped. One of the Elder Priests saw the crowd and asked, "What is going on? Why are you here?" This man, one of the men said was blind and now he says he can see! We think he may be lying and wanted to know if you recognize him. He said he was born blind! And now he can see!" The man finished.

"Really?" the Elder Priest said, looking at the man. "Is what they say true? Were you born blind?" The man stood still and was silent. The Elder priest looked him over. And looked at his eyes. He pushed up his eyelid and pulled his face left and right like he would look at a lamb. "Well?"

"I have told these people the Truth! And I will tell you as well." The man started. "Wait," they spoke aloud, "Johannan and the others come here! You need to hear this and judge!"

Soon, the man and the crowd increased by four Priests. And the Elder said, "Now, you may tell us."

He man pulled his arm away from the man holding him and stood straight and spoke confidently, "As I told them, I was blind from birth. And some of these people have known that for a long time. But the Man named Jesus came and made mud and wiped it on my eyes! And then he told me to go and wash my eyes in the Pool of Siloam! So I did. And now I can see!" He said with a hint of frustration in his voice.

The four Pharisees moved to one side and said to one another. "What is this? He was healed on the Sabbath? No godly man would do that!" "Wait how can a sinner do miracles?" "Yes, I agree! A godly man and one used of God, would not break the Sabbath!" "If the man wasn't used of God, how could it happen?" "Would God do this? On the Sabbath? Certainly not!" The Pharisees moved back to the crowd and said, "Well. . ." turning to the man ". . . what do you have to say for yourself, and this man?"

He shrugged his shoulders and answered. "I have told you. I was blind. Jesus put mud on my eyes. I washed and now I see. I say He is Prophet!" the man finished.

"We don't believe you! And neither does the crowd," answered the people. "Johannan, find this man's parents and Bring them here!" the Elder Priest said. "You people go home! We will question him and his parents! Go on!" Then the Priest said to him, "Why don't you go and clean up! And when your parents get here we will talk."

"I need clothes anyway," said the man. He moved to the place he knew where he could buy clothes outside the Temple. As the day wore on he came back to the Temple. He found the Priests again and his parents.

"Ahh, good," the Elder Priest said, "you are back, clean and good." The Priest turned to his parents and said, "Is this your son?"

Both of his parents together said fearfully, "Yes, this is our son. **Why?"**

"He was born blind. Since birth? . . . He can see now. How is that possible?" the Priest asked sternly.

"Yes, this our son. As to how he can see, ask him; he is of age. He can speak for himself," they said. His parents looked at him sheepishly because they knew what the Synagogue leaders warned everyone of. The leaders had said, **"If anyone claims Jesus is the Messiah, we will put them out of the Synagogue."**

The Priests and Scribes conferred together again. They wanted to clear up this matter quickly and quietly, and maybe trap Jesus as well.

The four came back and said, "Give God glory! For what has happened?" They said snidely, "This man, Jesus is a sinner!"

"I don't know if Jesus is a sinner or not, what I do know is. . . I was blind from birth, as my parents and I have said. And now I see." The man finished.

"How is that possible? What did He do to you?" They said.

"What do you mean what did He do? I have told you everything. And you didn't listen. Why do you need to hear it again?" he said in frustration. "Unless you want to be his disciples? Maybe? Are you going to follow Him too like the others?" He finished boldly.

Enraged the Priests and Scribes chided and mocked him. "You are one His disciples! We are Moses' disciples! And we know God spoke to Moses. But as for this Jesus, God didn't speak to this man! We don't even know where he is from!" The Priests acknowledged.

The healed man stood proudly and proclaimed smiling. "Well, that's just amazing!" The man looked at the Priests, all concern was gone. "You say you have no idea where He came from, and yet, He opened my blind eyes! Amazing!" he continued before anyone could interrupt. "You and others have taught that God doesn't listen to sinners. But, if they fear God, and do God's will, He would listen." He laughed, "From Adam to till now, I haven't heard of anyone opening the eyes a of a person born blind. Not even the Prophets. It's plain to me that if this Man was not from God, He could do nothing!"

The four Priests took his arms angrily and dragged him out of the Temple and said, "You were born totally in sin, yet attempt to teach us! We cast you out of the Synagogue!"

The four walked behind him as he came to the road. He stood quietly. He looked to Heaven and saw the blue sky and turned and saw the beauty of the sunset. The Priests waited. He smiled and enjoyed a view that he had never seen before. Word came quickly to Jesus about the man.

So, Jesus left where He was and found him outside the Temple. Jesus walked to him and took his arm. "Shalom, can we talk?" He stopped and said, "Sure. I was enjoying the sunset. I never saw one before."

Jesus took him by the shoulders and said, "Do you believe in the Son of Man? The Messiah?"

The healed man said, "Who is He sir, that I would believe in him?"

Jesus smiled. And said, "You have seen Him. And I am Jesus, the one talking with you."

He knelt down and worshipped Him. Jesus lifted him up and said, "I came into this world for judgement sake. That those that are blind, that don't see, may see. And those that see, will not see and be blind."

The Pharisees heard what Jesus said and confronted Him. And said smugly, "We are not blind as well are we?"

Jesus spoke with authority, **"If you were blind you would have no sin. But, because you claim and maintain that you see, your sin remains."**

****

Jesus came back to the present and pain! His body shook. The soldiers were still there. They pointed and joked. And bet on how fast the men and He would die.

I know You can't hear Me because I bear sin for the world. Father, I miss being with You. And I know We did everything to fulfill Scripture and prophecy, but there were times I wish We could have told them plainly like the disciples. Those parables, each one unique, and with purpose, just like everything We created. But the Enemy of men's souls still sought to kill, steal, and destroy. And men truly could not hear. And sometimes, even the Twelve. I marvel at how fickle even their faith was. In spite of the parables and miracles.

His mind raced back to the days before and the stories. . . Jesus taught the people whenever He could in parables to fulfill Scripture and prophecy . . . Jesus quoted Isaiah. He said, **"You will keep on hearing, but will not understand; You will keep on seeing, but will not perceive; For the heart of this people has become dull, with their ears they scarcely hear, and they have closed their eyes, otherwise they would see with their eyes, hear with their ears, and understand with their heart and return, and I would heal them."**

"A farmer went out to plant seeds. And as he planted his seed some fell by the roadside and the birds snatched them up and ate them. Some others fell in rocky places, and sprang up but had no root and sun rose and scorched them; they died. Others, landed among thorns and were choked out. But the rest fell on good ground and yielded a crop, a hundred fold, sixty, and thirty. He that has an ear let him hear."

Jesus continued, "The Kingdom of God is like a man casting seeds on the soil. He goes to sleep, gets up in the day, and sees the plant sprout and grow, but doesn't understand how it happened. Soil produces crops on its own. And when the harvest is ready, he cuts it."

"The Kingdom of Heaven is like a man that sowed good seed in his field. But while everyone was sleeping, his enemy sowed tares in the same field. And the enemy left. Now as the wheat grew, the man servants asked him, "Didn't you plant good seed in the field? Why are there tares here as well?"

"The man said an enemy has done this! His servants said, "Do you want us to cut them out?"

"No," the Man said. "Let them fully grow, so that we can see the difference. And the reapers can then take away and burn the tares, but save the wheat into my barn!"

"The Kingdom of heaven is like a mustard seed. A man sowed the mustard seed in his field; and it is the smallest of seeds. But when it is full grown it is larger than all the garden plants. And it is big enough that birds can nest in its branches."

"And again, it is like a woman that is going to bake. She had three pecks of flour. But she put in only a little leaven, but soon, all of her flour had leaven. Or the Kingdom of Heaven is like a man searching a field. On finding a great treasure, he buries it again, and goes and sells all he has and buys the field. And yet again the Kingdom of Heaven is like a merchant searching for the best pearls. And when he finds the one of great value, he sold everything, and bought it."

"Lastly, the Kingdom of Heaven, is like a great net cast into the sea. And this net gathers fish of every kind and is full. When the net is on the beach, they put the good fish in containers, but the bad fish they toss away. And so it will be at the end of the age, that the angels will come and separate, the wicked from the righteous. And they will throw them into the fiery furnace where there will be weeping and gnashing of teeth."

CHAPTER 13

TRANSFIGURATION, THE GOOD SAMARITAN, THE RICH MAN AND LAZARUS, AND MORE

Jesus and the Twelve were near Caesarea Philippi. He turned to the disciples and said, "Come with Me; let us go up the mountain and pray." So, Jesus led the way up the slope followed by Simon Peter, James, and John, his brother. Jesus walked quietly and took in the view, as they moved steadily upward. The trees stood tall and majestic and the blue sky and clouds made the trek even more peaceful and grand. Jesus stopped at a place just beyond a set trees, He could smell pine and other flowers and could see the very crest. He knelt and began to pray. The trio knelt not too far away and began to pray also. All that was heard were bird songs and a gentle breeze. Everything moved as if breathing. And Jesus prayed to the Father. The three disciples prayed. And the quietness truly rested.

Father, I came here to commune with You. And to let the three learn Your presence. And maybe even know you better. This is truly a beautiful place. And it is restful. He prayed.

Son, you could use a time refreshing. And maybe a bit more! Jesus thought He heard the Father chuckle. ***Maybe now the disciples will finally see. . .***

Soon Jesus felt the power of God and the Strengthening of the Holy Spirit; He then stood up. And there beside Him stood . . . **Moses**! Just as He remembered him! And **Elijah** on the other side! Jesus looked at his clothes and hands and the glory of God that was His before showed

231

all around! Jesus smiled and thought, *The only thing missing is some angels, huh Father.*

"Your Majesty, Son of God." Moses said, as Jesus turned and looked for the disciples. He found them awake and terrified! They were looking at one another in shock, amazement, and fear! Their prayer had stopped. He again looked over the mountain. He smiled.

This is the glory I held before the Universe was! Moses continued, "Elijah and I were to meet You the Light Father said, as a testimony not only to the future, and Israel now, but that your disciples could truly . . . even in this brief time see."

Elijah spoke to him now, "You know, Your Cousin was greatly used by the Father, though many don't see it yet. But we also came to fulfill Scripture. As of course you know."

And before Elijah could finish, Simon Peter, moved closer and said, "Lord, it is good we are here. If you tell me to I can make three tabernacles here. One for You, Moses and Elijah!" Jesus looked at Simon Peter and the others, and realized they were terrified, and Peter didn't understand.

In that moment; a glowing cloud covered the mountain side. And God the Father's rich, deep, powerful voice proclaimed, ***"This is My Son, My Chosen One; with whom I am well-pleased; listen to Him!"*** And all three fell on their face in fear!

Jesus moved to where the trio was and He touched them gently, speaking with authority, **"Get up all of you. And do not be afraid at all."**

As Jesus helped them to their feet, and they sheepishly opened their eyes, they saw. . . It was just the four of them now. And relief flooded them. Jesus saw them visibly relax. And sigh a deep sigh.

Jesus looked to the heavens and thought, *Well, that did something. At this moment I am not sure if it helped or not.* **I think it did!** He heard the Father. ***They needed to know. For a testimony and for greater faith on their part.***

As Jesus and the three disciples headed back down the mountain, He commanded them. "Do not tell anyone what you saw here today until I have risen from the dead." Jesus continued in silence, as they moved through the pines, and other trees to another level spot.

Then one of the three asked Jesus. "Why do the Scriptures and even the Scribes say Elijah must come first, before the Messiah?"

Jesus looked at the three, as He walked and said, "Elijah is coming to restore everything, as the Scriptures say. But I tell you Elijah already came; and they did not recognize him. And did to him whatever they wished. Just like him, they will treat the Son of God; He will suffer at their hands many things and just like him, being treated with contempt."

Jesus watched as realization dawned on the faces of the three. And He knew that they understood, as He talked of John the Baptist and Himself.

As Jesus and the three came back to the rest of the disciples, they saw a great crowd. Jesus watched as He was spotted by the crowd and many rushed to Him. He also saw the Scribes arguing with His disciples. The crowd greeted Him and He asked, "What are they arguing about?"

A Man pushed through and fell at his feet weeping. "I brought my only son to you. **Please!** Please, have mercy on my son. Many times he has seizures and is tossed to the ground, in water, or in the fire. He is so ill." He sobbed. "I came here and begged Your disciples to help. But they couldn't! They tried; but nothing happened! And my son is the same! It appears that my son is possessed by a spirit that makes him mute and takes him often, where he convulses and foams at the mouth. I didn't know what to do! And I have no more hope; it's impossible!"

"How long will I be with you? Bring him to me!"

Jesus watched, as the boy moved closer to Him. He saw the ghost image and dark smudge following the boy. His father held his arm, and just as He came near, the boy fell to the ground and began convulsing and foaming at the mouth!

Jesus said, "How long has this been going on?"

The father replied, "Since birth. If you can help us, take pity on us and help us please!"

"If I can? All things are possible to the one that Believes!"

"I believe!" the Father cried. "But help my unbelief!"

Jesus looked and the crowd was even bigger now. He turned to the boy and spoke with authority, **"You Deaf and Mute Spirit come out of him now! And never return to him!"** And Jesus and the crowd watched as the boy was healed instantly. And they all marveled at the greatness of God.

****

Jesus went all throughout Galilee and taught His disciples along the way. *Father, they need to know these things for later, even before My death. How can I teach them with such great need around me? I can't just let the enemy so rampantly kill, steal, or destroy. He has been very busy. Even as we travel, time and again. He has distracted and hindered. And the crowds, so many people, so many needs. How can I not be noticed! Father, I really do try. I do try and be discrete. But, the religious leaders are concerned only with here and now, not their souls. Nor for the peoples' souls either. I truly will be glad when We together can guide them with the Spirit and have them walk with Us, as We wanted.* His thoughts stopped. As they traveled, He began to warn them of the coming events to prepare for the future and theirs.

Jesus relayed to them this, "You need to hear this. . ." He said, "and it needs to sink into your hearts and ears. I, the Son of God, Son of Man, will be delivered into men's hands and the Priests, Scribes, and more. They will kill Me. Though I will rise again three days later. The will of God and Scripture must be completed. I know you may be frightened and saddened. But it must be done, at all cost, for the redemption and salvation of all mankind and creation."

Jesus was resting at the house in Capernaum with the disciples. The day was bright and clear.

There was a knock at the door and Simon Peter answered. Two men were at the door. They had on the robes and official garb of the Temple. And one of the men said to Simon Peter, "Shalom, we are from the Temple and we are here to collect the two drachma tax for the Temple. **Unless** of course, your teacher is intent on **not** paying the Temple tax!" The man paused, "He does **intend** to pay the tax I hope." He finished.

Peter replied, "Of course He intends to pay the tax. It must have slipped His mind. I will speak with Him and I will bring it by your office shortly."

The men bowed, turned and headed back toward the Temple. When Simon Peter entered the house, He went to where Jesus sat and before He could say a word Jesus asked, "So Simon, a question? Do the Kings and Rulers of the Earth collect taxes from sons or strangers?" Jesus looked with a grin.

Simon Peter paused a moment and replied. "I came to tell you the men from the Temple came about the tax. But you beat me to it. So I think they tax strangers."

Jesus smiled again "So, sons, would be exempt?" Simon Peter grinned and nodded. But Jesus held up His hand and finished, "I agree, but so we don't offend anyone. . . Go to the sea, and toss a hook in. And the first fish caught, open its mouth and take out the coin. A shekel and go find them at the Temple and pay the tax for us." Peter looked at Jesus and Jesus smiled again.

Peter finished. "Yes! I can go fishing!" He said laughing.

*****

As Jesus taught the crowds and the disciples, the disciples talked with one another. And a question arose, so they said, "Who would be the greatest person in the Kingdom of God?"

Jesus paused a moment and found among the sea of faces, a small child. He smiled at the little girl; she smiled back and He motioned for her to come to where He was. She hesitated. Jesus smiled bigger, nodded, and motioned again. So, she came to Jesus. He spoke to them all and said, "Unless you turn and become like a child, you will not enter the Kingdom. Humble yourself, like a child. He or she is the greatest in the Kingdom. And anyone who receives a child in my name, receives Me. I warn you though, anyone who causes one of these little ones to stumble, that believe in Me, it would be better if a millstone were hung around his neck and the person drowned in the sea. Woe to the world and its stumbling blocks! Because they will come, but worse, will it be for person who causes others to stumble!

Jesus continued teaching, "The Kingdom of Heaven compares to a King that wanted to settle debts, with his servants. There was one that owed him ten thousand talents, and he stood before the King. But he had no means to repay him what was owed. The King gave the command that he, his family, along with all he had, be sold, to pay the debt. When the servant heard this, he fell the before the King, face down and begged the King, 'Please! Have mercy and patience with me, and I will repay everything!' The King was moved with compassion and forgave all the debt. The servant left. As he was going he found a fellow slave, and seized him and began to choke, him saying, 'Pay me what you owe!' The fellow servant fell to the ground, pleading with him, 'Have mercy and patience, and I will repay you!' But he didn't listen. But took him to prison, and told them to keep him until everything was paid. The other slaves saw what happened. And they went before the King telling him everything. The King summoned him. The King said, 'You wicked slave! I forgave you all your debt! Because you pleaded with me. Why would you not do the same for your fellow slave?? And show him mercy!' In anger the King sent him to the torturers, so that he could pay back all he owed. My Heavenly Father will do the same if you do not forgive from heart."

Again he continued, "What about sheep?"

"If you had a hundred sheep and one goes astray, wouldn't you leave the ninety-nine on the mountains and go and search for the missing one? And when you find it; I tell you, you rejoice more over that lost one being found than the others that stayed. It is not the will of your Father in Heaven that any of these little ones perish. If your brother sins against you, speak with him in private. And if he listens to you, you have restored your brother and the relationship. But if he will not listen, take one or two people with you, so that by two or three witnesses, every fact can be established and confirmed. If he refuses you, then go to the Church, and if he refused the Church, treat him as an unbeliever. Truly, whatever you bind on Earth is bound in Heaven and whatever you lose on Earth is loosed in Heaven! If two or more of you agree on Earth about anything, it will be done for you by my Father in Heaven. And where two or three have gathered together, I will be in their midst."

Jesus continued in figurative speech, "I tell you the truth, anyone who does not enter by the door of the sheepfold, but gets in another way, is a thief, or robber. But if anyone enters by the door, he is a shepherd of the sheep. The doorkeeper opens to him. And the sheep hear the shepherd's voice. And he calls them by name, leading them out. The shepherd leads out all of his sheep. And all the sheep follow him. Because they know his voice. And they will not listen to strangers. I am the door of the sheep. And everyone who came before me are thieves and robbers and the sheep didn't hear them. I am the door; if anyone enters through Me, he will be saved. He will go in and out, finding pasture. The thief only comes to Kill, Steal and Destroy. But I came that they may have abundant life! I am the Good Shepherd. I lay down my life for the sheep. A hired hand does not own the sheep and is not a shepherd. So when the wolf comes, he leaves the sheep, and the wolf snatches them and scatters them! He flees because he is just a hired hand. He doesn't care for the sheep. But I am the Good Shepherd; and I know my own sheep, and they know Me. Just like the Father knows Me, and I know the Father. I lay down My life for the sheep. I have other sheep, not of this fold, and I must bring them in as well. They will hear My voice and become all one flock with one Shepherd. The Father loves Me because I lay my life down and I can take it up again. No one can take it from Me, but I lay it down on My own. I have the authority to take it up again. This command I received from My Father."

Jesus then turned to the disciples and said, "Blessed, happy are their eyes that see what you see. Many of the Prophets and Kings wanted to see what you do, and they didn't. Nor did they hear what you do."

After Jesus finished, a man stood in the crowd and asked, "Teacher, what do I have to do to have Eternal life?"

Jesus knew it was a test. "Since, you teach the Law, what does it say?" Jesus waited quietly.

He answered proudly, "You are to love the Lord your God with all of your heart, mind, soul, and strength, and your neighbor as yourself."

Jesus smiled at the man and said, "You answered correctly. Go and do this and you will live." Jesus looked at the man. Jesus could see his questions and concerns. And also his attempt to not do as He said. Because Jesus heard. "And who is my neighbor?"

Jesus chuckled, "I will tell you. There was man heading from Jerusalem to Jericho. And he was attacked by robbers. They beat him terribly; stripped him, and took all he had, leaving him half dead and alone."

"Soon a Priest came that same way. And seeing him, did nothing, and walked away. And not long after the Priest had left, there came a Levite. And he too saw him; did nothing, except when he left, it was on the opposite side of the road. Now, there came a Samaritan who had been on a long journey, he too saw him. Feeling compassion for the man, he bandaged his wounds as best he could, pouring oil and wine on them, even put him on his own horse. He led the beast and the man to an inn. Bought room and took care of him. The next day the man handed the inn keeper two denarii. And said. "Take care of him please. And whatever else is needed, when I return, I will pay you in full."

Jesus looked at the man and the crowd and asked, "Who of these three proved to be a neighbor of that man?"

The man said, "The one who showed mercy to him."

Jesus looked him in the eye and said, "Go and do the same."

As Jesus continued, a voice was heard shouting, "**Teacher!** Tell my brother to divide the inheritance with me!"

Jesus asked, "Who made Me an arbitrator or judge over you? Beware of greed because life is not found in the abundance of things, or money. There was a rich man. And he had a great amount of crops and goods and he said to himself, 'I have so much I can't store it. But if I tear down my barns and build bigger ones, then, I can store more crops and goods! And I will say you have enough for many years. Relax, take it easy, eat, drink, and be merry!' but God said, 'foolish man, even tonight death comes for you. Who will get what you leave?' so it is when people store up wealth and treasure to themselves and not God."

Jesus moved on from there and entered a village. As He was walking, Jesus met a woman named, Martha. She had heard of Him and asked that He and the Twelve come to her house. So, Jesus said He would. And soon, they were at her house.

She and her sister Mary lived there. So, Jesus entered the house. And sat down.

The house reminded Him of the house in Nazareth. It was large enough for a family, but not much else. And definitely not all the crowd that followed Him usually. *I am glad. Glad it was just the Twelve and I,* He thought, *or we couldn't have gotten in to sit down.* The house was warm and smelled of flowers; and something cooking that reminded Him that He needed to eat.

He smiled as Mary sat near Him and waited.

Martha spoke, "Jesus . . . I will bring water. And I will make something **more**." she laughed. "We, my sister and I, don't eat much. But I will add to what we have." She finished. "Oh, go ahead and talk or teach, if you choose."

Jesus watched as she moved off to the cooking area, and began to add to what they had. He could see the concern on her face. And her need to do well by her guests. *This is going to be tough for her. And my notoriety doesn't help.* He thought. *Well, since I am here and we have time, I could share some.*

Jesus said to His disciples, "Do not be overly concerned, or worry about your life. Don't worry about what you will eat or your body and its clothes. Why? Because life is more than just food. And more than just clothing. Look at the ravens; they don't sow or reap as farmers do. Yet, God your Father feeds them. And you are far more valuable than birds! Remember what I said before? So do not be afraid, little flock, for your Father has chosen gladly to give you the Kingdom. Sell your possessions and give to charity. Make for yourselves money belts that don't wear out and no thief can touch! Or moth destroy. Where your heart is, is where your treasure is. Be prepared and keep you lamps lit. Like the men who are waiting for their Master to return from a wedding feast. So they can quickly open the door when he knocks. Happy and prosperous are those that the Master finds ready. And the Master will have them recline at the table, and wait upon them. No matter if it is evening or midnight, even early morning. When he knocks, blessed are those men."

Jesus watched as Martha moved about, her face tight, with effort and stress. He watched, as she rustled about as He was speaking and even as He finished. She came to Him then. Leaned in and whispered to Him. "Lord, doesn't it bother you that my sister has left me here to serve alone! Tell her to help me!"

Jesus touched her arm, looked up at her, and said, "Martha, you are worried and stressed about so many things. But really, only one thing in all of this is necessary. She has chosen the best part and that will not be taken from her."

******

Jesus had gone out to pray at the Mount of Olives. *Father, it is nice to be with You anytime. But, sometimes, the beauty We have created just brings joy and peace. I will go in to the Temple and try to teach. Since it's a Feast day, hopefully the crowds won't be too bad.* He laughed. *We might need to get a bigger Temple!* He knew the Father was grinning.

Jesus walked slowly up the road to the Temple. And as always the road was filled with people. Some hurrying to sacrifice or sell. Others, walking and laughing together. He entered the Beautiful Gate, then entered one of the courts, and sat down to teach. When the people saw

Him, they came to Him and sat. He began to teach and share about the Kingdom of God. Jesus heard raised voices and saw people being pushed out of the way. A group of seven Scribes and Pharisees, angry and indignant, pushed through the group and threw a woman, barely dressed to the court floor! She lay in the dirt; wrapped in what possibly was a blanket, and what coverings she had. He could see bruises on her arms, evidence of the rough treatment of more than just the Scribes and Pharisees! *Father, here? Now? Has their false piety taken everything from them. Has pride? In their religiousness, no mercy or kindness??* Jesus saw her almost in a fetal position. Weeping and shaking in fear.

The Scribe in charge towered over her. And he turned to Jesus and arrogantly spit out his next words, almost as if they were poison!

"Teacher, this woman, has been caught in adultery, in the very act! Moses says to stone such women, what do you say?"

Father, both people were to be brought before the rulers. Not just one. Where I wonder is he? Could it be he was a Priest? A man of authority. And wants to hide his transgression, or is the trap simpler? He thought. *Father I will wait.* Jesus knelt and began writing in the dirt with His finger. Again, the Scribe repeated his accusation. And Jesus ignored the comment. And He kept writing in the dirt. Jesus heard the anger rise in his voice. The woman still was crying. The crowd, silent. He stood and spoke in authority.

"He that has no sin, go ahead, and cast the stone at her." Again, He knelt and wrote on the ground.

The tension was palpable. And the court now waited for the outcome. *Father which will it be? Will they offer forgiveness? Mercy? Kindness? We pointed the Law toward forgiveness and mercy first. Because that was Us. We held mercy and forgiveness and they were to model it. But, religiousness has no mercy! Pride has no tenderness. Just harsh reality of wrong or right. And they hold the right. And then judge harshly.* Jesus waited. The sun was hot; the smell of burnt sand, and sweat. It was quiet now, no Rage, no righteous indignation, just quiet. And he noticed the older Scribes and Priests; they looked at one another, then at Jesus, and conviction flashed on their faces, then slowly, one by one they turned and left the court. Time passed. Moments turned to minutes. Finally, Jesus looked up and tenderly spoke to the woman now sitting upright and quiet. Tears dried on her face.

"Woman where are they? Those that condemned you?" She looked around and at Jesus and in small voice said, "I do not know. They are not here. No one condemns me it seems."

Jesus reached down and lifted her to her feet. Looking in her eyes he said. "I do not condemn you either. Go from here in peace. But do not sin again."

****

Jesus spoke to the tax collectors and those marked as sinners by the Pharisees and Scribes. They were following Him more and more. Jesus heard the religious leaders grumble. And again say, "He receives sinner and eats with them!"

Jesus shared a parable. Again, to remind them all. He said "Who among you if he had one hundred sheep, and has lost just one . . . doesn't leave the rest, and search for it until he finds it. When he finds it, he puts it on his shoulders and carries it home. And once he is home, calls all his friends and neighbors and says, 'Rejoice! Rejoice with me; for I have found my sheep that was lost! But I tell you, even more important than this, there is more joy in Heaven when one sinner repents, than the ninety-nine righteous who do not need to repent. Or a woman who had ten silver coins and lost one, wouldn't you and she, light a lamp, and sweep and search the house, until it is found? When she does, she calls all her friends and neighbors,' and says, 'Rejoice! Rejoice with me; for I have found the coin I had lost!' The angels of God and all of Heaven rejoices over one sinner who repents."

Jesus continued, "There was man with two sons. And the younger said to his father, "Give me all that I will inherit from your estate and all my inheritance. So, the father divided the estate and all his wealth between the two sons. Not many days after, the younger son packed up all he had, and left. He left on a journey to a distant land. And in that land he squandered all he had. He lost everything in wild sensuous living. And after he was destitute, a great famine hit the land he was in. And he was so impoverished and in need, he finally broke down, and hired himself out as a servant to one of the countrymen. The countrymen sent him out to feed pigs. And he went to work. And as he worked because he was so hungry, he would have eaten even the scraps the pigs had and ate. But no one, not the countryman who hired him, or his friends, gave him anything. But when he came to his senses, he thought, *Wait, How many of my Father's hired servants, have more than enough bread to eat, and I starve in this place. I am dying of hunger! I know he said I will go home to my Father and, 'I will say, I have sinned against heaven and in your sight. I am no longer worthy to be called your son! Just make me like a hired hand.'* So he got up and headed back home to his Father's house. But before he even he got home, his Father saw him a long way off, feeling compassion for him, He ran to him. The Father ran to him and embraced him and kissed him! The son said to the Father, 'Father, I have sinned against Heaven and in your sight. I am no longer worthy, to be called your son.' "

"But the Father said to his slaves, 'Quickly, Quickly, bring out the best robe and put it on him. Also, put the ring on his hand and sandals on his feet! And then bring a fatted calf. Kill it and let us celebrate! Why? Because this son of mine was dead and is alive again, lost and has been found!' So they all began to celebrate."

"Now at the same time the older son having been in the field, came to the house, and hearing the music and dancing, asked one of the servants what was happening. The servant told him, 'Your brother has returned safe and sound, so your Father, killed a calf to celebrate.' At this the older son became angry! And he refused to enter the house and stayed outside. So, the Father came out and pleaded with the older son. And the older son said, 'All these years I have been serving you and not neglecting your commands, or wishes. And yet, you have never given me a goat, or calf to celebrate with my friends. But when this son of yours came who had devoured your wealth with prostitutes and sensuous living. You killed a calf!'"

"The Father said to the son, 'Son, you have always been with me, and believe me, all that I have is yours, but we had to celebrate and rejoice! Because this brother of yours was dead and has begun to live, was lost, and now is found.' "

  ****

Jesus was teaching in a Synagogue on the Sabbath. Jesus looked over the group and He saw a woman. And she was bent over and could not straighten at all. She was smiling and moving though, not without difficulty. Jesus asked about her and He was told she had been like this for eighteen years. Jesus looked at her. *Father, eighteen years, why?* **Son, look again**. He heard the Father say.

Jesus looked again and then He saw it. The faint almost imperceptible ghost image. He called her over to where He was. He looked at her and spoke with authority, **"Woman, you are freed from your sickness,"** after laying hands on her. He watched, as she looked puzzled. And then He saw, as she straightened completely upright, astonishment! She was overcome with joy. Her eyes took in the whole room from her correct standing. All the friends and neighbors looked in awe. She dared the unthinkable! She bent all the way over and touched her toes then straightened up again! No pain, no weight, no burden, just freedom of movement! She shouted, "Praise to God!" And Smiled and began dancing!

Jesus noticed the anger and indignance of the Synagogue official who in spite of what he had witnessed, scoffed and rebuked those around him.

"There are six days in which work should be done! So, come in those days, and be healed! Not on the Sabbath!"

Jesus answered him, "You hypocrites! You untie your ox or donkey and lead him to water, so he may drink! And this daughter of Abraham, this woman, who is more valuable! Whom Satan had bound for eighteen long years, isn't it right to be released and healed on the Sabbath! So, finally, she can truly rest?"

Jesus saw the official and all those opposing him sit back down and remain silent. They looked humbled, as the whole synagogue rejoiced and glorified god for the glorious things he did.

Jesus continued on also speaking to the disciples, "There was a rich man who had a manager and it was reported to him that the manager was squandering his possessions and money. He said to the manager, "What is this I hear about you? I want an accounting for what you have done. You might stop being my manager."

"What do I do?" "He thought since my master is taking away my job. . . I am not strong enough to dig. And I will not beg. I know what I will do so people will still welcome me.!"

"He summoned all his master's debtors. And he spoke to the first, 'How much do you owe my master?' "

"One hundred measures of oil," the debtor said.

"Quickly, take you bill and make it fifty instead," and the second and following "One hundred measures of wheat," "Mark eighty."

"And the rich man praised the unrighteous manager because he was shrewd. Because sons of this age are more shrewd to their own, than the Sons of Light. Make good use of what you have here, to prepare for your heavenly future. A faithful person in little will be faithful with much. And a person unrighteous in a little thing, is unrighteous in much. And if you have struggled in earthly riches, how can someone trust you with true riches? No one can serve two masters. He will hate one and love the other or be devoted to one and despise the other. You cannot server God and money."

And as Jesus was speaking; he saw the Pharisees, who loved money and taking bribes and more, scoffing at what he had said. "Understand this, you may justify yourself in the sight of men, but god knows your heart! And many of the things highly esteemed by men are detestable to God. So, be faithful in the little things."

"And again there was a rich man, dressed in purple and fine linen, joyously living in splendor daily. At the same time, a poor man was laid at his gate, covered in sores, named Lazarus. And Lazarus who was destitute; HE longed even to eat the crumbs that fell from his table. In such poverty, even the dogs came and licked his sores. And then the poor man died. And the angels came and carried him to Abraham's bosom. And the rich man also died. And was buried. In Hades, he opened his eyes and he was in torment! He looked and he could see far away Abraham and Lazarus near him. And the rich man cried out 'Father Abraham, have mercy on me. Send Lazarus, so that he would dip the tip of his finger in water and touch my tongue, for I am in agony in the flame!' "

"Abraham answered him, 'Child, remember in your life, you received good things, and Lazarus bad things, but now, he is being comforted and you are in agony. But besides all of that, there is a great chasm that is fixed in place. So that no one can leave either place! No one can cross to you or you to us.' "

"He said to Abraham, 'If the chasm is fixed, then can you send him to my father's house? I have five brothers. To warn them! That they do not come to this place of torment!' "

"Abraham said, 'No, they have Moses and the Prophets, let them hear them.' He pleaded, 'You don't understand! Father Abraham, I am sure if someone goes to them risen from the dead, they would repent!' "

"Abraham finished sadly, 'If they do not listen to Moses and the Prophets, they will not be persuaded, even if someone rises from the dead.' "

****

CHAPTER 14

LAZARUS, ZACHEUS, BARTIMEUS

Mary and Martha of Bethany, sent word to Jesus about their brother. "Lord, the one you love is sick." *Father, Lazarus is sick. What do you want Me to do?* **Son,** the Father said. **This sickness will not end in death. This is for my glory and Yours. Finish up here. Stay two more days.** *Okay Father, I will. Though Father I really do love them. And they follow after You too.* **I know Son. I know.**

Jesus said to the Twelve, "This sickness will not end in death. This is for my Father's glory and Mine." After He said this, He stayed two more days, and the work was done. He said to the Twelve. "Let's go to Judea again." Shocked, the Twelve said almost as one, "Rabbi, teacher; are you sure? The Jews there were looking to stone You, and kill You! And you want to go back?"

"Are there not twelve hours in a day? The one who walks in the day does not stumble. Because he sees the light of the world. But, if you walk in the night, you stumble because the light is not in him. But our friend Lazarus has fallen asleep. And I am going to wake him up!"

"If all that has happened is he fell asleep, he will recover." they said.

Jesus was speaking of Lazarus' death. But the Twelve thought it was literal sleep. "Lazarus is dead." he said plainly. "and I am glad for your sakes; I was not there, why? So you may believe. But let us go to him. "Didimus said to the Twelve, let's go with him. And die with if need be."

So when Jesus arrived near Bethany. Only two miles from Jerusalem; he noted many people heading to console Mary and Martha. And he found out Lazarus had been in the tomb four days. And Martha hearing Jesus was coming; rushed out, going to find him as soon as she could. Mary though stayed in the house. Martha moved through the streets and out to country side, passed the tombs.

Jesus walked slowly toward Bethany and the house. The road was full activity and those mourning or burying. He saw Martha coming up the road. He could see the urgency in her steps; and as she drew closer, the dried tears and ashes. She found him then; he stopped. He waited as she composed herself and said brokenly; full of pain, even anger. "lord. . . If you had been here; when we sent the message, my brother would not have died! But I know. ." She said breathing a sigh, that even now; whatever you ask of god. . . God will give it to you."

Jesus saw her anguish; pain, and even the anger. He spoke gently; surely, "your brother; will rise again."

Martha's head dropped as hopelessness; exhaustion, weariness, flooded her. She answered weakly " I know he will rise again; in the resurrection on the last day."

"Martha. . ." Jesus touched her arm and said "**I am the resurrection, and the life**. He that believes in me; will live even if he dies. And everyone who lives in me; and believes in me, will never die. Do you; believe this?"

Martha, shook her head as if to clear it. And said wearily "Yes, I have believed that you are the Christ, the son of god, come into the world." after she said this she went toward the house. Jesus watched as fear and faith battled in her heart as she walked away. *Father; her belief in me is true. But her earthly senses and circumstances, almost overwhelm, any growth in faith. No wonder people struggle so. People's sight is not normally one of faith. Satan has so blinded them to truth and even hope. No wonder; death is final. Human eyes see nothing else. And eyes of faith is seems see little.*

Martha came to the house and told Mary quietly, "Jesus wants to see you," so she got up quickly and left the house. And the mourners saw this and followed close behind.

Mary found Jesus just where Martha had left him. Jesus saw Mary, as she came closer he saw the mourning clothes and ashes. And the effects of dried tears on her face. And not far behind a large group for mourners, weeping. Jesus knew he wasn't close to their house in

Bethany. But more, as before in the countryside, close to the tombs, off the main road.

Mary fell at his feet weeping and looking into His face, spoke brokenly, "Lord, if only you had been here. My brother would not have died."

Jesus saw the pain; anguish, loss. And a flicker of hope. He looked from Mary to the mourning crowd that followed her. *So many . . . Lazarus and they have touched many.* **Son, I know this pain, you will know it too. But remember, this will not end in his death.** He heard the Father.

His heart and spirit felt their wounds, their pain, loss, and fear. He was troubled deeply. *Father, death separates, the gulf between them is wide. All they have are memories. They ache for those gone. And because of sin's destruction, and Lucifer's blinding, hope dies along with their loved ones. Even faith, weakens as reality hits. Only trust in God, in Us, can bridge the gap, and build hope again. But still, My* **humanness**, *wants to weep, and mourn a loss.* **Mourn**, *a voice created to make this world better, now gone. Yet,* **as God**, *I know they will see each other again. And live forever together! Yet, still, sometimes even their eyes of faith may dim, without help. And especially, without* **hope**. *No wonder I am to destroy all the works of the devil!*

Jesus took her hand, raising her to her feet, said gently, "Where have you laid him?" He followed Mary and the mourners. They walked to the tombs. They came to a simple hillside cave covered with a rough stone.

"This is where his body is." Mary said. "We couldn't afford more."

The hillside was red with sunset. And a gentle breeze blew. Jesus watched the grass, scrub brush, and wildflowers move. *Thank you Father. It is fitting You did this; You honored him. Now I understand.* His thoughts continued. Scenes of joy and laughter at the house in Bethany flooded His mind. The tears, the conversations of concern. Everything. Jesus wept. He let the emotions flow. He joined in their pain, sorrow, loss, frustration, anger even. Some spoke quietly in the crowd of mourners; Jesus overheard. "How he loved him." "Wait! If he could open the eyes of the blind. . . Couldn't He had stopped him from dying?"

Jesus, heartbroken, moved slowly to the tomb. He touched the rock. He felt the coldness of it. And caught the scent; and cost of sins existence, death. *Love was never meant to be separated; no one was to ever know this. This was never our plan. Sin's cost is great. No wonder in men's weakness hope dies. But hope will rise again here and on Golgotha.* He thought.

Jesus turned to Mary and now Martha, joining her and said to all there. "Remove the stone."

Martha touched Jesus arm and said, "Lord; are you **sure?** By now, he has been dead 4 days. There will be a smell." She shook her head slowly.

"Martha," Jesus replied. "Don't you remember what I said? That if you believed. You would see the glory of God?"

Jesus watched, as some men nearby and some the Twelve, went to the stone and rolled it away. They returned to Jesus side. The Twelve gathered around Mary and Martha. Mary held tightly to Martha, along with the Twelve touching them both. They and the crowd waited in silent expectation.

Jesus heard the Father, ***Son, this is the moment. You will glorify Me and I you. There is no going back now. We must complete what we have started. Oh, and just one thing.*** He felt the Father grin. *Yes,* Jesus thought. ***Just remember to call just Lazarus, not anyone else, yet.*** The Holy Spirit laughed too.

Jesus looked up to Heaven and spoke for all to hear, "Father, I thank you that you have heard Me, and always do. But for the sake of those here, so they can believe that You sent Me, I say this now." Jesus spoke with authority, loudly, **"Lazarus! Come out!"**

Everyone there, every heart and mind, focused on the cave entrance. Everything was silent and still. There was no breeze now, no bird song, just stillness and quiet.

Then those nearest the tomb heard a whisper. A muffled step and a muffled noise, and saw the entrance blocked by death clothes, and a body upright! The man Lazarus, still wrapped in death clothes, face covered, leaned against the entrance wall!

Jesus said, "Take off his grave clothes! And the wrappings, set him free!"

The nearest men and parts of the crowd did just that. As Mary and Martha wept and hugged for joy! As did the Twelve!

Jesus watched as they freed Lazarus. He looked astonished. And full of wonder! He looked at Jesus, smiled and now that one arm was free, waved in joy! Not only to his sisters, but to the crowd that once mourned! Now, they were celebrating with shouts, tears of joy, and claps on the back of neighbors and friends!

Well done, Son. Many here will believe. But the Pharisees and Scribes will not like it! And We knew it. They will be plotting Your demise. Do not be surprised.

No I won't be. Jesus smiled and moved to the group surrounding Mary, Martha and now Lazarus! Mourning, and death had been turned, as God promised, to joy and dancing!

****

Soon after these events, the chief priests and Pharisees convened a council. Discussing this among the group some said, "We need to do something about **this**! This **Jesus** is performing signs and miracles! But if He goes on as He is, many will believe in Him. And Rome will hear of it and come, remove us from power and destroy our nation!"

The High Priest Caiaphas stood and held up his hands for silence. The council chamber was filled with sound and murmurings. Discussion stopped. He moved out onto the floor; turning as he did so, regal robes flowed, as he took in everyone in the council chambers. Filled with Spirit of God, he spoke, "You all do not understand, nor see. It is important and vital from this moment on that only one man die for all the people. And that the whole nation will not perish! But bring together all the children of God, even those scattered abroad!" Caiaphas blinked, shocked at his own word. He had prophesied! And even in that, found a way to handle all their problems.

Dante chuckled evilly, as he heard the Priest. *Well, well ... we may not have to work hard to destroy the Light Father's plans after all! The Holy Spirit just told what He plans, so sorry we will end it short of what you plan!* ***Caiaphas,*** he whispered, ***since one has to die, we need to make sure Jesus/Yeshua does! And maybe, even someone that follows Him can help???*** Caiaphas took this thought as his own, and worked from this day forward to accomplish the death of Jesus.

***

Jesus was on his way to Jerusalem. He was on the road between Samaria and Galilee. As He entered a village, He saw off to His right, a distance away, lepers. He heard, as they cried as one, "Jesus, Master, have mercy on us!" He saw their disheveled look and their sickness, and He spoke with authority smiling, **"Go! Show yourselves to the Priests!"** He watched as they all turned and began the walk to where the local priests stayed.

And one of them, a Samaritan, seeing He had been healed and cleansed completely, shouted in a loud voice.

"Glory to God! Praise God!"

He turned back, rushing to Jesus. He fell on his face at Jesus' feet, weeping and saying, "Thank you, thank you!"

Jesus answered him, looking intently at him. "Did I not heal and cure ten?"

He paused, "Where are the other nine? No one returned to give God glory, but a foreigner??"

He reached down and took him by the hand saying, "Stand up. Go on your way. Your faith has made you whole." The man cured of leprosy smiled and laughed and danced as he went away toward home.

***

The Twelve privately asked Jesus, "Jesus increase our faith." Jesus was standing by a mulberry tree on the road to His house. And said, "If you had faith like a mustard seed. . ." He touched the tree, "You could say to this tree. . 'Come out of the ground, and fall into the sea!' And it would do so."

He made His way home to the house and sat. As crowds came by to listen and see Him, He again began to teach and share parables.

"There was in a certain city a judge who did not fear God or man. And it happened that a widow of the city came to Him and asked, "Give me protection and justice from my opponent."

"No," he told the widow. And he continued, "I am unwilling to help you."

"But daily, the widow would come and request his help. Each day his answer was the same. But one day he thought to himself, I do fear God or man! But this woman will wear me out with her request! So I will help her and finally be at peace."

"Did you hear what the unjust judge said? Will not God, the Father, bring about justice and more for His children and elect that cry to Him daily? Do you think that the Father would delay in helping them? I tell you truthfully, He will bring justice, swiftly for them. But, when the Son of God returns, will He find faith on the Earth? You should pray at all times and not lose heart."

Jesus continued, "There were two men, both going to the temple, to pray. One a Pharisee and the other, a tax collector. Now, the Pharisee stood and was praying to himself, "God I thank you, that I am not like other people! I am not a swindler, unjust, an adulterer, or even like this tax collector! I fast twice a week and pay tithes on all I get." Now the tax collector stood a great distance from the Pharisee. He didn't even look up to Heaven to pray. But head down and beating his chest, cried. "God . . ." he begged, "be merciful . . . to me, the sinner." I tell you now that this man went home justified before God, more than the other! He who justifies himself will be humbled. But, the one who humbles himself, will be exalted!"

Jesus thought to Himself after speaking, *Well Father, now I have done it. I am sure this will get back to the Scribes and Pharisees because you know, they trust in their own righteousness and pour contempt on everyone else!* He thought.

Jesus watched, as the crowds parted, and couples, men, women, came to where the Twelve were. Holding their children and babies, they asked to have Jesus touch them! The Twelve refused the request. Jesus heard it and said, "Let the children come to Me! Do not hinder them! Because the Kingdom of God belongs to such as these! I tell you the truth, whoever does not receive the Kingdom of God as a child, will not enter it."

After He had finished this, a ruler of the Temple, a young man who was rich, came to Jesus. He knelt before Him. "Good teacher, what can I do to inherit eternal life?" he said.

Jesus looked at the rich man and said, "Why do you call me good. There is only one good, and that is the Father. You know God's commands."

The young man stood in his finery and said, "Which ones?"

Jesus sighed deeply, and kept the frustration from His voice and said, "Do not murder, do not commit adultery, do not steal, do not lie, honor your father and mother, and love your neighbor as yourself." Jesus waited for the young ruler to speak. He could see the Law pass though his mind along with his teacher's words, his mentor's, and those ruling now. Jesus saw even a glimmer of his truly wanting to have eternal life.

The young man said, "All these I have kept from my youth," and Jesus knew it to be true.

So, out of love Jesus spoke, "One thing you still lack, sell all that you possess and distribute the money to the poor. And then you would have treasure in Heaven, come and follow Me."

When the ruler heard this, his head dropped, and he slowly walked away. Jesus knew he was an extremely wealthy man.

And Jesus said in amazement, "Truly, it is hard for a rich person to enter in the Kingdom of Heaven. It would easier for a camel to go through an eye of a needle, than a rich person to enter the Kingdom of God."

Those that heard this, and the Twelve, were astonished and asked, 'Who can be saved then?" Jesus looked at them all and said, "With men and people, this is impossible. But with God all things are possible."

Jesus continued, "The Kingdom of Heaven is like a vineyard owner. And he went out early in the morning to hire workers. When he found them, he hired them. And they agreed to work the day for a denarius. So, he sent them into his vineyard. He still needed workers, so he went back to find more workers in the third hour, found some standing idle and said, "Go to my vineyard and I will pay you whatever is right."" So they went. Still needing more, he went the sixth and ninth hours, and did the same. Now it was the eleventh hour, he went to the market place, and found others standing around. And said to them, "Why have you been here all day doing nothing?" they looked at him and said, "No one hired us." He said, "Go to my vineyard too."

"So now when evening came, the owner of the vineyard called the foreman and said, "Call all the laborers and pay their wages. Start with the last group first.""

"So those hired at the eleventh hour, came and received a denarius. Then when those he hired first came, they too got a denarius. But they expected more. And grumbled at the vineyard owner. 'These other men only worked one hour! And you gave them equal pay! But we bore more of the burden, and the scorching heat of the day!' ""

"The owner said to one of the men, 'Friend, I am doing you no wrong. Did you, or did you not agree to work a day for me, for a denarius?' The owner paused and finished. 'Take what is yours and go. But if I wish to pay the last man the same as you, can I not rightfully pay him what I wish? Or is it that you are envious because I am generous? The last shall be first and the first shall be last.' ""

***

Not long after this the sons of Zebedee and their mother, came to Jesus. She bowed at his feet and said, "I have a request."

Jesus saw James and John standing tall, and burly. He got a curious look on his face and he looked at the brothers, who shrugged their shoulders, but stood quiet. They held their hands up to forestall any conversation or comment. *They know their mother.* Jesus grinned. He looked at her and shook his head, thinking, what it must have been like in childbirth for a woman that small to bear something, so big. He smiled again.

"What do you wish?" He said.

"When your Kingdom comes, command these two sons of mine, sit on your right and left," she said.

Jesus looked at James and John, who again, shrugged and stayed silent.

Looking at their mother, Jesus answered, "You do not know what you ask." He spoke to all three now, "Are you able to drink the cup I drink?"

James and John said, "Yes, we are able."

Jesus said to them, "My cup you will drink. But to sit on my right hand, or left, that is not Mine to give. Those places are for those My Father has prepared them for."

And when the ten heard this, they became indignant! But Jesus called them all together and said, "The rulers of the Gentiles lord over them, and their great men exercise authority over them. But this will not be the way with you! Because the one here who wishes to be great among you will be your servant. And whoever wishes to be first among you, will be a slave. Just like I came, not to be served, but to serve. And give my life a ransom for many!"

***

Jesus and the Twelve had gone to Jericho. And when they were leaving a great crowd followed. And a blind beggar, known as Bartimaeus, the son of Timaeus, heard the crowd, and asked what was going on. Some of the crowd said, "Jesus, the Nazarene, was passing by. Bartimaeus thought to himself . . . *Jesus the Nazarene. Who . . . Who is that? Wait! I know, now! I cannot live like this. Too many days; too many nights, barely living, and all in darkness! I must say something! But can he hear with the crowd? He is too busy, too important, would He help?* Bartimaeus made up his mind! He had heard of miracles and wonders done by Jesus. And hope rose in his heart, and he dared! So, he cried out as loud as he could, "Jesus, son of David, have mercy on me!" He heard those in the crowd say, "Be quiet!" "Do not bother Jesus!" "Quiet beggar!" he heard their anger and felt their contempt.

He cried out again, with all he had! "Son of David! Have mercy on me!" As more thoughts raced through his mind. *I lost everything! I was an elder of the city, a good business man, and then darkness! I cannot live anymore like this! I barely live.*

His thoughts were interrupted by a man of the crowd that said, "Take courage; stand up! Jesus is calling you!"

Bartimaeus stopped. *Was it true? Did he hear him right? Jesus was asking for me? After all these years, can I believe it? Should I believe it! Come on Bartimaeus, if you don't move, you will never know!*

So Bartimaeus, threw off his cloak, got to his feet and came to Jesus. He stood in front of Jesus, after a helper or two, steered him right.

Jesus looked at him and asked. "What would you like me to do for you?"

Jesus waited quietly. He saw the years etched in his skin. He saw laugh lines, now heavier with grief and pain. His skin bore the years of the sun; yet, he looked strong. He looked like a man of prominence. Maybe the blindness caused him to lose everything.

Finally, Bartimaeus answered. "Rabboni, Lord . . . I want to regain my sight!"

Jesus smiled. And spoke with authority, **"Receive your sight; your faith, has made you whole."**

The crowd and Bartimaeus waited, as he moved his hands up to cover his eyes. And thought, *He said receive my sight! I guess I have to open them now! It's now or never Bartimaeus!*

He opened his eyes and moved his hands, then saw! No dimness, no fog, perfect sight! He looked all around. The crowd watched, as he spun in place, and shouted, "Glory to god! I can see!" He began laughing and dancing! And the crowd that had tried to silence him, joined him in shouting praise to God! He walked to one in the crowd and grabbed the man's shoulders and said, "I see you! I see you." The man smiled and embraced him. Bartimeus turned and walked with the crowd following Jesus. Then he went back for his cloak! "Ha – ha," he said. "I didn't trip!" as he kicked his empty alms bowl and watched it tumble over the small gully. Laughing, he turned and ran after Jesus and those that followed Him!

***

Son, He heard the Father, ***Go back; there is a little matter we need to take care of. It will be interesting with this crowd. There is one here besides Bartimaeus that needs You. Though he doesn't know it yet. And he wants to meet You. He is the chief tax collector, and quite wealthy. Though the people here almost despise him. He is in need of salvation and hope. He is big in business.*** The Father chuckled.

I will Father and he will hear of the Kingdom.

Jesus reentered the city gate and began walking up the main street. The Twelve were not surprised at all. They knew Jesus heard from the Father often. And as usual. . . plans changed.

The crowd adjusted and flowed with Him. Zaccheus had heard Jesus was here in Jericho and wanted to see Him. *I never have met a prophet before, or a miracle worker, as he has been called. Do they look different than we do? I mean, John the Baptist, walked around in a rough camel hair outfit. He had crazy hair and all. He ate bugs!* Zaccheus shook his head, *If that's true, then Jesus will be a sight for sure! I may need to talk with Him about presentation! And clothing! I mean you are what you wear!* He grumbled, as his sandal sunk in a puddle, and splashed up on his tunic and fine linen. *Ahh, every time!* He thought, *If not the puddles, then sheep dung or worse!* He looked and the street was busy as usual. But heard noise, the next street over, many voices and shouts of joy! *I wonder what happened.* He turned and crossed between two buildings. And there, he saw a large crowd. And more people lining both sides of the street. He paused. He looked up and down the street. The crowds was moving as one mass in his direction. But he wasn't sure. *Okay, think, think, Zacchaeus! Well, if they come this way, I won't see because of those lining the street. And of course, I can't push my way to the front!* He looked up the street and there was a sycamore to side nearest him. He looked back over his right shoulder and it seemed the crowd was moving his way.

Well, if they come close to that tree, I should be able to at least see something! And since there are not stairs nearby or roof access, you, Mr. Sycamore, are my only option! He thought, as he moved toward the tree.

Zaccheus ran ahead and touched the trunk. Looking both ways, he jumped and almost touched the lowest branch! "Grr," he said. "It doesn't pay to be short! How is it I have a good business and money, but I can't reach a tree branch!" Zaccheus backed up a step and looked at the gnarled trunk. Some of the bark had been torn away, and some places had knots that might help in climbing. So, he grabbed at a knot and pulled himself higher. He looked for footing and found it. And moved higher. He then grabbed a branch and crawled up and sat on the branch. "Whew! I made it," as he looked at his tunic and saw a tear! "Great! Not only do I have to clean this, I have to get it sewed!" he said aloud.

He looked back and he caught a glimpse of a man in front of the crowd. And they were coming closer. "Still can't see Him. Well, I better go up one more!" he said. Zaccheus grabbed the next branch up and sat on it. He watched from his perch and the crowd moved in time with the man in front. He noticed there was a tight-knit group of men a step away on his right. And they kept constant watch to see what He would do. The crowd grew closer and he saw the dust cloud build as they moved. And he heard clearly now, shouts of joy and praise to God! Zaccheus laughed aloud as men and women danced and shouted! *This is a party!* He saw one man laughing, shouting, and dancing! *I know that man! Or I think I do. No it can't be. . . Maybe it is? That man dancing and laughing that looks like Bartimaeus! That business man gone blind! But how is that possible? He was blind! Even the doctors said there was no hope!* He thought, as the joyous crowd was mere yards from the tree!

Now Zacchaeus could see clearly. And the man that was leading was now encircled by the crowd. He was smiling and embracing the one he thought was Bartimaeus. *He doesn't look wild and crazy like John did. He . . . actually looks normal. The prayer shawl and tunic are of good make. And His eyes . . . Jesus looked up to the tree. Zaccheus looked in His eyes. He looks kind and honest, even truthful. Probably too trusting. People could take advantage.* Zaccheus adjusted his seating on the branch, and watched as the crowd and this man Jesus came and stopped at the foot of the tree. His sycamore tree.

Okay Father, where is this one that needs help? You usually bring me right to them. And with this crowd, I could have missed him. Are we going to play a game like hide and seek? Or hot or cold? He felt the Father laugh. **No, Son, look up.** *Oh.* Then, He alone, heard the Father laugh.

Jesus looked up the sycamore tree and saw Zaccheus. Jesus looked at the chief tax collector and thought, *Yes, he certainly is attired well. And his clothes rival the priest in finery. And his feet, well-manicured. There's no mistaking him at all. Though, truthfully he is a small man.* Jesus smiled and said, "Zaccheus, I am Jesus, come down out of the tree quickly! I need to stay at your house today."

So, Jesus watched as Zaccheus climbed down from his perch on the branch and finally stood next to Jesus. Zaccheus smiled and shook Jesus' hand and was heard to say, "Of course! Of course, my house, yes. You will stay."

The crowd was not rejoicing anymore, nor laughing. Murmuring was heard, and then, loud cries! "Oh of course, Jesus will go to his house!" "Why don't you come to mine Jesus?" "He has stolen a lot from the city! Why him? Is he paying you?" "Why is Jesus going to stay at a sinners house?"

Zaccheus heard and felt their jibes and scorn. This was nothing new. But it didn't hurt any less. *Yes, I was shrewd. Yes, I was calculating. But business was business. I had always been good with money! I understood how the Roman mind worked. And even the greed of the city elders and priests. In all these years, not once did any approach me to dine at their homes. Or attend parties for children, births, or weddings. I worked tirelessly to make Jericho prosperous and safe for families. And free from the Roman garrison.* He thought.

Jesus watched as pain, rejection, regret, embarrassment washed across his face. Jesus could see the struggle. Zaccheus bowed his head, smoothed out his tunic, and cloak, stood tall. Then said, "Lord Jesus, I tell you now. I will give half my wealth to those poor, here, and the other cities. And if I swindled or stole from anyone . . . I will pay them four times what was taken."

The crowd was silent. Not a word, not a sound. They watched as Zacchaeus turned and began to walk toward his house. And Jesus laying an arm across his shoulders said for all to hear, "Today salvation has come to this house! Because he too is a son of Abraham. And I have come to seek and to save that which was lost!"

CHAPTER 15

PARABLES, TRIUMPHAL ENTRY AND MORE

The crowd followed Jesus and Zaccheus to his house. And as Zaccheus had food and drink prepared, Jesus went out to the crowd. ***Son***, he heard the father, ***these people; they believe that the restoration of the kingdom promised; ours and Israel's, will happen, now. It is not the time for that to take place.*** Jesus sat down and shared a parable.

"A nobleman was given a kingdom, in a distant land. He would go; and receive the honor, fulfill his duties, and return. So he called his ten slaves; and said to them all. "take the ten minas of money all of you. And do business with it until i return." the nobleman left; and citizens hated him. And they sent a delegation after him saying "we do not want this man to reign over us!"

When the nobleman arrived home; after his journey, he called his slaves to see how they did in business, while he was gone.

The first slave, came before him and he said "Master, I had ten mina. I have made ten more." the nobleman replied. "well done, good slave, because you were faithful with little, you will have authority over ten cities." Then the second came and said, "Master, your mina, has made five more," he answered. "Good, you have authority now over five cities." Another came and said, "Master, here is your mina. I kept it in a handkerchief; why, because I was afraid of you. I knew that you were a harsh, severe man. Taking what you didn't lay down or reaping what you didn't sow." The nobleman said, "By your own words, I will judge you. You worthless slave! If you believed these things why didn't you at least put my money in the bank, that I would at least gain, interest on it when I returned!" he turned to those watching. "Take away the mina from him! And give it to the one who has ten." They said, "Master, he already has ten?"

The nobleman finished, "I tell you everyone who has, more will be given. But, from one who does not have, even what they have will be taken away. But these enemies who did not want me to reign over them, bring them here! And slay them in my presence!"

***

Jesus and the Twelve returned to Bethany. The Passover was only six days away. They were there with Mary, Martha, and Lazarus. Jesus was reclining at the table with Lazarus, took in the scents of the cooking meal. And watched as Martha cooked and Mary helped. Jesus sighed. *I am glad we came. This feels more home, than even the house in Capernaum. As for now, it's quiet. But as always I am sure that will change. Since this house now has two famous people in it!* He laughed to himself and turned to Lazarus and said, "So, other than eating large amounts of Martha's great cooking, what is it like to be famous?"

Lazarus laughed and scoffed. "Well . . ." he said with a grin, "a lot like you! Crowds of people gawking, oohing and aahing, and angry Scribes and Pharisees picking apart a miracle God has done and parsing it down to find something wrong! How can these priests even sleep? They have no joy. I have never seen one laugh! And yet, when they come here, they still look on me as if I sin, for even being alive!" He finished the cup in his hand with a gulp and poured more in.

Lazarus looked deeply at Jesus. "I am sorry Jesus, I didn't want to ruin our dinner. And ruin the peace of the evening." Martha came by the table and said, "Yes, what he said is true. They have even said you cast out demons by their prince. So, Lazarus being alive, seems worse, to them."

"They have forgotten their charge. They were to seek God the Father, walk with Him, and help those around them. Not only to find their Heavenly Father, but have relationship with Him, as well. And from that, fulfill all the Law. The Law you know. **You shall love the Lord your God with all of your heart. And with all of you mind. And with all of your strength. And all of your soul. And your neighbor, as yourself.**" Jesus drank from his cup and smiled up at Martha, and finished, "They have lost their way. Their religiousness, and self-righteousness blinds them to truth. Even the very truth that they, even as they are, are deeply loved by the Father. It hurts Him to watch them miss out on what was, is and could be theirs. Real life, peace, joy. Not duty or regulation. But life."

The evening went on with conversation and laughter. *Martha has out done herself tonight. I cannot eat another bite!* He thought. And turning to Martha he said, "With cooking like this, I am surprised Lazarus, can even put on a cloak. Let alone, his tunic!" Jesus laughed and grinned. "I cannot eat anymore."

Lazarus patted his round belly with his hands, laughing. "I say, why get married, when your sisters cook like this!" The whole house erupted in laughter!

Soon after dinner Jesus was relaxing at his favorite spot, in the house, the mat for just a bit by the fire. Warm, but not too warm. He sipped from his cup and looked at his friends and disciples and thought, *Thank you Father for this. Thank you for fulfilling another promise. You said you would place the orphan, in families. Though I am not an orphan. This truly feels like home. Minus the angels and things.*

The room was quiet, all that was heard was the crackle of the fire. And the smell cedar and flowers. And everyone was relaxing and content.

Jesus watched as Mary, carrying a jar, came into the room. It was an alabaster jar full of nard. She walked quietly, almost reverently to him, and kneeled down. The firelight cast a warm glow on her face and clothes. The jar sparkled with reflection. He saw her head bowed. And tears, "Mary. . ." he started. She held up her hand. Jesus stopped. Mary was holding the jar now; she broke the seal on the lid, and poured the nard over his feet. Jesus felt the oil and smelled the perfume, which began to fill the house. He watched as she lovingly took her hand and spread it on his feet and sandals. He watched as tears streamed down her face. Jesus was going to speak, and then stopped.

Jesus looked at her; and then saw her begin to wipe his feet with her hair. *She honors me.* And the tender moment was shattered by Judas Iscariot's cry, "What are you doing! We could have sold that at the least for three hundred denarii and given it to the poor!"

Angry, Jesus answered, "Leave her alone!" he knew Judas was a thief and that he held the money box, and stole from it often. *Liar, you want to give the poor nothing!* He thought. He finished, "She is doing this for my burial. And she honors me. Leave this as memorial for her forever. The poor will always be here, but I will not be."

When large crowds of Jews learned that Jesus was at Bethany, they came. They came not only to see Jesus, or be with him, but they also hoped to see Lazarus because he was raised by Jesus form the dead. The chief priests and Scribes, however, planned to kill Lazarus and Jesus because many were believing in him.

***

Jesus woke early the next day. The time with Lazarus, Mary, and Martha was sweet. He got off his mat and stood. The others were still sleeping and even Simon Peter wasn't snoring. He quietly left the house, and stood in the early morning light. The sun was just cresting the hills behind him. He looked to Heaven and smiled. Then he bowed his head and said, "Father, good morning." He breathed in the scent of flowers, and the crisp early morning. He smiled, as he caught the faint scent of the perfume, still clinging to his feet.

"Father, I am glad you are here, and you too Holy Spirit. In my humanness, I am not so sure I am ready to do all that needs to be done." Jesus finished. Jesus looked around at the people still gathered around the house at Bethany. Some had left to go into the town and use the inn. But most, it seemed, had just slept under the stars. Since the weather was good at the moment. Jesus chuckled quietly and said, "And if it did change; I am sure they would ask me to make it sunny, and a bit cooler Father."

Son, if they ask, you can if you want. But I understand, this is a God size mission, and only you can do it. But from this day on, for you, it will not be easy. All these things must take place. Today, when you go into Jerusalem, you not are just Jesus the Nazarene as they call you. But you are according to Scripture, like the prophet Zechariah said rejoice greatly, O Daughter of Zion! Shout in triumph, O daughter of Jerusalem! Behold, your King is coming to you; he is just and endowed with salvation, humble, and mounted on a donkey, even on a colt, the foal of a donkey. Meaning as you know, you are truly the coming King. And you will rightly be praised by the people. But not by others. Because you are also the Messiah. . .a judge. Isaiah said the Lord arises to contend, and stands to judge the people. The Lord enters into judgment with the elders and princes of his people, "It is you who have devoured the vineyard; the plunder of the poor is in your houses. "What do you mean by crushing my people and grinding the face of the poor?" Declares the Lord God of hosts. Messiah is twofold. Not only as judge; but even as Daniel said seventy weeks have been decreed for your people and your holy city, to finish the wrongdoing, to make an end of sin, to make atonement for guilt, to bring in everlasting righteousness, to seal up vision and prophecy, and to anoint the most holy place. So, you are to know and understand that from the issuing of a decree to restore and rebuild Jerusalem, until Messiah the prince, . . .then after the sixty-two weeks, the Messiah will be cut off and have nothing. You will also be the Passover lamb. To do as Daniel spoke. And as King David spoke blessed is the one who comes in the name of the Lord, we have blessed you from the house of the Lord. They will rightly praise you. Because you are a priest and are fulfilling the law and prophets. Fear is the enemy's tool, and I know; he will try and stop you. But he does not know the whole plan. Remember these words. And my love. And don't forget; you also must bring first fruits, to the Temple, as part of the celebration.

Well Father, he thought, *we are near Bethpage; I could bring a small basket, the Twelve and those that truly believe. And they will be my* **first fruits!** *And I know the people are looking for a Messiah King to push out the Romans and defeat all of Israel's enemies. But our real enemy is sin. And the works of the devil. Like Daniel said for your* **people and your holy city, to finish the wrongdoing, to make an end of sin, to make atonement for guilt, to bring in everlasting righteousness**, *to seal up vision and prophecy, and to anoint the most holy place. Father I know the priests and elders will not like what must be done as a testimony to Israel and the nations; righteousness, must prevail.*

Jesus was filled with the Holy Spirit and power. He stood praying and communing in the early morning stillness. *The Father is right. If we do not complete this, all creation and all of mankind will perish. And we will have lost all we love. So, first I need a foal of donkey. . . Ahh thank you Father; you did say* **Bethpage.** *So, we can get the donkey and the Omer of figs. Well, when the others wake up, we will get started.*

Jesus walked back to the house and went inside. The house was warm, and the smell of the perfume still hung in the air. And some of the disciples stirred. Mary and Martha had already began getting fruits out bread and cheese. He smiled at them both, sat and drank water, and took bread and cheese. "Thank you," he said to both. Jesus bowed his head, *Thank you Father for this day again. I ask for an anointing to do all I am required. I will need strength and guidance. Especially, with this crowd, outside already here. Well, whoever wakes up first I will have them go to Bethpage and get the colt. And then get some figs and bring the first fruits to the Temple as the Law demands. And Father, one day all the first fruits will be brought in.*

More of the house was awake now. And they came and sat and broke bread. And Jesus turned to James and John and said, "I need you two to go and get something for me. And meet us in Bethpage."

James and John looked at each other and grinned. Jesus laughed. "When you are finished go there and you will find a colt of a donkey and its mother tied by a door in the street. One that no one has ever ridden. And when the owners ask you, 'Why are you untying them,' you will say the Lord needs them. And they will be returned to you.' " They looked at Jesus skeptically, then with a mischievous grin, shrugged. They both gulped water from their cups and grabbed a hunk of cheese, and headed out the door.

*Well, one thing done. Now to head to **Bethpage,** and get an Omer of figs. I wonder how many of the people here will follow. I am sure someone has let it leak that we will be heading to the first fruits and Passover,* Jesus thought.

****

So, James and John found their way to Bethpage. And the city seemed quiet, to the big burly brothers. They saw near a door a colt and its mother. They saw the door was open and people were moving around inside. They moved to where the colt and mother were. They looked inside. The people were eating and they heard the discussion about the celebration and Passover. James looked at John and said, "Well, there's a colt here, and momma just as Jesus said. I guess this is the one. Not sure how to tell if it's ever been ridden. But you know Jesus, normally whatever he says, goes." So, they began to untie the colt. And as they were untying the colt the owners came out. And asked, "Why are you untying the colt?"

James looked to the worried travelers, he smiled and said, "The Lord has need of them. They will be returned."

"The Lord . . . ," the man thought for a moment. And then smiled and said, "You may take them." And he went back inside. And sat down. James looked at John. John had an astonished look on his face. James, punched his brother's shoulder and said, "Are you surprised! Let's go. We need to get back to Bethany!" James took the mother and John the colt. The owners watch the two big men lead away their animals and smiled.

Jesus turned to the disciples and said, "We are going to Bethphage to get an Omer of figs, and go to the Temple and give our first fruits and James and John will meet us there." Mary, Martha and Lazarus hugged Jesus. And said they would try and follow them to the Temple as well. Jesus opened the door to the house and looked out on the crowd ready to travel. He laughed and said to everyone, "Well, it looks like we will not have to wait for anyone. Let's go the Bethphage and meet James and John."

Jesus led the Twelve and others up the ridge toward Bethphage. He moved through the tree lined road. And caught scent of pine and flowers and saw trees heavy with fruit. They walked enjoying the creation of God and each other's company. Every so often Jesus would turn and look back at the large crowd following behind. *Yes indeed! This is not a quiet trip.* Laughing to himself. As they came up the hill to the house at Bethphage, he saw James and John, waiting with the colt. He walked up to the two hugged them fiercely and broke the embrace.

"Here is what you requested Jesus," John said. Jesus looked at the colt and its mother not far away. And answered, "Yes, I see. Thank you." "Judas Iscariot, come here please," He called.

Judas Iscariot walked to Jesus and stopped. "Yes, Jesus."

Jesus noted that Judas' hand never left the clasp of the larger money bag they used on trips and travel. Jesus knew of course, he had often "stolen from the bag." Jesus looked at Judas. He was dark haired and curly. Average height and weight. And his clothes, were good fine linen and good colored. No tears or stains. Average. Except, his eyes. They were always shifting, and taking in everything. Like he was looking for advantage and ways to get something. *Like a thief. I was hoping he would change. After all he has seen. . . I will never understand. Just as Lightbringer/Lucifer/Satan could have repented. And has not. . .neither has he.*

"Judas, go into the house, and pay the owner for an Omer of figs, and for a basket. Please."

His eyes fell to the ground for a moment. And then he looked Jesus in the eyes and said, "I will," with reluctance. And Jesus watched as he walked toward the house. . . his hand never left the bag clasp.

Jesus turned, as Judas came out from the house, carrying the Omer of figs. He dropped it at Jesus feet. "Here is the Omer, Jesus," he said. "Though, I know I can't carry it to the Temple. Maybe, John or James can." He finished. Jesus looked at John and he smiled and picked up the Omer with ease. And Judas said, "And be careful with that! All of it better make to the temple for the offering, especially for what we paid for it!"

John gave Jesus a sideways glance; Jesus subtlety shook his head. And John stayed silent. "Well, Jesus said it is time to move on. Now understand this all of you. We go to Jerusalem, to the Temple, to offer first fruits. I as Messiah, King, Priest, and Judge of the nation. You will see the elders, priests and others react. But not you. Scripture will be fulfilled this day! Remember Zechariah and Isaiah and more. . ."

James moved to Jesus, and took his cloak off, and laid it on the colt. As did others. One the Twelve took the reins of the mother, and began to go toward Jerusalem and the Mount of Olives. The colt with Jesus on it, followed not far from his mother. Being led by James. John opposite James with Omer on his shoulder kept in step with his brother easily. They moved in silence. All the others followed behind as they made their way to the Mount of Olives. Jesus knew with every hoof beat of the colt and step the with the disciples and the crowd. He, as Messiah, King, Priest, Judge, Passover lamb was on his way to destiny. And at every footfall Scripture rang in His ears. **"FOR THE LORD GOD HELPS ME, THEREFORE, I AM NOT DISGRACED; THEREFORE, I HAVE SET MY FACE LIKE FLINT, AND I KNOW THAT I WILL NOT BE ASHAMED."**

Jesus rode quietly. And the crowd surged as they climbed the hill toward the mount of olives. And all at once a cry was raised, "Hosanna to the son of David; blessed is he who comes in the name of the Lord; Hosanna in the highest!" And again, "Blessed is the King who comes in the name of the Lord; peace in Heaven and glory in the highest!" "Hosanna!" "Hosanna!"

Jesus watched as the crowd surged around Him. And encircled Him. And they cried again, "Hosanna!" And with every cry Jesus heard the word of God in his ears, as each hoofbeat and footstep brough him closer to the Mount of Olives and Jerusalem. Jesus looked out upon sea of joy and jubilation! And shouts! And as those nearby came and touched him and shouted! And laid their cloaks on the ground before him and palm branches, mulberry, pine, and olive branches.

Jesus heard, "Seventy weeks have been decreed for your people and your holy city, to finish the wrongdoing, to make an end of sin, to make atonement for guilt, to bring in everlasting righteousness, to seal up vision and prophecy, and to anoint the most holy place."

Though he was on a small colt. He felt the steps reverberate through eternity! He thought back to when the Father decreed. . .*the Father of Lights looked intently at the Son and said, "We knew of this long ago and we searched far and wide to find the best solution to sin, he spit it out as if the poison of the word spoken would make its effect worse, 'and this dear son is our only choice.' He laughed ruefully, "Millennia from now hosts of angels and even the redeemed will question 'our choice' and the power of sin and its ultimate destruction. More so many will ask, why? That you Son, wanted to die for them. Their perceived value to creation and our world will have them question all of it just as Light Bringer, even how much we value them." He continued, "And redemption is necessary. Their creation, lives, joys, sorrows, pains, and exultation add more to the world, and their choice to love Us, than they will ever know. And for now, it must be. Remember; all that we have in store for them, and even their homecoming. To have them again, walk with Us out of love, even true companionship. Heaven and all that it will bring them, and Us, to the desired end. This must be done. . . At all cost."*

Jesus looked ahead, and saw the Mount of Olives and the crest of the hill. He saw palms waving! People dancing! Shouts of joy echoed in the hills! The crowd coming up the hill blended with those coming up out of Jerusalem! And the crowd expanded! And the celebration, shouts of praise to God for all the miracles! And all the things they had seen and what Jesus had done, echoed across the hills! In that moment, Jesus called James to halt the donkey. He climbed off and looked at Jerusalem!

One of the disciples came to him and said laughing, "Sorry Jesus, it seems someone, told those in Jerusalem you were attending the celebration of first fruits and Passover! I am not sure how we will fit through the gate!" Jesus laughed too. And then he saw the Priests and

Scribes storming over the hill! Amidst more shouts! "Hosanna! Glory to God in the highest!" and "Blessed is he who comes in the name of the Lord! Blessed be the King of Israel, Hosanna save now! Blessed is the coming kingdom of our father David!" and "Blessed is the King who comes in the name of the Lord; peace in Heaven and glory in the highest!"

Jesus turned to the elder of the Pharisees and Scribes, the man shouted, "Teacher! Rebuke your disciples! Tell them to be silent!"

Jesus looked at the Priest. He knew why he had said this and why he was sent before the crowd!

Full of the Holy Spirit and power, Jesus answered in authority. **"I tell you now; and all who hear, if these. . ."** he spread his arms to take in all the crowd, still rejoicing and praising God, and finished. . . **"fall silent, the very stones beneath the ground will cry out!"**

He looked intently at the elder, full of compassion. "You were to be guides, of the people. God called you and Isaiah, now rebukes you. "**I have kept silent for a long time, I have kept still and restrained myself. . . Hear, you deaf! And look, you blind, that you may see. Who is blind but my servant, or so deaf as my messenger whom I send? This is a people plundered and despoiled; all of them are trapped in caves, or are hidden away in prisons; they have become a prey with none to deliver them, and a spoil, with none to say, "Give them back!"** Jesus met the elders angry eyes; and in compassion finished, "The time for repentance is shortening. But God is full of forgiveness and mercy."

Jesus turned from the elder; and walked to the crest of hill, overlooking Jerusalem and the Temple Mount. The crowd parted as Jesus moved. No one spoke. Jesus bowed his head, as everyone looked on, and spread his arms wide and cried in a loud voice!

"Jerusalem! Jerusalem! If you had only known this day. And the things that bring peace! For the days are coming when your enemies will build a barricade and surround you and close you in on every side! They will level you to the ground and the people within your walls! And they will not leave one stone standing. All this awaits because you did not see, or even understand your time of visitation!" Jesus finished and stood there weeping.

Jesus walked past James, and got back on the colt, and headed down to Jerusalem and the Temple. Jesus watched, as the crowd picked up where they left off. They laid cloaks before him and palm branches still. And the shouts and dancing continued! Jesus watched the guards at the gate tensed. Then allowed them passage as the crowd ushered Jesus through the gate into Jerusalem! He then had James stop. And told him, "Thank you James! Now you may take the pair back to Bethpage. And thank the owners! Meet us at Lazarus' house in Bethany. I need john still to carry the Omer to the Temple! Go on now."

James smiled hugged Jesus and took the reins of both beasts, and headed back up the slope to Bethpage and Bethany.

Jesus walked with the crowd to the Temple. The crowd pushed its way through the streets at a good pace. And Jesus looked at John still carrying the Omer. And said, "How you doing John? Is your burden too much?" John looked at Jesus and smiled. "No, I am fine truly. This isn't even as heavy as the wood my mother makes me put in the house for fires in winter." Jesus laughed. "No," he said, "knowing your mother like I do, I would say I went easy on you!" John laughed again. "Okay, not that easy!" they laughed more as he moved further up the street.

Finally, they entered the Temple and walked to the court of the priests. And set down the Omer. And Jesus waited. Soon a priest came and said, "Is this for the celebration of first fruits and Passover?"

"Yes," Jesus said.

"Come with me and I will show you the place it will stay." John picked the Omer and followed Jesus and the Priest. They crossed the court to a storage area near the storages for grain. And they saw Omer after Omer of wheat, barley and more. Jesus stopped and said aloud, "Now, is the Scripture fulfilled. That we have brought the first fruits." Though Jesus knew he was speaking really of himself.

"Just a moment John." He said as he walked around the room and looked at the gifts and offerings. He saw the sun was setting and it was late. So, he now turned and called to John. "Our task here is finished. Let us go to Bethany and share another meal with our friend Lazarus and his sisters." John laughed and said "I can hardly wait! Martha is a great cook! Oh Jesus, don't tell my mother!"

Jesus laughed and grinned, "Oh, believe me John I won't! "

They both left in joy.

****

Jesus, as was his custom rose early. And he quietly stepped out of the house. The house in Bethany was quiet and still. He stepped into the early morning light, closed his eyes, and breathed deep. He smelt the wildflowers and heard the gentle breeze rustle in the trees. The early morning sun was warm on his face. He prayed, "Good morning Father; today is another day. And I commit myself, to finishing what we have planned." He opened his eyes and saw the glint of sunlight off the dew on the grass, and leaves of the trees.

Continuing, "Father, I need strength. Holy Spirit, I will need guidance, again. I know both of you are here. And will help. I would rather bring the people in by our great love. Even the nation, and the world. But that seems to be lost to all. Lightbringer/Satan has so twisted their minds and hearts with sin and lies. . .no wonder you said this was the only way."

He heard the Father, *Yes, Son, the only way. And sadly, today, you will have to be a judge. A judge over the Temple and the priesthood. Even the nation itself. Our first option is always love. Many are moved by it. Next is mercy, then grace, lastly forgiveness. Always before judgement. Just as in Isaiah and his day, I had kept silent for a long time, and restrained myself. But, now, it must be done. You must inspect the Temple and cleanse it, and call to account her Priests and Scribes and leaders.*

"Okay Father," He said aloud. I will. Though I truly wish I did not have too. It never should have been."

Jesus and the Twelve left the house and Bethany, and headed toward Jerusalem and the Temple. He enjoyed the walk with the Twelve. They talked amongst themselves and for once the crowd was not with them. Jesus relished the quiet. He felt the breeze and heard the birdsongs. And took in the beauty around him. He heard his stomach rumble. Then he realized he had not eaten and now he was hungry. As they walked through Bethphage, and over the crest of the hill, he saw a fig tree. Full of leaves. Hoping there was fruit, he walked to it, and searched.

Full of the Spirit, after he searched the tree. Finding nothing, He spoke in authority, **"May no one eat fruit from you ever again!"** Jesus turned and continued on toward the Temple. He knew the Twelve had seen and heard.

As Jesus walked with them, he said, "Today we go to the Temple. And as Messiah, Priest, King, I must judge. I may have to cleanse the Temple, as testimony against the Elders, Priests, and Scribes. Do not be surprised."

The Twelve took his words in stride and continued to Jerusalem. Jesus made his way through the gate past the city guard and began the long walk to the Temple.

Jesus and the Twelve walked past the Temple Guard and entered the beautiful gate. All the courts were full of people. He could hear the vendors and those buying. He walked into the court of the priests. He stopped. He and the Twelve watched as the priests moved to the altar and offered sacrifice. Jesus looked at the other priest and scribes. All adorned in their finery. Jesus then full of the spirit moved. The Twelve paused.

Jesus heard, as he moved, the Word of God thundering in his ears! And spoke aloud in authority, **"The Lord God has opened my ear; and I was not disobedient nor did I turn back. For the Lord God helps me, therefore, I am not disgraced; therefore, I have set my face like flint, and I know that I will not be ashamed. For zeal for your house has consumed me, and the reproaches of those who reproach you have fallen on me. My house shall be called a house of prayer but you are making it a robber's den."** He heard the words echo through eternity. The voice of the Father crying out through him!

He moved to the first of the tables and those selling and turned it over! The Holy Spirit maintained his strength and he cried out again, **"Thus says the Lord, preserve justice and do righteousness, for my salvation is about to come and my righteousness to be revealed. To the eunuchs who keep my Sabbaths, and choose what pleases me, and hold fast my Covenant, to them I will give in my house and within my walls a *memorial, and a name* better than that of sons and daughters; I will give them an *everlasting name which will not be cut off*. Also, the foreigners who join themselves to the Lord, to minister to him, and to love the name of the Lord, to be his servants, everyone who keeps from profaning the Sabbath and holds fast my Covenant,"** and another table. An animal pen. A vendor of doves. . . He continued, **"Even those I will bring to my holy mountain; and make them joyful, in my house of prayer. Their burnt offerings and their sacrifices *will be acceptable* on my altar; for my house will be called a *house of prayer for all the peoples*. The Lord God, who gathers the dispersed of Israel, declares, 'Yet others I will gather to them, to those already gathered.'"**

"My house shall be called a house of prayer. but you are making it a robber's den."

And Jesus sat down. And immediately the blind, lame, the sick came to him in the Temple. And he healed them. But Chief Priests, Scribes and Elders, saw all the wonderful things and miracles Jesus was doing; they became indignant. And they heard the children shouting in the Temple, "Hosanna! Hosanna to the Son of David! Save now!" The Chief Priests, Scribes and Elders stormed to where Jesus sat in one of the courts and said, "Do you hear the shouts of these children? What they say!"

Jesus stopped. He sighed deeply and looked at them, full of the Spirit and answered, "Yes, . . .have you never read? Out of the mouths of infants and nursing babies, you have prepared praise for yourself?" Stunned to silence, the Chief Priests, Scribes and Elders, talked among themselves. And began to try and find ways to destroy him. They feared him. And the whole temple marveled at what he said and the miracles he performed. They sought ways to destroy him. But they could not find anything. They could do nothing because the people were hanging on every word he said. Jesus quietly left the Temple with Twelve, and went back to Bethany and Lazarus' house.

****

Jesus again entered the Temple and sat down to teach. And the people came and listened. The Chief Priests and Elders of the people came to him and demanded, "By what authority are you doing and saying these things? Who gave you authority?" He looked them calmly and being full of the Spirit said, "I will ask you one question. And if you answer me, I will tell you by what authority I do and say the things I do."

He waited and he could see the Elder fidget and tense in irritation. "Here is my question. The baptism of John, what was its source? Heaven or from men?"

Jesus watched as the Elders, Scribes and Priests conferred. He knew their thoughts, and still waited. [*If we say from Heaven, he will reply why did you not believe him?*] Or [*If we say from men, the people regard him as a prophet.*]

Jesus watched their faces and could concern and fear upon them. But mostly, deception. He knew they dare not answer at all. But they would.

"We, do not know." They told him.

Jesus looked at them intently and calmly said, "Because you did not answer, I will not tell you by what authority or whose I do things by."

He continued speaking to the Priests and Elders. "A man had two sons, and he came to the first and said, 'Son, go work today in the vineyard.' And he answered, "I will not.' But, he regretted his answer, and went. The man came to the second and said the same thing; and he answered, 'I will, sir,' but he did not go. Which of the sons, did the father's will?"

The Chief Priests and Elders conferred again and spoke. "The first."

Jesus said, "I tell you the truth," shaking his head sadly, " the tax collectors and prostitutes, will get into the Kingdom of God, before you. Why? Because John came to you in the way of righteousness. And you did not believe him. But they did. And you, after seeing how they turned to John and his message. You felt no remorse or sadness, that you would then believe."

And Jesus continued.

"Listen to another parable. There was a landowner who planted a vineyard, and put a wall around it and dug a wine press in it, and built a tower, and rented it out to vine-growers and went on a journey. When the harvest time approached, he sent his slaves to the vine-growers, to receive his produce. The vine-growers took his slaves and beat one and killed another, and stoned a third. Again, he sent another group of slaves larger than the first; and they did the same thing to them.

The owner of the vineyard said, 'What shall I do? I will send my beloved son; they will *respect* my son. But when the vine-growers saw the son; they said among themselves, 'This is ***the heir***; come, let us kill him and seize his inheritance. So, they threw him out of the vineyard and killed him. What then will the owner do to them? He will come and destroy these vine-growers and will give the vineyard to others."

Jesus said to the Chief Priests and Elders, "Did you never read in the Scriptures, 'The stone which the builders rejected, this has become the chief corner stone; this came about from the Lord, and it is marvelous in our eyes'?" He spoke in authority, **"Now, I say to you, the Kingdom of God will be taken away from you and given to a people, producing the fruit of it. And he who falls on this stone will be broken to pieces, but on whomever it falls, it will scatter him like dust."**

The Chief Priests, Pharisees and Scribes understood he was speaking of them. They wanted then to seize him, but feared. The people considered him a prophet.

CHAPTER 16

PARABLES, THE FEAST, WIDOWS MITE AND MORE

Jesus spoke to them again in parables, saying, "The Kingdom of Heaven may be compared to a king who gave a wedding feast for his son. And he sent out his slaves; to call all those who had been invited to the wedding feast. And they were unwilling to come. Again, he sent out other slaves saying, "tell those who have been invited, "Behold, I have prepared my dinner; my oxen and my fattened livestock are all butchered and everything is ready; come to the wedding feast!" But they paid no attention. But they all began to make excuses. One said "I have bought a piece of land and I need to go out and look at it. Please excuse me." And another, "I bought five yoke of oxen and I need to try them out. Please excuse me." And another, " I have married a wife; and I cannot come. Please excuse me."

But the king was enraged and said, "The wedding is ready, but those who were invited were not worthy! Go out to the main roads, and invite any you find. So, his servants did so. His servant returned and said master, what you commanded has been done, and still there is room. And the king said to the slave, 'Go bring in here the poor and crippled and blind, and lame. Go out into the highways, and along the hedges, and compel them to come in, so that my house may be filled. Then the king came in and looked over the wedding guests; he saw a man who was not dressed in wedding clothes. And he said, "Friend, you are not dressed in wedding clothes; how did you get in? The man was speechless. The king turned to his servants and said, "Bind him hand and foot, and throw him into the outer darkness; in that place there will be weeping and gnashing of teeth.' for many are called, but few are chosen."

****

The Chief Priests, Pharisees and Scribes understood he was speaking of them. So, they watched him and sent spies who pretended to be right and act right, in order to catch him in what he said or did. To the sole purpose of turning him over to the governor or other authorities. Because if they did anything it would tarnish their office. And the Chief Priests, Pharisees and Scribes sent their disciples to him, along with the Herodians, and they said smoothly, "Teacher; we know that you are truthful and teach the way of God in truth, and that you do not show partiality to anyone. Is it right to pay tribute to Caesar? Or not?"

Jesus knew they were trying to trap him and deceive. So, he sighed deeply and said, "Show me a coin." They reluctantly, gave him a denarii. Jesus held it up; turned it front and back. And asked. "Whose inscription is on the coin?" They paused briefly looking at each other and replied. "Caesar's/"

Jesus tossed the coin to the priest and said in authority, **"Give to Caesar; the things that are Caesar's, and to God, the things that are God's."**

The chief priests; pharisees and scribes were unable to trap in his words, amazed, they stayed silent and went away.

The Chief Priests and Scribes were arguing and Jesus walked over and they asked Jesus, "What is the greatest commandment of all?"

Jesus smiled and spoke in authority, "Hear, O' Israel! The Lord our God is one Lord; and you shall love the Lord your God with all your heart, and with all your soul, and with all your mind, and with all your strength. The second is this, 'You shall love your neighbor as yourself.' There is no other commandment greater than these." The scribe said, "That is right teacher; you have truly stated he is one, and there is no one else beside him. To love him with all the heart, mind, soul, strength, and your neighbor as himself. . .is more than all the burnt offerings and sacrifices." Jesus understanding his answer said to the Scribe, "You are not far from the Kingdom of God." After that no one asked Jesus any more questions.

*****

Jesus again went into the Temple. And as always, people were buying, selling and giving sacrifice. Today Jesus walked through the Temple. And went past the court of women and sat down opposite the treasury. Jesus and the Twelve sat and he watched the people come and go. And he saw people put their offering in the treasury. The Chief Priests stood outside the treasury in all their finery.

Son, as Messiah you are to judge the priests and scribes, yes. Even the worship and sacrifice. Offerings were and are worship. And now. . . See. Look what it has become. And yet. . .he heard the Father.

Jesus saw people move passed the colonnades opposite him and he saw the offering boxes, and the offering trumpet flutes where the coins would roll into the box and be their offering. He watched the chief priests as people came by. Some, the priests bowed slightly too, due to position or power. The priesthood, in all its glory, on display for all to see. He watched as families, and entered and walked the colonnade and left their offering. Some, the priest, did not even smile at.

Many rich came through the colonnades and gave gifts. And they were greeted with great pomp and circumstance. *I am surprised Father that all these robes and tassels from the rich and the priests never get tangled or tied. Except, to buy favor. And better seat at a feast, or wedding. I was right to turn over the tables and chase them away. Look at them, truly, in all finery, naked. And poor.*

Son, look there; do you see the woman? She is a widow. Watch.

Jesus watched, as the woman moved along the colonnade. And came to the priest. He saw the priest, look briefly at her and caught, his disdain. Jesus saw the woman walk to the box. She closed her eyes and bowed her head. He could see her whispering, though he could not hear from where he was. She looked to Heaven, smiled, and opened her purse, and dropped two coins. She turned and walked toward the beautiful gate and down the steps of the Temple. Jesus watched her as she walked away. Her clothes were simple, clean, and untorn. Unlike the rich man there now blowing a trumpet, and pouring in a basket of coin! He was in fine purple, embroidered with gold, and his hands held rings and jewels. The woman, the widow, quietly, joyfully walked out the Temple.

Father, her clothes? Probably all she had. And her finest, right? And she really did worship. And she was thankful. He thought.

He heard the Father, *Son, remember my promise? Written down long ago. My promise was to the widow and orphan. Through Moses and others we set the in place, laws as you know. But you see, they have forgotten this priesthood. I remind only to have see again; why, you must do these things. I had said "You shall not afflict any widow or orphan. If you afflict them at all; and if they cry out to me, I will surely hear their cry; and my anger will be kindled. And I will kill you with the sword; and your wives shall become widows, and your children fatherless. I promised to execute justice for the orphan and the widow, and show my love even to the stranger, by giving him food and clothing. To be Father of the fatherless and a judge for the widows, me. El el yon, Shaddai, God in his holy habitation.*

Yes Father, I remember. And I understand. The priest have forgotten. Religion; and self-righteousness, seems to be rampant. The swallowing of a camel, yet, choking on a gnat. He thought. **Yes. But more so that widow. . . This is what she prayed. . .** *["and now, lord, for what do I wait? My hope is in you. "Hear my prayer, O' Lord, and give ear to my cry; do not be silent at my tears, I offer this to you freely. And with all of my heart, soul, mind and strength. You will have to be even more, my all. I have no family, no sons or daughters, . . .not even a kinsman redeemer to care for me. You must be my husband; provider, protector, of all I am. Thank you. That you are God and my God.]*

Jesus said to his disciples. "That woman, the widow that left."

"Yes, Lord, we saw." They answered.

"I tell you now; she has put into the treasury, and God's hands, more than all the rest. Even now, others give out of their abundance or prosperity. But, she, gave all she had. Those *two mites*. A *cent*. She gave out of her need. She trusts the Father, more than these here."

****

Jesus again spoke a parable in the ears of the people and his disciples. He looked out on the crowd and spoke.

"Then the Kingdom of Heaven will be comparable to ten virgins, who took their lamps, and went out to meet the bridegroom. Five of them were foolish; and five, were prudent. Because when the foolish took their lamps; they took no extra oil with them, but the prudent took oil in flasks, along with their lamps. Now while the bridegroom was delaying, they all got drowsy and began to sleep. But at midnight; there was a shout! 'Behold, the Bridegroom! Come out to meet him.' Then all those virgins rose and trimmed their lamps. The foolish said to the prudent, 'Give us some of your oil, for our lamps are going out.' But the prudent answered, 'No, there will not be enough for us, and you too. Go, instead to the dealers and buy some for yourselves.' And while they were going away to make the purchase, the Bridegroom came, and those who were ready went in with him to the wedding feast and the door was shut. Later, the other virgins also came, saying, 'Lord, Lord, open up for us. 'But he answered, 'Truly I say to you, I do not know you.' Be on the alert then, for you do not know the day nor the hour."

And he continued.

"For it is just like a man about to go on a journey who called his own servants, and entrusted his possessions to them. To one he gave five talents; to another, two, and to another, one, each according to his own ability. And he went on his journey. Immediately, the one who had received the five talents, went and traded with them, and gained five more talents. In the same way the one who had received the two talents gained two more. But, he who received the one talent, went away, and dug a hole in the ground and hid his master's money."

"Now after a long time, the master of those servants, came and settled accounts, with them. The one who had received the five talents came up and brought five more talents, saying, 'Master, you entrusted five talents to me. See, I have gained five more talents. His master said to him, 'Well done, good and faithful servant. You were faithful with a few things; I will put you in charge of many things; enter into the joy of your master. Also, the one who had received the two talents came up and said, master, you entrusted two talents to me. See, I have gained two more talents. His master said to him, 'Well done, good and faithful servant. You were faithful with a few things; I will put you in charge of many things; enter into the joy of your master. And the one also who had received the one talent; came up and said, master; I knew you to be a hard man, reaping where you did not sow, and gathering where you scattered no seed. And I was afraid; and went away; and hid your talent, in the ground. See; here it is, have what is yours. But his master answered and said to him, you wicked; lazy servant! You knew that I reap; where I did not sow, and gather where I scattered no seed. Then you ought to have put my money; in the bank, and on my arrival, I would have received my money back, with interest. Therefore; take away the talent from him, and give it to the one, who has the ten talents. For to everyone who has; more shall be given, and he will have an abundance. But from the one who does not have; even what he does have, shall be taken away. Throw out the worthless slave; into the outer darkness, in that place there will be weeping and gnashing of teeth."

****

Now, Jesus knew the time was near. And after he finished these things; he said to his disciples.

"You all know that Passover is coming in two days. And we need to prepare for it. And I, Messiah, Son of Man, will be handed over for crucifixion."

Later on, that evening, the Chief priests, Elders and Scribes were gathered in the courtyard of High Priest Caiaphas. The Temple Guard was near and watching over them. The evening lamps were lit. And the scent of oil burning filled the air; the braziers and hanging lamps, tossed shadows as the breeze touched the flame. Conversations were heard. As discussion about Jesus of Nazareth; and the needed solution to their problem, took place.

"The people believe he is a prophet. And he has done great signs and miracles." one spoke. "That is true," answered another.

"But if we do not do *something*, Rome will ride in and destroy us all!" cried another. Shouts of agreement rang out. And Caiaphas held up his hands for silence.

"Priests and Scribes, listen to me. We know how *crafty* this Jesus is. And how hard it has been, even to try, and catch him in his words."

"But know this; he must be stopped! And you heard my prophecy! We will lose, our prominence and authority, because of his teachings! And as to what the people have seen. Whether true miracles or pallor trick. They are following him, more than us. Our very way of life will be destroyed! So, we need answers. Think. YHWH has given us *wisdom, insight*, to guide this nation all these years! Only to have it all lost because of a new voice, a new face. A new bauble that attracts the eye!"

He closed his eyes and stroked his beard in thought.

The demon Dante grinned **Caiaphas and his underlings, were easy to guide. That's how it seems with these "religious." They strive for**

holiness, by doing, not by being. They push for position and power, and fail to really obey. All we need do is to stroke the pride, and place merit in following rules, then turn their eye in judgment on their fellows. We will end his attempt to take back this world. And these sickly, weak, creations. His plan will not succeed. And this Savior will die and all will be lost. His thoughts ended. He turned to a young priest nearby and whispered. The young priest took the whisper and made it his own. The young priest stood stiffly and proudly.

And spoke, "Your excellency, Caiaphas, if this Jesus must be destroyed. Would it not be wise. . ." he paused, "to seek out one of his own. . . And see if any would be . . . dissatisfied? Or maybe, . . . Take coin to offer us information or need I say it. Betray this false teacher. I am sure; there must be someone, we can speak too. And even. . . Encourage. . . With coin. . . Or something else."

Caiaphas clapped his hands and brought them to his lips as if to kiss them, but added, "We cannot take him during the festival or we face a riot! But, yes, yes my my priest. That may help us avoid, riot as well as Rome." Caiaphas turned to an acolyte and said get me the names of his twelve. By whatever means we can. And find out what you can. The Passover is soon. And they must celebrate it as we all do. Find where they dine. Or who they know. Find me; that weak one, and soon!" he finished. And then to everyone. "we may yet; come out of this untouched. . . .and with everything intact."

****

Jesus would teach during the day and he would go out and spend the night on the Mount of Olives. As the days of the Passover grew closer; Jesus went to Bethany and to the house of Simon the leper who had been healed.

****

Judas Iscariot walked casually through the market place in the Bethany. He saw the fruits, meats, and garments, all on display. And heard the vendors calling out deals. He smelled the spice and flowers. And heard the drop of coins in the business man's hands. His eyes surveyed the scene easily. And his eye; caught opportunity after opportunity, to easily take what he saw. And benefit. He tenderly caressed the bag and the tie. *Sure,* he thought; *I could buy anything, and Jesus and the others would not bat an eye.* But deep in his soul he heard the cry, [*but why pay, if you can have it for free*]. He had done business before. Worked hard and lost everything. And yet, by good fortune and chance, won again.

I like the finer things myself; but I can't wear them now, not with Jesus and the others. It would be out of place. And some would question it. And having extra is better than struggling. I don't know, what Jesus thinks. He certainly doesn't think as a business man, or even a priest. He laughed. *Even the priest; get paid to do the sacrifice. They eat; the other half of the ox or lamb. And as for money! They have more than enough. And the clothes! Oh the clothes. . .and power. Now; that! Is something i could use! Finally; to be in a place of wealth and power. . . Isn't that what we all want? Surely.* ... His thought finished as his hand touched the fine linen garment, embroidered with crimson and gold. The reflection off the white cloth, almost made him squint.

But; who am I kidding, really, Jesus says he is messiah and prophet, priest, king, he scoffed. *I see neither or any. If he was, he would have taken the priesthood by force! Like the Maccabees or raised and army to fight the romans and free us!* His thoughts were interrupted by an acolyte priest . . ."Shalom, you are one of Jesus disciples?"

Judas paused, looked around and hesitantly said, "Yes."

The acolyte in full dress of the priesthood said. "I have been sent by the priests to get some information, and the names of the twelve leading men."

Judas looked skeptical.

"What information? . . . The names you should already know."

"Well, I am told that, given the sensitive situation, this requires diplomacy. And it could be of benefit; to the one, who can help the priests in this endeavor. But of course; i cannot divulge, specifically who sent me. But I can say; it will be of benefit to that person that helps."

Judas took this in. And thought, *This is interesting. It sounds like a possible lucrative opportunity. And one must always find or make them, don't they.*

"If anyone would like to be of assistance, they can come to the temple and the court of priests tonight. Can you pass that along to any interested party?" the acolyte offered.

"Yes, yes I can." Judas crooned.

The acolyte moved off through the market. And Judas Iscariot; stopped and digested the meeting with the younger priest. He glanced around nervously; then, as casually as he thought he could, walked from the market.

The afternoon wore on and turned to evening as Judas Iscariot made his way to the temple. He laughed to himself, *I cannot believe Jesus really thought I was going out to make sure the meal for unleavened bread was set up. I did that the other day. He just doesn't appreciate me or my talents. We got a good deal too. And I did tell him the man's name. But telling him now I was gonna check on things made; it is easy to see what opportunity the priests have for me. And hey, working for the priests is working for God, right? They are the ones God talks too. I don't understand why Jesus doesn't use his powers to take care of things. I mean really. Stops a storm, but won't destroy the Romans and their taxes. Raises the dead, but won't take out the High Priest so he can have his office or money. Seriously, seriously, lacking, that man, lacking.*

Judas continued up the road to the Temple. The city streets were quieter than in the day. And no one noticed his passing. He climbed the steps to the colonnade where the priest court would begin. The braziers and lamps were lit and the flames danced on the columns and reflected off the inlaid gold of the vine on the columns. Judas made his way deeper into the court and the court of hewn stone.

There he saw the Sanhedrin and the Chief priests and Scribes. They were in full attire and were speaking among themselves. They were that intent on the discussion. He had to wait a few minutes in silence. Soon, one the priests noticed him. And came forward and asked why he was waiting. He said, "I was told to come." And the priest turned to go to the others and report; he saw the young priest from earlier. Who quickly got up and took him by the arm. And walked him to where the chief priest and scribes were seated in the room. And waited with him.

He watched the young priest; as he waited till the Chief Priests and Scribes ended their discussion. Then the young priest said, "Caiaphas, your excellency, our inquiry has produced fruit. I believe." He bowed his head and tapped Judas' arm and he too bowed his head. Caiaphas stood and looked at them. And spoke to the room.

"Ahh, my young priest, and who is this that we see in front of us?" Caiaphas waited. The young acolyte cleared his throat and standing tall, finished. "Ahem, this is a follower of the Nazarene, false prophet and the one who troubles Israel. Your excellency."

Judas watched as the young priest met Caiaphas eyes.

Caiaphas spread his arms and crooned smoothly, "Welcome, follower of this **Jesus**. I have been wanting to speak with him, here, in the Sanhedrin. And clear up some matters. But, he seems to have avoided us at every turn. It is a shame that he doesn't seem, to want to come and speak with us. I guess since there are no crowds, or those of simple minds he prefers."

Caiaphas stepped down and came close to them and stopped. "All I want to do is talk. I am sure that things are purely mis-understandings and oversights. Is there a way. . .I'm sorry, I didn't get your name. . ."

Judas looked at Caiaphas. *Here stands **God's authority** in Israel.* He thought *I am before **power**. And I must tread, every so carefully or I may meet the Temple Guard, and go missing.*

Judas met the Chief Priest's eyes, and spoke clearly, "I am Judas Iscariot," tilting his head slightly. "And at your **service**, your **excellency**."

Caiaphas touched his hand to the ephod, where the stones of the tribes were, and with a slight tilt of his head replied, "You are at **my**, service. I am also at the service of the nation. But thank you."

Judas watched as the braziers light and the lamps flickered off the gold and jewels of the ephod, and the jewels of government, on his shoulders holding the ephod.

"I carry all these before YHWH; and I am asking YHWH for wisdom, on how to best protect and keep the nation from trouble. And destruction. But I find no one following the **teacher**, that seems concerned or likeminded. Unless you are the one we need to speak to."

Caiaphas paused, reading Judas. Judas could tell the priests scrutiny, and search of weakness. He also knew what would come next. And depending on the results, he could be a wealthy man. Or a powerful one at least.

Caiaphas continued, "We need to handle things quietly. This happens often. All these would be prophets and teachers, many times they disappear. Or fade away when their followers grow tired. Are you tired Judas? I am sure he doesn't appreciate you. Or your insights. **Dante** whispered to Caiaphas. **Dante** whispered more and Caiaphas took them as his own. *"I am a shepherd of the people. And I must guide this flock. And as a shepherd I must defend those that are in danger. Since he seems hidden now; it would of great benefit to the Temple, if we knew where he was. But, if he will not come to us on his own, we need to help him, now, don't we? And as a business man, there is price. What might yours be Judas?"*

Judas smiled, "I am open to suggestions? If I can help you bring him here. . . Is thirty shekels weight, too much to ask?"

"I will confer with the council. Young acolyte take him to the door and wait. We will call you. With our decision."

Judas watched as the young priest bowed and grabbed his arm and moved him to the door. Judas allowed himself to be moved easily. He knew the negotiation was not necessarily done yet. He would have the money he knew, but what else might the Temple offer? He could do many things for the temple. And he could become . . .wealthy and powerful.

They waited together outside the chambers. Judas was so caught up in the whirlwind of possibilities; that he did not see the young priest leave, nor return, with his purse of silver coin.

"The Temple would ask that this task be handled quickly. So as not to disrupt things too much." The young acolyte said, "Thank you for assisting the Temple. You may go."

Judas bowed slightly and turned and left the temple. Whistling as he went. Tossing and catching the bag full of coin. Now, he thought, *I need to find the perfect moment to turn him in. And garner more favor and coin!*

****

That night after Judas Iscariot had left the Temple. And **Dante had whispered to and guided Caiaphas.** Caiaphas had turned in, not long after, and had fallen asleep. God the Father spoke into Caiaphas' dreams, as he lay still and quiet. *"I want you to know my heart. You were to be* *the Shepherds of Israel. The priesthood and Israel, were to bring the nation, and other nations to me. That they could be loved, cared for, protected. And I would be their God and all of them my people. But you and those before you. Did not listen. So, hear the words of the lord. . .* [the prophet Zechariah] *put the flock out to pasture. The flock doomed to slaughter. And all those that sell them and kill say, "Blessed be the Lord, I have become rich! Their shepherds have no pity on them. I will cause them all to fall into the power of another and not deliver. And I will raise a shepherd, that will not care for the dying, scattered, nor heal the broken, or protect the standing one. But a shepherd that will devour the sheep.* [and Ezekiel] *woe to you shepherds of Israel, that have been feeding yourselves! Are not the shepherds to feed the flock? But you, eat the fat and use the wool, without feeding them. You have not cared for the sick, nor healed the diseased, nor bound up what was broken, nor brought back the scattered, nor sought the lost, you with force and severity, dominate them. They have no shepherd and are scattered! They have wandered mountains, every hill, and no one searches or seeks them. Therefore, you shepherds hear the word of the Lord! As I live declare the Lord God. I am against you. I will demand my sheep and make them stop feeding my sheep. And the shepherds will not even feed themselves. And I will deliver them from their mouths. So, they will not be food for them.! Unless you repent, and do the works of righteousness. . . I will raise up shepherds over them and tend them. They will not be afraid or terrified. And none will be missing. Behold the days are coming, when I will raise up for David. . .a righteous branch. And he will reign as king. . .and act wisely, and do justice and righteousness in the land. Judah and Israel will be saved. And he will be called the Lord our righteousness! Turn and repent. I am full of mercy, full of forgiveness. . . "*

Caiaphas woke in a cold sweat, body shaking, and terror in his heart! *Did YHWH say that of me, and the priesthood? How is that possible? We have done righteous things. We have protected and cared for this nation.* He thought. He rubbed his eyes and face. Trying to understand what had happened. "It feels the same as when I prophesied. But why would I call woe on myself?" He spoke aloud.

"Surely, this was about that *Jesus! That Nazarene*. Not those in the Temple. How can this be? How can we be false shepherds? When we hold fast to the Law! And I am the *Law!* I carry the government of Israel on my shoulders before YHWH!"

His terror changed to anger and rage! Disbelief! He scoffed. "How can YHWH say those things of me?" **Dante whispered**. *You are right; YHWH did call judgement upon the false shepherds! And those destroying Israel! Fear not you are safe here. You are doing his will. He confirmed it in your dream! He will judge the false shepherds and raise a righteous shepherd!* To rule over the house of David and Israel! *Do you not rule now?* Are you not *the Law embodied?* You and the council guide Israel and *call all men to trust in YHWH God. Rest. And be at peace. . .*the demon crooned. *Rest. . .*

Caiaphas fell fast asleep. And God the Father wept.

****

The feast of unleavened bread was here and the Passover lamb needed to be killed. Jesus turned to Peter and John and said, "We need to prepare the feast. Check on the preparations."

Peter and John said, "Where will we prepare it?"

Jesus spoke in authority, "Go into the city. And a man will meet you carrying a large pitcher of water. Follow him. And when he enters the building, ask the owner, where will my disciples and I take Passover? And he will open the large upper room. Make sure things are ready there."

So, they left to do as Jesus commanded. And prepared the Passover meal for Jesus and the rest of the Twelve.

****

Evening came and Jesus with Twelve went to the upper room, and began the Passover meal. The room was large and well furnished. The room was expensive usually, but Judas had negotiated a good price; and Jesus knew, this would be a final time, to share with the Twelve and have Passover. Soon he knew he would be the Passover lamb. They had already put the settings at each place.

Jesus saw the cooked lamb and the elements of the seder.

Each plate had the beroa, the charoset, the maror, the karpas, and the beitzah. And the three matzahs covered in cloth. And each a small bowl of salt water. And a cup of wine for each person and one cup for Elijah.

Each place setting was perfect. And he sat and he took the wine and bread and looking to Heaven; he prayed and blessed the meal.

The Twelve were at separate tables and on mats per tradition. They with a small meal with lamb. The conversation was varied and lively. Jesus took in the room and looked at each in turn, smiling. *Father, thank you. Thank you for these men. And their lives. They are dear to me. I will finish what we started. I will do as you have asked. And I know of Judas and Caiaphas. I know it hurt you to have to remind Caiaphas of his call and duty and failure. But, soon, we will rescue and save many. And these will be scattered for a time. And even deny me.* He thought. He watched as they ate and talked among themselves. He had finished what he would eat and moved the seder plate near him.

The Twelve noted that he had taken his plate and was going to begin the seder. So, conversation shifted. The Twelve took their plates and they prepared to start the seder.

The candles were lit and they all prayed. . . "Blessed are you, Lord our God, king of the universe, who has sanctified us with his commandments and commanded us that we kindle the yom tov lights. Baruch atah ado-nai, elo-heinu melech ha-olam, asher kid'shanu b'mitzvotav v'tzivanu l'hadlik ner shel yom tov."

Jesus then holding the wine said, "Blessed are you, Lord our God, king of the universe, who creates the fruit of the vine. Baruch atah ado-nai elo-heinu melech ha-olam boreh pree ha-ga-fen."

Jesus continued, "We thank you God for giving us the gift of festivals for joy and holidays for happiness, among them this day of Passover, the festival of our liberation, a day of sacred assembly recalling the exodus from Egypt. Blessed are you, Lord our God, king of the universe, who has kept us in life, sustained us, and enabled us to reach this season. Baruch atah ado-nai, elo-heinu melech ha-olam, she-heche-yanu, v'kiye-manu vehigi-yanu la-z'man ha-zeh."

They drank the first cup, then washed their hands for the karpas, and recited, "Blessed are you, Lord our God, king of the universe, who creates the fruit of the Earth. Baruch atah Adonai elo-heinu melech haolam boreh pree ha'adamah," as they ate.

Jesus then broke the matzah and placed the other half in the napkin in the stack. And the others followed suit. And he recited the maggid the story . . .

There arose in Egypt a pharaoh who knew not of the good deeds that Joseph had done for that country. Thus, he enslaved the Jews and made their lives harsh through servitude and humiliation. This is the Passover which we commemorate tonight. So, Simon Peter is his baritone voice sang, "On all other nights we eat either bread or matzah; on this night, why only matzah? On all other nights we eat herbs or vegetables of any kind; on this night why bitter herbs? On all other nights we do not dip even once; on this night why do we dip twice? On all other nights we eat our meals in any manner; on this night why do we sit around the table   together.   .   .
Jesus and the others answered Simon, "We were slaves to pharaoh in Egypt, and God brought us out with a strong hand and an outstretched arm. And if God had not brought our ancestors out of Egypt, we and our children and our children's children would still be subjugated to Pharaoh in Egypt. We still are commanded to tell the story of the exodus from Egypt."

Jesus continued, "We commemorate Passover tonight because of what God did for us when we went out of Egypt. While the Jews endured harsh slavery in Egypt, God chose Moses to lead them out to freedom. Moses encountered God at the burning bush and then returned to Egypt to lead the people out of Egypt. He demanded that Pharaoh let the Jewish people go. But Pharaoh hardened his heart and refused to let the Jewish people go. That is why God sent the ten plagues."

Everyone there listed the ten plagues. . . And took drops from the wine cups as they spoke it.

"Following the slaying of the first born, Pharaoh allowed the Jewish people to leave. The Jews left Egypt in such haste that their dough did not rise, so they ate matzah. When Pharaoh changed his mind and chased after the Israelites, God miraculously caused the Red Sea to split, allowing the Israelites to cross safely. When the Egyptians entered the sea, it returned to its natural state and the mighty Egyptian army drowned." Jesus and all present sang:

"Ilu ho-tsi, ho-tsi-a-nu, Ho-tsi-anu mi-Mitz-ra-yim Ho-tsi-anu mi-Mitz-ra-yim Da-ye-nu

Chorus

Da-da-ye-nu,

Da-da-ye-nu,

Da-da-ye-nu,

Da-da-ye-nu,

Da-ye-nu Da-ye-nu"

"If God would've taken us out of Egypt and not executed judgment upon them,

It would've been enough for us—Dayenu.

If He would've executed judgment upon them and not upon their idols, it would've been enough for us—Dayenu.

If He would've judged their idols, and not killed their firstborn, it would've been enough for us—Dayenu.

If He would've killed their firstborn, and not given us their wealth, it would've been enough for us—Dayenu.

If He would've given us their wealth, and not split the sea for us, it would've been enough for us—Dayenu.

If He would've split the sea for us, and not let us through it on dry land, it would've been enough for us—Dayenu.

If He would've let us through it on dry land, and not drowned our enemies in it, it would've been enough for us—Dayenu.

If He would've drowned our enemies in it, and not provided for our needs in the desert for forty years, it would've been enough for us—Dayenu."

And Jesus had the scroll of Psalms and read it.

CHAPTER 17

WASHING FEET, GETHSEMANE, BETRAYAL

Son, He heard the Father, *the time has come. And remember you are My Son. and when all of this is done, you will return to Me. You will need to help the Twelve. They are still little children. and They will be frightened. and you do know Judas Iscariot is going to be the one to betray you. Even in that, I will give him space to repent. But as you know, this is what must be done. And this night will be a long one. Prepare your heart, mind and soul. But I will be with you as Always. Until the Passover sacrifice you make. When All the sins of mankind are placed on you.*

I understand Father, Jesus Thought. *Now, I must show what it is to be a servant to them. And to teach them to be servants and love one another.*

Jesus got up from the table, and removed his cloak and shawl. And took a towel, and wrapped another, around himself. And got a basin and filled it with water.

Jesus walked to far side of the hall, and knelt down before Thomas. He gently removed a sandal. And took Thomas' foot and with his other hand poured water over it. He then took the towel and dried that foot and repeated the process for the others. And spoke as He did so.

"Do not let your heart be afraid or troubled. You believe in God; Believe in Me. In my Father's House are many dwelling places. And I would have told you if it wasn't so. But I go soon to prepare a place for you. And Because I do this; I will come again and find you and take you back with Me. So, that where I am, you may be too. And you all know where I am going."

Thomas asked plainly, "But Lord, we really don't know where you are going. How would we know the way to go?" Jesus answered, "I am the Way, the Truth, and the Life. No one comes to the Father, but through Me. If you had known Me; you would know the Father, and from now on you will know him and see him."

Jesus walked to Philip and knelt before him and removed His sandal and washed his feet. And Philip said, "Lord, show us the Father and that will be enough."

Jesus chuckled and said, "Philip, have I been here so long, and you still don't know Me? The Father sent Me. and If you have seen Me, you have seen the Father. How can you say, 'Show us the Father.' Do you not believe that I am in the Father and the Father is in Me and We are One? I speak what the Father says or at least believe the miracles. But I tell you the truth: If you believe in Me, You will do greater works than I. And because I go to the Father, you will ask in My Name and I will do it so the Father is glorified in the Son. and if you ask anything in My name, I will do it. And Keep my commands if you truly love Me."

Jesus moved on to another of the Twelve and washed his feet. and continued, "I will ask the Father for you, that he would give you another Helper, a Guide and Companion and more. And He will be with you Forever! He is the Holy Spirit; the Spirit of Truth. The world cannot receive Him because the world does not see Him or know Him. But you do. He abides with you and will live in you. I will not leave you orphans. I will come to you. But after a while, you will no longer see Me. Yet, because I live, you will also. And I and my Father will be with you. And the one who Loves Me will be loved by My Father as well. And if you keep my Word, My Father, will love him and will come to him and make our home with him. And if you don't keep my Words, you don't love me. But the Words you hear; are not mine, but My Father's who sent Me."

I have said all these things; while I am here with you. Understand; the Holy Spirit sent by the Father, will teach you and bring to your memory, everything I said. Peace shalom; nothing broken Nothing missing, I leave with you. My Peace I give to you. My peace is not like the Worlds. Do not let your Heart be Troubled. Nor let it be fearful. You should rejoice; since the Father is Greater than I, Because I go to him. I told you this before it happens, so you will believe. And I do everything the Father commands."

Jesus went through the twelve and came lastly to Simon Peter. And knelt down before him and Simon Peter; touched Jesus's hand and said, "Lord, do you wash my feet?" Jesus looked at him and finished. "You all, may not understand, now what I do but you will afterwards."

"No, you will never wash my feet!" Simon insisted.

Jesus looked into Simon's face and said, "If I do not wash your feet, you will have no Part with Me." Simon thought a moment and then full of emotion said "Then; wash my Head and my Hands as well! All of me."

Jesus smiled and finished his feet and said, "Those that had a bath are clean, they only need their feet washed. But not everyone is clean."

Jesus locked eyes with Judas Iscariot. Who looked away quickly, still feeling the touch of Jesus, from his foot washing.

"I am the True Vine and my Father the Husbandman. Every branch in Me that does not bear fruit is taken away. But, the branch that bears much fruit he prunes, so it will produce more. Abide in Me and I in you. A branch must abide in the vine to produce fruit. And apart from me you can do nothing. if you do not abide in me, you are thrown away and dry up. and others, take the dry branches and burn them in the fire. If you abide in Me, you will ask whatever you wish and it will be done. My Father is glorified in this. and that you also bear much fruit and prove yourselves to be my disciples. Just as the Father loves me, I have loved you. If you abide in my love and abide in His love, your joy will be full. Love one another. and no greater love has anyone than this: that he lay down his Life for His friends. And you are my friends. If you follow My commands. You did not choose me, I chose you. and whatever you ask of the Father in My name, He will give it to you."

Jesus put the basin away and got dressed and sat back down at the table and said to them all. "Do you understand what I have done? You all call me Teacher and Lord; and I am and you are right to say it. I gave an example. If I washed your feet, you should wash one another's feet. A servant is not greater than his Master. And if you understand these things you are blessed. But not all of you. I know those I have chosen. And I say this now. . . One of you will betray me. As the Scripture says, "He that eats my bread has lifted up his heel against me."

All the disciples looked at each other. They all were searching for the One who would betray Jesus. And each in turn; including Judas Iscariot, said, "Surely, Not I Lord?" Simon Peter motioned to John who was closest to Jesus and said, "Ask Jesus who it is." So, John asked. And Jesus took the torn matzah and dipped it into the salt water and handed it to Judas Iscariot.

Judas thought. *He knows. Jesus knows. How? I didn't say anything. I made sure everything was normal. I hid everything well. No one suspected.* Fear began to build in his heart. He finished the matzah. *I have been in situations like this before, but why am I feeling fear??* Then he felt cold and clammy. It was as if his eyes were looking through a light fog or were unfocused. His fear grew to anger and rage. He had a hard time thinking and even opened and closed his mouth a few times. No Sounds. And Jesus turned to him and said, "What you do. . .do it quickly." Judas heard the words distantly and he looked at Jesus through another's eyes. He wanted to speak but couldn't. He wanted to reach out and touch Jesus but couldn't. He watched as he moved away from the table and out the door and down the stairs. And he walked into the Night. He felt familiar with the night now. He seemed to move faster, surer. Judas tried to cry out and couldn't! He wanted to turn back and stay with the Twelve. But He could not.

Jesus then stopped and took some bread again. He looked up to Heaven and blessed it. And he passed it to all the disciples and said, "Take this and eat. This is my body which is broken for you." He took the cup, blessed it again and spoke.

"Drink from it all of you. This is My blood, and the New Covenant. This is my blood poured out for many, for the forgiveness of sins. But I will not drink of the fruit of the vine till I drink it a new in My Father's Kingdom with you."

He thought of Judas and the coming betrayal and trials and spoke to them all. He stood arms wide and said, "Now, is the Son of God and Son of Man glorified. God the Father will glorify Himself and the Son immediately. Little children, I will be with you only for a little while yet. I know you will seek Me. And as I said to the Jews, I say it again. I am going, but you cannot come. A New Commandment I tell you. . .Love one Another, even as I have loved you. Love one another. Why? By this New Commandment; Love one another, All Men will know you are my disciples. If you love one another."

Jesus continued, "You will all be scattered and fall away. The Scriptures says, **"I will strike down the shepherd, and the sheep shall be scattered."** But when I rise from the dead. I will go ahead of you to Galilee." But Simon Peter said to Him, "Even though all may fall away, yet I will not." And everyone insisted the same thing.

Simon Peter concerned moved to Jesus and said, "Lord; where are you going?" Jesus looked at him intently, tenderly. Emotions rising in his heart. Not just for Simon Peter, but all the Twelve. He said, " Where I go, you cannot follow Me now, but later you will."

Simon Peter looked at Jesus, then the Twelve, more concerned. "Lord, why can I not follow you now? Right now?" Courage rose in his heart." I will follow you wherever you go! And I will even face death for you!"

Jesus placed his hand on Simon Peter's shoulder and gently Replied. "Will you lay your life down for Me? I tell you now, a rooster will crow after you have denied me three times."

The whole room was silent. And Peter dropped his eyes to the floor.

Jesus broke the silence of the room. He looked up to Heaven and prayed. The whole room seemed to vibrate with power and hush fell upon all present. The eleven stood transfixed as he prayed.

"Father, it is now time, glorify your Son, that your Son may glorify you. You have given Me authority over all men and flesh. And to all those you have given Him; He may give eternal life. This is eternal life that they may know you; intimately, the Only True God. And Me, Jesus Christ, your Son, whom You sent. I have glorified You on the Earth; and accomplished the work you sent me to do. Now Father, glorify Me with yourself, and the glory I had before world was. I revealed all your name to these men you gave Me out of the world. They were Yours and You gave them to Me. And they have kept your Word. And they understand everything I told them, was from You. And all the words I have spoken to them; they have taken them, and believed them. Believing that You have sent Me. I asked for them and not the world them. That as all you have is Mine, and all that is Mine is Yours, would be theirs also. Since I am leaving this world and they remain in it, Father God, keep them in Your Name! So that all You have given Me, will be one, as We are. And all You have given Me I have kept. And lost none. Except the Son of Perdition, that Scripture be fulfilled. I pray these things that My joy would be full in them. The world has hated them. Because they are not of the world, even as I am not. Do not take them out of the world, but keep them from the Evil one. Sanctify them in the Truth of Your Word. Just as you sent Me, I send them. I also do not ask just for these alone. But for all who will believe in ME; from their Words. Make them one as We are. Father; that just as you are in Me, and I in you, help them be in Us. So, the world may see and believe. May they be kept mature in unity; so, the world will know You sent Me. And loved them, just as you loved me. And I also want them to be where I am. So, they may see the glory that You gave Me because You loved Me, before the foundation of the world. Righteous Father, thank you for Your unfailing love. For Me and them."

Jesus finished the prayer and spoke to the Eleven. "Let us leave here. Now, the time for the Son of God to be betrayed is near."

Jesus left the upper room. The night sky was bright with stars and a full moon. Jesus felt the gentle breeze belying, the coming storm. Not only in his heart, but for the fate of all men and their redemption. He walked in silence down the road and turned to the Kidron Valley and toward the Mount of Olives. The night was filled with the scent of flowers and gentle sway of the tree's branches as they walked by. He almost wanted to go farther and grab a fig or date. But He walked the familiar path to His favorite spot in the garden. He had made this trip many times. The olive trees reflected the moonlight off their leaves causing a silver glow in the trees. and He smelt the woody aroma, amidst the olive trunks. Some were silhouetted even in full moon. But the time of prayer and communion with the Father and the Holy Spirit was needed these last days and hours. He knew he needed to talk to both of them and gain strength and more, for what was ahead.

He found he favorite spot. It was under and ancient tree. The tree had spread out its branches to make a simple canopy over a small patch of grass and flat top rock. That looked like it had been purposely cut to sit on. The light of the moon and the leaves sparkled and silver shafts of light cut to the ground. And the grass had become a mosaic of light and darkness. Even the rock was painted in silver and black.

He spoke to the eleven "I am burdened heavily. Pray with me. James, John, Peter stay over there nearby and pray as well. The rest of you find a comfortable spot and pray. And pray you do not enter into temptation."

Peter, James, and John found a spot a stones throw from Jesus and sat down leaning on a nearby trunk.

Jesus moved to the flat rock and knelt and began to pray. He prayed aloud, but softly. "Father, here I am. I feel *dread*. I am *anxious*. And I am *troubled*. I know I must face what is to come. But I cannot do this without help. Holy Spirit, I need you and your strength and the Father's. Is this what they feel when trouble comes? A dread, but one that might change with the moment or event?" Jesus looked through the canopy and caught the moonlight. He looked the eleven nearby dispersed in the grove.

Son, he heard the Father, ***Remember, this is Our Plan. The only way to redeem man and restore all that was stolen. I will have to place on you the sins of the world. No one else could bear it. Our Holiness and Righteousness demand sin's death. And all that sin. But, Our Love, and Mercy, won out over Judgement. If We had not chosen to bear sin's weight ourselves, everything We have made and Love so dearly, by Our Own Righteousness, would be forever beyond our reach. No, not that We couldn't reach them, but when Judgement is passed. . . there is no changing it.***

The person who sins will die. The son will not bear the punishment for the Father's iniquity, nor will the Father bear the punishment for the son's iniquity; the righteousness of the righteous will be upon himself, and the wickedness of the wicked will be upon himself. The Father paused.

And Jesus prayed. "I have never sinned. I know this flesh is fearful at your Words and the Truth. How can I do this?" He waited.

He stood up and moved to where Simon Peter, James, and John were leaning against the trunk underneath the nearby olive tree.

He looked and they were asleep. *Asleep? I don't understand. They have prayed before and not fallen asleep.* He thought.

He said to them, "Simon Peter, James, John. . . I am deeply grieved in My Spirit and Soul, almost to the point of Death! So, you men could not pray with me for one hour and keep watch? See that you do not become entangled with temptation. The Spirit is willing, but flesh is weak. Keep watch and pray."

Jesus moved back to the rock and knelt again and cried out "Father, if you are willing, remove this cup from me, but Your will be done. Abba, Father, please!"

He heard a whisper, faintly, dimly, and the moonlight seemed to shift. The darkness around him seemed to breathe, and move. He heard [*Why are you here? Are you afraid? Is the Lion of Judah, a kitten?*] A cold breeze touched his neck and covered him. He shivered. and looked around. *Nothing, No one. Well not no one.* He thought.

Jesus began to weep. His tears came in response to the anguish of heart and soul, as he faced the daunting task of bearing mankind's sin. And becoming the Sacrificial Passover Lamb for the world. *Father, is this what they feel? Helpless, powerless, that there is nothing they can do to change anything? My humanness cries for more. I am a carpenter. I build things. I would like a family, and more. Oh, this pain.* Jesus shook his head. *This would be a final thing for anyone else. Or what of man's sickness and disease? No wonder King Solomon wrote, everything is meaningless, without God and His love and care.*

He heard the Whispers again. [*You could tell your Father No, and even the thought of sin and death would be gone.*] He looked and black smudge moved nearby.

Jesus prayed louder "My Father, Abba, will you remove this cup from me?" He heard the Father, *No Son, I cannot. I will not.* Jesus groaned and wept.

His heart began to race. Fear mounted. He tried to concentrate and found his focus was lost. A **Whisper** [*The Sin of the world will touch you. What will it be, to know man's darkness? To know his evil.*]

Jesus stood and again walked to Simon Peter, James, and John, again asleep. "Simon! James, John. Can you not watch even a little while? Are you not able to pray . . . even for Me?"

Jesus numbly walked to the rock, and dropped, heavily to his knees. "Father, please, remove this cup. . ." He struggled in his Spirt; and in His humanness, he didn't want to be touched by evil. He felt the Father, pulling back away from him. And the enemy whispered more [*Are you sure about what the Father promised? Why do you want to help those who hate you?*] He wrestled with the question. . . [*Are you really the Son of God?*] [*Is dying for them worth it?*] more whispers, more doubts. [*Even if you die, will God keep his Promise?*] [*What if No one*

Believes after all has been done?] [Who will choose to believe in the Future? If your Message of Salvation and hope dies at the Cross?]

Jesus knew those things as the lies that they were, his mind knew it. Deep in his soul, he knew it, but at the moment, his emotions, seemed out of control. And reason and knowledge were powerless to change it. How do they live? How do they get through this quagmire of feelings and stress? Jesus groaned and cried. *I do not want to know sin. I do not want to lose my communion with the Father and Spirit. My Holiness cries to not go on. To let it go. And my humanness, sees no hope. Because death is final. But the Father promised!* He groaned. . .He opened his eyes and his hands felt drops like rain. He looked up and the moon was still there, the stars were still there.

He held his hands in front of his face, and saw blood! Drops of blood ran down his hands, to his cuffs, of his Tunic and he looked at the rock, that too was blood spattered. He reached a hand up and wiped his forehead. And it brought a fresh smear of blood on his fingers.

Suddenly, he saw a flash! And there stood Cenehard. The Angel came to him. Lifted him up from the ground. And began to encourage him and minister to him. "Cenehard, it is good to see you," Jesus said. "And thank you. In my weariness. . .I almost forgot."

Cenehard smiled and said, "The Father said to remind you of what is true. And to lean on his Word and Promise, from now on." And He embraced Jesus in a bear hug. Jesus laughed. "And I thought a hug would help too!" Jesus said, "Yes it did."

And then in a flash Cenehard was gone. And the garden was as it was. Jesus walked to Simon Peter, James and John. He looked again, *Asleep.* He laughed; *You guys missed it,* He thought. He Spoke to them. "Are you still sleeping? Come on get up. The Time is at hand, the Son of God is betrayed into the hands of sinners. The one who betrays me is Here. Let us go."

Judas Iscariot led the Roman Contingent, and the Temple Guard sent by the Chief Priest, Elders, and Scribes to capture Jesus. He walked the road to the Mount of Olives in silence. The High Priests voice echoing in his ears still. "I know what you *promised* Judas. But I do not *know you* well enough to *trust* your service. This Jesus of Nazareth has done miracles, and eluded us when he was standing before us, or even a crowd. I want No *Mistakes*! *I want Him*. And I will have Him. Because

God YHWH told me in dream, He will Judge him! I will send more hands to guarantee His capture and ***Our Success!***"

Fifty Men! Fifty Romans and the Temple Guard! All to bring a Teacher who does what? Heal the Sick, Raise the Dead, Feed the Poor. . .But threatens No one. Or takes or envy's position or Power. This is foolishness! Caiaphas did not see the need to be subtle. Seven Soldiers, could have moved quietly and Jesus would have been ours without fanfare, or effort. As it is, He will see us coming. With all these torches and lanterns, we shine like the noon day! And sound like a herd of oxen lowing to market! Judas shook his head. He stopped at the entrance to the garden. He took the arm of the Roman Commander, *What was his name again. Marcus.* "Marcus, we go this path to ensure Jesus of Nazareth does not slip by us! Your soldiers need to be quiet! And hold back, those with torches, till I signal you." He finished.

Marcus spoke boldly, "My contingent was sent by our Centurion here at the High Priests' request. We know how to capture criminals and rioters!"

"Yes, I am sure you do. But Jesus is different. So, caution is needed."

"Bah, a good sword and chains are what is needed. But I will pass the word. This better not be a wild goose chase!" Marcus went quietly to his men and they doused most of the torches and dimmed the lanterns.

Judas walked the path to where Jesus normally would meet with the Twelve. A place of peace, away from the crowds, and noise. Marcus and five Roman soldiers, moved silently with him. *Well, maybe we can actually capture Jesus, without a fight. Amazing, they do move quietly!* He thought, *Wait! what is Jesus doing here? Is he just walking into our hands??*

Jesus stood completely still. He was bathed in moonlight and his robes stood out brightly against the shadows. Jesus knew they were here to take him, to Annas and Caiaphas, and more.

Judas whispered to Marcus, "Remember the signal, I will kiss the one you are to take."

Marcus answered him in a ruff whisper, "Of course, do you not think I listen?"

Jesus spoke in authority, **"Who is it that you all seek?"** He watched, as Judas crossed the garden lawn, to where He stood. Jesus saw the

Roman contingent, yards behind, the five soldiers standing nearby. He also saw the Temple Guard. And soon, behind them, the garden was brightened by more torches and lanterns.

Jesus looked Judas in the eye and said, "Judas."

Judas mockingly cried, " Hail Rabbi! Master!" and leaned in and kissed Jesus on the cheek. Jesus Finished. "So, Judas, you Betray the Son of God with a kiss? Friend, do what you have come for."

Jesus looked at the soldiers, the Temple Guard, and Judas standing with them. Again, he spoke in authority, **"Who do you seek?"** The Temple Guard, Judas and Marcus, the Roman Commander said, "Jesus, the Nazarene." Jesus spoke in authority, **"I am HE."** Jesus knew power had left Him and the authority He held before the world was made, flowed out and struck the waiting crowd! And all of them were knocked back to the ground.

Marcus, was stunned! He didn't see Jesus move, nor any assault, or arrows, nothing! But yet, he had been pushed back to the ground in a moment! He looked to his left and it was same for the Temple guard and even Judas! For a moment he dared not move! Then, the years of training, and soldiering kicked in, and he was on his feet and moving!

Jesus said again, "I told you, I am he. And To fulfill scripture, I ask, let these others go."

Simon Peter, seeing the Roman Commander move, and the Temple guard as well, pulled his sword. Jesus heard a cry, "Lord, shall we defend you with sword?"

Simon Peter close to the Temple guard, struck with his sword, and cut off the guard's right ear! Jesus said in authority, **"Stop! Put away the sword."** "Simon Peter. Do you not think if I cried to My Father in Heaven that at once I would have here, more than twelve Legions of angels! Put away the sword. Those that live by it, sadly die by it. The Father has given me a cup to drink. . . Shall I not Drink It?"

Jesus walked to the place the ear had fallen; he picked it up, and walked to the guard, Malchus, touched him and healed him. Jesus turned back to the crowd and all present as he finished. "Am I a robber, or a thief, that you came here, with swords and clubs? I was with you all, daily in the Temple, teaching. And even then, you did not touch Me, or seize Me. But, this Hour and Power of Darkness is yours that the Scriptures be fulfilled." And all of the disciples fled away into the night!

Jesus watched as His disciples, friends, and believers, ran into the darkness. His heart sank. He remembered the Scriptures. ". . .Strike the Shepherd that the sheep may be scattered." *There they go Father. Just as We knew. Thank You that you are still here.* Jesus' thoughts finished as The Temple Guard that He healed, looked into his eyes, and whispered, "I do what I must. But I will not harm you." He then took Jesus hands and tied them in chords. And then Marcus, the Roman Commander said, "We need to put chains on him. I want the you five to surround him, and you Calitis, trail behind and watch for ambush. Dominicus, you scout ahead, and watch! Now move!"

Marcus looked into Jesus' eyes and said, "I also do what I must. I don't understand what they have against You. But You are not a rioter, or troublemaker. I will put the manacles on your hands. Do not flee or you will die. Though I doubt you would flee."

Jesus felt the heaviness of the manacles and the ropes underneath. He was thankful for the ability to walk freely. He looked at Marcus and said, "I will not. And I thank you that I can walk freely. Though later, I may not be free at all."

Marcus and his five moved with Jesus up the path, followed by the Temple Guard and Judas. The night was still cool. Nothing moved. No sound, but the armor of the Romans, and the flutter of torches. The pathway bright with moonlight; Jesus heard the drums of war, and destiny with every step.

Jesus found the manacles not too cumbersome. But, if they went a great distance, his arms would be tired.

Father, My Human heart, has great fear now. And though I have seen Romans before, they are formidable. Though, I know the enemy, is dancing with glee I am sure. I do not look forward to this. But the dread grows, despair beckons. And the drums of war ring. I know now why you said to stand upon Your Word to Cenehard! I will. I will call it to my mind, and if need be, recite it aloud. Even in Whisper.

So, Jesus began remembering **[The Lord God has opened My ear; And I was not disobedient nor did I turn back. For the Lord God helps Me, Therefore, I am not disgraced; Therefore, I have set My face like flint, And I know that I will not be ashamed.]**

Judas caught up with the Roman Commander and struggled to match the man's stride. But managed to get his words out.

"This is not the way to Caiaphas's Palace! Where are we going?"

Marcus turned to Judas and said, "It seems my orders have been changed momentarily. A runner came and said we go to Annas, the Old High Priest's house first. Not sure why, but orders, are orders. Maybe, he wants to see this celebrity before judgment?"

Jesus took another step and heard a whisper **[*You have lost, you go to die*]**. *Yes,* he thought *I do. But your fear will not work!* Jesus thought again. **[The Lord God has opened My ear; And I was not disobedient nor did I turn back. For the Lord God helps Me, Therefore, I am not disgraced; Therefore, I have set My face like flint, And I know that I will not be ashamed.]** He continued, following the Roman guard, in front of him and found they had entered the water gate. And marched the streets to Annas's house.

Marcus and his five neared the entrance to Annas's house, he stopped. And turned to Jesus. He checked the manacles and rope. He quietly said to Jesus, "It seems there are more people interested in you, than I was told. I tell you now, any move or resistance, I will execute you and save everyone the trouble."

Jesus looked Marcus in the eye and answered. "Though I will not resist you have only the power from those who sent you. And they may say otherwise."

Jesus was guided by the Roman soldier nearest him into the reception hall. Marcus turned to two of the men. "You two, guard the door. And no one enters that way, understood?"

"Yes sir," they said in unison as their fists struck armor. Marcus walked back to the door and the rest of the Contingent. and said, "Calitis, split the men, and send half back to the barracks and sleep. The rest, wait in the courtyard and keep warm and vigilant. Hopefully, we will not need them. It seems his followers have left him." Calitis replied, "Yes, commander, it will be done." With salute and a slight bow, he left.

"Now. . ." Marcus said turning to the rest. "Where is this Annas? I hope this will not take all night, Caiaphas, needs him at his house and the meeting with the Sanhedrin before daybreak."

Jesus watched, as the braziers were lit and hanging lamps and the reception room came alive. Jesus took in the opulence of the room in an instant. *Who knew. . . Being a Priest of Aaron would afford this. . . no wonder, The Father said through the Prophet.* **"Put the flock out to pasture. The flock doomed to slaughter. And all those that sell them and kill say, "Blessed be the Lord, I have become rich! Their shepherds have no pity on them. Woe to you shepherds of Israel, that have been feeding yourselves! Are not the shepherds to feed the flock? But you, eat the fat and use the wool without feeding them. You have not cared for the sick, nor healed the diseased, nor bound up what was broken, nor brought back the scattered, nor sought the lost. You with force and severity, dominate them."**

Jesus waited quietly. As did his guards and those of the Temple. Jesus watched as the Roman Commander approached him. He looked into Jesus eyes and then reached up and turned his face side-to-side. He released his grip and crossed his arms in thought. Looking at the floor. And then looking up again. He said, "Do I know you? I seem to recall, a young man in a carpenter's shop. And my Centurions home. The Centurion told me of meeting a carpenter's son, what was His name. . . Joseph, and he had a son, named. . ."

"Jesus." Jesus smiled. "My name is Jesus. And the Centurion, Perseus, met my father, Joseph. When Joseph was younger." Marcus said to him. "Your Father, Joseph. Hmm. I wish we had met on other terms. I am sure the Centurion would want to see you. But I know he is proud to own things of your father's work."

"Joseph told stories about the Centurion and his kindness, and his guidance in matchmaking."

Simon Peter and John had followed from a distance. They had passed unnoticed in the streets and now were at Annas's house outside the door.

The servant girl at the door recognized John, and opened the door. And Simon Peter was outside. John realizing that Peter was outside, turned and spoke to the doorkeeper, and they let Simon Peter in. John said, "I go to the reception hall; that is where Jesus will be. You may be able to watch from the courtyard nearby."

Simon Peter nodded and moved carefully to the courtyard. The men of the Contingent and the Temple Guard were warming themselves at a fire. Simon Peter stood with them. He wanted to see how things would turn out. And the servant girl, that had let him in at John's request said, "Aren't you also a follower, a disciple of this Jesus?" Simon Peter shook his head and said, "No, I am not." And continued warming himself.

Annas, the old High Priest, came down the stairs from the second floor room and walked to where he had a seat in the reception hall.

Jesus watched as his priestly robes caught the light of the lamps and shimmered as he moved. *Isn't Caiaphas the High Priest now? Jesus thought. He still has his robes? I guess the Priesthood, literally runs in the family. Oh, that's right, the Romans replaced him.*

Annas, the High Priest, looked Jesus over. He spoke to Marcus, "Bring him closer so I may see him better."

Marcus took Jesus' arm and led him closer to the Priest. "He hasn't been any trouble Marcus, has he?" the Priest asked.

"No, He has been quiet. I have him here at your request. Caiaphas needs him before daybreak. Though, from what I have seen, I do not, understand the orders. I saw no riot, or sedition, of any kind."

Annas looked at Marcus and smiled. "My Son-in Law Joseph, uh Caiaphas, can be sensitive. He takes things to heart. Unlike, you Romans and your Centurion, Perseus, how is he by the way? He needs to come by to dine."

"He is well Annas, older yes, but well. I will tell him."

"Oh, Marcus, make yourself comfortable. We may be a while with these questions I have." He finished.

"Now, Jesus, I have some questions. Will you indulge me, an old man and a Priest?"

Jesus answered, "Yes."

Annas began with questions, of worship of YHWH. And Jesus gave the classic answers. And the questions went on.

Simon Peter watched as Annas questioned Jesus. And a man warming at the fire, said to Simon Peter, "Are you not a disciple of this Jesus?"

Simon Peter worried now, and hesitant said, " No, I am not a disciple." Simon Peter watched as John standing near Annas, leaned down and spoke to a guard.

Time seemed to pass slowly, but Jesus answered every question. And then finally, tired of the charade, said. "I have taught and spoken openly, and freely to everyone. I taught in Synagogues and in the Temple, where all the Jews come together. I didn't say anything in secret, nor is anything hidden. Why do you question Me? Question the ones who heard Me, and what I spoke to them. They know what I said."

One the officers of the Temple slapped Jesus, "Is that the way you answer the High Priest!" Annas held up his hand, "Gentleness, Josiah, peace."

Jesus undeterred finished. "If I have spoken wrongly or disrespectable, show me My wrong! But if not, Why Did you slap me?" Jesus retorted.

Simon Peter looked on, and he flinched, as the slap echoed in the room. He watched as Annas raised his hand to interrupt Jesus. At that same moment, another man came to Simon Peter and said, "I have seen you; you are one of His followers! I know who you are."

Angry now, Simon Peter said, "I am not! I have no idea what you are talking about!" Just as the echo of his words died in the air, in the distance, Simon Peter heard a rooster crow! And Jesus, with sadness in his eyes, locked eyes with Simon Peter! Simon Peter turned quickly away and ran from the house weeping in bitter tears.

Annas turned to Marcus and said, "I am finished; take to him to Caiaphas!"

The Roman Contingent and Temple Guard moved Jesus quicky through the streets. They moved quietly in an unobserved manner. They came to Caiaphas' house. And they entered the house and went to the Great Hall. The Great Hall was where Caiaphas held banquets and meetings for important business when the Temple was closed. The Great Hall was bright as the twenty braziers and ten lamps along its walls burned.

Jesus looked at the crowd and understood. This was not a meeting in the Temple of the Sanhedrin, but now, a mock trial. The time day forbid judgment at night. But here he was. And all of the Sanhedrin was present. In a far corner, Jesus saw Nicodemus, looking concerned and conversing with another of the Sanhedrin.

Marcus turned to Jesus and said quietly, "I have been to battles far and wide, and battles where we were outnumbered twenty to one. . .But Now, Jesus, I am more nervous here, than any battle I have fought. I do not envy you, what comes next."

Jesus smiled at the big Roman and answered. "This is why I was sent here. My Father, knew it, and Joseph, would say he knew it."

Marcus turned from Jesus and went to where Caiaphas sat with many of the Elders and Scribes.

Marcus saluted, hand against armor, bowed slightly and said, "I bring Jesus the Nazarene, to you as requested. And all are safe. Even your Temple Guard. Centurion Perseus Quintis Nerva sent us at your request, to assist in bringing Him to you. And to remind you, that Rome will always help those in need." Marcus bowed deeply and turned on his heel and waved his contingent toward the door.

Jesus watched the big Roman leave with his detachment. And as their foot falls fell silent, He felt a coldness, and heard distant drums of war. And slowly, subtly, the tension in the room grew.

CHAPTER 18

MOCK TRIAL, JUDAS, PILATE, HEROD BACK AND FORTH

"DANTE! CIRILION! ALL Of YOU ATTEND ME!" Lightbringer/Lucifer/Satan called. The Prince and Power of the Air was pacing his domain. And anxious to verify the things he had heard and how they would fit in his plans.

Dark smudges and black smoke marked multiple entries of His Legions. He paced as he thought through his Plans and then stopped. Dante already was kneeling, head bowed. Cirilion, seemed to slide into place, head bowed as well. His dark eyes panned the host behind them. All heads bowed. And utter silence. *Good,* he thought, *Good, now we can begin.*

Arms wide he began, "As you all know, the plans we had to stop the birth of Jesus failed. And had it, not failed, the Light Father's Plan of the Redeemed would have stopped and we would have won! I know, I know, but worry not! It seems this Jesus is not as smart, as one would hope! He has even; it seems, without much help, found his way into the arms of the ones who hate him the most! Next to me of course. This sickly Priesthood and Temple, the ones who obtain favor by doing what we have guided! Everything, away from what the Light Father set down to become an empty, impotent, envious shell. They have an opportunity; to do what we could not. Now don't feel bad, you see, they, want him dead! And so do we! And what do I always say? Work together! But they are human. Sadly, human. So, they will need our help. So, all of you, go to the House of Caiaphas where they meet together, and assist in causing the death of God's Son! Because when He dies as a human, so dies the Light Father's Dream!" Lightbringer/Lucifer/Satan finished with relish. "Now Go! and end this swiftly, that we can return home to our rightful place!"

Caiaphas stood. Jesus noted He is in full regalia and anxious to fight. *Well let's see how this goes. Father again, I submit to your will. I ask for help; I ask for Wisdom and Strength.* Jesus prayed silently

He moved from his seat and calmly walked toward Jesus in the rooms center. The other Elders looked on seemingly unmoved, and immovable. He walked close to Jesus and with arms extended, bowed and said, "We of the Priesthood and Sanhedrin welcome Yeshua /Jesus of Nazareth to this Hall! And this meeting. We here, are to decide, once and for all, what we will do with you."

Jesus heard the whispers begin and murmurs all around him. Jesus Remembered the Father's words **["Behold, My Servant, whom I uphold; My chosen one in whom My soul delights. I have put My Spirit upon Him; He will bring forth justice to the Nations. He will not cry out or raise His voice, nor make His voice heard in the street. A bruised reed He will not break and a dimly burning wick He will not extinguish; He will faithfully bring forth justice. He will not be disheartened or crushed Until He has established justice in the earth; And the coastlands will wait expectantly for His Law.] [The Lord God has opened My ear; And I was not disobedient nor did I turn back.] [For the Lord God helps Me, Therefore, I am not disgraced; Therefore, I have set My face like flint, And I know that I will not be ashamed.]**

Dante raced to Caiaphas's side and whispered. *We need evidence. So, we may put him to death!* Caiaphas said aloud, "Bring out the witnesses!"

Caiaphas looked at the young Priest and those acolytes, who nodded. **Dante** whispered again, *I hope they were paid well. This needs to be done quickly if we are to complete Passover!*

One by one the witnesses came into the Hall. They all began to accuse Jesus.

Dante spoke to Cirilion, "We need to bring up the tension, or the Sanhedrin will not convict and call for death!"

Cirilion answered, "These *Humans,* are so ill suited for *ruling*. They can barely remember their names. I know; we want him dead, as the Master said! But How? look at them! From what I have seen, they only have   one   hope.   .   ."
Dante said, "And what is that?"

Cirilion crooned, "Have Jesus admit he is ***God's Son***. It is true, He is. But they will never *Believe* nor *Accept*, Him as Messiah! He has **hurt** them. Taken away their **reputation** and **power**, which all men crave. No, these paid witnesses, will just be an irritant and a delay."

One witness, "Healed on the Sabbath!" Another, "He raised the Dead." Another, "He gave sight to the blind." Still more, "Hearing to the deaf." "He made the lame walk." "He healed leprosy." "He set free the demon oppressed." "He healed a Roman servant!"

In all of this, murmurs and anger. But Nothing. ***This is nothing! No real accusation or story! This is going nowhere!*** Caiaphas thought, as Dante whispered.

"He goes against the Law!" Another said, "He Breaks the Sabbath!" More cries of agreement. "He eats with dirty hands!" Still more. "He touched a dead person, Unclean!" The crowd cried, "Yes! Yes!" Another, "He touched a Leper, Unclean!"

One witness said in seductive voice, "He ate and drank with sinners!" "Yes!" said the crowd. Another, "He ate and drank with tax collectors!" "Boo!" the crowd yelled! Witness after witness accused and yet, no real accusation was brought. After an hour of noise and angry accusations, the High Priest looked at Jesus and demanded, "Do you not answer? Do you not hear what they have said about You?"

Jesus in sadness of heart, knowing of the Priests and Priesthood, he heard Scriptures in his Mind and Heart. . .Confirming the truth. He stood as a silent witness. **[You have seen many things, but you do not observe them; Your ears are open, but none hears. But this is a people plundered and despoiled; All of them are trapped in caves, or are hidden away in prisons; They have become a prey with none to deliver them, and a spoil, with none to say, "Give them back! "I am against you. I will demand my Sheep and make them stop feeding my Sheep. and the Shepherds will not even feed themselves. And I will deliver them from their mouths. So, they will not be food**

**for them.! Unless you repent, and do the works of righteousness. . .
I will raise up Shepherds over them and tend them.]**

Caiaphas reacting to Jesus's silence and strength, cried out in anger.
"I demand you, under oath, by the Living God, tell us plainly. . . Are
You the Christ! The Son of the Living God!"

Jesus answered, "You have said it yourself. But, never the less, soon
you will see the Son of Man and the Son of God sitting at the right hand
of power and coming on the clouds of Heaven!"

Dante and **Cirilion** crooned, "Yes!"

Dante whispered to Caiaphas, *Look around the room. Meet their
eye and hold it! Find your supporters and paid voters! This must be
all one voice, or we lose everything! Our life, profession, wealth,
security and reputation! We lose even the nation!* Caiaphas looked
intently at each member of the Sanhedrin and Council, every Priest and
Acolyte. He circled around Jesus, as a hunter for prey. Caiaphas took
the whispers and suggestions as his own.

He noted only one descent. . . *I am not surprised, Nicodemus. Oh
well, so it means the vote will be ninety-nine. But we have him now! Now
for the show!* He thought. He let all his rage, impotence, and frustration
boil up and out in one move! Screaming! "He has Blasphemed!" He
grabbed his coat and tunic and pulled apart with all he had! He heard
the tear! And heard and saw the Ephod rip! And watched as the twelve
jewels clattered against the stones!

He dropped to his knees, as the jewels of the government, shattered
on the stones as well! And he finished, "What do we need witnesses for!
You have now heard, His blasphemy! Well, what say YOU!"

Jesus remained silent and still. He steeled himself for what he knew
would come next. As the Sanhedrin rose, almost as one, and rushed him!

Jesus heard the words ring in his heart and ears! **[The Lord God has
opened My ear; And I was not disobedient nor did I turn back.] [I
gave My back to those who strike Me, And My cheeks to those who
pluck out the beard; I did not cover My face from humiliation and
spitting.] [For the Lord God helps Me, Therefore, I am not
disgraced; Therefore, I have set My face like flint, And I know that
I will not be ashamed.]**

He felt a hand slap him! Fists, landed blows! He found His eyes wrapped in cloths! As the crowd's rage swept him up! He heard. "Prophesy! Who Hit YOU!" Slap! "Tell us Son of God!" the voice mocked! Punch! He was almost taken to the floor in the rage! **[I gave My back to those who strike Me, And My cheeks to those who pluck out the beard; I did not cover My face from humiliation and spitting.]** Priest after Priest came and spat in his face, and slapped or punched him!

Jesus' head, rocked side-to-side, with every blow! Pain and blood filled his mouth! The pain was like sharp knives, cutting flesh! His body almost crumpled under the onslaught, but He forced himself to stand! **[For the Lord God helps Me, Therefore, I am not disgraced; Therefore, I have set My face like flint, And I know that I will not be ashamed.]**

And as each blow fell, He heard laughter! And as the cloth was ripped from his eyes, he caught dark smudges, dancing around the room and the Council. As he lost consciousness, he heard the deep, dark laughter echo, as he met darkness!

****

Caiaphas, the Sanhedrin and all the Elders of the people had finished their debates, as the morning light broke. All of them agreed; that Jesus must die. And with the tentative calm between Roman and Judea, they agreed to take him to Pilate, the Governor. They bound Jesus with the manacles left by the Roman contingent and the Temple Guard, took control, and they made their way through streets, to the Governor's mansion.

***

Judas stood in the empty Reception Hall, at the House of Caiaphas. The room was quiet, except for the crackle and flutter of braziers and lamps. The light of the morning sun was in stark contrast to the coals and low lamps. He walked vacantly to the brazier nearest him. He heard the jingle of the coin purse. He scoffed. He felt the wait of the coin in his hand, *I forgot I had this still.* He looked at the brazier, the coals still burned, dark against the orange red embers, molten veins and crumbling bits. His face felt the heat of the fire. *Then a vivid image of the dread of Sheol.* Fear rose in his heart. *He didn't stand up to the Priests! He could have worked with them to free us! and He could have taken Caiaphas place and ruled.* He walked from the room into the morning sun. *The Council was adamant that Jesus Die! I didn't want him to Die! We could have been rich! All those crowds he fed and miracles, He would have need of nothing!* He walked the streets in the early morning light. He felt out of place. still distant from everything and everyone. He began to hear noises. and whispers. Nothing clear nothing concrete. He made his way to the Temple. He touched the door post of the Beautiful gate. And he heard **[Betrayer, Killer you you.]** Judas turned to his left and right. Nothing no one. Not even a Temple Guard was at the door. He walked through the Court of Women, *empty.* Though the lamps were lit and the morning light painted a path on the stones. **[You do not belong here.]** He turned and spun in place looking for the source of the whisper. *Nothing, no one!* He moved passed the Treasury and entered to where the Altar stood. and sacrifices never stopped. **[you have sinned]** **[you come here after what you have done]**

Judas felt a weight now, it was hard to think. He moved haltingly. His eyes dimmed and he saw through a fog again. He walked to the steps; where he could see the Sanctuary doors open. His heart filled with remorse and fear all at once. He couldn't move.

Judas saw a group of Priests coming from the Sanctuary. They saw him standing on the steps. He recognized them! They had been there at Caiaphas's House! Caiaphas; was nowhere to be seen, so He approached the Elder and said "I have sinned before God and Man! I betrayed an innocent Man, and innocent Blood! Here, take back your coin!" Judas held out the purse to the Elder. He answered "What has that got to do with us? it was *your Bargain!* You deal with it!" and they turned to walk away; as Judas threw the Purse, toward the Sanctuary, and ran from the Temple. He heard the coins ring off the stones as he passed the Altar, running even faster now! He made it out of the Temple and down the Road. Distraught; Broken, Fearful, Overcome in Grief and the Knowledge Jesus would Die! Not by his hand, but he had helped! The side of the road held vendors; He saw what he needed, and moved quickly to it. On the way He saw Dove Vendors, Sheep vendors, and more. The Vendor he wanted looked up from his task. "I need that. And this. How Much?" He asked. "For both?" the Vendor said in Scratchy voice "Seven shekels." He paid the man; and didn't acknowledge his thanks, or mention of happy Passover.

Judas eyes filled with tears! As he ran further down the Road. He ran till he saw a tree in a field. The tree was gnarled and ancient. He walked to it, weeping. The field the tree stood in was small and already plowed. Judas stopped; and leaned on the tree, trying to catch his breath. "God I am Sorry! I know Jesus was innocent! But he should have Used his power to Destroy Rome! He should have. . ." his voice faded. All at once; Judas felt cold! And the Tears were gone! His hands seemed to move on their own. His heart was full of Anguish and sorrow. The voices Returned [*You must pay for what you have done!*] [*You know there is no Forgiveness for You!*] [*Do it! . . . do it*] [*Innocent Blood Innocent Blood!*] His hand cut the rope. His hands tied the knot.

His hands, tied the end of the rope, around a large Branch. Judas Climbed. He went higher in the tree. And the found the spot. He laid the rope over a nearby branch. Looked at the ground; the distance was enough! The fog lifted from his Eyes. He saw the Rope; He put the Noose over his head, and stepped off the Branch! The rope became taught as his body moved toward the ground! The secondary branch and trunk held! Judas body Jerked once, and swung eerily in the morning sun. The only sound was laughter. . .

    ****

One of the Elder Priests, coming up the stairs to the Sanctuary, saw a smaller group in a heated Argument! "We cannot! That would not be Right!" one said.

The reply "Caiaphas, paid that Money! It should go back into the treasury!"

Answer, "But don't you see. . . that was blood Money! The Price of a Man. It would defile even the Treasury!"

"The treasury, would never know! Money is Money!"

The Elder Priest stepped close and said "Quiet! We must be more discreet, in the Temple!" He said in a harsh whisper!

"Stop both of you! Let us think this through shall we." He said.

"I know." The Elder said. "Take this money, and If I remember correctly, just outside that gate; just a bit down the road is a field. And it only has One Tree. An Old Gnarled one. Find the owner and buy it! We can use it; to bury strangers, or foreigners there. Or those who have no money!"

The two Priests left to do as he suggested. The Elder Priest walked into the sanctuary and began his duties there.

****

The Young Roman soldier, reluctantly, made his way to the Prefect's Chambers. It was too early; for the Prefect to be out in Barracks, or Training field. The Centurion on the wall had seen the group approaching, and went out to determine the situation. He found; the situation merited the Prefects Notice. And he had to send someone, and he, was that someone. It was not with a little dread; he was poised, to rap on the door, when Pontius Pilate, the Prefect opened the door himself. The young soldier quickly dropped his hand, to his chest armor in salute and bowed. Then he found his voice, "I apologize Prefect; But Centurion Niscilion, sent me to bring you to the Watch stairs. There is a situation that needs you." He finished smoothly.

Pontious Pilate smoothed his tunic and tightened his clasp on his cloak and said smoothly, "I understand Cestus, you will not be reprimanded or Punished for the seeming intrusion. I know of the Centurion's clear assessment of most situations. If He deems this important to send you to me, who am I to dissuade." Pilate indicated to the young soldier to lead the way, with a gesture in the direction he came from. Cestus saluted and bowed again, and spun on his heel and marched toward the Watch. The stones echoed each step made by both men. Soon they had reached the Watch. The Watch was one of four towers in Fortress Antonia. And they were met at the base of the stairs by Centurion Niscilion. Who also saluted Pilate and in his deep voice added, " Sorry to wake you Prefect, but there is a request; the High Priest and his group need to be answered."

Pilate smiled and held up his hand to forestall any objections or apology. "What have you found Centurion? What is the High Priests request?"

The Centurion hesitated only slightly, and finished.

"It seems Prefect; that they want you, to sentence someone to death."

"Interesting; I thought the Jews, condoned stoning or some such activity. . . I wonder what the Reason is." Pilate finished.

" I am Sorry Prefect. I did not intend to disturb you. But. . ."

"No, No Niscilion, think nothing of it. I couldn't sleep anyway. But; this does pose an interesting Question, why won't they Put the man to death themselves I wonder?"

The Centurion added, "I asked them to enter the Judgement Hall; so, things could be handled correctly, but it seems, they cannot even enter the Fortress. They claim; if they enter, they will be Unclean for their "Passover Celebration". So, I am sorry; but they requested you meet them. On the Portico stairs at the Entrance."

"Well, if their God deems us dirty; and Who am I to argue. I think it will be interesting either way. I will take Cetus with me if you allow it." Pilate Finished

"Of course, Prefect. Cetus is not in need of Training at the Moment." The Centurion finished. Cestus saluted both in turn and turned to move to the Portico.

Pilate moved into step with the young soldier. And said "I have seen may things in my Life; but I have never understood Religion. Even when Ceasar; Himself says things. What do you say Cestus? And you can speak freely."

Cestus turned to Pilate and said, "Well Prefect, I know Rome teaches to stand together for Strength and more, but in spite of The Caesars wishes, Belief is a strong thing. I am sometimes struggling, even to believe I am Soldier. But there are times, believing a God or even the Hebrew God is interested in what goes on in the day to day, would be a comfort of sorts. I say too Much, Prefect I am sorry."

"No offense taken Cestus. There are many things' Men do or don't. But Belief holds more power than Even Ceasar Admits. Though some may say I speak treason to Object to some things. We all are under someone; even I, I have the Ever-watchful Eye of Rome on Me. But; strength is good, but can fail, if hope is lost. That's why the Trainers and Centurions, Push you. To be the Best, but when the struggle even for you or the unit, is too Much, sometimes Belief triumphs odds." Pilate said as they began the long march to the Portico steps.

The Sun was bright and hot; even at this hour, as they made their way across the parade grounds to the entry. The hope for rain to cool things; was shattered by the clear blue sky, as Pilate made his way to the covered stairs and then outside again to the portico. And near his Judgement seat, when large crowds demanded space.

"Well Cestus, this better be worth the Trip Eh. What Rome does for those it conquers. . . " He laughed bitterly. He looked; and saw the knot of Robes and finery of the High Priest and His Entourage. And a Man, in chains and bloody. *Hmm* he thought, *it seems There has been prior questioning, I think. Well; he has caught someone's ire. Let us see if it is Justified.*

Pilate stopped twenty yards from the Judgement seat on the right. And looked at the Group from the top of the large set of steps. He smiled and thought, *would it have been better to bring more than Cestus I wonder?*

Pilate motioned them to come up and meet him. He watched as they climbed the steps and hauled their Prisoner up with them. He spoke in his Official Voice now; after glancing at Cestus; who stood, hand ready on his sword. *He is ready to defend me and die, Hopefully, that will not be the case today. Cestus seems a good Soldier, young, but good.* His thoughts finished. Pilate held up his hand and said Officially "What charges do you bring against this Man?"

He saw Caiaphas puff out his chest and retort " If he were not a Troublemaker and criminal, we would not have brought him Here!"

Pilate heard the arrogant boast of Caiaphas. and the quick agreement of the Others, and yet, the man in chains said nothing. He stood quietly, though a little unsteady at times. *He must have had quite a night. So; Caiaphas, did you question him all night? Those Bruises are not from swatting flies, and the swelled cheeks are not from Kisses I will wager.*

"If he is a Criminal and Troublemaker; as you say, take him Yourself, and deal with him according to your Law!" Pilate turned to go. He knew; something was off with all of this, but needed to hear more.

Caiaphas spoke again; anger and frustration evident "We cannot put anyone to Death, per Rome remember!"

That sounds like a convenience to me; that has never stopped you before, Why now? I wonder? He thought.

In desperation Caiaphas said "This man is misleading our Nation and is Forbidding others to pay taxes to Ceasar. And even saying he is Christ, a King! And He has stirred up the People all over Judea and from galilee to even here!"

Pilate turned to Cestus and said quietly "It seems Cestus; We cannot avoid involvement, go over and bring him into the Fort and Praetorium. I will question him there. Post a guard here and keep them here as well."

Pilate turned and headed back to the Praetorium and the Forts interior. Cestus took Jesus by the arm and walked him further up the steps and into the Fort.

Cestus looked at Jesus, who said nothing as they walked. They crossed the Parade grounds to the Praetorium. and He stopped in front of Pilate and who sat in His usual Place of Judgement.

Pilate looked at Jesus; now out of the hot sun, and saw even more clearly the evidence of questioning. *If he is a King, there are questions even Rome would ask. But no King would allow himself to be treated, thusly. Something doesn't seem right. But, I also need to protect Rome and myself; we need no help stirring up trouble it seems with these Jews.*

Pilate asked. "So, are you a King then?"

Jesus answered, "You have said so. Whether it is on your own or because of others."

"Are you a Galilean, then?" Pilate finished.

He turned to Cestus and said, "Cestus, take a few more men, and take this man to Herod. He is at the palace and let Herod deal with him! And as for Caiaphas and his lot, tell them, "I find him not guilty."

****

Herod Antipas was excited to hear Jesus was in his audience chamber! He had heard stories and hoped to see a sign or a miracle.

Herod lounged on his throne sipping wine and looking perturbed. "Jesus, Pilate sent you to me to question you about what Caiaphas, and the Elders have said. They have said, 'This man is misleading our nation and is forbidding others to pay taxes to Ceasar. And even saying he is Christ, a King! And He has stirred up the people all over Judea and from Galilee, to even here!' So, You are here, I only ask that you answer. And that Truthfully. Because, I understand my friend, Pilate, found you not guilty. But Caiaphas is young and sensitive! He is rash sometimes. So, will you answer their questions for me?"

He looked on clearly not happy. But Jesus knew not to respond. He knew Herod understood Caiaphas and the blasphemy charge, but, was only concerned with his own power and spectacles. He knew he wanted Him to do something never had done before. Or maybe turn more water into wine! So, he and his followers could be drunk and revel in it. *Father, I will not cheapen your power and name with theatrics! I know he will be angry, but I will not!* Jesus thought.

After an hour of silence, Herod turned to his guard, motioning him to come close, whispered in his ear and the guard left. Not long after, he returned and undid the manacles and stripped off his cloak and tunic, replacing the bloody clothes with a gorgeous purple robe that was embroidered! He stood and said to his guard, "Now he is dressed as befitting Him, this King!" He said in mockery, "Send him back to Pilate!"

So, Jesus and Herod's guards returned to Pilate. And they were met outside the fort on the portico steps, with a large crowd with Caiaphas and Pilate.

Pilate now was on the Dias and his Judgement seat outside the fort on the portico as Jesus was brought up the steps to stand near Pilate.

One of Herod's guards leaned in and whispered in Pilate's ear, and turned walked down the steps. He motioned for the rest to follow. Pilate in frustration called out to the growing crowd; "I told you before, I found no guilt in him!"

He continued, "You brought him to me, as one who incites the people to rebellion! And I have examined him, nor has Herod, one of your own, has sent him back to us, finding no guilt! He has done nothing to deserve death!"

While Pilate sat listening; to the repeated crimes He had heard before, a runner came and handed him a note. He acknowledged the Runner and Opened the note.

It smelled of Perfume and flowers; **His Wife**, he recognized her handwriting. He read the Note [*Pilate; Love, do not have anything to do with this man, He is a Righteous Man! I was tortured in My Dreams All night because of Him! Do not Judge this man!*] Pilate crumpled the note in His hand, and turned to Cestus and the other guards "Bring Him!" he said as He walked from the Judgement seat. and headed inside the Fort.

Pilate Now away from the crowd and noise; spoke to Jesus again. "Do you not hear what they say! Your Nation has turned you over to Me! what have you Done? I am not a Jew, Are you a King? "

Jesus said nothing except "If My Kingdom; was of this World, my Servants would fight, so that I would not be turned over to the Jews. But my kingdom is not of this Realm, but another."

Pilate answered again " So you are a King."

"You answered Truthfully that I am A King. This is what I was born for; and to testify to the Truth! Everyone, who is of the truth, Hears Me and My voice."

Pilate retorted "What is Truth?"

He turned to Cestus, keep him here. I will try and Speak to this rabble. Hopefully; we can find Peace today!"

Soon Pilate again sat down on his seat and said again "I find him not Guilty of the Charges or Accusations."

Dante spoke to **Cirilion** and said "We need this done. I will whisper to *Pilate*, you stir the Pot as they say, If He thinks there will be a Rebellion for real, He will do what We need, Now Go! And have the others whisper as well.

Pontius Pilate looked out on the Crowd. At the Forefront; Caiaphas and his entourage. And somehow the crowd had gotten even larger since he questioned Jesus now a Second time.

Dante whispered ***"You know; If Rome hears any of this, you will have to answer for it. The High Priest Caiaphas, has lost Power, Reputation, and Money of course! The people follow Jesus. . .***Pilate took the whispers as his own thoughts. And continued *Not only do I have to balance this Foolishness, but even my Wife's ire. If I condemn the man, I will lose my Wife, If I don't, I may have a riot or rebellion on my hands. I have met criminals and Insurrectionists before, This Jesus is neither. How can I come out of this with a Whole Skin. Think, think!* **Dante** whispered again, *this is their Feast! and We of Rome are Magnanimous always! I have released People before; I could do it Now. Maybe if I give them a Drastic Choice. . .maybe, they will choose and I will be free and no harm to Me or My Wife, it would be Out my hands! Thats it! Thats it!* Thoughts ended he turned to Cestus "Cestus, who do we hold in the Prison?"

Cestus leaned down and said "Many, why Prefect?"

"Remember I told you we may come out of this safely? I believe I have found a Way!" he paused "Who is the Worst we hold?"

Cestus thought a moment; He stepped back and spoke to another guard, who ran back into the Fort. Not long after, the guard returned with a Note.

He handed to Cestus; Cestus looked it over, and brought the note to Pilate. and said "Centurion Niscilion says the *worst* is *Barabbas*. He is being Held for Insurrection and Murder of Romans and more." Cestus finished.

At that same Moment **Cirilion** moved to Caiaphas the High Priest and Whispered ***"This is going to fail, unless something is done! Twice Rome; has had Jesus in its hands, and Nothing as Yet! If he does not die, all of our Lives will change! You will disappear into obscurity. And Lose you standing in the Temple, you know that Rome will question why you went to Pilate at all. The people will revolt and Rome will descend upon Jerusalem as a Hawk on mouse!"***

Caiaphas; thought a moment more, and said "If we do not cry to have Jesus Crucified, that weakling Pilate, will release Him! But we need to wait to know for sure. Spread the Word! Stir the Crowd." he finished in a Whisper to an Acolyte.

Pilate stood and raised his hands for quiet. And He panned the whole Courtyard. And spoke in his Official Voice "Today is Your Passover Celebration! and Rome is Benevolent, and kind to its Subjects! I have released to you at Passover before, those that you have asked. I offer the same again today! As My gift to you. . ." He paused. "I would release to You Jesus; King of the Jews! Or Barabbas! Whom you know as the Killer of Men and insurrection! Which shall it be!" Pilate waited. He hoped the People would choose well; but even he knew crowds, were not thinkers.

Dante smiled and said to **Cirilion** "Perfect! Now; we push the Crowd to Crucify Jesus! If he dies, the Light Father's Plan Dies as Well! Use anything and Anyone! Go!

Caiaphas grabbed a priest, and said "Call to crucify Jesus, and Release Barabbas! the Simpleton does not realize, he has done as We desired!"

Pilate asked again "Who shall I release to you? Jesus or Barabbas!"

The Crowd; Elders and Chief Priests, in one voice, said "Crucify Jesus! Give us Barabbas!" "Crucify Jesus! Give Us Barabbas!" Pilate knowing the Reason shouted "I found no fault in him! Why? what evil has He done?" **Dante; Cirilion** and others, pushed now the Crowd and Priests! They were filled with anger and hate! and Cried "Crucify him! Crucify Him!" It became the mantra of the Crowd! "Away with Jesus! Crucify him! Give us Barabbas!"

Pilate again held up his hands for Quiet. It took some minutes to bring the crowd to stillness. Pilate hung his head and thought *I do not want this man's Death on my conscience. Though none had bothered me before. Maybe I can just Punish him and release him! Maybe they would accept that.*

"I will Punish Jesus and release him!" The Crowd groaned at this.

Pilate called to Cestus. "Yes Prefect?"

Pilate shook his head. "These people want blood! There is no choice. But maybe I can use this to change their Hearts. Go and tell the Centurion to Scourge him lightly and bring him out to me!"

"Yes Prefect!" Cestus went into the Fort and saluted Centurion Niscilion and gave him Pilate's Orders. The Centurion walked from his Post to where Jesus and the other guards were. and said "Orders are to scourge the prisoner and then Bring him out. Scourge lightly. So said the Prefect!" Centurion Niscilion knew though that Orders and people sometimes, do not match up Perfectly.

He left the Praetorium and watched as they moved Jesus outside onto the grounds. The *"Post"* as it was called was a Stone with Metal Clasps and Eyelets for Manacles.

Jesus heard the Orders. His human heart tightened; as his mind realized, what was in store. He had endured, the pummeling of the Temple Guard, and the Council. But Now; this, was Rome! This would be harder than anyone could imagine! He quickly prayed to the Father. *Father; I am tired. and sore. I need you and the Spirit to strengthen me. Without you; this may not get done. And I do not want to fail! Father I do not want to fail!*

Dante called for **Lobhrach** "Lobhrach, as insurance, move the Romans to Blood lust. Because; if Pilate isn't moved enough, we may have to bring Jesus near death to help!"

Jesus heard and felt the ripping of his clothes. And the heavy hands, that tore it all away! And felt the heat upon his skin. All that was left was the loin cloth. and sandals. He was led to the *Post*. And the manacles locked in place. The sun was hot on his back and legs. He smelled sweat and hot sand as he waited at the post. The Centurion was seated behind him and the post, was open to view.

Jesus, could see soldiers marching, Practicing. all within his view. But no one looked at him at all. *I guess, this is a Normal thing for these Men. Father; Help Me now. Please.*

Jesus felt the power of God fall on him. And his strength returned. Tiredness gone. His Fear however, was still lurking in the shadows.

Jesus saw a big Roman come from the parade grounds and walked past him to the Centurion.

Centurion Niscilion called out. "Light Scourging, Not Fatal. keep him Alive."

"Yes sir. Though, I make no Promises."

"Those were the *Prefects* **Orders** Sergeant! Not mine!"

The big Roman walked to where Jesus was; and moved in, close. He reached down and tested the manacles and the Lock Eyelet. Jesus saw the chain links; and knew, there was no escape, from anything from now on! He felt peace in that moment. He knew God's Power was flowing through him. and He heard the Scriptures in his ears **[Behold, My Servant, whom I uphold; My chosen one in whom My soul delights. I have put My Spirit upon Him; He will bring forth justice to the Nations. "He will not cry out or raise His voice, nor make His voice heard in the street. A bruised reed He will not break and a dimly burning wick He will not extinguish; He will faithfully bring forth justice." "He will not be disheartened or crushed]**

The Roman Soldier turned to him and looked him in the eyes and said Quietly. "This will hurt. There is no shame, in tears or screams. I usually have people bite on Leather, but I was told to go easy, on you for now. move with the blows. that helps." He finished.

Jesus felt his rough hands touch his back and shoulders. " I will begin. Be ready."

He heard rather than saw; the Big Man go to a Bench, and heard him pull away something. He heard the bits of rock, glass, nails scratch the bench. He heard the Big man say "I begin."

Jesus heard the Scriptures **[Behold, My Servant, whom I uphold; My chosen one in whom My soul delights. I have put My Spirit upon Him. . .]**

He heard a whistling, felt a deep bite into his back and a searing pain! Then whatever flesh was cut, he felt the pull of the whip as it was drawn away! He leaned as the cat of nine tails was moved. Pain! But He heard **[I gave My back to those who strike Me, . . .]** as another fell! That was . . . on the left! Again, Searing pain! He leaned in to the right as the next Fell! **[For the Lord God helps Me, therefore, I am not disgraced; . . .]** and again to the left **[Therefore, I have set My face like flint, And I know that I will not be ashamed.]**

Again, and again, Jesus felt the Cut of the whip and the tear of removal!

The Big Roman heard whispers *[You must strike Hard! Strike and tear flesh!]* the Big man shook his head; wiped the sweat from his eyes and struck again. He saw his target fall to his knees and lean over the Post. Whispers *[Vengeance! Retribution! He must pay the Price!]* another strike! *[Every drop of Blood is our Due! This man deserves Wrath and Death!]* He stopped shook his head and was ready to strike when He was stopped by the Centurion who cried "Soldier! **SOLDIER!**"

He shook visibly; as the seeming fog, lifted! And He looked at the Whip in his hand and the Object of his wrath! He saw the man's body, marked up like a plowed field*! I have never disobeyed orders before! What happened!* He thought. He felt Centurion Niscilion grab his shoulders and shake hard! And screamed "**ENOUGH!** Enough! Take him to Pilate now!" He pointed to two other soldiers nearby. And then turned to the Big Man. "And you. I will deal with you later! Now I must keep the Prefect from sending us all to the Ends of the Earth!"

Jesus; was held between two, Roman Soldiers. As the group came back to the Portico. Pilate winced as he saw him! *I told them Lightly! Lightly scourge!* Anger and dread filled him as He watched them bring him Forward! *He is not standing well on his own. They are holding him up!* He thought. Pilate stood and motioned for Quiet and Proclaimed "See; I have Punished him Sufficiently; Now I will release him to you!" Before the words died in the air the Crowd already was shouting and screaming "Take him away! We will not have this Man!" "Crucify Jesus! Give us Barabbas! Crucify Jesus and give Us Barabbas!"

Pilate saw the crowd. And All of his training; and years of life, told him, He was looking at Rebellion! And if he did nothing else, He must stop that Rebellion and quiet the situation. he turned to a Guard nearby. and said "Bring a Basin and a Towel! Now!" The guard rushed off to do as he was commanded.

Pilate saw a soldier coming with pitcher, Towel and basin, he smiled. And looked at the Soldier. And said "Hold the basin please."

Pilate poured in water. And He set the Pitcher at his feet. He turned to the crowd motioned for silence. Again, he waited for quiet. He looked all the crowd over. He made sure he met as many eyes as possible. He made sure; He met Caiaphas eyes, and held them for a few Moments and His Entourage. Then raising his voice again he said " I find no Fault in Jesus called the Christ. I am innocent of this man's blood! I say that again to all who hear! I find him Not guilty! and I wash my hands of Blood guilt!" he dipped his hands in the basin and wiped the off with the Towel and said again. I am Innocent!"

As he finished; He heard near the crowd, as the Murmur started, the Shout! "His Blood be on Us! and Our Children! Crucify Him Crucify Him!"

He turned to the guard and Cestus and said "Take him to the Praetorium, then, take him to be Crucified!"

Pilate turned from the Crowd and his Judgement seat and walked into the fort in silence.

CHAPTER 19

PRAETORIUM, SIMEON, THE LONG WALK TO GOLGATHA

Pilate found Centurion Niscilion and raged! "I gave Cestus specific orders! Did he report them to you Centurion!" Pilate waited. "Yes, Prefect he did!" Came the answer. Pilate waved his hand toward the prisoner Jesus and finished, "Does this look like light scourging to you?" He glared at the Centurion.

Cestus, focused his eyes on the stones at his feet. Pilate continued speaking to Niscilion, "If that is, I may need to appoint another Centurion!"

"Yes Sir, I mean No Sir, that is not Light scourging. And Yes, Prefect you may need to replace me." he continued "I had Magnus scourge him. he has more control and has been here the longest." Niscilion finished. "I must relay this to you from Sergeant Magnus, He said He followed his normal routine and understood the order, but he was almost pushed to go beyond orders."

"He was pushed? by whom?" Pilate asked

"He said He felt a Cold Presence and heard whispers, his sight was foggy, and he acted out of control. He could not stop." the Centurion finished

"So, what stopped him then?" Credulous Pilate asked.

"He said It was like the Lifting of a Mist, suddenly! He has never disobeyed a direct order before. He has asked to be reduced in rank and will be in the Stockade for three days."

Pilate waved a hand and said "Fine, Niscilion, but do not Reduce his rank. And move Cestus up in rank and Let Magnus teach him. We do not want to waste what We have now do we!"

Cestus saluted hand on chest and bowed. "Thank you, Prefect, thank you."

"Don't thank Me yet, sergeant, you are to prepare the Prisoner for Crucifixion. And remind the Men in the hole to tread carefully. and Send a runner to Centurion Perseus Quintis Nerva. I need him for the Crucifixion."

Pilate turned to leave. Sergeant Cestus Marcus stood stunned. He looked at Centurion Niscilion and asked "Forgive me Centurion, But Is what he said true? Have I been raised in rank to Sergeant?"

The Centurion said "Yes"

"But Sir, I did nothing of import today. I just did as Requested." The Centurion smiled and laughed. "Sergeant, when dealing with People, Orders, and Prefects, doing what is requested tends to pay off. Now go and send that Runner, and take him Below. and Prepare him."

Sergeant Cestus Marcus, left Centurion Niscilion still smiling, as he headed to the Mesenger area of Fort Antonia. He remembered not long ago he had been a runner for Centurion Niscilion. He smiled to himself. And opened the door; and was almost knocked to the floor, by a young Runner and his Satchel. He dodged quickly and the Young man stammered "S-s-sorry Sir!" He smiled again. walked into the heart of the Forts Messenger Service. He saw the three stands and three Scribers as they wrote furiously. and barked names aloud.

"Gaius! You go to Herod, in Response to His request for Protection, when Returning home from the Palace in Jerusalem!"

"Yes, Aritos! " came a reply. Cestus moved to the man holding out the Papyrus. and said "Aristos; I need to send a Message to Centurion, Perseus Quintis Nerva. Centurion Niscilion; asks his Assistance with Crucifixion Duty, His Presence is requested here at the Fort. At His Convenience of Course."

Aritos looked up from his papyrus. And said "Ahh I thought I heard you Cestus! You need Centurion Nerva, Ok, it must be wonderful, to be in the latter years of service!" He laughed "then again, He did give Rome many victories. Crucifixions are far less dangerous than a Campaign Eh Cestus."

"Yes, Yes they are Aritos." Cestus looked around. "Whom are you sending?" "Uh Aniarches, he's really fast! almost as fast as you!"

Aritos took a Papyrus and wrote on it. and Looked up again. "When does the Centurion need to be here?" Cestus thought a Moment and said "I am not sure Prefect Pontius Pilate, gave the Order before he retired for the Day. And I haven't checked the Prisoner Yet, so, tomorrow morning?"

Aristos asked. "Did he say that it was Urgent?"

"No, the Jews frustrated, him by Accusing a Man of Rebellion. Which; The Prefect and Others, found Not Guilty. But they wanted Blood."

"Hah, No surprise there. What do they call this Seven Day Festival? the Passover. And they kill a Lamb and Eat. . ." Aristos finished.

"The Man was Jesus of Nazareth. A Local Rabbi, whom some have said does Miracles." He said with a smile. Aristos waved Aniarches over. and handed him the Message.

Aristos came around the stand to where Cestus was and said. "It will be in his hands in an hour. Since he lives in the country side now. And What is this I here? You are a Sergeant Now?"

Cestus shrugged and said " yeah, All I did was obey Orders. Nothing fancy or brave."

"Moving up in Rank, Better Pay and sleeping quarters is always good." he shook Cestus hand. And finished. "You do know where you are sleeping now right?"

"yes, I think so. But I need to check on that Prisoner. I haven't yet."

Cestus turned and walked out of the Messenger Post and Headed to the Prison House.

The Torch, reflected off the stone as Cestus made his way down the stair to the Prison. There were three large rooms; Cut into the bedrock, under the Praetorium. And the Fort. The Four Tower, Edifice stood against everything. Unmoved and Unmovable. He loved being up on the Towers. And watching the action at the Temple. He had always been curious about what the Jews believed and enjoyed his watch hours, even if others thought it tedious.

He came to the outer gate and the Guard Post. He saluted, and passed through. He made his way to the Inner gate and stopped. He saluted the two guards and looked for the Jailer. The jailer came out of a small alcove, looking tired, and worn.

Cestus stopped the man, who asked "What is it you need Soldier?"

Cestus let the question pass and said "I am checking on a Prisoner, one brought in Today, towards evening. The Rabbi the High Priest accused."

"Ahh, him. He is isolated in the side room there. He must have favor with someone, that he is not in Main Hold. Then again, I was concerned that He might not even make it to his Crucifixion. After what Magnus did."

"Prefect Pilate, sent him down. To await Crucifixion. I was supposed to Prepare Him." Cestus finished.

The Jailer shook his head, "Since it is evening, and He has passed out, I doubt Pilate would object to waiting for Morning. There isn't the same Spectacle Crucifying at Night as in the Day!" he moved to his Station and added. "I think if Pilate was in a hurry, He would have dragged him off the stairs be fore this! And with this Jewish Celebration going on, Moving at Night would be tricky.

Cestus looked at the jailer. And said "Will he be able to Bear the Cross to Execution? Or will We need to help him then?"

The Jailer coughed and said "He looked like a strong man, But, after Magnus, it's a gamble either way."

"Well, Then I will send a Runner to Update Centurion Nerva and We will leave at the earliest."

The Jailer shook his Head. "He must have done something really bad for Magnus to Disobey Orders like that."

"I may be Crucified myself, if He dies tonight! but so be it. I will be in at Dawn as will Centurion Nerva I am Sure."

Cestus shook his head. "All this trouble for a Rabbi, that Healed, and Fed People, but someone didn't like."

"Yes, someone definitely didn't like. I think the dirt in and sand might seal some cuts up. But Who knows." The Jailer agreed.

****

Jesus found himself in pain and Darkness. He felt the cold stone and sand beneath him. *The big Roman was not wrong. It did Hurt. And if that was Light, I would hate to feel what Heavy Scourging was! What day is this? humph, Is it day even? I cannot see in this darkness. Father; are you there? Holy Spirit, thank you for your Strength. Though, I know more suffering awaits. But; I hope I haven't missed parts of the plan. I hope that All my Future Brethren and Jews, know. . . That I will soon be that True Passover Lamb. I will need strength for sure. . . I am Tired Father. But I will Obey.* **Son**, He heard the Father, **you have not missed any of the Plan, but we had to Fulfill the Scriptures, and Some are not enjoyable at all. And there are more yet to be fulfilled. And Yes, for now, I am still with you. Though soon, I will have to turn my back. And look away. Rest if you can. . .Soon it will be Sunrise and the Long walk will take place.**

The Fathers Voice melted into Darkness and Silence. . . .

****

Jesus was rudely awakened by a Burly Roman hauling him to his Feet! And his snidely voice calling out "Good Morning You Majesty!"

As his eyes focused to the torches; he was moved out, into the Main Prison Area. He was surrounded Soldiers. The nearest grabbed his shoulders; pulling away his Blood-soaked tunic. As he did so; He felt the Cuts, of the Whip Tear! Searing Pain!

"You need to be Dressed your Majesty! You have to Parade! And wear your Crown! and Ascend your throne!" Another cried. And it was met with laughter. Another Soldier spun him and pushed him over, as another jammed the Crown down upon His Head. and Blood spurted from the contact points! More Laughter! The Room swirled; with dark smudges, and harsh Whispers, But He looked as another moved toward him with the Purple Embroidered Gold Robe Herod had Put on him before.

"Here is your Robe Your Majesty! Let me Help you put it on!" The Soldier growled in anger!

Jesus realized the manacles were gone! And His hands were free. He was unable to focus; as He was pushed to his knees, and a Soldier pushed the Robe over his head! and catching the Crown and pushing it deeper! Blood flowed into his eyes! Stinging!

He again was raised to his Feet; now fully clothed and Crowned! He was spun again and a heavy reed was pushed into his hand!

And all at once; the Whole room of Roman Soldiers, dropped to one knee and cried out! "Hail! hail! O king of the Jews!" and again "Hail hail King Jesus of Nazareth!" He felt himself Spun again and the Reed left his hand! And it landed hard; on his forehead, with a Crack! The Crown of Thorns; dug deeper in to his scalp and head, as blood shot from each Blow! He heard the Harsh Whispers [*Hail, King Jesus! O Great Majesty of Heaven and Earth! Imposter! Liar!*] [*You are no king!*] the Whispers cried! A Fist landed! Laughter! The Reed landed again! Blood and more Shouts! "Hail the King in Purple! The King of nothing!" the Soldiers cried. Jesus then heard the Scriptures in his Ears **[I gave My back to those who strike Me...]** and He flinched as spittle hit his Face! Laughter! A smash of a Fist snapped his head to the left! He forced himself to stand. and heard again **[I did not cover My face from humiliation and spitting. . .]** He heard their curses as the onslaught continued. "You are no King! YOU are Nothing!" a blow fell! The Reed fell. And Dark laughter was added to room. and more smudges swirled and whispers [*You will die Alone and Forgotten! For what? No one sees you!*] [*God has abandoned you!*]

He saw the whole cohort of Soldiers drop again to one knee and cry as one "Hail, Hail, the Mighty King!" Another blow fell and Jesus met darkness!

****

Jesus was shocked awake by an ice-cold water bucket! And the mocking words, "Sorry Your Majesty! This is not sleeping time! You have a beam to carry and the parade to walk!" The soldier laughed as he finished. "You may rest at the Cross!" Jesus, was roughly hauled to his feet and pushed to the door! He noticed the purple robe was gone and his bloodied tattered tunic, what was left of it anyway was back!

The two Romans flanking him were in full armor and ready for war. One of the cohorts behind, as they climbed the steps said, "Do not fret, your Majesty! You will not be resting Alone! You have two other subjects that are accompanying you! Ahh, it is too bad, the prefect released that scum Barabbas! You would have enjoyed him!" He laughed cruelly. The stone steps were cold and rough on his feet. He realized his sandals were gone as well. The manacles were in place and when Jesus struggled on the stairs and lost balance, he was summarily lifted by his two guards.

The sun was a shock as Jesus reached the parade grounds of the fort and was moved to the tunnels to the stairs. He looked out on the area of Pilates's judgment. And he shook, as the memories flooded back! He looked the courtyard was empty. But for a contingent of soldiers, a Centurion on horseback, and the Roman Commander, Marcus. The two other men already bearing the Cross beams waited by a single Roman, holding an upright beam.

That is for me. Father I will need Your strength, I barely made up the steps to here! Holy Spirit, I need you as well. His thoughts finished. And the two Romans flanking him, marched him down the steps, to the waiting crossbeam and solitary soldier.

The Soldier leaned the heavy beam onto Jesus's back. Jesus winched as the rough beam cut through, to his torn back! The Purple robe would have eased it some, but that was gone! His tattered tunic; did nothing, but cover what skin was left. And that almost none!

Centurion Perseus Quintis Nerva moved his Black Stallion toward the group. And Marcus Aquila his Commander and friend joined him.

"Marcus, those two I recognize, but who is this?" looking at Jesus.

Commander Marcus Aquila looked up at His Commander and Friend and said, "This man; . . ." He paused, ". . .or what is left of Him, Is Jesus of Nazareth, a Rabbi, Accused of Rebellion and more. I am sorry to say; but he is Son of Joseph, your favorite carpenter."

Perseus Quintis Nerva moved his stallion closer to Jesus, who saw the man approach on his horse. Jesus looked at the Centurion, He remembered, what Commander Marcus had said earlier. And memory of Joseph's voice telling of the Centurion's advice and the wedding of Mary! Jesus looked at the Centurion staring down at him. *He is looking tired Marcus, as you said. But I wonder if he knows I am Joseph's Son? It really doesn't matter; redemption is for all men. I am sorry to have you do this. But This must be done at all cost, as I and the Father planned.*

The centurion leaned down in the saddle and spoke to Jesus "You. Are you Joseph's Son of Mary? Truly?"

Jesus Answered "I am, He taught me well. I was with him when He built you the Tables and chairs for your new House in the Countryside."

The Centurion quietly continued "You are Jesus? The Miracle worker? The one who Healed my Servant."

"Yes"

"What have they done? What have you done to deserve this?" He finished. "My Servant Lives. And is Strong! He has been even a friend. As was Joseph, though I am a Roman."

"Well, . . .Jesus smiled back ", not everyone is Perfect Centurion. Do not fret Yourself. Do what you must. But understand; this you do, is for a great purpose. One set down, by God Himself. Do not hesitate or shrink back. Nor will I."

"As you will." The centurion Straightened and moved his horse back to Marcus Aquila. He looked at Marcus and said "It is time we Move. There will be crowds on the street. Being one of them killed family. Watch Jesus though. I am not sure He will make it to the Skull. Let us go. Sergeant, set your men ahead, we move now!"

Sergeant Cestus Marcus; and his three moved in front of the Centurion, and began the trek to the streets of Jerusalem!

Jesus; and the other two men bearing the Cross beams, were followed by Commander Marcus Aquila, and His five men. Jesus moved slowly; but he felt strong, as the Holy Spirit flooded him. And He heard the Scriptures with each step, ringing in his ears, drowning out the Dark Whispers. . . **[For the Lord God helps Me, Therefore, I am not disgraced; Therefore, I have set My face like flint, And I know that I will not be ashamed.]**

Jesus with every step felt the scrape of the rough wood on His shoulders and back. He felt the jarring tear as his tattered tunic did nothing to stop the continuous scrape of semi-dried wounds!

Jesus moved steadily along the narrow streets. And as the Centurion said the people lined both sides looking at the spectacle and jeering! Some threw spoiled vegetables and food! Jesus was grateful for the beam he carried. . . *I could not have made it with the full cross!* he thought, as He was pummeled with rotten figs and jeers! "Liar! Son of God. HA!" and it was countered with, "He is innocent! Why? What has he done to deserve this!"

A jarring step; the tear of his back, and Scriptures ringing in his ears **[He was despised and forsaken of men, A man of sorrows and acquainted with grief; And like one from whom men hide their face]** as spit and worse assaulted him! He looked at their faces, all in rage and anger! The cries were almost screaming! "Crucify Him! He lied to us!" "What now O' Son of God!" More steps; more scraping of his back and more Pain! Jesus heard distant laughter and the words! [*God has Forsaken you! You are alone!*] then [*They do not want you! All you did for nothing!*]

The crowd lining the street saw the criminals now too. Some of them, recognized the murderers and the insurrectionists. And found anything at hand from dirt, rocks, and spit on them as well! Commander Marcus Aquila, and his five deftly pushed back those that attempted to rush them, to exact personal vengeance! Jesus counted each step, and scrape that kept his back and the pain raw! He turned a corner and heard, "Jesus! Master! Rabbi! No! No!" and turned to see eyes weeping and grief! He kept moving; albeit slowly, if he fell behind too much, the guard closest would push him ahead and cry, "Move!" He had almost fallen once already, but held his own.

Jesus recognized the open market and the broader street. But that too; seemed just a seething mass, of people. He saw hatred, murder, vengeance on every face! and he closed his eyes and looked again. . . there floating from one person to another, he saw the fallen angels, one after the other whispering in the peoples ears! Then, He saw the High Priest and Elders in the mix of people, also being whispered too, by non-other than LightBringer/Satan/Lucifer! He heard the laughter, and the smooth almost melodic voice say: [***Ooooh, how far one has fallen! To bear a body as this. So far below your station and right! You hear their voice. . .You hear how they cry. . .All you have done, for nothing!***] *Father; remind me! Tell me again why I do this! I need to hear again!* **[He was despised, and we did not esteem Him. Surely our griefs He Himself bore, and our sorrows He carried; Yet we ourselves esteemed Him stricken, smitten of God, and afflicted.]** and then **[God so loved the world; that He gave His one and Only Son, that whoever believes in Him shall not perish, but have eternal life. God**

did not send the Son into the world to judge the world, but that the world might be saved through Him] *Thank you Father, Thank you.*

He was now moving outside the city gate and toward the grand execution site "The Skull". I am not sure why they named it the Grand Execution Site, maybe because of the open area. He stumbled and fell hard! The beam slammed against his body and head, driving the thorns even deeper! And more blood flowed into his eyes! He heard the crowd cheer! He heard the Centurion cry, "Get him Up! Get him up!" Marcus and his five roughly hauled him to his feet! And two soldiers grabbed the beam and laid it again on his back.

The fall had shaken him. He knew what strength He did have was almost gone! *Help Me Father!* He cried in His Spirit!

He moved on, as the group pressed, through the crowd! And to the clear road ahead. All except; for a lone man, heading toward the city.

Jesus fell hard again! And again, the beam pummeled his body! He heard the Centurion's horse rear and gallop back to Him, as Marcus helped Him up!

He whispered to Jesus harshly! "You cannot continue this way! I commend you; doing, as you have done. But I must *complete*, The *Centurion and I must complete* the task!" He grabbed the other two and said, "Hold him up if you have to! But get them there!" Pointing to the hillock and rough ground of Golgatha!

The crowd had moved in behind the group now, and was pressing forward, to them! "Sergeant Cestus Marcus!" cried Centurion Nerva "Conscript that man now!"

Cestus looked ahead at the lone man treading his way toward them, passed the Skull toward Jerusalem. "Yes Sir! I will!" Jesus; now steadier on his feet, watched as the three Romans surrounded the man. And he watched as the Sergeant told him, what he was to do. He saw the man object, and shake his head! Cestus grabbed the man's tunic and pulled him close! The man was thrown to the ground, and swords were drawn! The air was tense, even the crowd, was silent!

Then reluctantly, the man got to his feet, and made his way to Jesus. Disgusted and angry, as he passed Jesus he said, " I do not know who you are criminal! But I now bear, your Cross! You will make it to the Skull! And You will die! I will rejoice and be done with You!"

He watched as the big Cyrene easily took the beam on his shoulder, and walked behind Jesus. Jesus turned and caught Simon's eye. In a moment, his anger and defiance faded. His eyes fell to the ground as He bore the weight of the rough beam toward "Golgatha" the Skull. Marcus came close to Jesus and said, "That man is Simon of Cyrene. Be grateful he was there. You would not have made it!"

"I know, Marcus, but I think My Father, chose him to do it. So, I may finish what We have started."

Jesus looked at the ground and behind it a cliff face. Where tombs were. The rain and weather had battered the face; along with the attempted quarry, now gone. Jesus shuddered. He looked and yes; He could see the eyes and bridge of the nose, and the Patch scrub brush at the top, denoting hair? *Well, it is definitely a rough looking patch of ground. And it is on the Main road where all will see. The rise in the road adds to the picture. And it seems there are Tombs here.* he thought

The Centurion edged his Horse onto the rock-strewn hillock and broken ground. The Sun now high in the sky. The heat from the Sun, was met by the heat of the ground. The Centurion; even from horseback, could feel the heat.

He dismounted; onto the rock-strewn Hillock, its flattop and found the quarried holes that would bear the upright. The other soldiers tasked with the Centurion; already, had most things in place. They had three upright beams ready to bear the Cross beam once nailed in place. And they had everything else ready as well. Swords, Pikes, and other tools of death. They had ropes to pull the crosses into place easily.

The crowd moved into a semi- circle Opposite the Cliff side quarry. Perseus Quintis Nerva moved to the other soldiers and said, "Is all in readiness?" the soldiers as one; saluted hands-on chest armor, and said, "Yes."

Perseus looked at the Sky and shook his head. "We may have a storm. So, let's get this done!" he turned and called "Commander Aquila, to me Please!"

Marcus Aquila left Jesus and the Five and walked to his commander. "Yes Sir!" He saluted. And Perseus leaned in. "Post the Men, meeting that Crowds line. One every five Feet. And no one; But Joesph and Mary and a few, A few of his Followers, can be five feet from his cross. I don't like this! But; he should have comfort for a time. Though I too, am surprised he made it as far as he did."

Marcus said, "At Once Centurion, and the Other two?"

"There are three posts, and holes. Put Jesus in the Center. Oh; and Put the Sign up, that Pilate made. Here." Perseus handed Marcus Aquila the Flat wood and its writing.

Marcus Whistled! "This will cause a stir!" Perseus said in reply; Shaking his head. "Truthfully; Marcus, this whole assignment, is off somehow. I can't place it. But It feels wrong. All the way through. that's why I give Him, this Small grace. For Joseph and Mary's sake. No one should watch their children Die! No matter the Age." He finished.

"Yes, sir" Marcus said "And I too agree."

"Well, if Pilate hears, we may have to find other work." Perseus laughed bitterly.

Commander Marcus Aquila called to sergeant Cestus Marcus "Sergeant! Bring the two Prisoners here!"

Cestus; and the soldiers assigned to the duty, grabbed the first criminal. And moved him to the first, upright beam lying on the ground. He had carried the beam arms tied to it. The soldiers; took an end each, and forced him onto the Prone upright. The criminal cursed! and spit at the Soldiers; as they placed his Beam, at the top of the upright post. The Third Soldier; held a Short sword to the man's throat! Silencing his noise and movement. Another soldier stood over him, with a large hammer, and thick nails. He leaned down; and placed a heavy nail on the Cross beam, directly over the Centered upright and began to drive the nail into the wood!

The Man jerked every time a hammer blow fell! And soon one was in; then another! The soldier having created the T-Cross; moved to the man's legs, and grabbed his Foot! And other soldier, held his leg to the side, of the Center post. And The soldier with the hammer; began driving a long thick nail through his ankle and center post!

The man screamed with each blow! And each blow sprayed, droplets of blood on the hot rock and sand! The soldiers did the same for the other leg and foot. Now that one was ready, three soldiers lifted the base end of the post, tied rope around it, and dragged the man and his cross, to his assigned hole, over the rough ground. The second prisoner was brought to his upright and laid on it. And the process repeated, with screams and blood. Two were ready to be dropped into place! Both criminals had been dragged with their crosses, and all to their assigned place. Now, the ropes were switched and the bottom end of the upright was over the whole as they lifted the T-cross to a standing position! And a Roman soldier at the right moment kicked the base and it dropped with a thud and an accompanying scream of pain, as all the body weight landed on the spiked ankles!

Then the soldier with the hammer stepped up close to the man and place a small step near his cross. The soldier stepped up and grabbed the man's wrist! And drove a nail through it! Another soldier behind the cross; used and Ax to cut the rope, tying his arm to the top post! And the same for the other!

The soldiers did the same for the other Prisoner. And now Jesus stood alone!

Jesus looked at the men and realized he now was next. The human dread had reached a peak! And he shook visibly as he fought to stay upright! *Father, I cannot stand anymore! I need your strength and help! Please!* He prayed.

The Holy Spirit surged into him! And his Strength returned. He looked at Marcus and the Centurion in turn and waited. *Help them Father, to do what they must! And do not hold it against them Please!*

Simon the Cyrene had already laid the cross beam near the upright and quietly joined the crowd.

The crowd had been silent; as they watched the others being readied, and Crucified. Marcus Aquila; took Jesus by the arm, and laid him on his Cross! And whispered "I regret having to do this thing! Know the Centurion has voiced his regret as well. He said This whole assignment is Not right! What they do now, to you is not Right!"

Jesus smiled weakly. "That may be Marcus. But; When I and the Father, are done. . . Men will be free! Oh No, not from Governments or Orders, But from things far worse. Men will be able to Come home again! Do not fear! You can come home too.

"Me? a Roman? Home."

"Yes, Home."

"I don't understand."

"Marcus, you and The Centurion will. Speak to Joseph and Mary or even Simon Peter. They will explain."

The Soldier nearby them said "Ahem, Commander, we need to Proceed now, unless you need to speak to him more."

Marcus Aquila shook his head and said "No. You may Finish." He got up and moved to where the Centurion watched nearby.

The soldiers; then removed the tattered remains of his tunic, and even his loin cloth! He felt the heat over all of his Body now! and Shame began to well up in his Soul!

Jesus's Cross Beam was already secured in the T-position; they also had nailed the sign sent by Pilate to the Upper edge of the Cross beam. One soldier took Jesus left arm and pulled it out straight! And the Soldier bearing the hammer; knelt down on his arm, holding it in place. And drove the spike through His wrist! The soldier paused, looking at Jesus, amazed! He hadn't screamed! He stepped over his Body and went to the right arm and repeated the process. Again, no outcry was heard!

He motioned for help as He placed One foot behind the other, and Paused Looking at Jesus, with regret. And began to drive the thick nail through both feet, into the wood where the foot post was! Again, no Sound!

the soldier could see the pain register in his eyes and face as his body visibly shook in reaction!

The soldiers lifted the base; and again, tied it with rope, and dragged Jesus and his Cross, over the Rough ground to his assigned place. They took off the ropes; and switched to the Cross beam. And began to lift it from the ground; and again, at the right moment, a soldier kicked the center beam, into the hole and all of Jesus weight and the cross dropped into the hole! The crowd gasped as his body jerked in reaction to the drop! and then. . . they saw the sign Pilate had placed there. And first it was murmurings, then angry outcries! Jesus heard "What is the Meaning of This!" "What has Pilate done!"

The Elders and High Priests, now free from Roman reprisal made their way to the front of the crowd. and saw the inscription, they were filled with Rage and Screamed! "What has Pilate done! This is not what We Agreed!"

Above Jesus head for all the World to see was the inscription "Jesus the Nazarene, The King of the Jews"

The Roman soldiers watching over the crucifixion; now that the major work was done, began playing dice at the crosses. They had looked over the clothes of the Criminals and divided them amongst themselves. Herod sent over all of Jesus clothes; and another Robe, as mockery. The soldiers divided them. But one piece was beautifully crafted, so, they cast lots.

Jesus came back to consciousness and looked through blood-soaked eyes, and saw John, James, Mary his Mother and Mary Magdalene. He was glad to see them. The Centurion and Marcus had kept their word. His whole body hurt! And those that stood by; Screamed and threw dirt and spit at him, as he Hung there.

The Scribes, Elders and Priests, mocked him! He heard "You said you would Destroy the Temple and rebuild it in Three days! Hah! Save Yourself!"

Jesus saw the smudges of darkness and heard the mocking laughter even clearer now. *[You are alone now! You will be alone Forever!]* "Save yourself! Jesus!" came a cry and another man passed by "I can open Deaf ears But I cannot come down from a cross!" other men and Women came to see the Spectacle and said " King of the Jews! hardly!" and another "False teacher!" another "Liar!"

Jesus tried to rise up to breathe easier and helped some. Between the heat of the Sun and the Blood loss now, he went from consciousness to unconsciousness often. He cried out "Father Forgive them! The do not know what they do!"

Jesus heard more curses and Screams of hatred! and then He heard from His right and left "If you are the Son of God, Save Us! and Yourself!"

He watched as they waited; just as Herod for a Spectacle or Miracle! They were silent and even the crowd, was stilled. All that Jesus heard was the Tears and wailing of Mary His Mother and the other Women. He saw Lazarus there and the other Disciples, all but Peter. Time passed. Jesus was not sure if time, was passing at all! He could not tell. His whole World was pain, heat, and continual mockery! Even the Criminals hanging beside him cursed him! "Save us O Son of God!" Pain! Ache! Breathe! Pushup on the Heel and Hope for Breath! All at once. Amidst the Anger and curses of the Crowd he heard on the Criminals say "Jesus, when you enter into your Kingdom, Remember me Please!" The other said "Why? What has he done for Us! He didn't save Us!" "We deserve this! We do rightly and You know! But He is Innocent! Nor worthy of Death!"

Jesus pushed up on his heel and said to the one, "Truly, I say, now, today you will be with me in Paradise!" Jesus heard thunder heralding rain! *Rain would be welcome Father in this heat! Are you sending rain to cool me? . . .Father are You there?*

Jesus' heart froze in his chest as the truth dawned on him! The Father's Presence and the Spirit's was not there! It was gone! They were gone!

He heard more thundering and looked up through blood-soaked eyes, not a cloud in the sky! Just the burning sun!

****

CHAPTER 20

CRUCIFIED, FINISHED, HELL AND THE GRAVE

All at once He felt a coldness and fear wash over Him! And abandonment! Darkness descended and all went Black! The crowd was struck silent as more thundering were heard! *Where are you Father? I am afraid! I cannot See! Where are You!* The Darkness moved and breathed! He felt its clammy Touch! ***Despair! I am alone! I am Alone! No one No one! Alone!*** His Heart, Mind and Soul cried out as one Voice! ***Then Hunger! So intense He felt as if He was cut in Two! Hatred Raged! He hungered to Kill! and Maim! To Destroy! Then Jealousy! Intense! He would do anything! Say anything! To have! or not lose! Shame raged at his Nakedness! Fear of being Caught! Hunger to Steal so strong, He could taste it! Abandonment! No Hope! Despair! Deeper than Oceans crashed over him!*** His body spasmed as he remembered! the Fathers voice, was bitter sweet! As Heard him say **[Everyone like sheep; has wandered away! Everyone to his own Desire! But the Lord has placed Upon his Son, the Iniquity, and Sin of us all!]**

Then another onslaught! ***Urges, raged in him! From the height of Ecstasy to the Utter perverse!*** His body; shook in response, to Evil now! ***So intense and cold! Calculating! Searching! Seeking! Lusting! Power! Contempt! Disdain! Self-Righteousness! Pride! Arrogance!*** With every moment, His body shook! ***He could not stop! He had to See! To touch, to have! To drink! To taste! To be! Desire for Wealth and Power, so great as to block away Everything! Love, lost, Love gained! Hope gained! Lost!*** Jesus knew All of it! ***An Evil so dark and hideous! There was no name for it!*** And in the darkness; Jesus wept alone! *Forsaken! Abandoned! All for what?* In the darkness; the questions began. . . [*Why have you come to die? Why did you leave your place? Why did you choose to walk the Earth again! Why have you chosen* **These!** **These** *are your reward!* **These** *that Hide in Darkness!* **These** *that take life!* **These** *that tear and maim!* **These** *that hunger for what they can never Have!*]

And in the Darkness Jesus cried, "**Eli, Eli, lama sabachthani!** and Again! **My God, My God why have you Forsaken me!**" Jesus; could hear the whimpering of the Crowd! He could hear the Soldiers whispering! Time, seemed to stand still. Nothing moved. Nothing even breathed! Darkness! Heavy! Oppressive! weighing Everything down! Forcing people to the ground! and then Thunder! and the darkness was gone!

Jesus, cried out then, in A Loud Voice! "IT IS FINISHED! Father, into your hands I lay my Spirit!" Jesus gave up his Spirit and Died!

At that very moment! An Earthquake hit! The ground rumbled and The Cliff Face cracked and popped, as bits the quarry wall fell to the ground! The Centurion; and All the Soldiers, were thrown to the Ground in utter Terror! No one dared move or speak! Perseus; watched as his Stallion bolted, and Screamed in Fright! He looked for his Friend, Marcus Aquila! He too was on the ground, frozen in Fear! Slowly Perseus, pushed to his feet, and looked at Jesus! He was dead. He had seen Death before and knew. He looked back at Marcus, now on his Feet. And Said "That Man was innocent. He was the Son of God!"

****

In all of Jerusalem; things were tossed to the ground! The Temple shook, with Force! And Braziers, lamps, columns crashed to the Temple Floor! All the Priests fell to the ground! Then came a roar; like none heard before, as the veil of the Temple was torn in half! From the Top to the Bottom! And the Ark and the Holy of Holies lay Open! And the Priests and Elders huddle together in Fear! at what they saw!

Caiaphas; and the other Elders, got to their feet. Terror was lessening and reason, returning. Caiaphas, ripped and tore his Robes! and began sobbing! There; lay open for all to see, *The Holy of Holies!* Caiaphas stood stunned! The Veil stood sixty feet high, and thirty feet wide, and one inch thick, *was the Veil!* God himself; had called out the measurements for it to be made. Why? So that no one; all but the High

Priest, once a Year could enter and Be in The Most Sacred Place, Alone, with God! It took many priests to part the Veil. and No one could accidently enter and Die! The others came along side and held him up and he staggered closer to the Veil. *What did this mean? **YHWH!** You are **Exposed!** All Eyes Can see you! You said If any unworthy were to enter, they would die!* He thought, *"Now, look! Disaster! Ruin! All may see! Your Glory! The Ark! The Cherubim!"*

Caiaphas stumbled and crawled closer! the Priest followed suit and crawled with Him! Weeping! And groaning, He touched bottom of the Veil! He took it in his hands! Now on his knees! pulled it to his face and Wept!

All through Jerusalem and the country side, people saw saints, Prophets of Old! walking! All the Tombs surrounding Jerusalem opened! The Nation of Israel shook! Awe and Wonder! Terror and Fear mixed! And those at Golgotha; that had come for a Spectacle, walked away, beating their Chests!

Centurion Perseus Quintis Nerva called out to the Men! "Soldiers! Assemble!" Commander Marcus Aquila and Sergeant Cestus Marcus and their men formed Ranks and All as one Saluted Fists against their Chest plates! The Centurion brushed off the dirt and gravel, and wiped his hands. He turned to them and said "I say now, for all to hear! that man!" pointing to Jesus dead body ". . . Was innocent! and the Son of God! I do not know, all that happened here. Nor do I understand, but we are Roman Soldiers! and as such, we must finish our task!" He paused. His eyes met his friends, in that moment, they both knew, we must leave Soldiering. Marcus, gave a quick knowing nod. And He finished "Check these Men! All of them! If they are not Dead Yet! Break their Legs and Let us Go home and be done with this! cursed task!"

So, by twos, they went to each man on the Cross, and broke their legs! Screams! Crack of Bone! Choking and Death! Marcus Aquila; came to his commander and Friend, Perseus Quintis Nerva, standing before the Dead Body of Jesus. Marcus quietly said "He is Dead. Even, I can see. Shall I break his Legs per your Command?"

"No, " he said shaking his head, "No, There's no need! It is a sad thing Marcus. A sad thing, to lose good Men. And hope. He was both. I am sure Pilate knew. Caiaphas knew. This Man was betrayed, and killed for Jealousy, Envy, Power, and more! He deserves better!" The Centurion sighed deeply. And said "We are Romans, and a Job must be finished. Take a Spear, and run it to his heart! go in the side. You and I know, he is Dead. but I am sure, that Everyone else will need proof!"

"As you Command Centurion." Marcus turned, then back again. "Centurion, Jesus spoke to me, when I laid him on the Cross. I don't understand, what He meant. He talked of making Men free. And that I, even a Roman, could come Home! then, he said to Speak to Joseph or Mary or even Simon Peter for answers!" He paused again. "I do not know why the Words he spoke move me so. But I want to know."

Perseus; put his hand on the big man's shoulder, and said "You, may have questions, we can seek the answers together with those he said to see. But I for one. Know Now, without doubt, He was God's Son!"

"Yes Sir, thank you." he answered

Then Commander Marcus Aquila walked to the rack of Spears and took one in hand. He Walked solemnly to Jesus Cross. He then stood at attention! Saluted! Fist to chest armor, bowed partially. Looked up and Whispered "Thank you. I don't not fully understand yet. But I will seek answers. Forgive me! But I have task to complete." and with that; Marcus Aquila, drove the spear into Jesus side! and held it for a ten count, the pulled it free! He stepped back and watched as Blood and water flowed from the open wound!

He turned on his heel; and walked from the Crosses, and the dying criminals to the Centurion. and marched home to the Fort!

****

Jesus cried out "It is Finished! Father, into your hands I lay my Spirit!" Jesus saw darkness! Felt the deep dread of Powerlessness! Darkness and Death, swallowed him and Plunged him down to. . .What? Jesus could not see! He could hear the laughter and taunts as he fell and fell to the Depths of the Earth! Far beyond what he left on the sunbaked surface; lay darkness, Fire and Flame! He felt pain! Burning! His Skin, alive with Pain! Every nerve in his body cried out! He was burning! Though he could see nothing, but darkness! The Darkness as before; was heavy and tangible, even oppressive!

And he felt something crawling on his skin, and biting! in desperation He tried to wipe whatever it was from his Arms and moved to his Chest and legs. He felt the thing give! and fall! But another took its place! No matter what he did! Another would replace what he wiped away! Then He heard a Voice. . .Melodic, Hypnotizing, yet subtly tormenting! "Welcome Jesus! Welcome to your new abode." The voice was stronger now "Welcome, failed Messiah! Failed Redeemer! Welcome, Retch Lover! This is my Domain, and I Rule here!" Laughter, cold, cruel, biting, Laughter!

The Pain; Burning, Biting, were continuous, Unrelenting! His thoughts were spinning, *Despair, Darkness, Death, a Bleak Eternity* loomed! "So, you died. . .Your Father has *Forsaken you*! He is not here! There is No hope now! There is No Escape! I hold the Keys!" The voice rumbled and he realized he was in Hades! Sheol, the Place of the Wicked dead. He knew this place as God, the Place reserved for Lucifer/Satan and the Angels of Rebellion*! I must finish what the Father and I started! At All Cost! I must finish the Payment for Sin! and Its destruction! and the Redemption of Man and Creation!*

Time, was unknown in this darkness. Was it minutes, Hours, days, Jesus could not tell? He closed his eyes, actually, felt them close, because the Darkness was so black. And opened them again. Still blackness! Time however it counted, whatever Time, was here. . .Passed.

Then in a moment; brightness, light! He could see! He looked and saw soul after soul, bound to the ground! Kneeling, lying, cringing! amidst Flames, Pain, and Torment! He looked up and saw in the distance, A bright, inviting place! He looked deeper, and there was Abraham, Isaac, Jacob, Joseph and more!

The Voice returned "Why torture yourself. . . Why do you long for *Paradise,* when you will never cross the chasm! The lines were drawn! The war begun! And now, the war is over! The Light Father Has Lost! His plan to Redeem Man has died with you! You have failed! You are trapped here! You cannot Escape or Flee!"

Jesus felt the Power of the Holy Spirit; and heard the scriptures like a Trumpet blast, held long and loud! **[For You will not abandon my soul to Sheol; Nor will You allow Your Holy One to undergo decay!]** The darkness around him shattered! He stood to his feet! And the biting worms, fell away into the Flames! He felt No heat! No Burning! No pain! The Fire fled from him. As walked through Hades!

He raised his hands; and time, flames, pain, froze! He had to finish what they started! "LightBringer! Lucifer! Satan! Come to me! Now!"

The dark swirled and dissipated. Now the whole realm was awash with Light!

The Creator; of all there is, was standing in Hades! The Demons and Devils of Hell rushed in and fell at his Feet! All the angels of rebellion bowed! and Satan Bowed as well!

"Here at your Command, Majesty!" he choked out!

Jesus looked at them all and Spoke with authority. **You will release the Keys of Death and Hell, to me. now. You will release the Captives of Paradise! I will speak to those here, the Wicked Dead, to charge them, to Judge them. After I leave here. . .The chasm will be gone! And until that day! As need to fulfill Scripture. . . Therefore, Sheol has enlarged its throat and opened its mouth without measure; and All Men, who Reject My gift of Eternal Life, will descend into it!"**

Lightbringer/Lucifer/Satan and all the Rebellious host Shook. He turned to those now tormented. Tears welled in his eyes. He looked out on the vast array of souls! Now; forever and always Tormented! Not out the of Hatred, Anger, Doubt, Fear, but choosing to turn from God. Rejecting him; Jesus God's Son, and Messiah! He looked at each one. And as God knowing their Hearts! Each one had heard the Promise of Hope and Redemption! and turned from it! Choosing to live as they chose, them Alone! He wept. He would know for All Eternity; each and every soul, that had chosen.

"Know this all of you! We do not hate you. We do not Destroy you. We gave you; just as your Tormentors, choice! And We will honor your choice! No matter how deeply it cuts; into our hearts and Tears those we Love, away from us!"

Jesus then turned from the Group and walked toward the Chasm! He saw the Gaping crag and walked across to Paradise! The place of the Righteous Believers! and those that held onto His Hope, Even at Death!

Jesus saw All of them bow to the ground! He walked among them, raising them up, and with some, Embracing them! Abraham Friend! Moses Face to Face! Jacob Wrestler! He called all nearby. And they came.

"I am Jesus Son of God; Messiah, Savior, Redeemer, Lamb of God, Bread of Life, Great I am, Bright and Morning Star! Living Water! And more. But I speak to you now, to assure you, you will leave here! and be with the Father, I, and the Holy Spirit! You will join with all the Host of Heaven! Paradise; though great, will be replaced! and you will be moved to Heaven Our Home. So that you and All Future Peoples of Every Nation and Tongue, and Tribe will be with Us Forever!"

He said to them All. . . "Are you ready?"

"Yes!" came the united Shout!

Jesus and the Host of Captives Soared up from Paradise and They Entered Heaven! At the Same Moment!

Hades Shook! Rocks Split and the Chasm was gone! and the Whole Realm of Hades Reverberated with the Scripture! Never before, never again! **[Therefore; Sheol, has enlarged its throat, and opened its mouth without measure, and All Men, who Reject My gift of Eternal Life, will descend into it!]**

****

Jesus; Son of God, stood on Heavens Shore! He turned to those He brought with him and said "Welcome Home! Beloved Ones! The Angels; the Father, and Holy Spirit will Welcome you more, But I have work to Finish! I will return to you shortly!"

All of Heaven; and the Realm, rang with shouts of Praise! All those Captives; from Paradise Rejoiced! Giving Glory to God the Father, the Son and Holy Spirit! as Jesus left! Jesus; raced to Earth and the Final steps, of Man's and Creations Redemption!

As He left the Realm; He remembered all of it! His Life as Jesus; on Earth from the dawn, of Time till now! He was glad to know the Father's Presence; and the Holy Spirit in Full, as it had been. But there were a few things, left to be done!

****

Jerusalem was in an uproar! Terror, mixed with Awe had flooded the City! All over Jerusalem, Tombs had been shaken open! People saw Saints of Old walking the streets! The Temple was still reeling from the Events! Caiaphas was visibly shaken; as He remembered the Tearing of the Veil, and the Earthquakes damage! And Now; hearing reports of Prophets, and Saints long dead walking! *What is happening! What does this All mean! Are they Signs? Portents? YHWH help us! What am I to do now?* He thought. *I have no guide from you! You have Forsaken us! You have abandoned us! your Chosen!*

Caiaphas paced his quarters like a caged tiger looking to strike! He had put on New robes and had cleaned away the Dirt and Grime! The repair of the Temple had already begun. Acolytes, were repairing and even rebuilding broken Columns and Braziers and lamps. Caiaphas Froze! *If the Liar, Jesus, was God. If he was Messiah. . . the People cannot know!* **Dante** smiled as his whisper lodged in Caiaphas 's heart and mind! *If the People knew;* he continued, ***they would turn from The Temple and Sacrifice! What would YHWH do then? How would We Live? If there was no Temple how would We worship? Would all those Years from Moses to Now, be wiped away?***

Dante Whispered again. . . ***All you have and know, would change! Messiah; was to have freed Men, to Turn to YHWH! But how? No! No.... I cannot lose All I know! I will not Believe! I will not Believe, this Jesus, was sent by God! Not Messiah, Not Priest, Not King! Charlatan! Nothing more!***

Caiaphas conscience screamed! His heart; felt the Conviction, of Sin! and the High Priest, Pushed it away! And stormed from his Quarters and Headed through the Temple to the walk- way that led to Fort Antonia! Anger and rage had welled in his heart! and it grew with each step he took! His heart and mind fully affected . . . *I studied for Years! I memorized all the Scrolls! I was elected High Priest! I held the Power of the Temple! I held the Law of God! I alone! and now; A would be Messiah! and Strange Events! Bah! A flip of a Coin! a Turn of the Dice! The roll of the Urim and Thummim! No. He was No Messiah! But I will not allow Jerusalem or Israel, to sink below an ocean, and be swallowed up by the Gentiles! Or another False Messiah!* He paused a Moment. And then continued on, and to plan!

***

Joseph had left the council and changed clothes. He had work to do. He knew the Council; had plotted against Jesus, to destroy him. He and Nicodemus knew. They had tried to dissuade the Council; but failed. And now they wanted to honor God and at least take care of Jesus body.

Since Joseph was on the Council, He could approach Pilate, but he was reluctant to do it. But Nicodemus, had encouraged him to try. So, he made his way through the rubble strewn streets, to the Fort Antonia.

He walked up the large steps passed the Judgment Seat and into the Fort itself. Joseph felt the chill again and heard the words! "Crucify Him! Give us Barabbas!" He also knew*; Pilate, had given into the crowd. He had gone against them before; why hadn't he then, was he afraid Rome would question? Because, Joseph; knew the claim of king, was not enough to bring Romes ire! They have dealt with Insurrection before. And Jesus did neither. He was not freeing Men from Rome; But Freeing Men, to God.* He thought.

Joseph walked to the main gate and spoke to a guard.

"Joseph of Arimathea of the Council, to speak to Prefect Pilate, Please." The Roman turned to his partner nodded. The other left to see if Pontius Pilate would see the Councilman. Joseph knew that the Romans left Bodies hanging for Days; and weeks, to prove their Power and a Point. He shifted on his feet as he waited. He had dared to come this far. *Would he have favor of God even, to bury God's Son?*

Soon the other Soldier returned and opened the gate and said "Follow Me. I will take you to him." The Fort seemed quiet, for evening. He had been here before and had seen the training and exercises of the Cohort in full Battle Gear! It was a sight! Joseph was led by the Soldier to the Praetorium. And to Pilate himself. Pilate was sitting near a desk with maps and a lamp was lit. It looked as if He had been writing.

Pilate looked up and said, " Joseph of Arimathea, Welcome, to what do I owe a visit from a Prominent Member of the Council?"

Joseph bowed slightly to Pilate. Then he straightened. He pushed through the nervous feelings and said, "Prefect, I have a simple Request. I know you gave the command to crucify Jesus of Nazareth. And I understand; it is Traditional, for you to leave Criminals on their Crosses, till they are Dead. But he is also a Jew; of some import, at least to those that knew him, and knew him well. His Family; and a few followers would ask, if We might take him off the Cross, and bury him Properly. I know it is asking allot, but would it be Possible? I even could pay to have him removed."

Pilate held up his hand and said, "No Joseph, No. There is no need for you to pay anything. I too, had questions about all of it. and Why, after what. . . Three years, of Teaching, and if true, Miracles! No, you may have him. My wife; even dreamt of him. Even she warned me. But the Crowd had cried for Blood." He dropped his eyes. "I will write a message to the gate. Take it, and take his body down. I truly regret what happened. " He finished.

Pilate wrote the Message quickly and handed it to Joseph. Who bowed slightly and said, "Thank Prefect, Thank you."

Joseph turned; and left the Praetorium, and made his way across the parade ground and to the steps. Only then; did he truly, give a sigh of relief. He was many things, But, bravery, was not normal. But Decency was. *Now to find Mary and Others, and bring them to the Cross and the Tomb, before Sabbath starts!*

"I am sure I will need help, taking him down. And someone, must buy the Spices. The Women; can do him the Honor and Re-wrap him after the Sabbath. I will have him put in the Tomb. It will be only a Day. And the coolness of the tomb will keep enough!" he said Aloud as he made his way to Golgotha and the Cross.

Joseph and men, he hired came to the Crosses. They went straight to the center Cross. and with a Stool and hammer. Took out one by one the spikes.

The men having done this before had a large bolt of pure white linen. and had taken a good length of it and wrapped around Jesus's torso. and had laid the other end over the Cross beam, and Then, pulled tight. Jesus body; now suspended, could have the spikes removed, without fear of His body crashing to the ground or anything uglier.

When Joseph had gone to hire the Men; somehow, the women had known and followed to see where he would be laid. So that after Sabbath, they could finish the Burial.

Gently, the Men lowered Jesus body to the ground, and wrapped him quickly in the Linen. Joseph and the Men; came to a tomb. The tomb; had a garden, and bench outside the Tomb. Joseph touched the name plate. It held his name. Joseph of Arimathea. He looked at the Engraved Letters, touching them. Then he smiled and said "I will change the name after Sabbath. Men, we Must hurry it is getting late and Sabbath is going to be upon us, in full. The Two Men carried Jesus inside the New Tomb.

"The Workers have just finished; only days ago. It large enough, for my Whole Family. Oh Well, I give it to the Teacher and Messiah."

The men, laid him on the raised stone bench. Joseph put the remains of the Bolt of pure white Linen nearby. And looking at the Women, He said "There is the Wrap. The Spices have been paid for; so, you can get them, tonight. and Bring them after."

The women agreed. They hugged him, and he them. Mary, touched the wrapped face of Jesus, lovingly. She then turned and walked out. The Men; pushed the stone in the track, and closed the Tomb.

****

Caiaphas stormed to the gate of The Fort. He and two other Elders. He looked at the fading afternoon light and said "I need to Speak to Pilate Now! It is an Urgent matter! If he cannot come to Us, We Must go to Him!"

The guards at the gate did not hesitate to open it for the High Priest and his Entourage. But sent a runner ahead, to warn Pilate of their Arrival.

The group, found Pilate on His Seat of Judgement, in the Praetorium. He was sipping wine and looked up. "Ahh. . ." He said "It seems, The Council Loves me." He finished with a grin.

"What might I do for you Caiaphas and Friends?"

"Prefect; you have been told how the Liar and False Messiah, Jesus said that in three days, He would Rise! Since He deceived All of Us, we would ask you to Post a Guard! and Secure His Tomb! Because; If his Followers, were to come and Steal the Body away, The Deception would be worse! and Cause, you and Us more Grief!"

Pilate thought to himself *You are the one worried Caiaphas, aren't you? You know more than you are saying. If what Joseph said is true. and he does Rise. . .That, would end the temple quickly wouldn't it.*

"I will Post a Guard. And Seal it with Rome's Seal. You have your Request." Pilate Finished.

"Thank you." Caiaphas said sincerely. "Sleep well, Prefect."

Oh, I will. He thought as they left. *I will. Though I am not sure about you Caiaphas. Not sure at all.*

Pilate watched the Sunset shine through the Window. And sipped his wine.

****

Sergeant Cestus Marcus; addressed the four Soldiers, before him. All in full Battle armor.

" I know you do not like this. But This has come from the Prefect, himself. Though I do not believe it. The Hight Priest; is afraid that, the Nazarite's followers, will attempt to steal his Body and claim "He rose from the Dead!"

He finished as the Soldiers laughed.

"Now; make no Mistake. This is an assignment. However, tedious. You will Guard that tomb. You will insure no one disturbs it. and most of all, no bodies be stolen! Is that understood?"

As one; the Soldiers saluted fist against Armor, and cried "Yes Sir!"

"Good!" he said "Now, it has been Reported that His Body, is in a New Tomb at the Crosses from Days ago. The tomb, was for A Joseph of Arimathea. A Rich Man of the Council. The Tomb bears His Name. Put on it; the Roman Seal, and the Prefects! Now go!"

"Yes Sir!"

The Four left the Praetorium and made their way to the Execution site. Sergeant Cestus Marcus, shook his head in wonder at the strangeness of it all.

The Four Soldiers found the Tomb. They saw the garden and the bench outside. And the stone closed over the tomb. They first tested the Stone. It would take at least two men; strong men, to move it. So; they started a small fire, away from the garden, and heated the wax and prepared the papyrus.

They walked to the tomb and laid the Papyrus against the Stone and wall, and poured that wax on it and Pressed the Seal!

The tomb, was sealed Officially now! and they now had their duty!

"So, Caius, how are we to do this? Two by the Tomb at all Times. Only to eat?" One said.

Caius, the Oldest of them, said "That is Fine. If this is longer than two days, we may rotate shifts. Do we have Provisions enough?"

One of the others said "Yes"

Caius shook his head. "It never ceases to amaze me. How someone, claiming to know God, can afford this! That plague alone was a week's wage! Then again, Rome is tight with Money!" they Laughed. "Well, time settle in boys. it will be a long night. Prepare."

****

Jesus was in Darkness. Not the harsh; cold, unforgiving darkness of Hades. But Darkness of Death. He now, held the Keys. *All he need do, is open his eyes. And He would free forever, Men from Sin's grasp and Death's hold! No more, would they have to fear! Sin; will be vanquished! And Men; finally, truly free! Free to choose Life, and that abundant! Choose to Love God, with all of their Heart, Mind, Soul and Strength, and to actually accomplish it! Now I must break Death's hold completely! And Finish what We started!*

He felt the grip of Death again! Its clawing hands trying to keep him trapped! Darkness of the Grave, Despair of the Soul! **No! it screamed! You cannot! You must not! You are Mine!** *No, I am not.* He thought *I am The First and Last! The Beginning and End! I am the Great I am! The Lion of Judah! The Perfect Lamb sacrificed! I am . . .the Risen KING!*

And Death and Hell wailed! The bonds Of Sin and Death; lay shattered on the Tomb Floor, like the Linen he was wrapped in! He found the Head wrapping and folded it neatly on the stone bench where his body used to be. And turned to the door of the tomb!

At that very Moment an Angel of God streaked to Earth! And landed at the tomb! The force of his landing shook the ground in an Earthquake! The Guards; were tossed. as leaves in the wind! and lay Terrified and Powerless!

They saw the huge Angel burning bright with Light! and Power! Speechless, and Frozen, they watched! **Cenehard** looked at the Soldiers, smiled and walked to the tomb. He touched the Stone, and with a flick of his wrist, it was moved away! Another joined him. And they walked into the tomb!

Jesus looked and saw Cenehard and Gabriel enter! They bowed on one knee. "Sorry We were late Your Majesty! The Father sent us to Greet you and Open the door!" they laughed.

"No, you were not late." He hugged them. "The task is almost finished. "Remind, those that come here, that I will go as Promised to Galilee. And that I will see them soon! Oh, there will be Women, coming to Prepare my body for Burial. Jesus laughed. "Don't scare them too bad. But remind them." he finished.

"We will your Majesty."

****

Mary couldn't sleep. She had tossed and turned. Finally; she just got up, dressed and left the house. It was still dark. But the dark no longer made her fear. Not after what Jesus had done! He had seen. He had heard. *Hmph* she thought, *even that shame is now gone!* He knew what held her. He knew she was desperate! No one wanted her. All those years of Trying! and then, the Darkness came! Her soul had cried out! *She had heard of YHWH, but Her life was not one He would accept! surely. Or at least, that was what she had told herself.* She absently made her was to the place of the Crosses. and the tomb.

No one saw her, no one stopped her. Her memories came flooding back! All the struggle and rejection, fear and Doubts, All the years, of Torment! *The days and nights, of powerlessness and observing, as She or her body, moved and did things, dark and Perverse! Then **Jesus came**. In Gentleness, Truth, Love. And with one word! Everything changed! The torment, the fears, Doubts, all of it gone! She could **breathe!** She could **laugh** and **Dance again!** move freely again. She had a New Life! And what was it. . . **Hope!** Hope, after what We saw? What the High Priest and Elders of the People did! and the Romans! We saw him die! Well, at Least I will be near where his body lays. I can at least, be there. In the Dark. everyone needs to not be alone!*

Mary Magdalene, reached the Tomb! She stood outside weeping! *Jesus, why have you gone? What will happen now? Will the Tormentors return? I believed you. I trusted you. The One and only person, that did as he said. Is gone!* Mary wept. *I am glad you freed me from the Seven. But, now, have I the power to make sure they do not return?*

She opened her eyes, wiped her tears and saw An Angel sitting on the Stone, the tomb lay open! She saw the Guards fallen and huddling in Terror! she stepped across the Road to the garden. It was cool and Peaceful, Quiet. in spite of the Angel sitting on the Stone. Feet dangling; as boy would, waiting for Friends. She came quietly, fearfully, to the tomb and looked inside.

There in the Tomb; she saw two more angels, sitting at where his Head had been and feet! But the Body was gone! It dawned on her! *His*

Body Gone! Fear gripped her! *Where is it? Where could they have taken Him!* Desperation claimed her again, as she frantically, look about and rushed outside the tomb. She spun in a circle, looking, searching, hoping! *Nothing!*

She turned and saw a Man. *maybe He is the Gardner! He could tell me where Jesus body is!* The man said, "Woman I heard you weeping."

She wiped eyes again and said "Yes, I was. Can You tell me Please, **Please**, where they have taken the Body, of my Lord Jesus the Christ?"

She stood trembling in sorrow and tears.

Then she heard her name. And the Voice; as no other, and she heard her Name again, as only he could say it! "**Mary**, *Mary*."

She spun and saw Jesus! Joy flooded her Soul and her whole Being! He was here! He was Alive! *How? But Alive!* She fell at his Feet, kissed them and held them and hugged his legs.

Mary heard a noise and there was Salome and the other Mary! They all grabbed on to Jesus's feet and Worshipped him! He said. "Go on ahead and tell my Brothers and Sisters I will meet them in Galilee. Do not be afraid! I go now to Your Father, and My Father. To complete what We started. I will be back soon."

The women again entered the Tomb and the Angel said "Go tell the Disciples and Peter. He will meet them in Galilee! Go Now!" They rushed from the Tomb and the garden and made their way to where they had gathered to Mourn! They were laughing and shouting as they went!

Soon they had come to the Upper room where they were mourning and Hiding. Because of how the Crowd had been. Mary Magdelene and the others told them what had happened and Jesus had said.

"No this can't be true! We saw him Die! How can this be!" Some of them said. But Simon Peter and John, ran to the Tomb!

CHAPTER 21

RESURRECTION! DAYS AFTER,
AT ALL COST'S END

Simon Peter, and John ran through the Streets in the early morning light! *Did they actually see Jesus? Or was it something else? How did they see in the Tomb? the Stone Joseph said was heavy and secured, He said even by Pilate and Rome! what is happening!* Simon Peter thought as he ran! John was not far behind.

Now at the Garden; they both, saw the Stone rolled away, and the Tomb open! They rushed inside! and found it Empty! Just as the women had said. Stunned Simon Peter and John looked at each other and remembered what Jesus had said.

Simon Peter; walked to the Entrance. And reached up and touched the Name plate. Feeling the carved words, and the wax Seal of Rome! Smiling to himself, Simon Peter, walked away from the Tomb. He walked toward home, in wonder and awe.

****

The guards at the Tomb; had fled after the Angel, and had made their way to the Temple. And to the High Priest and Elders. They knew eventually; they needed to go to the Fort and Report. But were afraid. Caiaphas and the others already had a plan in place and said the them.

"Listen closely. When asked tell those asking, that his Disciples came and stole the body away, as you slept! And if the Pilate hears, we will Persuade him as well. And We will make sure, no harm comes to you. From Rome, or any of your Commanders! Here, take this Money! Take all of it!"

Caius and the three were stunned at the Amount they saw. Caius thought there is enough here, to buy four Tombs greater than the one We saw! He spoke with the three Men; and they agreed to tell the story, to any who would ask!

****

Word had spread, that Jesus had Risen! Many doubted, but more believed! And as two disciples; were on their way to a city, called Emmaus, they were discussing the amazing Events of the last days!

Cleopas was saying "Can you imagine what it must have been like in the Temple, when the Veil tore! Can you believe that Veil weighs hundreds of Pounds! and was Split! How can that be! I am having a hard time understanding it all, Let alone the report of the Women at the tomb! That his Body was gone! And then that they saw him! it is almost too much!"

"I know, I know" said the Other disciple.

Jesus came up beside them and walked them. And he asked " I couldn't help but overhear your conversation. Who were you talking about?"

Cleopas said, "Who were we talking about?" He laughed as did the other Disciple.

"Are you the Only Person in Jerusalem, that hasn't heard of what has happened with Jesus of Nazareth and the Christ?"

Jesus answered, " What happened?"

Cleopas and the other disciple repeated again the exploits and wonders, surrounding Jesus. And sadness gripped them. "We were hoping, that He would have Redeemed Israel and set us free from the Romans and more! But the Chief Priests; killed him in Jealousy and Now. And now. . ."

Jesus said, " Is it so hard to believe what the Prophets and the Word of God Proclaim?"

Jesus shared from Moses to that day what was said of Him. They turned to ask him to stay with them. But he was gone.

****

Time passed slowly as they all Huddled in the upper Room. They were afraid to leave. Many were not sure; just what might happen, if they walked freely in Jerusalem.

Suddenly Jesus stood before them! He said "Shalom, and Peace to you! " They were stunned to silence. Fear and Awe mixed, with questions not asked! He showed them His hands, feet and side. Slowly, almost laboriously, they realized it was him! Jesus! Alive! Their hearts were full of Joy!

"Receive the Holy Spirit!" and Breathed on them. And said "If you forgive any Sin, it will be Forgiven. But if you don't, it will not be." They left that place and found Thomas and told him what Jesus had said.

He shook his head and said "Unless I see his hands and feet; even touch them, and Put my hand in the Spear hole. I will not believe it!"

****

Jesus appeared again Eight days after that; when they were in the Upper room. The doors were locked and Shut. And Thomas was there. He smiled and said "Shalom and Peace to you all! Thomas, come here and see. Touch and feel; My hands and Feet, and my side! Do not Doubt, but Believe!" Shy and afraid; Thomas came to Jesus.

He reached for his wrist, held it. Thomas saw the Spike hole and torn skin. Jesus watched as wonder destroyed doubt! Then Thomas; touched his Side. and cried

"My Lord, and My God!" weeping! Jesus embraced him and said. " Blessed are you. But more blessed are those who believe and will believe, who haven't seen!"

****

Jesus appeared many other times; over the next days, even to Five Hundred at once. Jesus came to Galilee as he Promised.

Simon Peter; one day said, " I am going Fishing!" and a few of the Others Chimed in and said "We will go with you!"

So there on the sea of Galilee, Simon Peter and the others fished. They fished All night. And caught Nothing! Discouraged they turned toward Shore.

The sea was quiet and still. Simon Peter looked there was a Man on the Shore; and He heard him ask "Do you have any Fish?" Peter, answered back "No."

Peter was pulling in his net and heard "Put the Net on the right side of the Boat and Try!"

Peter looked at John, shrugged and dropped his net on the Right side and the Net was Full of Fish! John whispered to Simon Peter; I think that was Jesus!"

Simon Peter put on his outer garment and jumped into the Sea and Swam for Shore! The others in the Boat turned it and headed for the Shore behind Simon Peter.

Once Simon Peter was on shore, He saw a Fire and Fish cooking! And he Heard the man say, " Bring some of the Fish you caught and Come, Eat Breakfast!"

So, Simon Peter and the Others pulled in the net, so full of Fish, yet it held.

No one said anything; but they ate and were full. They didn't dare ask if it was Jesus. . . Because in their hearts, they knew. As the Fire slowly became coals, Jesus turned to Simon Peter. He looked him in the eye and said "Simon; Do you Love Me, more than these?"

Simon Peter said, "Yes Lord I do." Jesus said, "Feed my Lambs."

A second time Jesus asked "Simon Peter, do you Love Me?"

Simon answered again "Lord I do." Jesus said again "Shepherd My Sheep." Simon Peter was concerned and felt very awkward.

And Jesus said a third Time "Simon Peter, do you Love Me?"

Simon Peter was heartbroken, that He had asked a third Time. Simon answered full of anguish "Lord, you know All things. And you know I love you!" He answered almost weeping.

Jesus looked at him intently and Finished "Tend my Sheep."

****

The next day Jesus appeared to them again. All of them. and said, "Follow me." He led them to Bethany. And the Mount of Olives and stopped. He held up his hands, and blessed them! And a cloud came down, and lifted him up toward Heaven.

As Jesus was taken from their sight. . . They saw and heard the two men, standing nearby robed in white, saying, "Men of Galilee, why are you here staring at the sky? This same Jesus will return, just as you have seen Him leave!" They rejoiced and worshipped God!

****

Jesus, the Son of God, was home again! The Realm resounded with shouts of Praise! He had come home. He embraced the Father and Holy Spirit.

The angels all bowed. Jesus entered the Temple of the Realm. He walked to the Altar. And saw again, the Mercy Seat. He bowed His head, and made a fist, then opened His palm.

There in His palm, was a small cup. The cup held Blood. His Blood. His Sacrifice. He smiled. He spoke aloud, "I know the work has been completed already. But what I do now, I do, as a symbol for all Eternity! For All time! Past, Present, Future! I lay on the Mercy Seat, the Altar of God, My Sacrifice and Blood! For the Atoning of Sin! And the Complete Redemption of Mankind, and Creation itself! To Restore all that was, is, and shall be forever! Sin is vanquished! Man is free to choose life! And is free by faith to live with Us here, always, never to depart!

Jesus poured the cup on the Mercy Seat of God. And all of Heaven rang with a shout!

All of Heaven; and the Realm, even Creation itself, heard the Father's Words!

"All Who hear, listen! Swing wide the Gates! Open the Doors! And let My people in! Those that were lost, have now been found! Those who were orphans, now have a home! Those far and wide! Those of every tongue! Those of every nation, tribe, and kindred! Those forsaken, broken, hurting, and desperate! Any who come, and receive this gift of Life in My Son Jesus! Let none be barred! Let none be stopped! I will be their Father! They shall be My Children! Now, forever and always! I will dwell with them. And they with Me!

Sin's Cost has been paid! The act of Redemption finished! Any and All may come! Unafraid, unhindered. None unwelcome! We have done this!

We did just as we said! **AT ALL COST!"**

AUTHOR'S NOTE

If you have made it this far, then you have read the book! Thank you! But there is more to this story "AT ALL COST" was just not a rewrite or novelization of the Bible. Truthfully, I was compelled to write it. You see, people need to hear this very message.

Everything in this story was an attempt to show everyone who God is and His character and love. Not religion, but relationship, one that anyone can have with God Himself.

So, here's the deal. . . God is calling to you. He is waiting for you. He did all He could for YOU! Knowing God is simple. Being Forgiven by God is simple. Having Life Eternal is simple.

Step 1: ADMIT YOU are a SINNER.

Step 2: REPENT of YOUR SIN

Step 3: ASK FORGIVENESS of GOD and JESUS

Step 4: RECEIVE GOD'S FREE GIFT of SALVATION

If you confess with your mouth, Jesus as Lord, and believe in your heart that God raised Him from the dead, you will be saved. For with the heart a person believes, resulting in Righteousness, and with the mouth he confesses, resulting in Salvation. For the Scripture says, "Whoever believes in Him will not be put to shame." For there is no distinction between Jew and Greek; for the same Lord is Lord of all, abounding in riches for all who call on Him. Everyone who calls on the name of the Lord will be saved. **(Romans 10:9-13)**

Pray something like this:

Dear Jesus, I know you are God's Son. And that you died on Calvary to destroy sin, my sin, and set men free. Forgive me of my sin, come into my life and be my Lord and Savior. Thank you for loving me and saving me. In Jesus' Name Amen.

www.ingramcontent.com/pod-product-compliance
Lightning Source LLC
Chambersburg PA
CBHW060859140726
47996CB00001B/47